The Light We Guard

Aurora King

Cover by Miles Ross.

Page illustrations and matching star elements included in the cover by Morgan Teal.

Made with human intelligence.

Edited by Mae Gaynor.

To Deborah Willis,
The greatest teacher I've ever had. I learned about so much more
than just music from your class.
I will carry your memory in my heart forever.

Dear Reader,

The Light We Guard is a fun, action-packed and heartwarming urban fantasy. While none of the content featured is inherently suggestive, the author would like to avoid any possibility of triggers or moments of discomfort.

This book contains depictions of neglectful and/or narcissistic parenting, manipulation, alcoholism, physical violence and abuse, gun violence, mild use of substances, torture, and kidnapping.

Don't worry, even in its darkest moments, this story remains grounded in the light.

Enjoy!

 4

1-Alyssa

Our world is a place of conflict. It's a place filled with life that's doomed to, one day, meet its end. It's a place where you confide in someone that means *everything* to you, until, one way or another, they have to go. Order balanced by chaos, light balanced by darkness. And I seem to always get myself caught in the middle.

My life is a constant whirlwind of conflict. It's gotten better since I moved out of my uncle's house, but that doesn't mean it's been perfect.

Ryan, my teenage brother, lives with me in my apartment. He comes from school every day covered in bruises and spends all his time in his room. I know this is typical for teens, getting in fights, shutting people out, constantly being mad at the world, but I still worry about him. Today was no exception.

He comes home, slamming the front door shut as per usual. In a rush of avoidance, he grabs a plate of the spaghetti I'd just finished making for dinner. Ryan keeps his head down, his hood hiding his face. Suspicious, I pull his hood down to reveal his left eye, beaten and black.

"What happened?!" I ask, grimacing as my volume is higher than I intended.

Ryan swats me away and quickly puts his hood back up.

"Don't worry about it, Lyz," he says.

But I refuse to let him wave off the subject. "*Don't worry about it*? No! Who's doing this to you?"

I grab an ice pack from the freezer.

He takes it, and presses it against his eye, wincing at the cold touch against the wound.

"I guess I just pissed off a couple of guys from my class. It's not a big deal," he answers without looking in my direction.

"What does *that* mean?!"

"Just forget it, Lyz!" He takes his dinner in one hand and holds the ice pack over his eyes with the other. Before letting me interrogate him any further, he stomps down the hall to his room without saying another word.

I let out an exasperated shout into the fridge. Suddenly, I'm not very hungry anymore, in fact I feel sick to my stomach. The mere thought of eating anything right now is enough to make me gag, so I grab the plastic containers from the cabinet at my feet and begin putting away the food.

He *always* does this. Whenever I see something wrong and try to ask about it, try to *help,* he just shuts down or explodes in my face. He acts almost as if *I* was the one who punched him.

I can hardly blame him, though. When we started living with our Uncle Will, it didn't take long to realize that he wasn't exactly the nurturing type. Will worked as a police officer at the Turnerville precinct and always took an unnecessarily large number of cases that kept him working late. He almost never had time for us, which meant *I* had to step in. At ten years old, I was cooking for my brother and I *and* doing everyone's laundry.

When I turned eighteen, through saving all my tips and most of the money from my restaurant job paychecks, I was able to put a down payment on a small apartment. The place is in a decent, quiet part of town. Before I left, I asked Ryan if he wanted to move in with me so he wouldn't have to rely on our lazy-ass uncle. He said yes almost immediately, and I've been taking care of him ever since.

Turning on the news for some background noise, I start on the dishes. While viciously scrubbing the burnt marinara sauce off the pan, something the reporter says catches my attention. I turn to read the headline:

'The Riot' gang burns down Turnerville Credit Union. Multiple workers injured.

The Riot. A group of criminal menaces that have been terrorizing this town for years. Sometimes they'll just rob a place and leave, but a lot of the time, they cause some serious damage. These are the cases that kept Will at work so late — he's been chasing down the Riot's leader, Jacob Reeves, for *fifteen years*. Anytime Ryan or I asked him about it, he would just give us the same practiced, generic answer: *These are bad people, who do incredibly bad things. They need to be stopped by any means necessary.*

Apparently, 'any means' hasn't been very necessary yet if he's still looking. The police are still no closer to stopping them than they were when they first showed up all those years ago.

I remember the day they first appeared pretty well. The Riot appeared out of nowhere and rampaged every store on one of the farther streets downtown. Stealing their money and other goods, holding employees hostage. A few of them even got shot, and some people *died*. It was horrible. But the thing I remember the most was Will coming home after having dealt with the hold-up.

He walked right past me when I tried to ask questions, grabbed a beer from the fridge, and locked himself in his room the rest of the evening. I heard him all night through his bedroom door as he screamed at someone through the phone.

My train of thought is abruptly interrupted by the reminder of dirty dishes stacked in the sink behind me.

When the kitchen clean-up is finally done, I grab a mug from the cabinet beside me and fill it with water to make some tea, maneuvering toward the pantry to get a bag of chamomile. While waiting on the microwave, my phone suddenly vibrates in my pocket. The name on the screen reads 'Madison Love' — my best friend since high school.

"Hey Lyz," she says, "you left your wallet at work."

"I—what?!" Running to my purse, my hands fraughtfully dig inside. I shove through old receipts, a couple of chapstick tubes, and spare change in a desperate attempt to feel for the black leather of my wallet. When I can't find it, my heart skips a beat.

"I can bring it up to you! My shift ends in an hour," Madison reassures.

Thank God for her.

Madison and I have been friends since tenth grade. She's the only person in my life that drives me crazy in a *good way*. Every time she pined for the school jock that was all brawn and no brains, every time she complained to me about a bitchy customer, I supported her, because she's supported me for years in ways I could never imagine. She brings me food from work when I forget to eat. When Ryan fights with me, she lets me talk about it and tries to help. Also, like today, she keeps me from losing my head when I forget something so absent-mindedly.

"Thank you, Maddie," I sigh, "you're amazing."

"No problem. Did you have enough to get groceries for dinner today?" Madison asks.

"Yeah." I can feel myself starting to choke up and try my best to hold it back. "I did."

A moment of silence. I can tell she can see right through me, but she doesn't provoke the situation. Not yet at least. "Did you actually *eat* the dinner you made?" she asks.

"No," I admit. My stomach knots, once again making me feel too queasy to eat anything.

"Alyssa, you can't keep starving yourself when you're upset," Madison says, "and you *definitely* can't keep punishing yourself."

"I'm not." Tears slowly roll down my face as I speak. My voice fails me, the sound comes out quieter and more broken. "I—I'm fine."

"Oh honey," she says in that sympathetic tone of voice that I've heard from her before, "what's wrong?"

"Nothing, it's...it's okay." I clear my throat and steady my voice, attempting to be convincing. "Ryan had a bad day and he just kind of snapped at me, but I'll be okay."

Of course, she doesn't believe me. We talk for a minute before the muffled sound of someone calling for Madison on her end of the phone interrupts us. Given that she's still at work, it's probably Logan, our manager.

"Shoot, I've got to get back. But I'll be there right after my shift, I promise," Madison says hurriedly.

After she hangs up, I move sluggishly to the bathroom to clean myself up.

Usually around this time, I would just go to bed. But as much as my muscles ache from exhaustion, I can't bring myself to begin to rest just yet.

Instead, I lay on the couch with my phone and listen to music through my headphones. With each song that rolls through my playlist, each melody, each soft lyric, I start to feel some level of calm.

Sometime later, there's a knock at the door.

Is Madison here already? Did she blackmail Logan again to get off work early?

I yank out my earbuds and get up to answer the door. Instead of Madison, the presence at the door sends me back. Nothing could have prepared me for the gruff man suddenly standing at my doorstep.

"Uncle Will?"

My uncle waits at the door with a hardened expression. His eyes stern on the ground until he looks up at me. Streaks of gray run through his chestnut brown hair and beard. The age lines in his skin, as well as tired eyes, make way for his sullen personality. His hands dip into both pockets of the brown bomber jacket he wears over a forest-green T-shirt. His blue jeans are frayed at the hems, and spotted with dark stains, probably from alcohol.

"Hello, Lyz," he greets as he walks right past me and into my living room.

"Um, hold on a second. What are you doing here?" I ask him.

Ryan's quick and frantic footsteps make their way toward us. As my brother sees Will, he stands frozen in disbelief.

"Hey there, Ryan," Will addresses him, almost dismissively.

Ryan's brow furrows. He opens his mouth to say something, but nothing comes out.

"Will!" I snap to grab my uncle's attention. "Why are you here?"

"I'm still Ryan's legal guardian, I'm supposed to be keeping an eye on him, so that's what I'm doing," he says as if it were the most obvious answer. "No need to be unreasonable."

"*Unreasonable*?" Ryan scoffs.

"Hey, you don't need to be here for this," I tell him.

"I..." he shifts uncomfortably, crossing his arms, "you shouldn't be alone with him, Lyz."

"Why not? You like to be alone, locking yourself in your room every day," Will retorts. "Why don't you go do that? I need to have a grown-up conversation with your sister."

Ryan's face is red hot with anger. I shoot a glare at Will.

"Ryan, go to your room."

I don't want my brother to be involved in this mess. He's sixteen, he doesn't need it.

With a beat of hesitation, he glances at Will before heading back to his bedroom.

Once he leaves, I turn to my uncle. "Okay, listen," I start, my fist clenched so hard that my nails dig into my palm. "You haven't shown this much interest in us in the last *year*, so I don't know what this is really about, but I don't care."

"Well—" he tries to interrupt.

"I have been taking care of Ryan my whole life, whether it be under your roof or mine. So I don't need you to *keep an eye* on us."

"Oh really?" Will asks, crossing his arms and inching closer to me. "Because I've seen his grades this year. You don't even have enough time to help a sophomore with his algebra homework?"

"He never asks me to help him! And he refuses to go to tutoring! You know that!" I shout in defense.

"Yes, I do know that. But *you* should be making sure that he goes," Will points out.

His glaring blue eyes read as equally serious and distant as he speaks, "*You* are the one who claimed you could raise him better than I could."

"And? Does that mean *I'm* supposed to be blamed every time Ryan acts up?" My face feels warm as the anger wells up inside of me.

"That's called being a parent, Alyssa," my uncle retorts.

"I'm not his parent, Will! I'm his sister!"

Our parents were in a car accident when I was eight, and Ryan wasn't even a year old. After that, it didn't take long for Ryan and I to be put in our uncle's care.

"Then I don't know why you wanted this," Will says quietly.

"It wasn't about what I wanted, it was about what Ryan *needed*," my voice strains.

Will's expression is irritatingly familiar. It's the same sneer he gives when deciding that *he* knows best. Everyone else's feelings be damned. Years back, when I was a teenager still living under his roof, it made my blood boil. Seeing that sneer in front of me today, it feels no different.

Will stiffens up and adjusts the collar of his jacket.

"Well then, here's what he needs: I'm still his legal guardian. If you want him to stay here, you need to show me that you can be responsible," he says. "I'll be staying here for a bit and keeping an eye on the two of you until you can prove to me that you can."

"Like hell you will! This is *my* apartment!" I shout.

"I've let you take responsibility for Ryan because *you* said you could handle it." He points at me. "Legally, your brother is still my responsibility, so if you want to fight me over this, we can get a judge involved."

The mention of a judge makes me freeze in my tracks. He's right, Will has every legal right to just take Ryan back. Hell, he has the right to keep me from seeing my brother at all. I can't fight him on this, if I do, he could take Ryan away forever. But...if I play along with Will's request for a little while, hopefully he'll *finally* leave us alone.

Forcing myself to take a steadying breath, I begrudgingly agree with Will's terms.

He grabs a bag of clothes from his old green truck. Since my apartment doesn't have an extra room, he claims the couch as his bed.

Exhausted and over it all, I head to my room to try and get some sleep. Before I can make it down the hallway, there's another knock on the door.

"Are you having a party or something?" Will asks as he throws a spare blanket over himself.

Ignoring him, I answer the door. Madison stands there with a styrofoam to-go box.

Before she can say anything, I slip outside and close the door behind me, putting at least some sort of barrier between me and Will.

"Hey, what's going on?" Madison asks, looking past my shoulder to try and catch a glimpse of the situation.

"My uncle is here," I answer.

"*Will*? Why is he here?" Her nose contorts in disgust.

"Long story," I say before changing the subject. "Do you have my wallet?"

"Yeah." She pulls it out of her big leather purse and hands it to me. She gestures to the box of food in her other hand. "I also got you the french fries that you like from work. You need to eat."

My hands reluctantly reach for the box, and she wraps her arms around me in a comforting hug. I *truly* don't know what I'd do without her.

"Are you okay?" she asks me.

It's a hard question to answer. At first, I can't form the words. My brother is growing more distant, and I feel like there's nothing I can do to help him.

My uncle is keeping us under surveillance, and if he finds anything wrong, he might never let me see Ryan again. I'm barely making enough money as a server to manage anything. My life is a mess, and it's only going to get worse.

So, no, I'm not okay.

"Lyz?" Madison's voice is concerned but demanding.

It's not until she speaks that I notice the tears rolling down my face.

Madison drops her purse onto the ground and wraps me in a long, comforting hug.

We end up talking for a while as I eat the fries she brought me. We almost don't notice the sky shift from an orange-pink sunset to a dark, star-sprinkled night. The two of us say our goodbyes, and soon enough it's time for me to soldier back into the apartment.

Will has passed out on the couch, so, thankfully, I'm able to skip another cynical conversation and quietly make my way to my bedroom.

Standing on the sidewalk in the middle of downtown, right on Milam Street, I turn around, noticing two different buildings behind me. Edgar's Baked Goods Emporium, and the Herb Shop. There's a dirty, trash-filled alleyway between the two stores. An out of place structure in the alley suddenly catches my attention.

A red wooden door, painted with golden-yellow lace-like designs along each edge, stands in front of me. No walls are there to surround it — the door is held up by a matching red frame that wraps around each side and plants itself sturdily on the ground.

This is ridiculous. I don't understand it. My heart pounds in my chest at the sight. Something about this feels so wrong. *But...it's also...mesmerizing.*

As if an invisible force were pushing on the door, it opens on its own. Behind it, a blinding yellow light shines through the entry. The intensity makes my eyes sting. Turning back around to shield myself from visual impairment, a blur of red whips past me. I watch as it flies above my head and lands on a metal bench on the sidewalk across the street. Upon landing, the shape of the blur clears to reveal a small red bird. The ends of its wings and tail feathers are so silver that they almost resemble a mirror. Behind the melodic chirping of this strange creature, I feel a sense of caution. It's almost as if the bird is trying to...warn me about something.

In an instant, I'm shifted to a different setting. Surrounding me now is a forest, more vibrant and green than any I've ever seen before. It feels like some kind of wonderful, strange magic. Nothing but trees and plant life for miles. Focusing my gaze outward, I spot a wooden cabin in the distance. While making my way towards it, the sun's warm and comforting rays gently press against my back. It offers temporary, soothing relief as I get closer.

Stepping up to the front porch, I knock on the door. Nobody answers. The door handle seems to be unlocked, offering no resistance.

The interior of the cabin is beautiful. Smooth quartz countertops, sand-colored carpeted floors, mostly birch kitchen furniture, and three worn brown sofas circling a stone fireplace against the wall in the center of the room. Against the side wall to the right, next to the dining room table, is a velvet-red painted wooden chest. I start to make my way toward it, but, before I can, a familiar voice from behind makes me jump.

"Don't open that," my Uncle Will says.

I turn rapidly to see him standing just a few feet behind me. The sunlight from outside creeps in from the windows and shines over his face.

Will's arms are crossed, sturdy and stone-cold as I know him to be.

"Why? What's in it?" I ask.

He stares out the window, as if looking for something. "The responsibility that comes with opening this thing... I wouldn't ask it of anyone," he says. "You're strong, but I don't think you're quite ready yet, Lyz."

"Ready for what?" I ask.

He chuckles instead of answering my question. "You'll find out soon." His smile quickly shifts to a frown. "I just hope I'll be able to protect you and your brother when you do."

"Protect us from what?" The pitch in my voice grows higher.

"I can't explain just yet," he says, "not until it's time."

"What?" I say, completely perplexed. This whole vague show of theatrics is very out of character for him. My uncle is self-centered and crazy, but this is just plain psychotic.

The natural sunlight begins to fade around us. Shadows loom over in their place as dark clouds can be seen covering the sky outside. Will looks around, eyes wild with fear.

"Will, what are you talking about?!" I ask him, now shouting.

"Find the door," he says, once again dodging my question. Before he can say any more, the darkness grows, swallowing the room. The image of Uncle Will begins to fade as everything in my line of sight blurs to black.

"ALYSSA!" My uncle's voice echoes as he disappears into the black shroud. The shadows around me grow deeper and darker until it's impossible to see him, or anything else.

The darkness is suffocating. It's impossible to speak, let alone breathe. The freezing air sends a cold shiver up my spine. An indiscernible sound seems to be coming from every direction. Like an echo that moves aimlessly through the air. An uncontrollable feeling *of anguish floods through my skin as the echo's volume increases. It gets louder and louder, until suddenly it comes to a stop. And a deep, booming voice calls my name.*

"Alyssa... Haller..."

I try to respond, to say anything at all, but no words manage to escape. Something that feels like thick smoke fills my lungs, blocking my airway and leaving me to gasp for air with what little space I have.

"William tried to silence me..." the voice echoes. Whoever he is, he doesn't show his face. "I do not take it personally. He was but the last of many who dared."

The last of what? What could Will have possibly done?

"You will soon try to silence me too..." he says, "you and your compatriots."

What compatriots? I don't understand. I don't want any part of this.

It's all just a dream, none of this is real. I can wake up and forget about all of it by morning. My eyes shut tightly, focusing on waking up safely in my bedroom. The voice erupts into laughter. Taunting me, mocking me as I try to force it out.

Wake up... come on, wake up!

My plan doesn't seem to have worked like I'd hoped when I open my eyes again. Looking around, the familiar sight of my living room fills me with both ease and confusion. I feel a wash of relief, but I still can't help the dread starting to crawl up the back of my neck.

This nightmare isn't over.

All of a sudden, Ryan creeps slowly through the hallway. His expression is blank, and his gaze is set behind me, as if I were invisible to him.

"Ryan?" I call out.

He stops in his tracks and, as he turns around to face me, my heart skips a beat. Ryan's face is pale and sickly black veins run along his neck. His eyes are unnaturally hollow like the night sky. When he speaks, I take an unbalanced step backward.

"There is no more Ryan. He belongs to the Darkness now..." Ryan speaks, but the words are coming from the same menacing voice from earlier.

Another shiver rolls up my spine, returning to that sense of utter terror.

"No!" I choke through tears. "Please!"

Ryan blinks rapidly and looks up at me, ghastly fear apparent on his face. He looks around the room for a second before turning back to me.

"Alyssa?" he calls in his own voice.

I extend my hand to reach for him, but before anything else, he starts gasping and choking.

"Help...Lyz," he says between breaths. Ryan grips his neck with both hands.

I try to run to him, but a heavy weight presses onto me, keeping me frozen. Keeping me from saving him. I try to scream, but just as before, the feeling of thick, ashy smoke prohibits any sound from coming out. With nothing left to do but watch, tears stream down my face as Ryan's body goes limp, and his knees buckle to the floor.

"You cannot save him..."

My alarm goes off, jolting me awake. I sit up, noting the familiar environment of my bedroom. My light gray comforter covers my body from my waist down. Sunlight shines through the blue striped curtains. Without a second thought, I throw the comforter off and run to my brother's room.

Flashbacks of my dream whip through my racing thoughts. The ghostly white of his skin, the black in his veins. His eyes...

It can't be real. It just can't be.

Can it?

As I swing the door open with no warning, Ryan stands there in a T-shirt and boxers, midway through pulling up a pair of jeans.

He screams, his voice shrill with shock. "What the hell?!"

"Sorry! Sorry!" I say, covering my eyes.

"*Knock* next time!" he shouts after I close the door.

My hand lingers on the doorknob for a short moment.

I'm okay, Ryan is okay. It was only a nightmare.

Taking a few deep breaths, my eyes dive down to the clock on my phone.

It's 6:31 a.m., soon it'll be time for me to drive Ryan to school. I get dressed into a pair of blue jeans, a light pink T-shirt, and my dark gray sneakers.

For the next hour, Ryan and I are running around the apartment to make sure he has everything he needs for the day.

Meanwhile, Will spends the entire time sitting at the kitchen table drinking his coffee, observing our morning routine. He appears to be extremely tired this morning. His face is sickly, as if he hardly slept at all last night.

Soon enough, the two of us are ready to head out the door.

Conveniently, Will chooses this time to intervene.

"Where do you think you're going?" he asks — his tone could be easily mistaken for blatant offense.

"I'm taking Ryan to school, he has to be there by eight o'clock," I answer, clear haste in my voice as I try to wrap up the conversation as quickly as possible.

"Oh no you don't. You've got to get to work," he says.

I shoot him a confused glare. "My shift doesn't start until nine."

"Don't argue with me, I'm taking him to school," he insists, grabbing his keys out of his pocket. "Come on, Ryan."

Ryan looks at him, his nose scrunched with disgust. He doesn't want to go with him, I can tell that much, but Will is persistent.

"Ryan," he orders sternly, "let's go."

My brother turns his head and looks at me behind him, silently asking me what to do.

"Will, what are you doing?" I ask, tired and annoyed with the entire ordeal.

"Spending time with my nephew." Will crosses his arms and keeps a firm police-like stance. "Do you have a problem with that?"

I don't know what Will is up to, but something in the insistence of his voice seems different. A hint of desperation or urgency is apparent in his tone.

Could this behavior have anything to do with the dream from last night?

I quickly cast away the thought. As bad as last night was, it was *just a dream.* I have to remember, if I play along with Will, he'll be gone sooner rather than later.

"It's okay." A sigh of defeat escapes as I drop my purse from my hands.

Ryan is clearly not pleased with my answer, but our condescending uncle certainly is. Ryan huffs and pulls his hood over his head before stomping out the door.

As Will begins to step out, he stops to face me again.

"I need a favor. Can you go down to the Herb Shop downtown before you pick him up?"

I pause, dumbfounded, remembering the Herb Shop from my dream last night. "Uh... why?"

"I need a bottle of magnesium supplements. That store has the only brand that works," Will claims.

Unbelievable. Now I'm running errands for him?

"Can't you do it yourself?" I ask, crossing my arms.

"I have to work. I have a meeting with Officer Miller and the chief about the Riot. It's gonna keep me busy all day," he explains, glaring at me as if I were a child refusing to do a household chore.

Typical. *This* is why I moved out.

"Fine," I answer, biting back my annoyance as much as physically possible.

"Thanks, Lyz." He ignores my obviously hidden objection. Without another word, he leaves the apartment and drives away with my pouting brother in the passenger seat of his truck.

After an hour of torturous solitude with the house to myself, it's time to go to work. Will should have been back from dropping

22

Ryan off a while ago, which is strange. However, Will is trying to prove himself to be a more worthy authority figure. He wouldn't have sabotaged Ryan getting to school. And honestly? That's all I care about.

As soon as I clock into work, Logan immediately starts lecturing me. He goes on about how I didn't clean the disgusting bathrooms yesterday, along with my inability to cash out the servers' tips before leaving.

For the record, I *did* clean the bathrooms that morning. Also, cashing out tips is the owner's job. I neither have the authority nor the knowledge to do it.

My guess is that Logan was drunk again last night, and he's barking at us because of a hangover.

Madison catches up to me as soon as she finishes showing a couple to their table.

"How'd things go this morning?" she asks me.

"Not great," I sigh, grabbing the sanitizer spray and a towel to wipe down a dirty table in my section. "Will practically shoved Ryan out the door. He *insisted* on taking him to school today."

"*What?*" Madison scowls. "Why?"

I shrug. "I wish I knew."

My next five, seemingly never-ending, hours are spent serving tables.

Finally, after what feels like an eternity, I reach the end of my shift. Despite the shorter hours I'd taken ever since Ryan moved in, my feet still ache. Picking him up from the car-riders line is at the forefront of my mind, until I remember Will's request. With about twenty spare minutes before pickup time, I drive to the Herb Shop downtown to get the magnesium he had asked me for.

A small part of my mind is suspicious at the thought of entering the Herb Shop right after seeing it in my dream last night, but I force the overly intrusive thought out of my head to focus on the task at hand.

Walking up to the door, I tentatively peek into the alley between the Herb Shop and the bakery. There are no doors, birds, or flashing lights. Just rusted metal trash cans, a few abandoned black garbage bags, stray food rotting on the ground, and... is that a *used* toilet seat?

Okay, nope. *Disgusting*. I shake off the nerves that have been looming over me and curse myself for being so ridiculous.

The moment my hand pushes open the door to the Herb Shop, the combined smell of spices and medicines surrounds me. I wave hello to the elderly woman at the register and scan the shelves. Having only been to this store a few times, I don't exactly know where to find the magnesium. After a moment of searching, the elderly lady leads me to a shelf towards the back, and a pack of two bottles for about twenty dollars sits at the top shelf. I meet the woman at the checkout and pay in cash.

My fingers grip the handles of the plastic bag as I walk out the door. Before making it to my car, a flicker of light coming from the alley catches the corner of my eye.

I shake it off, trying to ignore it, and continue towards my car when a familiar sound wisps past my ear.

The light sound of a chirping bird makes me jump. When I direct my attention to the alley again, my jaw drops in disbelief.

The door. The same one from my dream.

The painted velvet red, with the gold lace-like designs look the same as before. Elegant and bold in contrast to the grimy trash-filled alley it stands in.

Cautiously, I step closer, peaking around the back of the door. Nothing is there. The chirping sound appears again, this time coming from the other side of the door. My heart beats furiously in my chest. The air around me thickens, making it hard to breathe. I should run, go home, pretend none of this is happening. I can forget about all of this and go back to my car right now...

But something, some *force*, pulls me closer. An instinct buried deep within my soul. It's like every nerve in my body wants to trust it.

I grip the golden doorknob with a shaky hand, willing forth any last shreds of courage, and open the door.

✦2-Alyssa

Vibrant green trees engulf my surroundings. The forest feels so alive and pure, as if it was untouched by civilization. Strong and healthy tree branches sway with the gentle summer breeze. There's no sign of animal life anywhere. The air is peaceful and silent.

It looks just like it did in my dream.

Is that what this is? *Am* I dreaming?

Something catches my eye. A wooden structure out in the distance that fills me with unease and cuts me out of my trance. The cabin.

Going near that cabin is the last thing that I want to do. My dream from last night, Will's warning, it's all too unnerving. The pull from earlier that forced me in here is no longer present. There would be nothing stopping me from simply turning around and leaving.

But if this forest and that cabin are real, could everything else be?

This might be my chance to get some answers. I turn around to ponder my exit, only to find that the red door is gone. All that remains are miles and miles of forest.

Out of the corner of my eye, a light gleams in the air.

I turn to finally see the silver-winged small red bird flying through the trees. Tentatively, I follow the creature as it weaves through the forest and up the small hill until I reach the cleared dirt pathway leading to the cabin's entrance.

Approaching the first few steps of the wooden porch, I hesitate. The things that happened in my dream were not exactly...*pleasant*.

A sudden noise makes me jump in my skin.

It's the bird again. It chirps vigorously as it disappears into the bright sky right before my eyes.

"Hey! Wait!" I say too late. Scanning through the deep sea of forest surrounding me, the bird is nowhere to be found. I take a breath, gather my courage, and step inside.

The interior of the cabin is exactly the same as I remember it. The three tattered sofas surround the fireplace. The birch dining table sits behind the living room to the left. To my surprise, the chest that my uncle had stopped me from opening in my dream isn't there this time.

I wander through the room, trying to remember the other details. Will's mysterious warning, Ryan with the black veins pulsing through his pale skin. The thought of the voice that haunted him makes my skin crawl. Seeing half of my dream come to life right in front of me carves a pit of dread in my stomach, thinking about what that could mean for my brother.

My thought process is quickly interrupted by the sound of creaking footsteps coming from upstairs. I freeze in a panic. As they get closer, whoever is up there loudly calls out for someone.

"Daniel? Is that you?"

My breath catches. The weight in my chest nearly holds me in place, but I force myself to make a move.

Frantically, I scan the room. My eyes lock onto an intricate iron candle stick, about a foot long, sitting on the windowsill. I quickly grab it, remove the red wax candle, and hold it over my shoulder like a baseball bat.

The man rushes down the stairs, stopping on the second to last step. He appears to be just a few years older than me. His shaggy brown hair falls a little past his chin. The long sleeves of his maroon shirt are rolled up just below his elbow. The ratty light blue jeans he wears are too short, stopping just above his ankles. His eyes grow wide when he sees me and my makeshift weapon, rather than this 'Daniel' he'd called for.

"Whoa!" he exclaims when he sees me standing defensively, raising his hands in defense. "How did you get here?"

"I...uh..." I stammer.

"What's your name?" His tone is soft and gentle. Not angry, but cautious of the strange girl invading his home.

"It's, um...Alyssa." My voice wavers.

The man gasps. He inches closer to me, approaching me carefully like handling a spooked animal. "Alyssa Haller?"

My stomach drops. Heat rises in my cheeks. How does he know my name?

Panic sets in immediately. I back away, dropping the candlestick on the floor. Without giving him a chance to say anything else, I run.

Sprinting out of the cabin, the sound of the man calling for me quiets, like an echo fading into the air as I get further away. Now, trailing back through the woods, my pace quickens. My lungs are burning inside my chest. My heart beats faster than a ticking clock.

I have no idea where I am, but right now that doesn't matter. All I need to focus on is getting away from him.

I come to a stop to catch my breath, now a decent amount of distance from the cabin. As I search the forest for an exit, a chirping sound ripples in my ears. I look around, trying to find the little red bird. Though the bird is nowhere in sight, the door appears a couple feet away from me as the chirping fades. Not even bothering to question it, I make my way out the door.

Back in the alley, my eyes land on my car on the far end of the parking lot. My hands stagger, trying to unlock the door and get in as soon as possible. Once inside, I dig through my purse for my phone. The notifications reveal twenty-eight texts from Ryan and eleven missed calls from Will.

Oh no.

Driving away as quickly as possible, I force the events from today to the farthest corner of my mind.

Nothing happened. It's not real. Just get home, get to Ryan, and deal with Will. That's *all* that matters right now.

Once at my apartment, I quickly toss my purse onto the coffee table.

"Ryan? Will? Is anyone home?"

"In the kitchen, Alyssa," Will's voice calls, stern and uncompromising as ever.

Following it, I walk tentatively into the kitchen to find Will sitting at the table with his partner from the police department, Officer Kat Miller.

"Funny story," my uncle says, crossing his arms. "Ryan got out of school today and waited for you to pick him up."

"Will, I can ex—"

He cuts me off before I can finish.

"He waited outside for over an *hour* because you didn't answer your phone, and he didn't have my number. Luckily, Kat passed by on her way home and offered to drive him."

"They were keeping me at work," I lie. He wouldn't exactly believe that I was stuck in a creepy magical forest. I would sound completely delusional, and he'd drag Ryan away without a second thought.

"I don't want to hear it!" Will dismisses, raising his voice.

"Sir," Kat speaks quietly, her words a calm disruption to my uncle's storming anger. "Things like this happen—"

"Stay in your lane, Miller," Will snaps at her, "this is a family matter."

Kat Miller has been Uncle Will's partner for over three years now. She's twenty-seven, a little older than me, but we used to get along pretty well back when I was living with Will and seeing her around more often. Her wavy blonde hair was almost an inch past her face. When she's nervous, like she is right now, she gathers all of her hair and holds it in her hand on one side, as if almost forgetting it's too short to stay there. Today, instead of her uniform, Kat is in dark colored workout clothes. Her blue top falls tightly over the waist of her black yoga pants.

Will has always treated her harshly, even when she was only trying to help. She's as used to his callousness as Ryan and I are. Today, however, she seems more irritated with him. She glares at Will with a clear distaste in her deep green eyes.

"Yes sir," Kat says, a hint of passive-aggressiveness in her tone. She stands up from her seat at the kitchen table. "I'll just be on my way home then."

Will just nods. Kat leaves with a scoff, but he doesn't appear to notice, not even turning his head in her direction.

"Alyssa, what you did today was completely irresponsible," Will continues.

"Hey, you have no room to talk!" I yell. "You used to leave the two of us at school for *hours* after dismissal almost every day!"

"*You* are the one that wants to prove you're better for Ryan. You didn't do that today!"

My skin feels hot as my cheeks flush red. Unable to compose myself, my palm slams the table. "I was trying to get out of work, it wasn't my fault!"

Will holds his hand up in a stopping motion.

"That's enough!" he orders, standing tall as if he were speaking to a child. "I think you need to leave."

"I'm sorry, are you kicking me out of my own apartment?" I ask, flooded with utter disbelief and rage.

"I'm giving you time to calm down. You should be thanking me, young lady," Will insists.

"Are you crazy?!" I shout, my voice hoarse.

"Hey!" he snaps back, his finger pointed at me like a warning. "I can make one phone call, and Ryan can be moved back in with me by tomorrow, do you want that?"

"I..."

"I *won't* tell you again."

"Where am I supposed to go?" Tears well up in my eyes. It takes every ounce of restraint to keep them from spilling.

"You're an adult," he says. "Figure it out."

Will watches by my door as I pack. Two duffel bags from the bottom of my closet are stuffed with clothing and other belongings in an unorganized fashion.

Soon enough, Ryan enters to see what all the fuss is about. Needless to say, he was *not* happy about the situation.

"You're just going to leave me with him?!" Ryan angrily gestures a hand to Will.

"It's not permanent," I tell him. Though I'm not even sure if *I* believe that. My eyes turn hopefully in my uncle's direction, who silently nods in agreement.

With the expression on his face, he seems to agree with me. At the same time, he almost looks...sad, regretful. Although, the atmosphere in the room sends a different message.

The hurt on Ryan's face fills me with dread. He pulls my arm away from my bags. "Why are you doing this?"

"It's not like I want to," I say, "I don't have a choice."

"Yes, you do!" he yells, his voice strained. "You can *choose* to say no!"

"Ryan!" I shout. I grip my brother's shoulders to meet his eyes. "I *have to*. Do you want a judge involved? Do you *want* them to take you away?"

"No, but—"

"Then I have to play by his rules," I continue, glaring at Will. "I'll be back, I promise."

I look over at Will once more.

He leans against my door with his arms crossed, not saying a word. He doesn't have to. He knows that I've made my choice. He also knows that if it means being able to see my brother again after this mess is over, I'll stick to it for his sake. Part of me expects to see him happily smiling over there in his corner, quietly celebrating his victory, but the corners of his mouth remain neutral. Any delight he might be taking in this is completely unreadable.

"Whatever," Ryan scoffs, "do what you want." As he leaves the room, he curses under his breath.

Neither Will nor I bother to discipline him for his language right now. My head droops to face the half-packed bags on my bed.

Outside, I throw my bags in the back seat of my car before tiredly slipping into the driver's seat. On the phone with Madison, every muscle in my body is trying to fight through tears while explaining what happened.

"Are you kidding me?! Will is such an *asshole!*" Madison screams into the phone.

"Maddie, I messed up," I let out through a sob.

"Lyz, oh my god," she exclaims. "Why don't you come stay with me for a while?"

Shaking my head, I grip the phone in my hand. "No, I... I couldn't do that to you."

"Do what?" Madison asks. "Spend some time with your best friend while we plot against your piece-of-shit uncle? Get your ass down here, it's okay."

God, I love her. She's always been there for me, even at my lowest point.

"Okay," I laugh, "I'll see you in a minute."

Her place is a small two-bedroom house in an older neighborhood. Once I pull into her driveway and knock on the door, Madison is there almost immediately to wrap me in a hug.

"Come on in," she says, taking my bags from me.

She has an unopened bag of Chinese takeout on the table. Madison insists on sharing with me, even though she only has enough for herself. We sit down, and she listens to me go into detail about everything while we eat.

"Your uncle is *crazy*," Madison decides while opening her container of egg rolls, "he's using Ryan to control you, and Ryan is being a brooding teenager about it because he doesn't know what else to do."

"It's my fault," my voice quivers. While clutching the box of noodles, the fork in my palm slowly hovers over the food. I can't bring myself to take a bite.

"No," Madison stops me, "do *not* say that. You did the right thing when you took Ryan in. None of this is your fault, Lyz."

"I don't know how to protect him," I admit.

I've done everything I possibly could for Ryan. I got him out of Will's house, and enrolled him in a better school district. I *tried* to get him into therapy, but it got really expensive after a while. It's never been easy, but all of it was for *him*, to give him the best shot at life that I could.

How could one *stupid* nightmare erase all of that so easily?

"You do," Madison says, snapping me out of my daze. "Will just doesn't want you to know that."

The two of us sit there for a while, just talking. The hours of the evening slip away as our conversation trails on. At the end of the night, Madison tries to get me to take her bed, but I insist on the couch. I don't want her to sacrifice more for me than she already has.

I don't dream that night, and after everything that happened today, that scares me more than any nightmare.

The next morning, my eyes open, slowly and sluggish, but it takes me a while to work up the energy to actually get up. The time on my phone lights up when I touch the screen, showing 9:34 a.m.. We need to leave for work in about an hour. I manage to peel myself off the couch and go to Madison's room to check on her. She's still passed out, snoring.

Migrating into the kitchen, my hands work on autopilot to brew a pot of coffee for both of us while my mind is still half asleep. Once the pot is done, I make myself a cup with some creamer and step out onto the front porch.

Sitting on the old metal outdoor chair, my train of thought turns to my dream from the other night. As if I can even call it that now. At this point, it's more like reality.

How? How is it possible that any of it could be real? The door, the forest, the cabin, even that god-forsaken bird. I couldn't see it, but the constant chirping in the distance told me plainly that it *was* there, watching me. Drawing me toward the cabin.

What does any of this mean? Or does it mean anything at all? Is it possible that I'm just crazy? Was I imagining all of it?

"No." I say to myself under my breath.

There was too much coincidence to diagnose myself with insanity. Everything I saw yesterday was *real*.

And dangerous.

One thing is for sure: if my dream was real, some of it is connected to us. Will, Ryan...and me.

Before I can finish that thought, Madison meets me on the porch with her own coffee mug.

"Good morning," she says, clearly not awake enough yet. A yawn escapes her mouth as she sits down next to me. Her charcoal black hair hasn't been brushed yet. A few knotted strands stick outward. Her bangs are split to the side, which I know she hates because it's hard to center them neatly on her face after they do that. She clutches the mug in her hand with an appreciative smile. "Thank you for making this."

"No problem," I say.

"How are you feeling?"

"Like crap, but...it's fine." The sigh that comes out is more ragged than I was hoping.

She groans. "You know I hate it when you do that."

I just shrug. "When I do what?"

"When you wave it off and say, 'it's fine' like that," Madison clarifies. "It's okay to say that you're *not* fine."

"I know that," I say quietly.

Madison quietly rolls her eyes and takes a sip from her mug.

A quick glance at my phone shows the time as 9:50 a.m.

"Come on, we've gotta get going," I tell her, standing up to leave the porch "Logan's not gonna be happy if you're late again.

Madison scoffs. "When is Logan *ever* happy unless he has a bottle of bourbon in his hand?"

We split off to get dressed and prepare for the day. Per my insistence, we take my car so that Madison can save a little gas. After everything she's done for me, it's the least I can do.

We arrive at the restaurant, packed by the lunch rush. Logan jogs up to the two of us as we clock in, more than likely to deliver a criticizing lecture.

"Both of you are late!" he yells, clutching his clipboard. He pushes his circular glasses farther up on his nose. A bead of sweat trickles down his dark skin. The sneer across his face is a look I know all too well. It makes him look like he caught the smell of garbage, and it personally offended him. His red polo shirt reeks of alcohol and Pine-Sol rather than his typical cologne.

"It's two minutes past eleven!" Madison doesn't make eye contact with him. She puts her purse in her locker, sneering at his accusation.

"Are you arguing with me?" he asks. "You both are on the morning shift. We opened an hour ago and a rush came in. You should have been here by then!"

"We were on the schedule for eleven o'clock," I point out, gesturing to the old clock in the corner of the entrance hallway.

Logan sighs in defeat, knowing he can't argue. He doesn't make the schedule, that job goes to the general manager, Eric. Logan can't be bothered to check the staff's schedule more than once to confirm who's coming in. His tired, drunken eyes lay on me irritably before he gives in.

"Just get to work," he orders, "Madison, I need you serving. Alyssa, I need you to clean the drink machine and restock the bathrooms before you hop on the register."

Of course he would stick me with the busywork.

I start with the drink machine, since it's the quicker chore, but my hand accidentally hits a few of the knobs, and various drinks spray my arms and uniform before the job is done. The sticky sugar of sweet tea and multiple different sodas clings to my skin before I'm able to make the time to wash it off. Restocking the bathrooms is more of a pain than it should be, as the jagged metal key refuses to unlock the paper towel dispenser without me having to jam it inside.

They hardly even need to be restocked. There's still a full roll of toilet paper in each bathroom, and the paper towels were only half-empty. Logan is just freakishly particular.

Finally, I slip away to the register. Admittedly, it's not my favorite part of the job. Ringing up customers, most of which can be difficult to deal with, is pretty rough, but it's better than running around with endless chores assigned by Logan, who'll find any excuse to keep us busy.

Despite the restaurant being really busy today, my time at the register isn't so bad. That is, until I see someone I recognize.

Moving forward in the line of people in front of me is the man from the cabin.

"Alyssa?" he asks.

My heart races in my chest when I see the rugged cabin man walk up to me. He's joined by someone else. This other man is wearing a black leather jacket, a plain white T-shirt and blue jeans. His short hair is a bright, sand-like blonde, with messy strands falling in front of his face.

"What the hell?!" I mutter under my breath, panicking as they approach the register.

"Alyssa Haller?" the blonde man asks.

My pulse quickens even faster. "How do...what is..."

"It's okay! We just want to talk!" The first man calmingly raises his hands in caution.

The beating in my chest feels so loud that I swear everyone in the restaurant can hear it. I stand there, frozen. Unsure of what to do. Heat flushes in my cheeks as I take a slow, ragged breath before questioning them.

"H—how do you know my name?" I ask them.

"Alyssa!" Logan yells from his office behind me. "What's going on over there? You're holding up the line!"

Customers begin glaring at the three of us, restless. The disdain in the atmosphere is increasingly obvious.

"Nothing. Sorry Logan!" I shout back before turning to face the mysterious strangers and rubbing the bridge of my nose. "You have to go, I can't be getting in trouble right now."

"Wait, Alyssa, please! I can explain everything! Just meet me in the alley after your shift." asks the blonde man.

"I..." I start.

I don't even know these guys. There's *no way* I can trust them.

But the blonde man's gaze is fixed on me, and something about him stands out. The sincerity in his bright green eyes is overwhelmed with desperation, too raw to fake.

Somehow, that same desperation makes its way to me. Despite how badly I want these men to leave me alone, to let me go back to my life without adding more insanity than I can handle, that desperate feeling seems out of place. Like it truly isn't mine.

Two women in line get fed up with waiting and leave. An elderly woman whispers to her husband with a sour expression. The thick tension in the air urges me to wrap up the conversation and get back to work.

But there's too many questions, and these men are offering all the answers. The conflict between duty and morbid curiosity is intense like a battle waging on a repeated loop in my head.

Cautiously, I dare to test the waters. "What's your name?"

The blonde man smiles, as if my question filled him with the hope that my decision had been made, when, in fact, that definitely wasn't the case.

"It's Daniel," he answers. He gestures to the man I met at the cabin, "this is my friend, Kyle."

I recognize Daniel's name from Kyle calling to him yesterday. Kyle himself is shifting nervously, acknowledging the awkward atmosphere of the situation.

"We just want to help you," he assures.

Sighing, I wave him off. "I don't know what you know about me, but I *need* you to leave."

Daniel sighs and exchanges a mournful look with Kyle. He then turns back to me, and nods. "Just think about it. Please," he says. "We'll be waiting."

With that, both turn to make their way out the door without objecting any further. Before stepping out of the restaurant, Daniel stops once more, turns his head toward me, and flashes yet another genuine smile in my direction.

Honestly, I can't tell if I find that comforting or unsettling. The knot in my stomach decides on the latter.

The customer behind them is a middle-aged man with a prickly look on his face that resembles Will a little too closely. He steps up to the register and rolls his eyes in disgruntled relief.

"Kids are too distracted these days," he says matter-of-factly. The man then looks at me expectantly, waiting for me to either apologize or agree with him.

"How many in your party?" I avoid either option, moving on and quickly getting back to work.

The rest of the day fills me with nothing but dread before finally making it to the end of my shift. By the time I clock out and start towards the exit, my feet are aching furiously. Madison and I both grab our purses and prepare to leave, but before exiting the building, my anxious mind brings me to a pause. Should I go talk to those guys? The two strange men that seem to have all the answers?

No. I can't afford to take any more risks. I don't even know them, but they're obviously connected to something dangerous. For the sake of my brother, I choose to avoid the answers to my burning questions, at least for now. Madison and I walk together toward the car, and we head straight to her place. For a brief moment, driving past the restaurant, my line of sight finds Daniel and Kyle by the dumpsters. They wait patiently for someone who will never arrive.

Meanwhile, several questions churn through my mind, waiting for answers that will never come.

It's better this way. It has to be.

When we get to Madison's place, the sun is starting to set. Bright pink and orange hues paint the sky. A familiar car is parked in her driveway. Kat steps out of her car and starts toward me.

A beating in my chest storms over all my other senses. I can only think of one reason why she'd come here: my brother. Quickly, I swing my legs out of the driver's seat of my car to meet her.

"What are you doing here?" I ask her, panicked. "Is Ryan okay?!"

Kat nervously fidgets with her hair before she speaks.

"Your uncle wanted me to ask—"

"Well then don't waste your time. Just tell him I listened to his second-hand lecture," I cut in as Madison gets out of the passenger seat.

"He wants you to come back," she says.

The words bring me to a stop.

"Wait...what?" I ask her.

"He got called into a case. There's a new lead on the Riot's location. He'll be gone for a couple of days," she explains, straightening the waist of her uniform pants. She must've just finished her shift at the station. "He wants you home to look after Ryan."

Unbelievable. Will's audacity never ceases to surprise me. He kicks me out of my own home, lectures me about who is a better fit to take care of my brother, and then leaves and asks me to come back just to *babysit*? All of this for a criminal gang that he hasn't been able to find in fifteen years.

This is ridiculous. It feels like I'm back at Will's house, left once again to pick up his slack.

My first instinct is to tell her no, so that he'll finally take some initiative for once in his damn life. But I can't do that to Ryan. As absurd as the situation is, I need to be there for him, since Will clearly won't.

Kat's car follows me to my apartment. I don't know why. My impression was that she was going to head home after asking me to watch Ryan. What else could she need from me?

It doesn't take long to find out. When we both park at the complex, she calls my name.

"Alyssa! Wait!" she jogs up to me.

"Kat, I'm really tired," I say, my shoulders slumping back with the weight of my bags in my hands as I pull them out of my car, "I just want to check on Ryan and go to bed."

As we talk, the vibrant sunset colors begin to fade into the darkness of the night. A couple of streetlights in the distance start to turn on behind Kat.

"I know, I just—" she starts, struggling to find the words, "Will is an ass."

"Obviously," I scoff.

"But he *does* care about you and Ryan," she says.

"He has a funny way of showing it," I say, rolling my eyes.

I can barely hear her next words when she says them in a low mutter.

"There are worse ways."

Kat blinks, noticing my curious look. "The thing is, he's your family. He took you and Ryan in and raised you."

Staring wide-mouthed at Kat while she said something wildly out of pocket was not something I thought would happen *twice* today.

"Will is a *drunk*," I say, "for fifteen years he made it clear that he would rather sit on his recliner with a beer in his hand or scream and have constant meltdowns locked in his bedroom, than pay *any* attention to us. Just because he's family doesn't mean he's a saint!"

"So you're just going to ignore him?" she asks, somehow offended.

My arms spread outward into the air despite being weighed down by my duffel bags.

"Would if I could, Kat!" I say, a little louder than intended, spreading my arms out.

Kat grunts, her eyes meeting the ground below her. "Unbelievable. You're just like him."

"*Excuse me*?" I say, baffled by the implication.

"Not Will," she says, looking back up and scanning me as if watching an ungrateful child throw a tantrum over getting a new smartphone for Christmas. "You're as stubborn as my brother."

The comparison feels out of place, and honestly it infuriates me. I don't know what situation she might be dealing with at home that led her to make that connection. Truthfully, I never knew she had a brother. But unfortunately, right now, I couldn't care less.

"Goodnight, Kat."

Inside, I let my bags fall from my arms and land on the floor in front of me. I call for Will, but there's no answer. Instead, Ryan comes out of his room, looking tired and pale. The exhausted expression on his face shows clear resentment as he faces me.

Ryan huffs and pushes past to get to the kitchen. "Save your breath, he's not here."

"Are you okay?" I ask him.

His tired baggy eyes drag between me, his phone, and the floor below him. He moves around the apartment like an aimless zombie. I place a hand to his forehead to check his temperature, but he swats it away.

"Like you care," he retorts, half-heartedly stomping away from me to get to the kitchen. He grabs a soda from the refrigerator and slips back into his room without another word.

I scroll through my phone to find somewhere to order dinner for the two of us. Alfonzo's has always been one of Ryan's favorites. I order a pizza for us to share and get back to straightening up the place. Turning on my TV for background noise, the first thing that comes up is the news channel. I scoff at the headline.

The Riot Gang: Ongoing Police Response.

Yeah. No shit.

Despite his insistence that he knows what's best for Ryan, Will is still pulling the same crap that he did when we were living with him. I'd thought he'd given it up years ago after we moved out, but *clearly* that's not the case. Chasing after Jacob Reeves is *still* more important than his niece and nephew.

What a hypocrite.

The apartment is an absolute mess thanks to Will, who left cans of beer and half-eaten takeout everywhere. After discarding his trash, I start running loads of laundry. A few minutes into the washer's first cycle, I hear the doorbell ringing.

I quickly grab some cash from my wallet and answer it, expecting to find the delivery driver. However, to my surprise, the one holding the pizza is the man from the cabin, Kyle.

"Are you serious?!" I shout, crossing my arms.

"You didn't show up after work today," he says.

"Yeah, and you two didn't *take the hint*!" I shout again.

Daniel emerges from the cover of the evening's darkness and stands behind him, stuffing an old cellphone into his pocket.

"Alyssa, I'm sorry, but we *need* to talk to you," he pleads.

"Look," I sigh, "I don't know what's going on, but I *really* can't do this right now. My uncle is on my case, and I can't afford to screw up again. He could take my brother away from me."

"I...we didn't know that." Kyle's eyes widen with sympathy.

"No, you didn't," I snap. "Because I don't *know* you. You guys clearly know who I am, but don't you see how this looks? To me, you're just two strangers who won't leave me the hell alone!"

Daniel and Kyle exchange looks with each other, seemingly just now realizing how all of this appears.

"We're not trying to hurt you," Daniel explains. "We just want to explain what happened back at the cabin."

"I gathered that. And believe me, I'd *love* to get some answers," I admit. "But right now my hands are tied. I'm sorry, but I need you guys to leave, *please*!"

I start pushing the door shut, but Daniel blocks it with his forearm before it reaches the jamb.

"Wait, please! I can tell you about the dreams you've been having!" he says urgently, his eyes reflecting that same desperation from earlier.

The feeling subtly creeps up my spine, making me stop in my tracks. Panic quickly sets into my stomach.

How? How could he possibly know that? I never told anyone, not even Madison.

With one look into Daniel's eyes, the realization hits. If he knows about my dream, could he maybe help me make sense of it all? The constant yearning for answers grows stronger with each passing second.

As tempted as I am, though, my thoughts immediately turn back to Ryan. He comes first, always.

"I—I'm sorry, I can't help you."

Kyle tries to object, but Daniel raises a hand and stops him, his expression now shifted from imperative pleading to gentle understanding. Kyle sighs and hands me the pizza.

"It's okay," Daniel assures with another gentle smile. "Have a good night."

He closes the door. I can hear Kyle's muffled voice arguing with him as they step further away.

I set the warm cardboard box of pizza on the coffee table in the living room.

With a heavy sigh, I call out toward the hallway. "Ryan! Food's here! Come eat!"

After twenty minutes, Ryan still hasn't come out of his room. Knocking on his door, there's no response, just dead silence. I can't shake the feeling that something is wrong.

His door is unlocked, and, although I know he hates it, I open it and step into his bedroom. There are clothes everywhere, and his video game on his computer is turned on, but nobody is there to play it.

"Ryan?" I call out.

No answer.

I scramble around the apartment looking for him. All the windows are still locked from the inside, so he couldn't have climbed out. The front door is the only other exit point.

I would've seen him. There's no way he could've left unnoticed, but still, he's gone. There's no sign of him.

"Ryan, this isn't funny!" I shout.

My sight blurs. I can feel the gaps in my breath. Clutching my chest, my knees give in, causing me to crash onto the floor. My hands grip the rough carpet of the living room. Heat swells around me, suffocating and impossible to escape from. An unstoppable swell of tears streams down my face as I cry out for my brother.

Where could he have gone? Is he safe? Why did he leave?

There are two answers to that last question. He's had to live with Will again for a whole day. I ran away a couple times myself because of our uncle when I was his age. Or maybe... could he have left because of me? He was so upset when he found out I was leaving.

The rest of my thoughts start to clear, with one left to echo in my mind on repeat: Ryan thinks I abandoned him. It's all my fault.

3-Daniel

Sweat drips down the side of my face. The beating in my chest could give a drummer in a heavy metal band a run for their money. My feet stay positioned firmly on the ground. I watch him closely for any falter in his movements, any sign of sloppiness. As if there's ever been any. No one even gets close to touching the great Jacob Reeves without regretting it later. There's no point in trying to beat him, even if my head was really in the game today.

"Don't be shy, Danny," he taunts. His smile prods me on, like a bullfighter waving a flag.

I lunge at him with my fist.

He dodges easily, grabbing and twisting my arm. His laughter rings in my ears. Mocking me. Judging me.

With my free hand, I grab his wrist in an attempt to free myself, but with his other hand he pulls it away.

"What do you do now?" he asks me as if he were a teacher giving a pop quiz.

But I was never a stellar student. Frustrated, I throw my head forward, colliding with his and causing him to let go. The impact makes me a little dizzy. My vision starts to cloud, but I force myself to focus and inch closer to him as much as I can.

After a short pause to collect himself, he's back in, seemingly unphased. That snarky, knowing smile spreads across his lips as he readies himself. He jabs his fist forward, but I block him. We move in a fast-paced rhythm around the room, throwing and blocking punch after punch, until something suddenly catches me off guard.

My phone buzzes in my jacket pocket on the bench behind me. All it takes is for me to glance back for a second before his fist collides with my jaw, knocking me off balance and onto the floor. Groaning, I rub my cheek. The impact of his punch stings the left side of my face.

The towering man standing over me, who never misses a hit or a chance to lecture me, offers a hand. The disappointment across his face is crystal clear.

"What did I tell you? *Never* let your guard down!" he says, "Maybe start listening to me, Danny. It'll do you some good."

"Yes sir." My response is almost monotonous while taking his hand to pull myself up.

The phone goes off again. I didn't put it on silent on my way back. Crap.

"Who's calling you?" he asks me.

"It's just Zane. I asked him to grab some stuff for me on his supply run." Lies come so easily nowadays. So effortless.

He huffs, crossing his arms. "*Stuff*?"

"I wore out the sharpening stone for my knife," I tell him, "he's getting me a new one."

"Hmph," he grumbles. It seems like he buys it, but I still get the famously passive side-eye. Before he can question me any further, though, one of the guys from outside pokes his head through the door.

Like most everyone, he avoids my father's gaze, remaining too nervous to interrupt.

Noticing the daunted look on the guy behind him, Dad turns his attention away from me.

"What is it, Jeff?" he asks, running a hand over his buzzed blonde hair.

Jeff clears his throat before speaking. Sweat drips from his bare scalp, plain for the room to see.

"Hey—uh, Jacob?" Jeff's eyes widen as he corrects himself before he can *be* corrected. "Uh, I mean, *Sir*! Some of the other guys were wondering about the plan for tomorrow's job in Herald?"

"Yeah, yeah, I'm coming."

Before he leaves, my dad turns back to me, pointing his finger right in my face. "Distractions make you weak. You've got to get your head out of the clouds, Danny. I've been telling you that since you were eleven."

"I'm sorry, Sir."

The second he leaves, I sprint to my phone and open it to find a missed call and a text, both from Kyle.

911. Get to the cabin. Now!!!

Shit. Something's wrong.

I grab my black leather jacket lying on the floor and pull my arms through the sleeves as quickly as possible. My sneakers push through the halls of the old metal warehouse, squeaking with every rushed scuffle on the floor. Several other Riot members try to stop and talk to me as I weave between them, but my blank and determined stare repels them from engaging. It's a tactic I don't like to use. It's cold, it's heartless, it's *Jacob Reeves's* stare. But today it's a necessary tool. I can't run out of there without causing suspicion, so this is the only way to leave the Riot base as quickly as possible.

Once out of sight of the old warehouse, I sprint off toward town. The alley is only a few blocks away from Riot headquarters. It's a long run, but it's not impossible.

Finally, on Milam Street after a long-winded run, my lungs are burning. I dip into the alley between the Herb Shop and Edgar's Baked Goods Emporium. After taking a few steps into the alley, the red door with golden painted designs appears in front of me.

Once inside the quiet sanctity of the forest, my pace slows, and I take a relaxing breath. From here, it's just a simple walk to the cabin.

Inside the rustic wooden building, my friend Kyle stands in the living room. He looks at me, eyes wide like he just saw a ghost.

"What's going on?" I ask him.

"Remember that girl we've been looking for?"

I shoot him a sarcastic glare and fold my arms. "Oh, you mean Alyssa Haller? The girl that I've spent five years of my life looking for because the magic cabin says she's important?" I say. "*Nope,* doesn't ring a bell at all."

Kyle strokes his chin with his hand and paces the living room. I've never seen him this worked up.

Finally, he looks back in my direction. "She was here."

"Wait...*what*?"

We've been trying to find this girl for years. I don't know how she could've found us so easily, but clearly our luck is finally changing.

"She walked right into the cabin!" He gestures to the door behind me.

I look around, anxious. "Well, where is she?"

"She kinda...ran off." Kyle's admission is quiet. He avoids eye contact with me completely.

"*What*?!"

"I don't know what happened! When I said her last name, she just bolted!" Kyle says frantically.

"Did she *tell* you her last name?" I ask him, realizing the issue.

Kyle's long, silent pause answers my question.

"You didn't..." I sigh, bringing my fingers to my temple.

"A stranger broke in here and said her name was Alyssa! I wasn't thinking!"

"Kyle!" I shout, "You scared off our one chance to—" my voice trails off before I finish. "To save everything!"

Kyle runs his hands through his brown hair. "I'm sorry, Dan."

"Has she been in town this entire time?!" I wonder aloud.

My thoughts spin with places we could've potentially run into her over the years. The Light Door entrance is *right* in the middle of downtown. How many times has she passed by it without us knowing?

"It's a possibility," Kyle says.

That brings up a different question, though: Why now? Alyssa must have found the door because it appeared for her. So why did it take so long for the Light Door to sense her?

A chirping noise sounds from behind the front entrance. Through the small stained-glass window, a little red bird hovers outside, waiting to be let in.

I open the door, and as he flies through, sunlight reflects off his silver wingtips and nearly blinds me. He circles the living room twice, then lands on Kyle's shoulder and puffs out his feathers.

"Hey, Peck." Kyle gently pets our little friend, stroking his back with his pointer finger. He then notes the gold band around his own wrist. "Oh, here's your bracelet."

He slides the band off of his wrist and tosses it to me.

The golden bracelet is engraved with my name, and similar designs to the Light Door in the alley. I found it when I first started out at the cabin. It's the only useful Guardian tool I have. If my father, or anyone else in the Riot found it, they'd take it, and I'd be screwed. Kyle holds onto the bracelet for me when I'm at the base. Otherwise, I keep it on me.

"We know now that she's local, so what can we do?" I ask while spinning the band around my wrist.

"I'm not sure," Kyle says honestly, "it's not like we can go door-to-door looking for her all over town."

"Yeah, I know," I sigh.

The framed photo on the wall behind him catches my eye. A woman basking in the summer sunlight, holding a little boy in her arms. The woman's caramel hair glows under the light. Her blue dress shifts in the direction of the wind. The boy is about ten years old. The breeze pushes his blonde hair in front of his eyes, and his green shirt is stained with chocolate ice cream. I look back at the woman, her warm smile is so happy, so gentle. And yet, the sadness in her bright green eyes is so clear.

Kyle comes up behind me and puts a hand on my shoulder.

I don't turn away, my focus fixed on the portrait of me and my mother.

"I know how important this is to you," he sighs.

Peck takes off from Kyle's shoulder and flutters his wings toward my hands.

I catch him and snap out of my daze.

"We *need* to find this girl." The heaviness in my chest leaves me feeling almost hopeless. This is too important to risk.

"Look man, I know," Kyle says. "But there's nothing we can do right now."

"Are you giving up?" I raise an eyebrow toward him.

"Never," he replies with a reassuring smile. "I'm just saying, we should regroup tomorrow once we have a plan."

As much as I hate it, he's right. We could search the entire town, but it would take forever. We need a solid plan, but if I don't get back to the Riot soon, my dad might just *literally* kill me.

It's still wild to me that Alyssa had just *shown up* here.

When I found out five years ago that there was somebody else like me, someone chosen to be a Guardian, it was like a weight was lifted. Spending most of my time trying to find her has been driving me nuts. And then she *finally* turns up, only for Kyle to scare her away?

I can hardly blame him though. From what he told me, the interaction was very sudden, and the fact that she was just standing there was dumbfounding. It threw him off. What Kyle did was stupid, but honestly, I probably would've been that stupid too.

"Fine, we'll meet back here tomorrow," I decide. "Bright and early."

"Yeah, sure dude. *Bright and early* for you is lunchtime," Kyle retorts.

I smack the backside of his head, and he just laughs.

That afternoon, I rush back to headquarters by myself.

The moment I push open the rusted metal door of the old warehouse building, a few of my dad's men come up to talk to me.

"You goin' with your dad on that job later?" Landon's cigarette bobs in his mouth.

"Which job?"

"He won't tell us the score yet. He hasn't clued you in, Junior?" Henry asks me, snarking with my nickname.

"I haven't heard anything," I answer, glaring. Pushing past them, a low growl escapes my throat. "And *don't* call me Junior."

On the way out, a few other Riot members pass by me, but they don't bother me with more than a "Hey," simply acknowledging my presence.

In the crowd, my older sister is talking with Maria, the new recruit that she's been training.

Walking further towards my room, Zane crosses my path with a wrapped-up sub sandwich in hand. I grab his arm and turn both of us around to speak to him.

"Hey! Zane, wait!" I call out.

"What's up, Daniel?"

"When's your next supply run?" Hopefully I can take care of the lie I told my dad earlier today.

"Tomorrow morning," Zane answers. He looks exhausted, like he wants to end this conversation as soon as possible and eat his dinner in peace.

"Perfect!" I exclaim. "Can you get me a new sharpening stone? Mine sucks right now, it wore out."

"Yeah, man," he says, "I've got you."

Patting Zane lightly on the shoulder, I send him off. "Thanks! I owe you one."

Finally alone in my room, I take my jacket off and toss it over the metal folding chair that sits in the corner by the door. I kick my shoes off and shove them under my cot. On top of the bed lies one pillow with no sheet covering it, and a thin blue cotton blanket.

Yep, home sweet home. If I could spend even one night at the cabin, sleeping comfortably in the queen-sized fortress of wool blankets, without my father getting suspicious, I would. Not that the flat mattress of the cot is too uncomfortable for me.

Laying down on the low-standing bed, I stare up at the ceiling for a while. My mind is lost deep in thought before eventually drifting off.

Morning comes and I jolt upwards in my bed.

The nightmares.

The *worst* part of this job.

They never make any sense, but they almost always come back to haunt me. Shouting *I told you so* in my face like a damning prophecy.

My mom told me once that the dreams were Peck's way of talking to us, that he was trying his best to protect us. I'm not sure how that works, but those dreams don't feel very protective. They feel like they're just meant to scare me.

Hurrying out of the warehouse again, I don't look back for a second.

Soon enough, back in the alley, the Light Door appears. Before I step through, my phone buzzes in my jean pocket.

"Hey, I left to get breakfast. Do you want to meet me there?" Kyle asks.

Starving, I eagerly reply. "Yeah, where are you?"

"I'm walking over to that old cafe over on Church Street, do you know where it is?" he asks me.

"No, but I know where Church Street is. I'll be right over."

"How do you know where a street is, but not what's on it?" Kyle wonders, his tone filled with judgement.

"By not paying attention," I smirk. "I'm on my way."

It's just a short walk to get to Church Street. When I get close enough, Kyle calls out to me from the other side. I jog to meet up with him.

"Where's the fire?" Kyle laughs.

"Shut up."

Kyle and I take our seats in the cafe. We each order coffee with half and half cream. It's flavorless and dull but adding a couple of sugar packets makes it tolerable. By the time our food comes, we've finished about five refills of coffee between the two of us.

Kyle's plate is loaded. Three pancakes pile up next to a portion of eggs, topped with a thick slice of ham. The waitress hands Kyle his food, and then my plate of two plain pancakes is placed in front of me. Kyle frowns, and gives me his ham. Then, he splits his eggs with me. At the end of the meal, he takes the check, and then we head out.

I've always felt guilty about how much Kyle's been willing to share with me. I don't own a wallet, let alone have five dollars in my pocket. My dad uses any money we get from jobs to fund exchanges and other business deals. Kyle was briefly homeless a few years back and shouldn't really be able to afford to pay for anything. He always assures me that it's fine, he has a savings account that he uses to help out. I can't imagine that there would be much in that account, though.

As we make our way to the cabin, we pass by a local restaurant. From the window, a hoard of people pushing through and waiting for their tables engulfs the entrance.

Kyle spots something through the glass and stops dead in his tracks.

"That's her!"

"Who?"

"The girl at the register! That's Alyssa!" he shouts, excited.

Through the window, I can see the waiting area of the restaurant, where a girl stands at the computer on the register table. Her long and wavy hair is a unique mix of amber and brunette. She looks sad and dazed as each customer passes through her line. As if something were pushing her down, and any hope she had of release was drained a long time ago. Still, she looks...beautiful.

My chest tightens in a manner I've never felt before. Her deep brown eyes are yearning for *something*. Part of me desperately wants to know what it is.

"That's Alyssa? Are you sure?" I ask Kyle, not losing eye contact with her.

"Absolutely."

I gather up my courage and walk inside the restaurant behind Kyle.

When she sees us, Alyssa looks terrified. She flicks her eyes between Kyle and me.

"What the hell?!" she quietly panics as we approach her.

As we try to talk to her, Alyssa seemingly grows increasingly frantic. At one point, her boss sees us holding up the line of customers and asks us to leave. Before we do, though, I beg her to meet us in the back of the building after she gets off work.

I can see the doubt in her eyes when I ask her. Something is keeping her from wanting to learn more about her situation. Fear, maybe? The nightmares? Whatever it is, I can tell that it's bad.

Nevertheless, she's curious. "What's your name?"

I turn back to her. A faint smile tugs at my lips. "It's Daniel."

Her eyes light up, as if she recognizes me. Even if she *is* scared, she still wants to know more, I can tell. But she obviously has a lot going on, and she needs to go at her own pace.

"Just think about it. Please," I ask her. "We'll be waiting."

With that, Kyle and I exit the restaurant and start toward the back.

"You know she's not coming, right?" Kyle says as we walk.

"I know," I say, "but on the chance that she does, I'd rather talk to her in a place she's familiar with so that she doesn't freak out in the cabin."

"You mean *again*?" he sighs.

"I didn't say that."

Kyle lifts his head, looking at me apologetically. "So, we're all good?"

"Of course, man," I tell him.

We wait outside for a few hours, even when it becomes increasingly obvious that she blew us off. I don't care. Leaning against the brick wall that corners the dumpsters, I fiddle with my bracelet, deep in thought.

I found her, after *five years*. I've been a guardian for almost fifteen at this point. Even with Kyle around, I've spent *so long* feeling isolated in that role. Like the weight of the entire world was on my shoulders, and *mine* alone. But it's not, there's someone else to carry it with me.

But is it fair to ask Alyssa to take on a weight like that? *Of course not*, I know that. Nobody wants to be told that they're responsible for the well-being of every source of life on the planet. It's going to be impossible for her to come to terms with her role. Hopefully I can be of some help, the way my mom helped me when *I* was first chosen.

Eventually, Kyle grows so impatient that he insists we leave, so the two of us head back to the cabin.

When we get there, Peck is fast asleep in his little nest by the front windowsill. Kyle helped him make the nest a while back by giving him shreds of newspaper. Those two have been close ever since I told Kyle about this place three years ago, when he left the Riot.

My dad was *furious*. He would've killed him.

I helped Kyle out by bringing him to the cabin and giving him a place to hide.

He's been here ever since, keeping an eye on this place when I can't be here.

Peck was *not* a fan of Kyle at first. He attacked him with his little beak the second he walked through the front door. But I guess the two of them have bonded over the years. They've spent so much time together that I often come back from the Riot base to find Peck nestled atop Kyle's hair as if it were a nest.

There's no way of knowing where Peck really came from, but he's been protecting this cabin way longer than I have. He pretty much stays in the cabin or in the surrounding woods. He's never gone outside the Light Door before, to my knowledge.

"Do you think she'll turn up again?" Kyle asks me suddenly.

"She has to," I respond. "Our type of job has a lot of pressure, and I *hate* putting that on her..."

"But it's necessary. I know," Kyle says.

"It's not fair," I say to myself.

My job in this cabin isn't always easy. When I found out that someone would be sharing that job with me, it was a total relief at first, not having to do this alone.

But now it just feels cruel adding so much onto Alyssa's plate. I have to break the news to an innocent girl that the weight of the universe is on her shoulders. She was already so broken when we met her today. So obviously burdened by *something*. How will she react when she learns exactly what we're fighting against?

My eyes meet the kitchen, the entry to the basement just beyond, where the Dark Door lies.

My mother's words ring in my ears. A ghostly memory.

"The magic behind this door is dangerous, Danny," she'd said. *"Letting it out could destroy the world. It's* our *job to keep it trapped right where it belongs."*

The Dark Door has gotten weaker over the years, cracks blistering through the rotting wood, making it easier for some of its magic to slip through. Voices haunt me in every nightmare, the dark forces infecting Peck's dreams. It was the same for my mother. I'd be shocked if Alyssa wasn't also having those nightmares.

If that force of power ever got out, it would be the end of everything. Our world would be nothing but a void of destruction and chaos. The dark magic would demolish every life, every building, every ecosystem, reducing it all to a pile of ash. That's why we protect this cabin. *That* is what we're fighting for. To stop the darkness from wiping out everything. It's what makes this cabin so important. What makes *Alyssa* so important.

I found out about Alyssa all those years ago in a dream. One of Peck's *methods of protection*.

She was on the floor of the cabin, kneeling over a teenage boy. Her eyes were red with tears. It looked like all the energy had been sucked out of the boy's body.

His veins were so black that they popped out under his pale white skin. She turned to look at me, and when she spoke, my heart sank in my chest.

"Help him... help him! That's your job, right?"

After that, the room darkened as seamlessly as a blown-out candle. Then, something else spoke through Alyssa. I could feel the shift, the power of the darkness overtaking her.

"This Guardian will fall much quicker than the last," she had said, *"and you will fall with her."*

Before I woke up, the last thing I heard was my mom's voice. She whispered a name to me: Alyssa Haller.

Since then, all I've been doing is trying to find her. Alyssa is connected to this, not just through her Guardianship, but through something bigger. The worst part? Based on our interaction today, I don't think she knows anything about what she is.

My phone buzzes in my pocket. It's my sister again.

Kyle frowns. "You should get back to the base. She's probably worried."

"Yeah," I sigh.

"Do you need a ride over there?" he asks me.

Shaking my head, my eyes find Peck. He's picking through the peanuts and raisins in the trail mix Kyle had left on the coffee table, leaving only M&M's and pretzels. He fluffs his feathers in a giddy motion as he eats his snack.

"Nah, I'll be okay," I tell Kyle. "Besides, you shouldn't risk being so close to the base."

I give my bracelet back to Kyle and start back to the Riot base.

It's a long walk out of town, and by the time I reach the old warehouse, my legs are killing me, but it's better than risking Kyle's safety.

"I should've taken the damn truck," I huff under my breath as I pull on the door handle. I couldn't have taken it, though. The

Riot would recognize it pretty quickly, since Kyle and I stole it from them.

Inside, some of the members stop to greet me.

"Hey, kid! What's up?" Charles asks with a smile. He's one of the older members, one of my dad's army friends. His gray hair is short and curly. His age doesn't take away from his skill. Charles has never been one to question an order from my father. All things considered, though, he's a pretty nice guy.

"Not much," I say, "have you seen my dad?"

He shrugs. "Jacob left about an hour ago, he said he had a meeting."

"A meeting? With who?"

Charles clears his throat.

"Not sure. I just heard something about a *potential business partner*."

Well that definitely doesn't sound good.

"Have you heard anything about the job he's been working on?"

He looks outward in both directions, checking to make sure nobody is listening.

"I heard him yesterday in his office making a call, he said something about targeting somebody."

My brow furrows. "Who?"

"I have no idea." Charles shrugs. "But if you ask me kiddo, I think it has something to do with this new business partner of his."

"What gives you that idea?"

"The secrecy," he answers matter-of-factly.

A job that Jacob Reeves won't tell anyone about, and a business partner that nobody has met before. Not to mention the timing, with everything happening all at once. What could this mean?

"Thanks, man," I tell Charles, shrugging the thought away and starting upstairs.

Maybe while my dad is gone, I can go into his office and see what I can find.

The room is dimly lit by a single nearly burnt-out light bulb. The sullen gray walls are bare aside from the wooden bulletin board behind his desk where he posts his maps, shipment orders, and other lists.

Crossing the room to examine the board, the bottom of my shoe squeaks across the floor. The sound makes me jump, mistaking it for a surprise entry from my father. I examine the papers on the bulletin board, lifting some of them up to read the ones underneath. The rush of adrenaline from the illicitness of my situation makes it hard to focus on the words on each page. Nothing indicates anything about a *potential business partner*.

Turning around, my eyes meet the desk behind me. I open each drawer, digging through any other papers or files inside.

Nothing.

I could check my dad's phone for his emails...if I had a death wish. He pretty much always keeps it on him anyway. No doubt it's currently on his person while he's at that meeting.

A call from Kyle interrupts my train of thought.

"What's up, man?" I ask when I answer.

"Something's wrong with the Dark Door!" His voice is rushed and panicked.

I push the office door open and shuffle out of the room. "Another crack?"

"A big one. You need to get back here now to patch it!" Kyle says.

A few of the Riot members pass me by as I rush through the crowded hallway.

Charles, being one of them, eyes me curiously as I pass.

"Whoa, kid! Where are you rushing off to?" he asks.

Ignoring him, I maneuver past the obstacle of bodies as quickly as possible to get to the exit.

Once outside the warehouse, I start running. The three miles down to the alley is nothing I haven't done several times before. But today, when I'm the most desperate, the journey feels significantly longer. Adrenaline rushes through me, keeping my movement seamless. Tunnel vision focuses my sight on the road directly in front of me.

Run. Get to the cabin. Don't let the crack get worse. You *can't* let the crack get worse.

Passing by Fairplay High School, I almost make it to town when something causes me to stop. An eerie sense of dread fills the air. Through my jacket, the hair on my arms stands up.

Something is here.

The heels of my black sneakers turn as I veer away from the road and towards the cluster of surrounding trees.

A low, nearly indiscernible sound echoes through the forest. the growl of some sort of animal.

Slowly stepping closer, I push through the branches, trying to locate the source of the noise. Eventually I'm so deep into the stretch of trees that the road is hardly visible.

Something dark is hiding in these trees. Something *evil*.

A final faded growl reverberates in every direction before the chill subsides. The feeling is gone, and there's no more trace of the dark presence.

Oh god, it's the door.

Something got out.

Whipping around, I carry myself back to the road and continue towards town. After what feels like ten more minutes of running, buildings and busy cars on the street become visible. Construction workers at the site for the new parking deck glare at me as I whip past them on the sidewalk. Finally, Milam Street comes into view.

I don't stop running when the Light Door appears. I cross immediately into the mystical bright forest. Though the muscles in my legs start to burn, my quick pace is consistent all the way to the cabin porch.

Inside, Kyle lets loose a heavy sigh of relief when he sees me. "Thank God!"

"Has it… gotten any worse… since you called?" I huff from exhaustion, taking the gold band from him.

"Not really, but it's still in pretty bad shape," Kyle answers. "It's getting stronger. I don't know how much longer the Door can keep this up, Dan."

"Shit," I growl under my breath.

Kyle follows behind me into the basement. The sudden waft of dark magic energy hits us in an intense wave. Immediately the chill returns, creeping up my spine, making sure every nerve in my body knows what I'm walking into.

The basement is pretty much empty aside from the Dark Door, the barrier between our world and the prison world that keeps the dark magic at bay...for the most part.

The blackened, old wooden door *should* be too weak to hold anything back. The magic of the cabin keeps the Dark Door *just* sturdy enough to hold it. But it isn't enough. The door grows weaker every day. Cracks form in the wood on occasion, giving way for something to slip right through. Often without us noticing for a while.

The newest crack is *huge*. It runs in a slanted line nearly all the way across the top of the door.

My eyes narrow toward the crack as an orb of light forms in my palm. My golden Guardian bracelet glistens with the light as it forms the orb in my hand. Every second I take to focus my energy makes the orb grow larger until it's the size of a basketball.

It doesn't hurt me. It never has. Though the light orb is essentially a ball of *fire*, it's a comfortable temperature. Like holding your hand out in front of a warm fireplace.

I aim the light at the Dark Door and concentrate the energy toward the crack. It shoots out of my hand, forming a beam of the light. The orb itself shrinks in my palm, the energy transferring to its target. When the ball of light disappears, the beam leaves with it. The crack is now filled with that same light energy, patching the hole and keeping any dark magic from escaping.

Kyle has seen me do this several times before, and yet his mouth hangs open in total awe.

"That never ceases to amaze me."

Kyle can't use the bracelet, it won't work for him.

I was chosen to use this power. By what? I wish I knew.

Upstairs in the living room, an orange glare shines through the windows. It's getting late.

My stomach growls. When was the last time I ate?

Kyle picks up his wallet from the coffee table.

"You want pizza?" he asks.

"Uhh, sure."

The two of us venture down the sidewalk downtown to the nearby pizza place, Alfonzo's. After we order and Kyle takes out his wallet, I take a look around the lobby. A giant stack of pizza boxes waits on the counter to be delivered. Each box has a white printed tag on the side with names, addresses, and phone numbers labeled on them.

Upon a closer look, one of the names suddenly catches my eye: *Alyssa Haller*.

I point the pizza box out to Kyle.

He gets his phone ready to take a picture, but before Kyle can get it in time, a delivery driver takes the box in his hands.

"That one is a little far out, the others are a lot closer," one of the other workers tells the driver. "Take that Haller order first, then come back and take the rest."

With that, the driver nods and leaves with the pizza. Our one lead to finding Alyssa again.

Kyle sighs in defeat, but I have an idea.

"Let's go," I whisper to him.

He picks up the box of pizza we had ordered and then walks behind me, hesitant, probably assuming that whatever plan I have is going to be incredibly stupid.

He isn't wrong.

I rush into the driver's seat of Kyle's truck.

He glares but climbs into the passenger's seat regardless.

As the delivery driver pulls out of the parking lot, I trail behind him.

"So we're adding stalking to our list of criminal activity?" Kyle asks, narrowing a brow at me. "Lovely."

"I'm not proud of it," I admit, "but like you said, it's necessary."

We follow the driver to an apartment complex about fifteen minutes out. When he parks near one of the buildings, I pass him by and park at the other end of the lot. We're far enough to avoid suspicion, but close enough to watch the driver ring the doorbell at an apartment on the first floor. After he leaves, we get out of the car.

Before I get the chance to go with Kyle to the door, I feel my phone buzz in my pocket. I take it out to look, it's my sister.

"*What*?" I answer with more irritation in my voice than I intended.

"Daniel, where are you? Dad is about to lose it," she says, "you need to get home *now*!"

"I got held up. What happened?" I ask her.

"You left and nobody knows where you are! That's what happened!"

"Just keep him busy," I say, "I'm on my way."

"You'd better be," she demands.

With that, I hang up the phone.

I didn't lie to her. I *am* on my way...after we talk to Alyssa.

Running to meet up with Kyle at the front door, Alyssa looks plenty angrier than the last time we saw her. We talk to her for a minute, but once again, she frantically tries to wave us away.

"My uncle is on my case, and I can't afford to screw up again. He could take my brother away from me," she says.

Her evasiveness finally makes sense now: she feels tied to her uncle, like I feel tied to my father.

She feels like she can't escape him, despite how badly she wants to, with so much at risk.

"I...we didn't know that." Kyle says, his head lowering with sympathy.

If I had known that Alyssa was dealing with *this*? I never would've approached her. She *already* has the weight of the world on her shoulders. Piling the Guardianship on top of that would crush her.

"—Don't you see how this looks? To me, you're just two strangers who won't leave me the hell alone!"

Shit. She's right. *What have we done?*

I try to assure her, to offer an explanation, but she shoots me down. I don't even want to bring her to the cabin right now, I just want her to have the truth. What if the presence I felt in the woods finds its way to her? Alyssa would have no idea what she was dealing with. She'd be a sitting duck. There's one thing that *might* convince her to talk to us, assuming I'm right.

As she starts to close the door, my arm flies upward to block it from the jamb.

"Wait, please! I can tell you about the dreams you've been having!"

That gets her attention. By the look on her face, she knows exactly what I'm talking about. Alyssa *has* been having the nightmares. She wants to know more, but something is stopping her. From the looks of things, it's probably her brother.

"I—I'm sorry, I can't help you," she says.

I can see it in her eyes, she has too much on her plate.

I can't explain it, but I can almost feel the sense of dread that looms over her. All of the stress that she's dealing with becomes apparent to me, like it's my *own* burden to bear. Guilt creeps up inside of me for adding onto the crushing weight of her problems.

Kyle starts to speak up, "Alyssa, please just let us—"

I hold my hand up in front of Kyle to stop him.

He shoots me a confused look and then sighs before handing Alyssa her box of pizza.

"It's okay." I nod. "Have a good night."

Closing the door, I drag Kyle to the truck with me without any further objections.

"Why would you do that?" Kyle asks, dumbfounded.

"I'm giving her some time."

"We need her help, Dan!"

As we head to the car, something makes me pause. I can sense something, a familiar presence known only from my nightmares. The dark magic has made its way here somehow. I start to walk towards the pull of the somber presence before Kyle's voice snaps me back into reality.

"Dude, am I taking you back home or not?" he says, grabbing my arm and pulling me forward.

The eerie sense is gone now. There's nothing there, but the green shrubbery planted against the building.

As he drives me back to the Riot base, Kyle and I eat our own box of pizza. He parks a few blocks away so that nobody can spot him. It's a good call. If someone *had* seen him, he'd be killed on sight.

"Text me if you need me," Kyle says. "If your sister called, it's probably not good."

"I will. Thanks, man."

I hand him back my bracelet before he drives off.

Inside the warehouse, I sneak towards the room where my dad usually has his meetings. Though, before I can reach it, my sister corners me.

"Took you long enough!" she says.

"Where's Dad, Kat?"

She stands there, still in her ridiculous police uniform. Her arms are folded as she narrows her eyes at me. She definitely *acts* like a legitimate cop. Kat has been undercover for the past few years. It was our dad's idea. He said it'd be *useful* someday. He pulled any strings he had to get Kat enrolled in the police academy under the alias 'Kat Miller'.

A bit on the nose if you ask me. He didn't even change her first name.

"Doing weapons inventory for the job we've got coming up," she answers.

"Do you know what he's planning?" I ask, feigning curiosity.

"Oh, so you haven't heard?" she says. "Well maybe if you actually *showed up* to a meeting, you wouldn't be so out of the loop."

Rolling my eyes, I shove past her and turn to the weapons room.

"I don't know what the job is," Kat shouts to get my attention.

I turn around. "What do you mean?"

A beat of silence fills the distance between us before she answers. "He didn't want me at the meeting."

"That's ridiculous, you're always there with him."

"Whatever he's planning is big, and he's keeping it completely under wraps right now," Kat tells me. "It's...strange."

Kat is basically my father's right hand. If he kept her out of the meeting, then something serious is going on. A small part of me is hoping I can talk to him and figure it out. However, the rest of me knows that it will never work. The moment I talk to him, he'll turn the conversation around to what I've done wrong in his eyes. Normally, I would hate it when my dad confronts me, but every now and then I let him yell in my face while I tune him out just so I can get him off my back.

Just the typical father-son bonding stuff.

Kat walks off without another word, so I continue forward. When I get to the meeting room, he isn't there, so I just head straight to my bedroom. He'll catch me tomorrow, I bet.

Worn out and exhausted, I turn my bedroom light on.

"Busy day?" asks my father, sitting on my cot.

"Shit, Dad!"

His arms are crossed, and his mouth is curved into a disapproving snarl. He leans over the edge of my bed, his brow arched curiously.

"You wanna tell me where you were?"

"Since when are you that interested?" I ask, avoiding the question.

"Since you started disappearing for hours at a time and don't tell your dear old dad what you're doing," he answers sternly.

Pfft. Right. How long did it *actually* take him to notice I was gone?

Dad looks at me expectantly, waiting for an answer. When I don't give him one, he sighs and unfolds his arms.

"Look Danny, my work here is important," he says. "You know that, right?"

"Yeah, Dad."

"And this crew is like your family," he continues. "Your sister and I *are* family, and family shouldn't keep secrets."

"Okay, then tell me about the meeting," I say. "What are you planning that you won't even tell Kat about?"

Dad just stands up and chuckles, resting both of his hands on his hips.

"Since when are you that interested?" he asks, mocking me.

"I just find it funny that you kept the golden child out of the loop."

"Aww, come on Danny," Dad retorts. "You don't really think that about your sister, do you? You know I love you both."

"Of course not," I chime in quickly. "Now that you've avoided the question, what's this secret job?"

He stands up and inches closer to my face until there is barely any space between us. It's an intimidation tactic, one that I know well. The way his mouth is curled in disgust, it looks like he's about to scream, or throw something, to make me nervous. But I'm betting that he's about to head for the door, taking the last word. After a few seconds of grueling silence, he finally speaks.

"If I didn't want you kids in a meeting, there's a reason," he states, his face cold and rigid. "That's *my* business."

He then walks out the door.

I should've bet money on it.

I scoff, take off my jacket, and lay down on my cot. I close my eyes and think about the conversation with Alyssa to distract myself until I can finally fall asleep.

Upstairs in the cabin, I hear something. Whatever it is, it's muffled. Distant. It's coming from downstairs. Cautiously, I follow the sound to investigate.

The closer I get, the more I can make out the sound of a girl crying, until she's finally in my sights.

Alyssa Haller is standing in the middle of the living room floor, tears streaming down her face.

"Alyssa?" I call out.

"I can't...no...I can't...there's too much..." she mutters. Her fingers clutch the side of her head in an anxious motion. She lightly sways back and forth, as if she were seconds away from losing her balance.

"Too much of what? What's wrong?" I ask, putting my hands on her shoulders in an attempt to keep her steady.

An unfamiliar female voice speaks, the sound coming from every direction of the room. It's similar to the voice behind the dark magic, except...lighter, somehow. "She needs your help, Daniel."

Alyssa's gentle tears turn into a slightly louder sob. Her breath shakes as her body begins to tremble. Suddenly, she melts to the floor.

"Hey, it's okay!" I say, bending down to her level. "Let me help you."

"Find her. Bring her to the cabin," the woman's voice says again. "Bring her to the Light. It's this world's only hope..."

Alyssa shivers. Her cries grow more broken and breathless. She's in pain.

The only thing I can think of to do for the time being is wrap my arms around her. As I hold onto her, I can feel her body begin to relax, her breath steadying. Soon after, the crying stops. I let go of her to meet her eyes.

"I've got you," I say. "It's gonna be alright, I promise."

She takes a deep breath, then flashes a weak smile.

Alyssa's mouth opens to say something, but before she can, a blackening darkness falls over us in a quick movement, like flipping a switch. When the light returns to the room just as quickly, Alyssa's state is worse off than before. Her trembling has worsened uncontrollably. She gasps for air with a shaky breath, unable to get a word out.

"Alyssa!" I shout, gripping her shoulders. "Hey, hey! You're okay!"

Menacing laughter echoes in the air. My face grows red hot with anger. The laughter grows louder and louder, filling up the room.

"She hasn't done anything to you! Leave her alone!" I shout toward the ceiling.

"STOP!"

The woman's voice drowns out the laughter.

Suddenly, a blinding light shines over my eyes, and for a second I can't see anything. When my vision clears, Alyssa is gone, but someone else stands in front of me in her place.

A woman looks at me with a warm smile. Her hair is a bold red color, like a ruby. Her skin is so pale that it almost blends with her simple white dress, laced with a golden trim.

"Who are you?" I ask.

"That's not important right now, Daniel," she says, her voice kind and gentle.

"But... I've never seen you before."

"I have been there for you every step of the way," she says, "even before you brought your friend to the cabin."

I'm confused. In all my time at that cabin, I've never come across this woman before. My mother definitely never told me about her.

"What?"

"Alyssa needs a guiding hand. She needs someone to show her the way to the Light," the stranger tells me.

"But how do I—"

A more well-known feeling shivers up my spine.

Oh god, the source of the magic. It's found its way back.

The woman senses the presence too, she looks around the cabin, her expression clear with disdain.

"No," she says. "No, you barbaric—"

I wake in a cold sweat.

That was one of the easier nights.

Sluggishly, I get out of bed, grab my jacket, and make my way to the cabin.

By the time I get there, I'm a little late.

Kyle is sitting on the couch in the living room with a cup of coffee. He's reading the sci-fi novel I picked up for him a while ago as he sips from his mug.

Peck, of course, is nuzzled on his lap.

"You slept in," Kyle remarks, taking my bracelet off his wrist.

"Shut up," I tell him as I put it on.

He just smirks.

"Is there any left for me?" I ask him, pointing at the coffee pot in the kitchen.

He nods without taking his eyes off his book.

I make my way into the kitchen and grab a mug from the cupboard. As soon as I have my coffee, I join Kyle in silence, drinking from my cup, and trying to enjoy the quiet morning.

Early mornings here are always really beautiful. In the window by the kitchen door, the pink-orange sunrise peeks in through the forest.

Kyle looks up from his book, closes it with a bookmark, and sets it on the cushion next to him. "So, what's the plan?"

"What do you mean?"

"We still need to get Alyssa over here, man."

"I know that," I say. "I was just thinking...maybe we should give her a break for a little while, you know?"

"*Give her a break*?" Kyle asks.

"Kyle, you heard what she's going through at home. And you saw her face last night. I don't think she needs all this right now."

"Yeah, but we do. *You* do," he retorts. "Look, you're right, she has it really rough right now. But both of you are Guardians. She has a purpose here."

"I *know*," I repeat. "I just don't think she's up for this right now, we should give her some time."

Kyle narrows his eyes. "What's up with you? Until yesterday, you were hell-bent on bringing her here."

Sighing, I set down my mug. "It's just—"

Out of nowhere, someone knocks on the front door.

"What the hell?"

Quickly, I stand up to answer it. When the door swings open, Alyssa Haller stands on our front porch, her cheeks red and streaked with tears.

"I need answers."

4-Daniel

"Come on in," I tell our unexpected guest.

Alyssa's eyes are heavy and dark. She looks as if she didn't get any sleep *at all* last night. Her baggy red t-shirt falls well over a pair of dark gray yoga pants. Her auburn hair is in a disheveled bun, like it hasn't been brushed.

Closing the door behind her, my eyes meet her curiously. "I thought you didn't want anything to do with us?"

"Well...I didn't," she sighs. "But things have changed. I have too many questions."

I gesture for her to sit on one of the sofas in the living room. She follows, slowly.

"You look tired," Kyle points out. "Are you okay?"

"I had a rough night," her eyes stay fixated on the floor as she answers.

"I'll get you some coffee," he says, already making his way to the kitchen.

I lean against the back of the couch, watching her with a regretful knot in my stomach. "What's going on?"

"My brother is missing," Alyssa says. She sits down with a long sigh, holding back tears as she continues. "He took off last night. My uncle isn't answering his phone, and the police have looked everywhere in town. Nobody can find him."

"Oh god. I..." I want to say something else, *anything else* to comfort her, but the words won't come. Not that I would be of much help. What comfort could *I* possibly give her?

"I had a dream about him the other night," she continues. "The same dream that led me to this place."

Leaning in a bit closer, I cross my arms.

"I just thought that maybe—" she pauses, her voice breaking. "Maybe if I took a chance with you guys, things might be a little bit clearer. You knew about my dreams. That...means something, right?"

In truth, I have no clue where her brother is. But if Alyssa had a dream about him, a vision, maybe we can help her in some way.

On the other hand, do we really want to pull her into all this with everything she's going through right now?

"Yeah. It means something." I circle around the couch to sit across from her. "I want to help you. But you *have* to understand, what we do here is serious. It'll change everything for you."

Kyle comes back with a ceramic mug and hands it to her. The meaning behind the silent look he gives me is clear. *I thought we weren't going there yet?*

"I was going to back off...for at least a little while, after everything you told us yesterday. You *do not* have to do this right now," I assure her.

Alyssa gives me a hopeful look that makes my heart ache. "Will it help me find my brother?"

"I think it's possible."

"*But* we can't guarantee that. It's just a theory," Kyle chimes in. "The choice is yours, but Daniel could really use your help."

Alyssa weighs her options for a moment, focusing her eyes on the coffee in the mug in front of her. Finally, she looks back at me. "Tell me everything."

Kyle and I lead Alyssa to the front porch for some fresh air.

"Okay, where to start?" I groan, trying to think.

Suddenly, Peck swoops in from behind me and lands on the porch railing. He sees Alyssa with us and starts chirping relentlessly. His little voice is somehow so loud that a slight echo shifts through the trees.

"Peck, calm down! It's okay!" Kyle says, going in to help.

Alyssa watches Peck, completely awestruck. "I've seen that bird before, in my dream..." she says. "I heard it too, when I first came here."

"Yeah, Peck was my first dream too," I tell her. "I'm sorry about him. He's *really* protective of the cabin."

"Why do you call him Peck?"

Kyle steps in to answer. "Because he attacks anyone new that comes in and..." he pinches his fingers together and taps the back of his head in a showing motion. "*Pecks* at them. That's basically his way of saying *stranger danger*."

"Oh...cute," Alyssa tentatively rubs her index finger along Peck's back, petting him.

Peck happily accepts the gesture.

"But if that's the case, why didn't he attack me when I got here?"

My hand rests against my chin as I ponder the question. "You said you've seen him before?"

"A couple times, yeah," she answers.

"I'm pretty sure he knew you were chosen. He didn't see you as a threat to the cabin."

"I guess that...makes sense," Alyssa nods. "But what is he?"

"Peck is the guardian of this place. He's been here for a long time, protecting it from the people in the outside world," I explain.

"What exactly *is* he protecting though?" she asks. "I mean, I get that it's some sort of magic, but...it's just a cabin in the woods. What's so important in here?"

Kyle gives me a questioning look, and I nod in response before turning back to face Alyssa. "Let me show you."

We lead her back into the house and over to the kitchen. I open the wooden door across from the pantry to the stairs of the somber basement. As soon as the door swings open, a waft of cold air pushes out from the inside. A shiver runs up my spine, either from the cold, or the effect of the dark magic.

"Not creepy at all," Alyssa remarks sarcastically.

"Oh, don't worry. It's about to get creepier," Kyle says.

Alyssa lets out a nervous laugh.

"Seriously, Kyle?" I elbow my friend in the ribs, then quickly turn to Alyssa. "Nothing is going to happen to you down here. I promise."

She smiles at me, clearly still apprehensive, as the three of us work our way down the steps.

Upon seeing the rotting, brittle state of the Dark Door, Alyssa looks mortified. Waves of black magic emanate from the Door like thick smoke. Her eyes are wide with disbelief. "What is this?"

"*This* is what's so important," I say. "This door keeps back a dangerous, *living* dark magic. If it got out, it would destroy *everything*."

Alyssa's staggered eyes don't tread from the door. "Oh my god..."

Kyle exhales sharply. "We don't entirely understand how it works," he says. "But we know that the Dark Door is getting weaker. And every time a crack forms, something gets out."

Alyssa swallows hard. "It... cracks?"

"Our job, you and me," I continue, "is to guard this door and make sure that it stays shut. To protect our world from whatever danger manages to get loose. We're the Guardians."

"Wait, wait..." Alyssa says. "I thought Peck was the guardian?"

"Well, yeah. Think of it this way: I'm *a* Guardian, you're *a* Guardian, and everyone before us was *a* Guardian," I tell her. "Peck is *the* Guardian, he's the main source of the cabin's magic, as far as we know. But he can't keep this door shut on his own, he needs help from people like us."

Instead of saying anything else, Alyssa trudges upstairs.

Kyle and I exchange a look and then follow her back into the living room.

"This is...*a lot* to process," she says, circling the kitchen.

"Trust me, I know. But—"

"Why me? Why am I a part of this? I don't understand."

A lump forms in my throat. "I don't have a clear answer to that," I admit. "You were chosen to help keep the Dark Door closed, just like I was. That's really all we know."

"The dream, Daniel," Kyle says. "Tell her."

Alyssa looks at me for clarity.

I tell her about the dream I had five years ago, where my mother whispered Alyssa's name to me.

"That was all we had to go off, until you showed up here the other day," I explain.

"*Five years?*" she murmurs under her breath. Her fingers pinch her temple as she tries to wrap her head around it. "You guys were nearby this whole time. I had no idea."

"Yeah well, to be fair, a lot went down in that time. We were a little busy," Kyle remarks.

"What do you mean?"

Only then do I realize Kyle is talking about the Riot.

"Just some family drama," I add in quickly before he can elaborate.

Alyssa takes her hair down to fix her bun. I watch her run her fingers through her long brown hair, brushing it out before twisting the hair tie back in again.

She tugs at a second hair tie around her wrist, fiddling with it between her fingers. "Was there anything else in that dream? When you found out I was chosen?"

God I was hoping she wouldn't ask that question.

The twist in my gut reminds me of what happened yesterday. The Dark Door, the giant crack, the looming dark presence outside her apartment.

"I, um, I saw you," I start, "you were leaning over someone, this younger kid. He was sick. Pale. Like something had sucked all the life out of him, and the veins in his arms were—"

"Black," Alyssa finishes, her face full of pure shock.

"You saw it too?" I ask her.

"That was my brother." Her voice quivers when she answers. Tears well up in her eyes as the realization hits.

"Crap." Kyle's hand covers his mouth.

"Oh my god, Ryan..." Alyssa says, breathing heavily. "What happened to him?"

The words land heavily. My stomach drops. This is all my fault.

"I, uh...I don't know. But it *definitely* came from here," I say, gesturing to the Door behind us.

"But something like that would take *a lot* of dark energy, right? When did the Dark Door get that unstable?" Kyle asks me.

My fingers rake through my hair as I search for the words. "Yesterday?"

"You don't think—?" Kyle follows me.

Alyssa's eyes shift quickly from terror to anger. "What are you talking about?!" she demands.

My gaze shifts to the wall behind her, a desperate attempt to avoid facing her directly. With a sigh, I begin to explain the events from yesterday.

"Something got out," I say. "And...I felt something last night, right before we left your place. Something dark."

"No..." Alyssa whispers, breathless.

"I think that whatever got to Ryan—" a wave of guilt weighs in my chest, making me pause before the rest of the sentence finds itself, "—got out because of me."

Alyssa's breathing grows heavier. Tears start to form. As quickly as the first time, she bolts through the kitchen door.

Kyle and I follow her to the front porch.

"Alyssa, I'm so *so* sorry," I say.

She paces around the porch, trying to find her breath. Her hands are trembling, her face is drenched in tears.

Kyle stops, deciding whether to approach her or give her space.

Meanwhile, I inch closer without a second thought.

"I can't...no...I can't...there's too much..." Alyssa gasps.

"Hey, hey, it'll be okay!" I try to reassure her. "We can figure this out."

The words from the woman in my dream.

A guiding hand.

"H—he's gone...I c—can't pr—pro—"

I try to reach my hand out in comfort, but she shoves it away.

"S—stop, just stop. STOP!" Alyssa screams. She thrashes away from us and storms back inside, sobbing.

As she heads up the stairs, I try to go after her, but Kyle pulls me back.

"Just let her have some time, man," he says. "She'll be fine."

"Will she?"

We both decide to give Alyssa some space.

Kyle leaves the cabin to get lunch for the three of us.

Sitting on the middle couch in the living room, I tear apart an old newspaper and hand the pieces to Peck to help him add to his nest. After a while, I hear Alyssa's footsteps creaking down the stairs.

"Hey," I say softly, jumping up from the couch to greet her. My eyes meet hers, scanning her expression to get an idea of how she's feeling.

Her eyes are red. Her hair is now completely down, falling messily over her shoulders. She takes slow, ragged breaths, grounding herself. A numb feeling dulls the air in a way that I can't quite place.

"Hey," Alyssa looks around the room, "where's Kyle?"

"Oh, he went out to get us some food."

She nods, her voice cracking a little. "Hey, um I—"

My phone buzzes in my pocket. I take it out, expecting to see Kyle calling me. A shiver runs up my spine when the screen lights up.

"I'll be right back," I tell Alyssa, barreling towards the front porch.

"O—okay," she answers before I close the door.

Heat fills my cheeks. My hands move faster than my mind can catch up as I answer the buzzing flip phone.

"What is it?" An unintentional growl escapes my throat.

"Should I even *bother* asking where you are right now?" Kat snarls back at me. "You need to get home."

"Why? What's going on?" The question comes out sharp. Irritable.

"That job that Dad was keeping from us? It's happening *now*," she says.

"And I'm guessing he wants me to be there?" I sigh.

"No," Kat corrects. Her tone grows more nervous. "He's going alone."

"*What?*"

"He said it was a one-man job. He won't tell me anything else," she explains. "Do you know anything about this?"

"Of course not," I answer. My eyes lock onto the cabin's front door behind me, then to the window at its side. Alyssa paces through the living room, anxiously.

"Look, I'll be over there soon, okay?"

"Daniel, wait—"

I hang up the phone and grip the doorknob to start back inside. Before my foot even reaches the hardwood floor of the cabin, a red blur zips outward past my shoulder.

"Whoa!" The sudden hurl of air almost sends me doubling backward.

Inside, Alyssa jolts up from the couch.

"What happened?!" she asks, bewildered.

Peck zooms into the forest like a hurricane of bright red feathers. The Light Door appears, letting him loose into our world.

I run after him without a second thought, and Alyssa hurries behind me.

We follow Peck outside, back to the alley, but from there, he's nowhere to be seen. All I notice is the worn blue truck, still parked in front of us. My feet are stiff on the ground, heavy with realization.

"What is it?" Alyssa asks, noticing the worry that is no doubt plastered across my face.

"That's Kyle's truck," I explain, curiously stepping forward to look through the windows, "it shouldn't be here..."

"Maybe he walked?" she suggests.

"He took his keys with him," I remember.

"Well," her eyes dart around the alley, searching for another explanation. She spots something on the ground and bends down to the corner of the alley to pick up a set of keys.

I feel a knot form in my stomach.

"Those are his."

"What do we do?" Alyssa asks, holding the keys in her hand like a fragile piece of glass.

It's an impossible choice. Peck is too important to the cabin to let him run rampant in town. If somebody sees him, or if he gets caught...

But Kyle is my best friend. Something has obviously happened to him. The growing punch in my gut makes it obvious that I already know where he is.

As much as I hate leaving Kyle at the mercy of my father and the Riot, I know what Kyle would tell me to do.

"We're going after Peck."

"What about Kyle?" Alyssa asks.

"As soon as we get Peck back to the cabin, I'll go after him."

Getting in the truck, Alyssa hands me the keys and we take off.

I drive us around town for a while, looking out for Peck.

Eventually, Alyssa spots a flash of silver and red. "There!" she calls out, pointing.

We follow it to a dumpster behind a motel, thankfully out of sight from other people for the most part.

Only there does Peck stop in his tracks and start chirping furiously at the brick wall behind the dumpster.

"He senses something."

"From all the way back at the cabin?" Alyssa wonders.

"Whatever it is, it can't be good," I answer.

A deep thrumming sound comes from behind the dumpster, like a dog growling. Peck's relentless chirping only angers it further.

Slowly, the canine comes toward us from behind the dumpster. Alyssa and I back up, tentatively. We have a full view of what is *clearly* not just any regular dog, but some kind of demon.

"What *is* that thing?!" Alyssa gasps.

The raging demon dog's skin is like charcoal. Rough in texture rather than fur and black as the night. His eyes are bright and fiery orange. The angry canine is fuming, with tufts of smoke releasing from his back. His growl echoes in every direction around us.

"I've never seen this before," I admit.

Alyssa's eyes are fixed on the dog, frozen with terror as the creature approaches, gnashing his teeth with a ferocious hunger.

The dog hunches down, preparing to pounce.

I cover myself with one arm and Alyssa with the other, closing my eyes as he lunges forward.

Only when the sound of metal clanging and high-pitched whimpering rings in my ears do I realize I haven't become the dog's chew toy. I look up to see a golden shield attached to my bracelet.

"How did...?"

But I'm too stunned to get the rest of the question out.

The demon dog shakes himself off and whimpers, turning around and running for the streets with a final bark.

"How did you do that?!" Alyssa almost yells in disbelief at the giant golden plate attached to my arm.

"I have no idea." I stare off in the direction that the dog ran.

Why would it just *leave*?

The shield still rests at my side. I hold it up to examine it. The metal is smooth to the touch. I recognize the lines and intricate details welded into the gold material. It's the same pattern on the Light Door. Centering the design of the shield is a picture of a sun.

The shield is surprisingly light for how thick the metal is. But based on the feel from earlier as the dog bounced against it, the shield's weightlessness doesn't take from its power.

After one last look toward the street to see if the dog came back, the shield disappears in a flash of light.

"Come on, let's head back," I tell Alyssa.

On the drive back to the cabin, Alyssa lets Peck sit in her lap.

He nuzzles comfortably and lets out a happy chirp.

"Where did you get that bracelet?" she asks, petting the bird's back with two fingers.

"My mom gave it to me." I don't meet her eyes to answer her question.

"Your mother?"

"She was a Guardian. When she found out I was next, she brought me to the cabin. I was ten years old at the time."

"Well, if she's a guardian, then why do you need me?" she wonders.

My stomach drops at the question. I swallow hard before answering her, my knuckles gripping the steering wheel.

"She died," I sigh, "a few months after she brought me in."

Alyssa is left speechless. Her eyes lock onto the road in front of us without a word of response.

"It's alright," I assure her.

"I'm so sorry..." she says.

Finally parking in front of the alley, my hand reaches for Kyle's keys to turn off the ignition. Before opening my door, I turn to face her.

"I do this for her, the door in the basement, the cabin, I protect it," I explain. "I come here every day, patch any cracks in the Dark Door, Kyle and I take care of Peck, we keep the cabin clean, and we look for answers in places we've been *a hundred times*. All of it so that I can do right by my mother."

With that, both of us get out of the car, and the Light Door appears in the alley as we continue talking.

"I get it now," Alyssa says, moving a strand of hair out of her face and behind her ear. "I understand why all of this matters so much to you guys, and I want to help. But I *have* to think of my brother first."

"We'll do everything we can to find him, Alyssa."

We walk up to the porch of the cabin. As I open the door, Alyssa grins at me softly.

"You can call me Lyz if you want," she says.

I can't help but let out a smile. "I'd like that."

She shifts nervously, about changing the topic. "What are we going to do about Kyle?"

"I know where he is. I'm going to go get him, but I need you to stay here," I say.

Alyssa doesn't seem to like that answer. Her brow furrows determinately. "I can help though! Do you want me to call someone?"

"No. Don't call anyone, just stay here and stay safe, *please*," I urge her.

She looks down at her feet for a short moment, thinking. Then she looks back up at me, clearly disgruntled. "Okay, fine."

"Thank you," I say as I head back out the door, "I'll be back soon."

During the drive, my mind races to the last time Kyle was at the Riot base.
The Croft incident.
His past has caught up to him, and now the thing I've been trying to protect him from for *three years* has finally happened.

Finally, at the base, I park the truck a little further away, so nobody sees it. The heavy metal door groans open, and a quick and steady sprint carries me through the warehouse halls.

Everyone is there getting weapons ready, and for a single, horrible moment I worry that all the preparation is for Kyle. The thought brings a chill up my spine before I remember that Dad was going solo on his job. Hopefully that's where their focus is instead.

Shifting through the halls, I look for where they might be keeping him. Upstairs maybe? Not the basement, they wouldn't take him down there until Dad gets back. Before I can search for very long, Ben, one of the Riot's weapon experts, stops me.

"Hey there, kid!" he says. "Where were you today? You missed all the fun!"

"I was..." searching for a quick excuse, I stumble in my words. "Erm...running errands. What did I miss?"

"Your old man is leading a massive strike on—"

Before he can finish, an alarm sounds. The screeching beeps reverberate throughout the room. It can only mean one thing: Dad is back from the job.

Everyone, including Ben, quickly heads toward the meeting room, giving me a chance to continue forward.

Quickly, I bolt up the stairs. At the top of the second floor, Kat exits the room to my left and stops me in my tracks.

"What are you doing?" Her voice breaks as she wipes a tear from her cheek.

"Where is he?" I ask, winded from all the running.

Her eyes narrow irritably in my direction. "Dad wants us to wait until he gets back before we do anything," she says, sniffling. "You'll get your turn."

Kat thinks that I'm as mad at Kyle as the rest of them.

To play it off, I sneer toward the door she exited from and cross my arms.

"Then why does it look like you already took yours?"

At that, she scoffs. "I just needed to blow off some steam, I didn't touch him." She looks away from me, over the railing. "Yet."

She seems really bothered. What happened in there?

"I'll bet he was *real* disappointed then."

Kat sneers at the remark. Her gaze still turned away from me. "Just leave him alone until Dad gets here, Daniel," she orders, making her way past me.

"No problem," I say.

She walks off, and my stomach twists at the earlier comment. "Wait!"

"*What?*" she asks, annoyed.

"I'm sorry, Kat."

I'm sorry for the comment. I'm sorry she's hurting. I'm sorry for lying to her. But there's no way for me to say the rest out loud.

She smirks and tilts her head in a short nod, the closest I'll get to forgiveness, before leaving.

I turn into the room Kat came out of. It's empty, with nothing but a table, a closet...and Kyle.

He sits in a metal chair, his hands bound behind his back, and his ankles tied to the legs of the chair with zip-ties. His mouth is duct-taped shut. Thankfully, it doesn't look like he was hurt. He sees me and tries to speak, so I rush over and take off the duct tape.

"What happened?" I ask him.

"They grabbed me the second they saw me outside...I didn't even make it to my car." His tone is tired, most likely wary from the drugs that the Riot uses in hostage situations.

Disgust rises in my throat at the cruelty of my father's men. No doubt my sister also had a say in Kyle's condition.

"Did they see the door?"

"I don't think so, nobody asked me about it."

"Let's get you out of here," I say, grabbing the knife in my jacket pocket.

"But Dan—"

Both of us pause when the sound of footsteps approaches. A couple of Riot members, Landon and Miles, it sounds like, walk past us down the hallway. Kyle and I keep quiet as they pass.

"Did they say where Jacob went for the job?" asks Miles.

"Nah, but that score better be good if he was hell-bent on going solo," Landon exclaims.

Their voices quiet as they walk further down the hall. Finally, they're gone.

Shuffling behind Kyle, I cut the zip ties binding his wrists together. As I maneuver around the chair and bend down to cut the ties at his ankles, something makes me pause. One of them has already been cut.

"Daniel," Kyle warns.

"Who are you?" says an unexpected voice.

Turning around, I see Alyssa pointing a gun at my chest. It looks like my pistol, she must have gotten it from the cabin.

"Alyssa..." I say gently, dropping my knife on the floor near Kyle's still zip-tied foot. "Put the gun down. I know you don't want to hurt anyone."

"My uncle is a cop, I know how to use this," she bites before repeating her question. "Now, *who are you?*"

"She was hiding in the closet when Kat came in," Kyle says, "she heard everything."

"Why was Kat here? Where are we?" Alyssa asks, switching the safety off.

The guilt makes every muscle in my body tense. There's no getting around this now. No other options.

"We're at the Riot's base of operations," I sigh in defeat.

"The Riot? Kat..." she processes as her arms fall, the gun lowering with them.

"Alyssa, I know you have a lot of questions, but we need to get Kyle out of here!" I try my best to reason with her.

Her eyes are frantic with a hundred different thoughts. Her teeth grit as she raises the trembling gun back up at me.

"Why should I trust you?!" she yells.

I raise both of my hands in surrender.

"Alyssa, *please,*" Kyle attempts to plead with her.

She tries to regain her composure, despite the tremors in her hands. She takes a few breaths, glaring daggers right at me as she attempts to straighten up in her stance.

"Tell me the truth," she orders.

I let out another sigh, unable to look her in the eye as the words come out. "My name is Daniel Reeves. Kat is my sister."

"Reeves..." she repeats. "As in *Jacob Reeves*?"

"He's my father."

Alyssa's eyes widen. She chokes back a sob. "No..."

The shaking in her hands gets worse. She loses control of the gun and accidentally pulls the trigger.

The bullet grazes just below my left rib. The pain shoots through my side like a sudden strike of fire, causing me to double down to the ground. The burning in my abdomen makes my eyes water. Blood soaks my hands as I grip the wound.

Kyle takes the opportunity with the shock of the moment to grab my knife in front of him and cut the last tie. While Alyssa stands, frozen in the weight of the gunshot, Kyle takes the firearm out of her hand.

"We've got to go." He offers a hand to help me get back on my feet.

"No! Go without me. I'll slow you down!" I grunt through the pain, still sprawled on the floor.

"I'm not leaving you here, Daniel!" Kyle insists.

"You need a cover story, I'll be *fine*!" I say through gritted teeth.

Reluctantly, Kyle agrees, and leads Alyssa out the window.

I can barely think straight. My vision blurs as they leave. I lay flat on my back, clutching my wound with both hands.

One of Dad's men comes in and finds me on the floor. He leads me down to the medical bay, slinging my arm over his shoulders and grabbing me by the waist in support.

A couple hours go by sitting in the medical bay, but it feels more like days. As I'm getting stitched up, the events from today replay in my head in a furious loop.

Alyssa heard *everything*. I can only imagine how hurt she is right now. She probably never wants to see my face again. The thought of her shutting me out hurts worse than the bullet, but...if I'm being honest? I wouldn't blame her.

Why did I think I could keep this from her? If I had just told Alyssa the truth from the start, none of this would've happened. I was so ashamed of my background, of the Riot. I thought it would be easier if she didn't know.

Easier for her? Or easier for me?

Oh god. What have I done?

Soon enough, both my dad and sister come to talk to me. Kat just stands off to the side, looking down aggressively at her feet.

My dad sits down at my side and looks off to the wall in front of him. He stays silent for a minute before finally speaking.

"So Willis came crawling back?" he asks, still not looking in my direction.

Pierce, the medic, nervously keeps his eyes away from my father as much as possible while he stitches me up.

"I—I heard that they took him in, yeah," I answer my dad. I wince at the pain as Pierce tugs on a thread.

Dad glances at my side, then finally looks up at me. "How'd that happen?" he asks plainly.

Wow, thanks for the concern.

"He shot me," I say. "To clear the way to escape."

"Hmm," he raises an eyebrow. "How'd he get out of the zip-ties?"

"He must've gotten hold of a knife somewhere, I don't know," I say irritably. My tense mood is directed at my father. But, given the situation, it's easy to make it look like I'm directing it at Kyle. "Did you forget that you trained the guy?"

My Dad examines my expression.

I stare him down, keeping a stern composure. Putting up a brick wall, built high enough to stand level with his own. That wall blocks away the man I used to proudly call my father. Lately, when I look at him, I don't see a father anymore. I see something cold. Harsh. Ruthless.

Knowing that Alyssa saw the same thing in me today fills me with dread.

Finally, Dad stands up and starts to leave the room.

"Where were you tonight?" I ask him before his hand reaches for the doorknob.

He pauses, deadpan and still in a way I've never seen before. As Dad turns his head toward me just slightly, he doesn't look scared. The grin curling his lips, the arch in his brow. He looks *proud*. "Visiting an old friend."

A chill runs up my spine. Exactly what kind of *visiting* took place?

With that, he leaves.

Kat pushes herself off the wall and glares at me. "You let him go, didn't you?"

"I don't know what you're talking about," I grit through my teeth as Pierce tugs a little too tight on the stitching.

She lets out a light scoff. I half expect her to object, or threaten the truth out of me. Instead, she turns away from me and exits the room without another word.

Some time later, Ben, the crew member that found me upstairs, walks in to check on me. After chatting with him for a bit, he chuckles to himself.

"Man, your old man did a number on Haller today," he laughs.

The name makes me freeze in my tracks.

What did he just say?

"I heard about that," Pierce remarks. There's a slight snark in his tone, though he's mostly blank-faced and focused on my stitches. "I'd be surprised if the man didn't flatline on the spot."

"Who?" I ask, trying as hard as I can to keep a neutral expression.

"The guy he went after on that job this afternoon," Ben explains. "He was leading an attack on some cop he said he used to know. Some guy named Will Haller."

5-Alyssa

"I'll be back soon," Daniel says as he rushes out the cabin door to rescue Kyle, leaving me alone in the cabin with Peck.

Daniel wouldn't tell me what he and Kyle were up against, but he was clearly worried. The thought of him going in alone scares me. Sure, I just met these guys, but they're the only ones that seem to have any answers about Ryan. I can't risk losing that. Besides, I feel like I owe it to them, to try to help them somehow.

Bolting up the stairs, I look for anything to take with me for defense. There's no telling what I could be walking into, or how much trouble Kyle could be in. To follow Daniel, I have to be quick. At the top of the wooden stairs, there's a hallway to my left with two rooms on each side. The first door on my right is wide open. Inside, I scan the room for anything helpful.

In the top drawer of the white dresser beside the bed, a gun rests in its holster, hiding underneath a small cluster of socks. The brown leather holster has a name written in black ink. "Daniel R." Taking it out to examine, the black pistol feels heavy in my hands. Yellow accents on some of the plastic detailing stand out against the rest of the weapon's color.

I hesitate. Will taught me how to shoot a gun *years* ago, but there's never been a need. My thoughts shift to Kyle. I don't know what kind of danger he's in, but that's exactly why I should take precautions. Grabbing the gun, I rush to the cabin's exit.

In the alley, Daniel is hurriedly peeling off the parking lot in the truck.

I rush to my car and pull out after him.

Daniel drives out of town, about forty minutes away from anything familiar.

I follow him, keeping a far enough distance away from him to ensure he doesn't see me.

He parks between the side of the road and a grassy, unkept field.

hurrying to get out of my car, I run behind him about another mile towards an abandoned warehouse.

Daniel heads towards the front.

Before making another move, I pause when Kyle's shoulder length mop of brown hair comes into view from the second story window.

I have to find some way to get to him unnoticed. Looking around for a different entrance, I find a cracked open window on the other side of the building. The creaking noises send a chill up my spine as I open the window and climb through.

The window leads me to a wide-open hallway of rustic metal infrastructure. The stairs and ceiling above me look as if they are about to collapse. Several men dressed in black combat clothes tread throughout the building. There are two sets of stairs on the other side of the hall leading to the second story.

Daniel is stopped by one of the men before he even gets halfway up the steps.

A crowd of people block the path between me and the stairs. I'm trapped. There's no way I can get through without anyone seeing me. Before I can turn around, an alarm blares throughout the building. Everyone moves quickly towards the sound, leaving the path to the stairs completely clear. I run as fast as I can to get upstairs. A room comes into view with the door flung right open. Before I can sprint inside, a woman's voice stops me.

"Where have you been?" she asks.

She sounds oddly familiar, but I can't place it.

"Trying to avoid *this*."

Kyle.

"Me?" the woman asks.

"That's not what I meant," he says.

"But it's what you did, Kyle."

"I did what I had to!" he insists.

"You could've...!" she starts, choking up, "you could've stayed...with me."

"Not like this," Kyle says, "I won't hurt anyone else."

There was a moment of silence before the woman spoke again.

"You *did* hurt someone," she says.

The sound of footsteps marching out of the room sends me into a panic. There's a door to a closet on my right. I hide in there quickly, making sure not to shut the door completely, fearing she'd hear the doorknob click. I listen as the woman walks away, but she stops and I hear another voice.

Daniel.

"Where is he?" I hear him ask the woman.

Snap out of it. They're close. I still need get to Kyle.

Keeping my head down, I bolt into the room as fast as possible. Luckily, both of them are too busy with their conversation to notice me. When I get inside, Kyle is tied up in a metal chair.

"Kyle!" I whisper.

He makes some noises behind the duct tape that I can't make out. Reaching into my pockets, the only thing I have is Daniel's gun concealed on my waist, which I avoid touching for the time being, and my keys.

Perfect! I take out my apartment key and thread it behind the zip tie on one of Kyle's legs. After a little bit of pulling, the plastic tie breaks off with a snap.

"I'm going to get you out of here," I tell Kyle.

"Just leave him alone until Dad gets here, Daniel."

Wait a second, that voice again. I know that voice, it couldn't be...

I creep towards the edge of the door and take a quick glance at the woman talking to Daniel. I see the back of her short blonde hair.

"I'm sorry, Kat." Daniel says.

A shiver of fear creeps up my spine. Kat is with these people? The men that captured Kyle? And Daniel knows her. How? Is he involved in this? A million questions run through my head, washed over by an overwhelming feeling of anxiety that I can't explain.

From the shadows in the corner, I watch as Daniel rushes in to help Kyle. Something comes over me. My hands move to the hilt without even thinking about it. I pull out Daniel's gun and aim at his chest. The weight of the pistol makes it unsteady in my trembling hands.

"Who are you?"

Daniel snaps his head around at the sound of my voice. He's slow and cautious when he sees me with the gun. He speaks softly, trying to settle me like calming a wild animal.

I dismiss his efforts, keeping the pistol pointed at his chest.

Kyle says something to Daniel, but I don't hear it. The noise is muffled in my ears by the ache in my head as the questions keep coming. The only thing I can make out is when Kyle mentions Kat.

"Why was Kat here? Where are we?" I ask them both.

Daniel's guilt-ridden face drops as I switch the safety off on the gun and straighten my aim.

"We're at the Riot's base of operations," he sighs.

"The Riot?" I repeat the words in my head, the dots connecting. The gun lowers in my hands. "Kat..."

Daniel holds out his hands in defense.

"Alyssa, I know you have a lot of questions, but we need to get Kyle out of here!"

I look between Daniel, Kyle, and the door, not sure where to focus my attention. The shaking in my hands worsens, leaving the pistol more unstable in my grip. Kyle and Daniel both plead with me to listen to them, but I can't. A tidal wave of unanswered questions keeps me frozen in place, fearful of the answers to come.

And then it does.

"My name is Daniel Reeves. Kat is my sister."

Flashes of Will's countless investigations of the Riot come to mind. "Reeves...As in *Jacob Reeves*?"

"He's my father."

The pounding in my chest skips multiple beats. "No..."

My hands tremble uncontrollably like the surrounding ground of an active volcano. A heavy weight forms in my chest. I feel breathless, gasping for air. I can't stop it. No matter how much I try to calm myself down, to steady my breath and calm the sensation in my hands, nothing works. My fingers fumble around the hilt of the gun until it goes off. The loud bang rings in my ears. My chest falls, and I stand there, motionless at the weight of my actions. Then I see Daniel crumble to the floor, clutching his stomach as blood soaks his white T-shirt.

In the stunned silence, Kyle takes Daniel's knife and cuts himself free. He comes up behind me and takes the gun out of my hand.

I don't fight him. I wouldn't even if I could.

He reaches a hand towards Daniel, who grips his bleeding abdomen with gritted teeth. They speak, but I can't register the words. Eventually, Kyle leads me out the window, without Daniel.

A flight of metal stairs below takes us both safely to the ground. Once both my feet are on the grass, Kyle grabs my wrist.

"Run."

Our feet pound on the pavement as we move, but my heart pounds even louder in my chest. I follow Kyle for half a mile down to the road where both of our vehicles are parked.

"Hey! Hey, are you okay?" Kyle asks, the man that was literally just kidnapped not five minutes ago, as he grips my shoulders.

"I shot him..."

That shot could have killed him. This is my fault, how could I be so *stupid*?

"He'll be fine," Kyle assures me, "they have medics."

I gasp for air through tears.

"Alyssa, look at me," he meets my eyes with a sense of urgency, "do you want to go back to the cabin, or do you want me to take you home?"

I can't go home, not like this. Will hasn't called me or anything this whole time, but if he sees the mess I've gotten into, if he knows that Ryan has gone missing, I'm done.

"The cabin," I answer.

I follow him back into town, and we both park next to each other in front of the alley. Just like that, the door appears as soon as we step into the trash-filled gap.

Kyle's eyes dart to me and then back to the door, as if he were formulating an idea. Though I didn't ask, he explains the sudden appearance of the door, possibly to distract me.

"The Light Door only ever appears to a Guardian or former Guardian," he explains, "I can't get in without yours or Daniel's help, which is why I live here...away from them."

I nod absent-mindedly. My attention is on the Riot and everything that just happened. Is Daniel going to be okay on his own? Do I even want him to be? He's Jacob Reeve's *son*. How can I trust him?

Why would he lie?

When we get inside the cabin, I offer to make some tea. Kyle directs me to a small antique silver tin in the cabinet.

"It's made from the leaves in the forest right outside," he explains in another attempt at taking my mind off things, "it has some sort of healing properties."

While I prepare it in the kitchen, Kyle plops down on the couch, exhausted. Peck flies over and lays down on his lap.

A few minutes later, I come back into the living room and hand Kyle his mug before sitting down. He takes a sip and gags.

"I don't usually drink this stuff. It tastes like rotting broccoli to me," his face scrunches in disgust, "but it'll help. And I know Daniel would have my ass if I didn't drink it."

Sitting down on the couch across from Kyle, I grab the navy-blue knitted blanket crumpled in the corner next to me. I wrap it around myself, sighing into the comfort of the fabric.

"How're you doing?" Kyle asks me.

How can I possibly answer that? Daniel lied to me. He *completely* failed to mention that he was part of the group that my uncle chased after for over a decade. His dad is their leader, and he didn't think I should know about this? We only just met yesterday, sure, but if Daniel expects us to be partners in whatever magical destiny tied me to this cabin, he's off to a horrible start.

And Kat. She came to Ryan's middle school graduation. She's my uncle's partner on the force. Will has no idea that he's been working side-by-side with a criminal for *years*.

Criminals. Is that what they all are?

My head is spinning. I bury my head in my hands in exasperation.

"Hey, it's alright," Kyle says. Pushing himself off the couch, he kneels to meet me at eye level and places a hand on my shoulder in comfort.

"Why didn't he tell me?" My voice breaks.

"Because he was scared," Kyle sighs, "Daniel just wants to help you. We both do. He knew you wouldn't trust him if he told you."

"I don't know if I would, but...he didn't give me the chance."

The gun on Kyle's hip catches my eye. I don't know what happened. It was like I wasn't in control of myself. My mind waivers between being angry at Daniel and being scared for him.

Sitting down next to me, Kyle takes another sip of his tea before he talks. He ignores the gag in his throat at the taste.

"Look, Jacob has always had some twisted grip on his kids," he says. "Daniel has been lucky enough to slip away when he can, but he still can't really escape him."

I don't say anything, staring down at the hardwood floor.

"He hardly ever goes on missions for them anymore."

Hardly, but he still does.

Kyle stays silent next to me on the couch, letting me process everything.

After a few breaths, I muster up enough sanity to ask him another question. "Why did the Riot take you?"

Kyle sighs and takes another sip. "I used to be one of them."

"Used to?"

My eyes meet his knowingly, trying to get him to elaborate.

He looks away, suddenly interested in the wall to his left as he recovers whatever memory he keeps hidden.

With a wide arch in my brow, I press on until he gives in with a nervous chuckle.

"It's not a pretty story," Kyle starts, "but if you're willing..."

"I'm curious," I admit, adjusting the grip on the blanket around me.

Kyle glances at Peck, who is fast asleep on his lap. He pets the small bird with his free hand.

"I joined to help a friend," he begins, "he got into some trouble, and he owed a debt to Jacob. That debt was never paid off."

I can only guess what that meant for his friend. "So what made you stay?"

"Well, either way there's no leaving, and I didn't have anywhere else to go anyways," he answers, "but I met someone on the crew that made things easier."

"Was it Daniel?" I guess.

Kyle just laughs. A splash of tea falls on his jeans.

"No, but we met around that time," he says, wiping his jeans with his shirt sleeve. "It was a girl."

"Oh."

"Yeah," he says, still smiling. "Anyways, we'd been together for about two years when my training was done, and Jacob sent me on my first real mission."

I shift in my seat on the couch as he continues.

"Basically, Jacob had ordered me to kill a man," he tells me. "It's not easy, disobeying an order from that guy, but I put my gun down. He was innocent, a convenience store owner that just owed Jacob money...I couldn't do it."

"Oh my gosh..."

"Jacob had a lot to say on the matter," Kyle continues, "but all I knew was that I didn't want to be a part of it anymore."

"So how does Daniel and the cabin fit into all this?" I ask him.

Kyle pauses, and glances out at the door for a moment. In the short pause, he watches the door like he expects someone to walk through it. When nobody does, he continues.

"Daniel saw how I resisted his dad. He brought me here to keep me safe from the Riot, and to help him out," he finally answers. "Keeping a magical cabin a secret for so many years makes a guy lonely."

I let out a nervous laugh, thinking about how the guys had begged me to help them with the cabin just yesterday.

"When I first got here, all the crazy light magic stuff was a lot to take in. And the responsibility?" Kyle frowns. "Being a Guardian isn't easy, that's why Dan needs your help. But it's also why we've been trying to ease you into everything, including the Riot."

I nod, shifting uncomfortably in my seat, and change the subject. "What happened with the girl?"

Kyle's face falls into a painful frown.

"Leaving her was the *hardest* thing I've ever had to do," he says. "I don't regret my decision, but I'll always regret how much I hurt her."

"Do you ever miss Kat?" I ask.

He looks at me, dumbfounded.

"I was there, remember? I heard your conversation."

Kyle just laughs again, this time more gentle and sad.

"I miss her every day."

We keep talking for a while. When my eyelids begin to droop from exhaustion, he offers me the spare room upstairs to stay for the night. I thank him and pass out on the bed.

The next day, I wake up and check my phone. There are several texts and calls from Madison. I can't tell her where I am. It would jeopardize everything for the guys. But Madison has been there for me through everything. She was there for me all through high school, and when I moved out of Will's place, when Logan gave me trouble, and especially when Ryan went missing. As much as I hate it, I can't talk to her right now.

Still half-asleep, I trudge downstairs where Kyle is already in the kitchen with a mug in his hand.

"Good morning," he says, "there's fresh coffee in the pot over there."

While making myself a cup, Daniel limps through the door, seemingly exhausted and out of breath. The second he looks in my direction, I can see the sudden burst of remorse in his eyes.

"Hey..." he greets.

"Hey," I say half-heartedly, turning my head away to avoid looking in his direction.

"Why were you running?" Kyle asks. He looks down at his wrist, then looks back up at Daniel in fearful realization.

Daniel catches this and pulls out his bracelet from the pocket of his black leather jacket.

Kyle sighs a breath of relief.

"Something...happened..." Daniel huffs, he clutches at his ribcage at the spot where the bullet pierced him last night. The wound is more than likely what makes it harder for him to breathe right now.

I take my coffee mug and take a step up the stairs. I'm not really in the mood to deal with Daniel's Guardian issues today.

"Wait!" Daniel begs.

Reluctantly, I stop in my tracks.

"Alyssa, I know you're mad at me, and this probably isn't going to help," he starts, "but you need to know about this."

"Like I needed to know about the Riot?" I roll my eyes.

The corner of his mouth lowers, but he shakes it off and moves closer to me. The roots of his sand blonde hair are sweaty from running. His bright green eyes are full of hope, but at the same time, the expression on his face is serious. Whatever he wants to tell us isn't good.

"I won't lie to you again," he promises. By the determination in his voice, I can tell that his words are sincere.

Against my better judgement, I humor him. Letting out a sigh, I take a sip of my coffee. "What's going on?"

Daniel offers his hand.

I refuse to take it, to his disappointment.

The two of us meet Kyle in the kitchen.

"My dad was working on this job, and usually he takes a group with him, but this time he was being really closed off about it," he starts.

I scowl at the mention of his dad's chosen line of work.

"Last night I found out that he was going after someone," he continues.

"That's never good," Kyle says. "Who was it?"

"Someone named Will Haller." Daniel turns to me.

The name hits me like a truck. The beating in my chest grows louder, more forcible.

"That's my uncle."

"The one you were having trouble with?" Daniel remembers.

"Oh no," Kyle says quietly.

"What..."

I'm not even sure how to finish that question. What happened? What does Jacob Reeves want with my uncle?

What do I do now?

"Alyssa, I'm so sorry," Daniel says.

My blood boils with anger. My chest heaves as Will's name echoes in my mind. The same overwhelming strength in my emotions from last night returns to the surface. But it's different this time. It's not fear, it's anger.

I slap Daniel across the face.

"*I told you,*" I say, choking up, "I told both of you that I couldn't do this! I had a life! A brother! And now..." Tears start rolling down the side of my cheek. "Will was...complicated, but he was the *only* family I had left!"

Neither of the boys say anything at first. Daniel rubs his cheek.

"He's not dead. I checked, he's in the hospital," he finally says.

"Which hospital?"

"Piedmont North," Daniel answers.

I march upstairs to grab my purse from the spare room and head for the door. Before leaving, I turn to Daniel and Kyle.

"If *either* of you show up at my apartment again, I'm calling the cops," I warn them, "and I'll tell them *everything*. Stay away from me."

I drive to the hospital holding back tears.

When I finally get there, the elevator leads me to the floor where his room is, 312C.

On the way up, my stomach turns. All the fights I'd gotten into with Will come rushing back to the forefront of my mind. I think about the last time, when Ryan decided to move in with me. What it must have felt like watching his niece and nephew, his dead sister's children, walk away. At the time, it was the best thing we could've done.

I still believe that...I think. Right now, however, I can't help but feel sympathetic.

In the room, my uncle lays in the hospital bed. He's unconscious, hooked up to multiple tubes and needles for life support. Will's skin is pale, his breathing so light that it's almost not there. Upon a closer look, I notice multiple bruises all around his arms and neck. He looks like a bus ran over him twenty times, not that I'd blame the bus. Even still, seeing him like this is unsettling.

"I guess you can't lecture me right now," I start choking up.

Silence. Nothing but faint breathing and beeping machinery.

"I lost Ryan. I don't know if I have what it takes to get him back, I don't know if—" I pause, "I don't think I can trust the people that can help me."

Pausing as a nurse walks by, I feel embarrassed basically talking to myself.

"I just feel so alone. I thought I knew what that was like before, but I was *so wrong*," I admit. I hear footsteps come to the door behind me. A small part of me, in the back of my mind, hopes that it's Daniel and Kyle.

"You're not alone, Alyssa."

I turn around, disappointed and frightened at the sound of Kat's voice.

"What are you doing here?!" I ask harshly.

"I...I just came to pay my respects," she says. Kat holds a bottle of bourbon in her hand, more fitting to set at Will's bedside than flowers.

"If you need me to leave, I can come back later," she offers.

She doesn't know that I was at the warehouse. She has no idea that I know the truth about her and her brother, I have to remember that. Though, I realize, both of us are keeping a cover right now.

"No, you can stay."

Kat pulls a chair up from against the wall and sits down.

"I heard about Ryan, I'm so sorry. How are you holding up?" she asks.

Her question infuriates me. The only reason I'm in this mess is because of her and her dad.

Daniel's dad.

"I'm—" I sigh, "I'm fine."

Kat just shakes her head.

"You know you can talk to me, Alyssa," she says, "I'm here for you."

Yeah, right.

"Thanks," I answer.

She takes a deep breath before she speaks again. "I don't think I've told you this, but my mom died when I was younger."

Intrigued, I perk up and listen.

"Someone broke into the house, they had a gun, and she thought she was alone folding laundry," she says, choking up, "they saw her and..."

So *that's* how she died.

Putting a hand on her shoulder in comfort, I can't help but feel sorry for Kat in this moment.

"Why are you telling me this?" I ask her.

She clears her throat and wipes away a tear.

"Because, like I said, you're not alone," she says. "I know exactly how you're feeling right now."

She doesn't know how I feel. She has *no idea* what I've been through. *She* did this. Her and her dad. Anger wells up inside of me.

I have to ignore it. I have to...

I can't.

"I have to go."

"Alyssa—"

Before she can say anything more, I bolt out of the room.

Should I talk to someone? The only person I can think of is Madison, but I can't tell her everything. I would have to make up a story beforehand when she asks where I've been.

The lies. The manipulation. It all just makes me think back to Daniel and Kat. I'm sick of it.

Inside my car, I take a deep breath. My leg bobs up and down in a fast-paced anxious movement.

As I come to the decision, my face is buried in my hands. I know who I need to talk to about this. As much as the thought fills me with dread, they're the only ones who will understand.

I pull up to the alley.

When I get up the stairs of the cabin porch, I hesitate. The things that I said to them, to Daniel.

Oh god. I shot him. Do they even want to see me? I don't know if I can stomach the guilt.

They must have seen me lurking, because Kyle opens the door.

"Hey, you're back?" he says.

"I...I need help," I stutter.

Kyle nods, smiling softly. "Come on in."

✦6-Alyssa

Daniel is standing in the kitchen eating a sandwich. When he sees me walk through the door, he chokes on the bite in his mouth.

"What are you doing here?" he asks through gasps of air, confused.

"Kat showed up to the hospital," I tell them.

"What?! Are you okay?" Daniel immediately puts down his lunch.

"*No.* She didn't hurt me, I just..." The words come out weaker than I mean for it to. I exhale sharply, crossing my arms. "Seeing her struck a nerve."

He looks at me, his green eyes full of remorseful concern.

I let out a long sigh of exasperation before continuing. "Daniel, I still don't know if I can do this, but...I'm *all alone.* I can't talk to anybody about what's happening except for you guys." I hesitate and reluctantly add, "as much as I hate to admit it, I need you."

His face softens, but he doesn't rush toward me.

Kyle watches carefully, like he's waiting for me to say something else, but I don't know what else there is to say.

Daniel straightens up as he approaches me.

"I don't know if I'll ever be able to make up for how I hurt you, but I meant what I said earlier. No more lies." He locks eyes with me. "I *promise.*"

Kyle then takes this moment to step in. "And you are *not* alone. We're here for you."

I don't know if I can forgive them yet, or if I'll ever be able to. But one thing is clear to me now: I don't have to go through this pain on my own anymore.

Daniel rubs his hand over his wound and winces, and my heart sinks.

"Oh god. I can't believe I did that, I'm so sorry," I plead, "I've never lost control like that before."

"Honestly, I deserved it." He tries for a convincing smile.

I shake my head. "No one deserves to get shot, Daniel."

Kyle snorts. "Tell that to Jacob."

That afternoon, the three of us sit down and talk about what happened yesterday. We tell Kyle about the demon dog we encountered, and the shield that had come to our rescue from the bracelet.

"*Wow*," Kyle's eyes widen, "did you know it could do that?"

"I think I would have told you if I did." Daniel gives him a side eye.

"You said your mother gave you that bracelet?" I ask him.

Daniel nods, twisting the golden band around his wrist.

"So, shouldn't there be another one?" If his mom was a Guardian, and that bracelet came from here, it would make sense that any Guardian would have one.

"Possibly, or it could just be an artifact that she found," Daniel says. "There might just be one."

"It has your name on it," I point out, "it's got to be connected to the Guardianship."

Kyle snaps his fingers, nearly jumping from excitement over whatever he's thinking. "What if there's *another* former Guardian out there that still has it?"

Daniel and I share a look of realization.

Another Guardian? I hadn't even thought about that.

"Are there usually two Guardians?" I ask.

"One or two, I think. Mom said it was kinda random. But she never mentioned having a partner," he answers.

"Do you think it's possible?"

"Maybe?" Daniel's eyes meet the window to his left, thinking.

As he ponders, my train of thought shifts back to the demon that attacked us. "Where do you think that dog came from?" I ask.

"I don't know for sure," Daniel says, breaking his gaze, "but it looked like it came from..." He looks in the direction of the door leading to the basement.

"You think something got through without us knowing?" Kyle asks.

"God, I hope not," Daniel says, "but yeah, maybe."

I let out a giant sigh. "All of these 'maybes' are getting ridiculous, I wish we had some more answers,"

Daniel perks up, like an idea had just come to mind.

"There was something," he starts, "I was taking a nap on the couch after you left, and Peck showed me something in my dream. It's a long shot, but it might help."

"What did you see?" I asked him, intrigued.

"A gazebo, somewhere out in these woods. It had these hidden stairs," Daniel remembers. "I think if we can find it, we can get some more information."

"I've been through miles of these woods," Kyle says, "several times. I've never seen any gazebos."

Daniel shrugs. "It couldn't hurt to check."

"Agreed," I say.

Peck tweets with approval.

Kyle opens his mouth to say something and then closes it. He rolls his eyes in exasperation before finally speaking. "I guess I'm outnumbered."

We take a moment to pack for the journey. Kyle insistently pushes a walking stick into Daniel's hands after watching him limp through the upstairs hallway.

Soon enough, the three of us, with Peck on Daniel's shoulder, are hiking through the woods. A gentle breeze passes by, combing through the vibrant green trees as the branches sway. A ray of warmth surrounds me, but when I look up, the sun is nowhere in the sky.

Daniel seems to notice me looking for it. "Yeah, there's no sun here, but the atmosphere mimics it, making it look warm and sunny year-round."

"That is so weird."

With everything going on, there was never a chance for me to take in the beauty of this place. I hadn't really looked at it since I first got here.

"It's like a perfect summer home," Kyle says over his shoulder a few feet ahead of us.

After the first two miles, I start to lose my breath. The muscles in my legs feel like they're burning. I look over at the guys.

Daniel looks like he's about as tired as I am, though the grip he has on his side reminds me how much more he's struggling. Sweat beads down his cheek and on the neck of his white shirt. His heavy gasps for air are rasped and seemingly desperate. He moves slower, almost forcing each step, a white-knuckle grip on the walking stick. I match my pace with his, not only to keep from leaving him behind, but also to give myself a rest.

Kyle, however, is still marching on unbothered.

"Dude...how are you still not...out of breath yet?" Daniel asks through a huff.

"I used to do a lot of hiking when I was younger, plus I've done a little bit of exploring through here too." Kyle shrugs, "I'm practically stuck here, what else am I gonna do?"

We trudge through the forest just a little bit longer. Daniel's taken off his black leather jacket for the hike and has it tied around his waist. So, for the first time since I've known him, his arms are out, toned and slim.

When I realize how long I've been staring at his biceps, I quickly turn my head and force my sights on something else. Luckily, in that moment, Peck starts chirping frantically, directing everyone's attention.

"I think...he senses something," I gasp, exhausted, "we must...be close..."

Peck leaps off Daniel's shoulder and zooms ahead of us.

Kyle runs to follow him, while we slowly saunter behind them.

When we finally do catch up to Kyle and Peck, they're examining a glittering white marble gazebo. Beautiful vine-like designs are etched into it, and the gazebo seems to have a very faint yellow glow.

"It's just like my dream," Daniel points out.

"How did you *not* know this was here?" Kyle asks him.

"I've never been very far from the cabin, I thought that was all there was."

What else is here outside of the cabin that we don't know about?

I walk up the couple of steps and stand in the gazebo while Peck sits on the railing. Our little bird friend fluffs out his wings and lets out a whistle. Without any warning, the floor below me opens up. The lack of support where I'm standing sends me falling about six feet. As I land on the cold stone floor, a snap, followed by a burning shock of pain, shoots through my nervous system in my left leg. My eyes water as a scream escapes my throat.

"Alyssa!" Daniel shouts from outside. "What happened?"

I try to speak, but all that comes out is a loud groan through the tears streaming down my face.

Peck lets out an alarmed twitter, but cuts himself off and flies away in the direction that we came from.

"Hang on! I'm coming down!" Rapid footsteps scurry down a flight of stairs that descend in front of me until they stop for only a short moment. The next thing I know, Daniel leaps from the steps and is right next to me in an instant. He winces as the impact brings attention to his bullet wound but shakes it off.

Kyle scuffles down the steps and glares at Daniel with his hands on his hips.

"Dude, the stairs were *right there*! What is wrong with you?!"

"Are you okay?" Daniel asks, ignoring Kyle's remark.

"I—I don't know, it's really bad," I tell him frantically.

"Can you stand up?"

He helps me as I try to plant my feet, but as soon as my left foot starts to press down on the floor, pain shoots up through my nerves, making me scream. It's definitely broken. I steady myself with winced breathing as the guys pick me up.

They carry me to a bed in the room in front of us. The ache in my muscles starts to fade as I sit on the velvet bedspread. When my foot hits the marble floor, I cry out again.

"Okay, okay!" Daniel gently puts me down. "I've got you, just breathe."

Following his instructions, I take a few deep breaths. It eases the pain temporarily, allowing me to think straight.

"Where are we?" Kyle asks.

I look around at our surroundings. The queen size bed I'm sat on is dressed with a velvet red cover against the right-side wall. A desk to its side is drowned in papers and writing materials. On the other side of the bed stands a tall wooden wardrobe. One of the doors is open, revealing the wardrobe to be completely empty. The smooth walls of white marble are covered with banners of red and gold. Next to the desk, I see a golden pole, a perch meant for a bird. It's probably for Peck.

"Whose room is this?" I wonder.

"I'm not sure," Kyle says, wandering in. He walks over to the desk and picks up a book.

The leather-bound cover is red with golden thread woven around the sides in an intricate design.

Kyle opens the book and starts reading.

"It belongs to some girl...*Mala*," he reads. "That's weird. This thing switches between English and some other language."

Mala, was she another Guardian?

Daniel glances at me worriedly.

"I'm gonna check it out, are you okay for a second?" he asks.

When I nod affirmatively, his brow furrows with concern before he walks up to Kyle and takes the book out of his hands. He skims through the book before stumbling across something he finds intriguing enough to read aloud.

"These words. I can't make out some of it, but look," Daniel says, pointing at the next page, "Kaedrik grows stronger...don't know what that says...the Dark Door grows weaker."

"Kaedrik?" I ask.

The weight of the words holds over the atmosphere in the room.

Who is Kaedrik? What does he have to do with the Dark Door?

Suddenly, Kyle's head bolts up from the pages of the book. "Guys, what if the door isn't holding back dark magic?"

I follow him. "It's holding back *Kaedrik*."

"It's a prison," Daniel says under his breath. "But...why wouldn't..."

The meaning is clear before he finishes his thought: *why wouldn't his mother tell him that*?

A strange, unfamiliar sensation runs through my thoughts. Anger. Sadness. Heartbreak. Why would Daniel's mom keep the truth from him?

But also, why do I suddenly feel so strongly about it?

The air feels heavier as the truth hits us all at once. For a moment, none of us speak. It feels as if the entire world has stopped turning.

Daniel then takes hold of the book and skims through the pages before finding something else. "What the hell is all this? Taken by his darkness...only way...kill them...the host can be freed...when blood is shed."

"The darkness...in Ryan." My eyes widen with horror as I make the connection.

"The only way to stop Kaedrik from infecting Ryan is to kill him." Shocked, Kyle has a hand over his mouth when he speaks.

Daniel slams the book shut and angrily throws it across the room.

"*Damn it*!" he shouts.

My hands start to tremble again. I lose control of everything. I feel a pain in my chest like it's on fire. This can't be happening. There has to be some kind of mistake.

"Alyssa!" Daniel calls out, rushing to help me.

"I—I... I can't..."

I feel cold. My entire body is shivering relentlessly. And yet, my eyes burn from the downpour of tears that fall on my face. Everything hurts. I cross my arms tightly, trying to warm myself, steady my shaking, *anything*. Nothing works. It won't stop.

This *can't* be the only way. Killing Ryan can't be the only option. He's my little brother. I've spent my entire life taking care of him. I can't. I *won't*.

The harder I hold onto myself, the emptier I feel in the pit of my stomach. It's not enough. There's a yearning in my chest for a weight, an anchor. Something to keep me grounded. I can't find the words, let alone the strength to ask for some sort of comfort.

"Hey! Look at me! You're okay." Daniel places his hands on my shoulders. "You're okay, Alyssa, just breathe."

Kyle tries to pull him back. "Daniel, give her some space."

Daniel shoves him away, keeping his eyes on me.

"It's gonna be okay," he repeats softly, wrapping his arms around me.

I melt into his touch, letting the warmth of his body calm me. His breaths are apparent this close to his chest. I follow the rhythm, the rise and fall of his lungs, to steady myself. After a few seconds, I pull away and take one last deep breath before speaking.

"It's alright," I tell Kyle. Then I turn back to Daniel. "Thank you."

"Of course," he says, "I figured you needed a little comfort."

"How did you..."

Before I can finish my thought, my eyes catch something glowing in the left drawer of the desk.

"What's that?" I ask.

Kyle opens the drawer and rummages through it. He then pulls out a small glass bottle with shimmering golden liquid. A note is tied to it with string. Kyle reads the note out loud:

"Healing tonic, H.O."

"What does that mean?" I ask.

"I'm not sure," Daniel admits.

"Guys, this is a healing tonic...in a magical underground room, in a magical hidden cabin in the woods," Kyle points out.

Daniel quickly catches his meaning. "Do you think it could heal anything? Better than the tea leaves can, like—"

"Will," I realize, "we've got to get it to him."

Daniel and Kyle exchange a look.

"I don't know, Alyssa. We're not even sure if this thing works," Daniel says.

"We have to *try*!" I plead. "*I* have to try. *Please*!"

Something shifts suddenly in the air around us. A silent understanding. I see the look in Daniel's eyes, and for some reason, I know exactly what it means. He agrees with me.

"But how are we going to get you back to the cabin?" Kyle gestures a hand toward me. "You're hurt."

Daniel thinks for a second and then jumps back up on his feet.

"I have an idea. I'll be right back."

Kyle and I wait in a curious silence as we listen to Daniel doing...whatever he's doing.

After a minute, he runs back downstairs with a thick tree branch about a foot long. He rushes toward the banners on the wall to rip one of them off. After one tug, he winces over the stretch on his bullet wound, and Kyle comes in to help. Once they get it down, Daniel leans down and puts the stick against my broken leg, and wraps the banner around it, making a brace.

"There," Daniel says, "that should help, and I can carry you on my back down to the cabin."

I shoot Daniel a hesitant look.

"Are you sure you can do that?" I ask. "It's a couple of miles away."

"You have no idea what kind of training exercises my dad made me do," Daniel replies, chuckling. "I used to carry a backpack across the woods behind our old house that was filled with a bunch of weights. This is nothing."

"Hey show-off," Kyle raises an eyebrow, "you're wounded. Stop trying to impress the girl and let me help."

Daniel blushes. "I wasn't—!"

"Mm-hmm," Kyle cuts him off snarkily.

Both of the guys assist me in getting to the cabin.

Daniel hands me his walking stick that he had left on the ground near the gazebo. I lean onto the stick with one hand while he drapes my other arm over his shoulder for support.

Kyle walks right behind us, ready to catch me if I stumble.

By the time we get back to the cabin, Daniel's out of breath, but he keeps hold of me without faltering. Anytime I ask him if he needs a break, he just shakes his head and pushes on. But I don't miss the exhaustion written on his face. His cheeks flushed red with heat.

Once we get past the porch stairs and to the front door, I ask Daniel to put me down. I don't want to tire him out any longer, and I'm perfectly capable of hopping to the couch. The second we get inside, I hear something dropping to the floor upstairs.

"What was that?" I ask.

"Someone's here," Kyle notes.

"Alyssa, wait here," Daniel orders, "we'll go check it out."

I do as he says and lean against the wall next to the front door, ready to make my escape in the case of a dangerous intruder.

"Who are you?" I hear Daniel ask.

"Stay back!" a familiar voice shouts.

"We don't want to hurt you," Kyle says softly, "we just want to know how you got here?"

"I said *stay back*!"

I nearly lose my grip on the walking stick and tumble forward when I realize who it is.

"Madison?!" I yell toward the stairs.

Daniel and Kyle shuffle downstairs with my best friend nervously following a few feet behind them.

Peck glides in the air with them, next to Madison.

"Alyssa? What are you doing here?!" she asks, "Why didn't you answer my calls?" When she sees the handmade brace on my leg, her eyes light up in horror. "And what…"

"Maddie, what are *you* doing here?" I try to speak calmly.

"I was looking for you!" she says. "I have your location on my phone."

"You didn't turn that off?" Daniel asks frantically.

"I…"

I have no excuse. I've been so focused on everything going on here that I didn't think about it. Plus, it wasn't like my family would be looking for me.

"Okay but aside from that, I thought only Guardians could get through the door," I remember. "How did you get in here?"

"I don't know," Madison admits, "the door just *appeared*."

Daniel, Kyle, and I all exchange uneasy looks thinking about what this could mean.

"Is she another Guardian?" I wonder.

"I don't think so, we would've known," Daniel says, "my dreams had been telling me your name for *years* before we actually found you."

"So how did she get here?" I ask.

"I don't know," Daniel answers sheepishly.

Peck chirps happily, fluffing his feathers.

When I found the cabin, Peck was following me, so he knew I was supposed to be here....but why didn't he attack Madison?

"Lyz," Madison interjects, "what's going on?"

I look over at Daniel and Kyle. The two of them have been keeping the secret of the cabin for a long time.

I've left Madison in the dark for days. She's always been the one constant in my life that I could count on. I've been so focused on the cabin, and finding my brother, that I forgot about my best friend.

"I have to tell her," I say to both of them.

Kyle looks unsure, but Daniel nods approvingly.

"It's alright," he says, smiling.

I turn back to Madison, ready to tell her everything.

7-Daniel

Alyssa sits in the living room to talk to her friend.

Migrating to the kitchen, Kyle frantically paces in circles while I grab the metal container of forest tea leaves.

"Why are we letting her tell this random girl all of our secrets again?" he asks, chewing his fingernails nervously.

"Because this *random girl* showed up here, so she knows about the cabin—"

"—which is insane," Kyle adds.

"*And* because she's Alyssa's friend. She needs this," I tell him. "You know how important it is to have that kind of support."

Kyle sighs, stopping in his tracks. "Fine."

Microwaving a cup of water for the tea, I grab a small silver leaf infuser from the cabinet. When the microwave beeps, I insert the leaves and let them steep for a while.

"I could've boiled some water on the stove." Kyle glares at me.

"This is faster," I shrug.

"It's lazy," he scoffs.

Ignoring him, I dig in the pocket of my jacket and take out the vial that we found in the gazebo. My fingers fiddle with the paper tag tied to it.

This vial could help wake up Will Haller. Alyssa's uncle will be back in her life. I know they have a rough relationship, trust me, I can relate. Regardless, without her brother, Will is the only family Alyssa has left. she was given the chance to save him, and she's taking it. I only hope she gets that same chance with Ryan, no matter what that *damn* book says.

I look over at Peck, who is contentedly sleeping on the kitchen counter. He was there when we saw Madison in one of the bedrooms upstairs. Does our little bird friend know something that we don't?

With the leaves finally steeped enough, I take a sip of the tea. It has healing properties, like the tonic, but it isn't very potent. It helped last month when I had a bruise Kat had given me during a training session. The tea made it fade away instantly. However, when Kyle got a really bad sinus infection that same week, the magic in the tea only lessened his symptoms.

The drink sends a gentle warmth through my stomach. After a few sips, the aching in my abdomen starts to subside. It's not fully healed, but it feels much better. The sharp pain in my side is nearly gone.

I feel a buzz in the back pocket of my jeans. I pull out my phone and open it to find a text from my sister.

Dad's asking for you again.

I let out an exasperated sigh.

"Kat?" Kyle asks.

"Yeah." I put my phone away. I can't deal with this right now.

The Riot put Alyssa's uncle in a coma. I'm sure my dad has celebrated over the victory of his 'mystery job'. The thought of going back there makes me sick to my stomach.

"Dude," Kyle furrows his brow, irritated, "you do know that when she texts you it means she's worried about you, right?"

He crosses his arms like he's disciplining a child.

"Worried for *me*?" I wonder. "Or worried about Dad?"

Kyle walks closer to me, until he's an inch away from my face. He's close enough for me to feel his breath brush against my nose. "You. Always."

At that point, Alyssa hobbles into the kitchen with the walking stick, Madison sheepishly behind her.

"Is everything okay?" she asks, giving us a worried look.

"Uh, yeah," I say, "we're fine."

Kyle backs away as if nothing happened.

Madison tucks a strand of her charcoal black hair behind her ear.

"Are we heading to the hospital?" Alyssa asks me. "For Will?"

"Yeah," I tell her, "of course."

"I'll get my keys," Kyle says.

I help Alyssa into the truck as the four of us pile in.

She leans on the side of the truck, holding the handle above.

I pull her arm over my shoulder, allowing her to shift her body weight into the seat with her good leg. As soon as she presses onto me, the strain from shifting her weight makes my wound flare up.

I grunt, accidentally letting go of Alyssa. Luckily, she's far enough into the truck that she pulls herself in without any issue.

"Are you okay?!" she asks frantically.

"I'm good!" I assure her, clutching my side and breathing through the pain. After a few moments, the burning fades, and I slide into the seat next to her.

On the way to the hospital, we try our best to answer any questions Madison has. Alyssa already explained a lot of it, so most of her questions are about the cabin. There's only so much we can explain to her before we realize how little we really know ourselves.

"So, wait," Madison stops us, "if you knew that Alyssa was a Guardian five years ago, why did she only find out just now?"

I pause, thinking for a second, to no avail.

"I, uh... that's a good question."

One that none of us has an answer for.

At the hospital, one of the nurses offers to take Alyssa to get her leg taken care of. She declines, eager to get to Will, but the nurse insists. If she doesn't get her leg looked at, the bones in her leg won't heal like they should.

"It'll be okay, we got this," I tell her.

Alyssa stares at the vial in her hand for just a moment before handing it to me.

The nurse is visibly annoyed at her hesitance. Her dark messy curls fall in front of her face as she watches us impatiently.

"Bring him back," Alyssa says before she and Madison leave with the nurse.

Kyle and I get Will's room number and head up in the elevator.

When we get to the room, the sight makes my skin crawl.

An older man lays in his hospital bed. Multiple tubes and machines are connected to him, making odd noises and keeping him clinging to life. Looking closer, the bruises on his arms match the one on his swollen right eye.

What the hell did Dad do to him?

At that moment, I remember what Alyssa had told us. Kat had shown up to this very room. She saw Will in this condition. Did she have the same thought? Or was it worse for her? She'd been undercover as his partner for years. She knew Will. She knew

Alyssa and Ryan. She was there, by Alyssa's side when she came to visit him. I can't imagine the guilt she must have felt. It was probably several thousand times worse than what I'm feeling right now.

Kyle shifts anxiously against the wall to my left. I never knew that hospitals made him so nervous.

Sitting on the edge of the bed, I open the cap and tip the healing tonic toward Will's mouth. I'm not sure how much he needs for it to work, but I don't take any chances. I give Will the entire bottle.

"What are you doing?" Kyle asks. "That was our only one. What if we need it later? Like for Alyssa?"

"He's in bad shape," I explain, "part of the bottle might not be enough." I step back, waiting for something to happen.

For a few painstaking minutes, everything is quiet. Then, without any warning, Will wakes up with a deep gasp. He sits up on the bed, frantic.

"Shit!" I shout. The sudden movement causes me to shift backward in surprise, making me fall off the bed.

Kyle straightens up and comes to help me.

"Who are you two?" Will asks.

The man is groggy and tired, yawning and running his hand through his brown salt-and-pepper hair. The bag of his good eye is dark, making him look older than he actually is.

Kyle is the first one to fill the stunned silence.

"We're friends of your niece."

"I'm Daniel, and this—"

"Daniel? Daniel Reeves?" Will asks me.

"H—how did you..."

"Where's your father?" he interrogates, stepping out of the hospital bed. "Is he with you?"

"N—no, he has no idea," I tell him.

"What are you doing here, kid?"

I feel a buzz in my pocket. It's another text from Kat.

Kyle shoots me a look.

Where are you?

"Just text her back, man," Kyle insists.

Will looks at the two of us with equal confusion and annoyance. He stands there, wearing nothing but a hospital gown, waiting for answers.

I quickly text Kat back.

Be home soon.

Though it may or may not be true.

"Okay look," Will says, "I don't know what you're doing here, but I need to get back to my family."

"Alyssa's here," Kyle said, "the doctors are checking her out."

"Checking her out? Where's Ryan?" Will asks.

Both of us go silent at the mention of Alyssa's brother. How are we supposed to explain that to him?

Will notices the grim expressions on our faces. He sighs, and strokes his scratchy, unkept beard. "He got to him, didn't he?"

I perk up in confusion. "Who?"

"Kaedrik."

A feeling of shock floods through my nerves. For a moment, I can't hold on to a thought long enough to put it into words.

Kyle is equally as speechless as I am.

"How do you know about him?" I finally manage to ask.

"Same way I know about that cabin of yours," he answers. "I've been in your shoes, kid."

"You mean..."

"I was a Guardian."

As the doctors and nurses scramble to check Will's vitals and pepper him with questions, the words repeat in my head on a loop.

It's been years since anyone else knew as much about the cabin as I do.

Then I realize something. The last person that knew about the cabin before any of us. The dots are starting to connect.

When Will is finally out of bed and dressed, ready to go, I ask him.

"You were my mother's partner?"

Will sighs, his breath shaking ever so slightly as the words come out. "Yes, I was."

"This whole time, *you* were the other Guardian."

"What..." says a voice behind me. Alyssa stands at the door, holding herself up with crutches. Her left leg is now in a white cast.

Madison stands at her side.

As Alyssa looks at her uncle, her eyes are sad. Hurt. I don't know how long she was standing there, or how much she heard, but she probably has more questions for Will than any of us.

"Lyz...what happened to you?" Will asks.

"I was going to ask you the same question," she says, "but clearly that's not the most important detail right now."

"Lyz, listen to me..."

"I'm gonna go tell the doctors to start the paperwork and get you out of here," Alyssa says. She hobbles out into the hallway with her crutches, Madison following behind her.

As we check Will out of the hospital, the staff try to ask more questions, but he stays silent. He shows them his gold police badge and promises to give a report in the near future. Though I'm not sure how much truth will be written in it.

"I guess we're taking him back to the cabin, right?" Kyle asks.

"Yeah," I say. "Yeah, I think we need to."

Maybe Will can fill in some of the blanks we've had. If a former Guardian can shed some light on what's been happening, maybe we'll be better off.

Kyle drives all of us back to the cabin. The entire ride, everyone is stone cold silent. Nobody knows what to say right now.

When we get to the alley, Will is the first to step out of the truck. As Alyssa opens her door, he comes around to try and help her.

Alyssa refuses, already grabbing her crutches from Madison and trying to do it herself.

"I've got it," she insists.

Will's expression saddens.

But as I get out of the car and walk over to Alyssa's side, she slips, one crutch falling to the ground. I rush to catch her before her casted foot hits the pavement.

With one arm securing her waist, I quickly lift her injured leg by sliding my other hand beneath her thigh. Her hands press on my chest to brace herself. Feeling a slight twinge in my wound from supporting her weight, I ignore it to keep her steady.

"You good?" I ask her.

"Yeah." She takes a reeling breath to refocus herself after the fall.

Her brown eyes stare into mine, as if bewildered by such a simple act of kindness. Her gaze is broken when her uncle tries once more to help by offering Alyssa her crutch that had fallen. She takes it without saying a word and lets go of me to find her balance.

We follow Will as he walks up to the alley. Right on cue, the Light Door appears in front of him, solid proof that his story is true.

"Home sweet home," he says.

One by one, we all go inside.

Madison is still mesmerized by the lively trees shifting in the warm sunlight.

It still baffles me that she was able to get here by herself. Clearly, it means she's connected to the cabin in some way, but how?

As Peck zooms over in a red blur, Will catches him in his palms, and the little bird chirps at him with delight. "Hello old friend," he says.

Once inside the cabin, all of us gather in the living room, ready for Will to explain.

I have a question to start with that has been itching inside for the last hour. "How did you know my mother?"

Everyone else looks over at me.

Will lets out a sigh, his expression filled with regret. "Hillary, Jacob, and I were friends in high school," he starts. "We grew up in the same town, went to college, and moved here together."

Will's eyes sadden at the memories that were no doubt swirling through his mind.

"When we hit junior year, the Light Door showed up behind my house," Will continues, "I stumbled upon it, and naturally I was curious enough to go through."

"Wait a second, it was at your house?" Kyle asked.

"Once the cabin finds its Guardians, it can move to wherever it needs to for their convenience."

"So, how did my mom find it?" I wonder, fiddling with my bracelet in anticipation.

"Well, as I'm sure you know, Peck communicates with us Guardians through dreams..."

"You dreamt that my mother was the next Guardian," I realize, "just like I did with Alyssa."

Alyssa's eyes widen with shock, and I realize that we hadn't yet explained her Guardianship to Will.

Madison slaps my kneecap in frustration. "Dude, TMI."

"It's okay kid," Will says, turning to look Alyssa in the eye, "I already knew."

"What? How?" Alyssa asks in utter disbelief.

Will lets out another sigh. "The night that I first came to your apartment," he explains, "when you had your first dream of the cabin."

"How could you possibly know about that?" Alyssa wonders.

"Lyz, you weren't just dreaming of me there...I *was* there."

Alyssa looks like her head is going to explode. Everyone is frantically waiting for an answer.

"The more connected a Guardian is with the cabin and their partner, the more they start to gain... *abilities*," he says, "they start to feel each other's emotions, and then, at a certain point, Guardians can enter each other's dreams."

I had never known that we were capable of something like this. I've been connected to the cabin for about fifteen years, and I've never been able to do anything like that. And soon, Alyssa and I will both be able to do it? It's almost hard to imagine.

"I had lost my connection with the cabin years ago," Will claims, taking Alyssa by the hand, "but somehow, you pulled me back in."

Alyssa pulls her hand back. Her brow contorts, frustratedly. A short, yet unmistakable quiver in her bottom lip forms before she speaks again.

"How did you know that Kaedrik took Ryan?" she asks him.

"I saw the rest of your dream, when he took over," Will explains.

Madison rests her head on Alyssa's shoulder in comfort.

Tears start to form in Alyssa's eyes as she remembers her dream. She didn't tell me much about it, but it must have been bad, especially for her first one.

Something else about the whole situation has been pestering me since Will woke up. "Yeah, that's another thing," I add. "You said *he*. You know about Kaedrik too?"

Will raises a curious eyebrow. "How much did your mother tell you?"

Heat fills my cheeks, and I can't bring myself to answer him. My eyes meet Alyssa's. She gives an empathetic glance in my direction.

Kyle steps in for me. "We didn't know what was behind the Dark Door, only that it was powerful, and dangerous. We thought it was some kind of living dark magic."

"In a way, yes," Will answers in a low voice. "Kaedrik is an entity of dark magic. He controls it, and everything in its domain. Darkness, the night, destruction...and death."

"Jesus," I let out.

"Kaedrik is hell-bent on destroying our world," he continues, "Mala trapped him in that prison to stop him for as long as possible. Us Guardians? This cabin? We're the failsafe."

Alyssa quietly frowns at Will's sentiment of *us Guardians*. "Mala. We saw her name in the journal, who is she?"

"Kaedrik's opposite. The entity of light and creation," Will explains. "She enlisted the cabin and the Guardians to keep Kaedrik's demented ass right where it is in that prison."

"Well, where is she?" I ask, my tone harsher than I intended. "We damn well could use her help right now."

"I, uh...I don't know," Will admits. His eyes dart away from us. He watches Peck, who sits contently in his nest on the coffee table I had helped him with earlier.

Madison grips Alyssa's hand before speaking up. "What did you mean when you said you lost your connection with the cabin?"

I'll give her some credit. Given the circumstances, she's doing a hell of a job keeping up.

"When Lyz's parents died, my sister and brother-in-law...I renounced my Guardianship to look after their kids," Will says.

"Look after us?" Alyssa scoffs at the sentiment. "You left us at home all day to go to work, or sleep in with a hangover. We missed school half the time because of you, and when you *were* home, you were drunk."

"Alyssa..." Madison tries to calm her down.

"*No!*" she yells. "Excuse me for not handing you the 'Parent of the Year' award on a silver platter!" Alyssa takes her crutches and heads to the kitchen.

Will starts to get up, his mouth open like he's about to call out to her, but he gives up, his eyes sullen and apologetic.

"I'll talk to her," I tell him.

Will nods and sits back down. As it turns out, he understands the Guardian bond more than any of us.

Following Alyssa into the kitchen, I find her brewing water in a tea kettle on the stove, tears rolling down her face. On the counter next to her is an old blue ceramic mug and the forest tea leaves, probably for her leg.

"Got enough for two?" I ask, rubbing my side. With all the stress I've been putting on my bullet wound lately, the tea can't really do much. but another cup couldn't hurt.

She nods her head.

I grab another mug from the cabinet.

She takes it and sets it down next to hers without saying a word.

"You know, you're not the only one that was raised to be an example of bad parenting skills," I remind her.

She lets out a nervous laugh. "I didn't mean it like that."

"I know."

"I just...he's always said that everything he did was to protect us, that he was going to make things better," she tells me.

"It never was. He thought he knew best, but he only ever made things worse. This Guardian thing doesn't feel any different."

"Hey, I get it," I say. "My dad thought the same way, that only *he* knew how to protect us after mom died. That's how he started the Riot."

Alyssa's gaze sinks down to the floor at the mention of my father.

"Does it ever get any easier?" she asks.

"I'll let you know if it does," I smirk.

At this point, the kettle whistles its high-pitched tune.

Alyssa lifts it off the stove and pours it into both mugs.

I prepare two tea infusers and dip them into each cup.

Once we've both sat down at the kitchen table, Alyssa takes a sip and immediately gags.

"Kyle was right," she says, her face scrunched, "this stuff is *disgusting*."

"See, I don't get that," I laugh, "it's never bothered me."

"Seriously? It literally tastes like old broccoli."

"Not to me," I shrug.

She laughs and takes another, though much smaller, sip of her drink.

I run my fingers through my hair before continuing the conversation. "Here's the thing that I've noticed," I gently set my mug on the table, "we both were on similar paths, and we dealt with it pretty much the same way."

"How so?"

"Well, my dad started leading a criminal gang and tearing up multiple cities around the state, so I ran away to the cabin whenever I could. Your uncle wasn't around for anything, leaving you to basically raise yourself, so you took Ryan and moved away."

"Should I have just stayed put?" Alyssa asks, her brow arched as if waiting for me to continue with something offensive.

I take a quick sip of the tea before answering. "I'm not saying it wasn't justified, I'm saying that *now* maybe there are certain things to stop running from."

My phone buzzes in my pocket again. It's another text from Kat.

I need you to come home, Daniel.

"Is that Kat?" Alyssa asks.

"Yeah," I sigh, not sure how else to answer.

"Kyle told me you've been avoiding her." She says sympathetically before taking another small sip. "Look, as a big sister with her own dodgy little brother, I think you should take your own advice."

"I'm working on it," I say with a nervous chuckle.

Once Alyssa starts to feel better, we start to make our way back toward the living room. Though she pauses at the doorframe, hesitant. Her hand reaches for the door, but she doesn't move it much further, as if afraid of what will happen when she reaches the other side. She's anxious. Somehow, strangely, I can tell.

My hand reaches out to touch Alyssa's shoulder. She flinches at the sudden contact, and my cheeks immediately flush with heat, wondering if that was the right move. But she doesn't pull away. The moment feels very similar to her panic attack in the gazebo this morning. She's looking for comfort.

"It'll be okay," I tell her.

Alyssa smiles, takes a deep breath, and opens the door.

Will looks relieved to see his niece come back and shoots up off the couch immediately ready to speak. "Lyz, I'm so sorry—"

"Thank you, but I'm not ready for any of that yet." Alyssa holds a hand up to stop him. "I'm gonna need you to give me some time."

Will looks resistant, like he desperately wants to say something, but I step in.

"How about we take you downstairs," I say, "I'm sure you want to see how the Dark Door is holding up."

Kyle and I lead Will downstairs to the basement. I offer to Alyssa to stay upstairs with Madison, given her reaction the last time she was there. Although she appreciates it, she insists on joining us.

"I'll be okay," she says, "I feel like I need to do this."

The Dark Door looks more rotten and desolate than the last time we were here. The waves of dark magic emitting from the wood have spread further. The golden door handle has started to rust. A few chips of the desiccated wood have fallen to the floor.

"Whoa," Madison exclaims, turning to Alyssa, "it looks creepier than you described it."

"That's because it is," Alyssa realizes.

"It's in worse shape than ever," Will says.

"I checked it last night," Kyle states, "it's been like this since you guys rescued me from the Riot."

Will's head snaps around to Alyssa with horrified disbelief.

"You went to the Riot's base?!" He gestures at Alyssa's cast. "Is that how this happened?"

"No, it's not," she tells him, "Kyle was in danger, so I helped him."

"You put yourself at risk with Jacob!" Will yells.

"So did you!" Alyssa points out, "and we rescued you from that too! *You're welcome*, by the way!"

Will shoots Alyssa a stern glance, then pinches the bridge of his nose with a heavy sigh. "I just don't want you getting hurt," he says, his eyes on the door, "my mistakes have already affected your brother, I don't want to lose you too."

Neither does Alyssa, I realize. Why else would she save this man that has done nothing but neglect her? Will and Alyssa only have each other.

It makes me start to think about Kat. Throughout all the hell that our dad has put us through, my sister has been the one to look out for me. But anytime she tries to get me to come home, I shut her down. The Riot is not my home, but Kat has been the closest thing to it.

Kyle is right, I haven't been fair to her.

Alyssa's head lowers, anger stewing around her. "You lost me the day I moved into that apartment," she says. "I did everything I possibly could to give Ryan a better life, and the second you barged in, everything went wrong."

"I wasn't trying to barge in," Will claims, "I was trying to protect you."

"Okay, that's a load of crap!" Madison chimes in, standing firmly in front of Alyssa like a shield to glare at Will. "You kicked her out of her own apartment. She came to *me* when you threw her out like trash!"

"I kicked her out so that she *would* be protected!" Will shouts.

"What does that mean?" Alyssa's expression changes, still mad, but growing with curiosity.

Will buries his face in his hands, cursing under his breath. "Lyz, I saw your dream," Will reminds her, "you were chosen as a Guardian."

"And?"

"*And* I knew that was why you didn't pick up Ryan from school," he states, "I kicked you out so that you could find the cabin again, and to try and keep Ryan out of it."

"Why would you..." Alyssa quivers.

"I thought that if you were away from Ryan while learning about this place, then I could protect your brother. Obviously, I only made things worse," Will says, his voice low with shame.

Something about his explanation bothers me. "Why didn't you just tell her about the cabin yourself?" I ask him. "My mom was the one that helped me get started, you could've helped her."

Will turns back to Alyssa and crosses his arms. "If I had, would you have believed, let alone *trusted*, anything I would've said?"

Alyssa doesn't even hesitate. "If you had shown me the cabin? Yeah, I would have. Because this is bigger than me," she says, "but instead, I had to rely on two strangers."

What would things have been like if Will had shown Alyssa the cabin? Meeting us still would've been a surprise, but Alyssa would've had more support at the start of her Guardianship than even I had.

The tension in the room, along with the eeriness of the Dark Door, makes everybody uncomfortable.

We head back upstairs, and I fidget with my bracelet again with a nervous feeling in my stomach.

Will notices. "Is that your mother's?"

"Yeah," I answer, "she gave it to me before she died."

"Do you have one of those?" Kyle asks.

"I do," he says, "I keep it in an old chest back home."

"A chest..." Alyssa says, "was it the red one you told me not to open in my dream?"

"That's the one."

"You told me that I wasn't ready," Alyssa remembers.

Will walks up to Alyssa and puts a hand on her shoulder. "You are now. Let's go get your bracelet."

Will sits in the front seat of Kyle's truck, giving directions to his house.

Alyssa's head hangs low, nervous at the thought of returning to her uncle's home.

Madison looks almost as uneasy. Based on her reaction, I'm assuming she's never been to Will's house before.

Will leads Kyle to a gravel road in the woods, a few miles outside of town.

His small brick house is old and rotting in the ceiling. A wooden porch leads to the front door, the wood stained gray and green by years of rain and wood rot. There are trash bags at the steps, ripped open by some sort of critter. Bushes in front of the house are untouched and overgrown, the leaves starting to brown.

The inside is even more of a mess. It smells like whatever critter chewed up the trash bags died inside the house. Beer cans cover every table. The furniture looks like it was bought in the nineteen-fifties, down to how worn it is.

"I see the housekeeper never left," Alyssa jokes without smiling, "thanks for that mess you left in my apartment, by the way."

Will just grunts and heads down the hallway.

The rest of us follow.

In his bedroom, Will opens the closet, where a wooden chest painted dark red sits on the floor. Dragging the chest out of the closet, he then moves over to his bed. He lifts the mattress and pulls out a key, unlocking the chest. Leaning down, he digs through the chest for a minute, his brow furrowing in frustration.

"Where is...? Gah!" he exclaims. His eyes dart to Alyssa for a split second.

Will continues searching through the chest for a minute, then soon pulls himself back up to hand Alyssa a thick golden bracelet, identical to mine.

"I've held onto this bracelet for over thirty years," he tells her. "I trust you'll take good care of it."

Alyssa handles the bracelet like a porcelain teacup filled to the brim that she's afraid to drop. She then carefully twists it around her wrist and examines the treasure that was long thought lost. "I will," she says.

Will smiles at his niece, and when he glances over at me, there's a small jump of realization. "Oh, Daniel. I have something for you."

He goes back to digging around through the chest, then pulls out a sealed orange manila envelope. I break open the seal. Inside is about seven pieces of paper. I take one out and read what it says.

Will,

I heard about what happened, I'm so sorry. Angie was a good woman with a beautiful family. I know that you'll take good care of her kids...

I recognize the handwriting. A tear races down my cheek as my eyes scan through the letters.

Kyle looks over my shoulder, sees what I'm reading, and gasps.

"What is it?" Alyssa asks, concerned.

"They're from his mother," Kyle replies.

As I read her words, a feeling of warmth washes over me that I haven't felt in a long time. I remember her soft eyes and the flowery smell of her perfume. The hint of vanilla in the scent made it sweeter, more welcoming.

Snapping me out of my haze is an aggressive knock at the door.

"Kyle?! Is that you?" says a familiar voice. "I can see your truck outside!"

"Kat," I say.

"What is she doing here?!" Alyssa asks.

A moment of panic sets in. Kyle steps toward the door. "I'll go," he offers, "I can handle her."

"No!" I object, "what if it's a trick, and you get taken again?"

Kyle sighs and pushes past me to head out the door before I can say anything further. He turns around before he leaves.

"I'll be okay, Dan. Let me do this."

When he leaves, I put my ear to the door and listen to the conversation.

"What are you doing here?" Kat asks Kyle.

"Oh, just house-sitting," Kyle replies with a sly tone of voice.

Kat is not convinced. "How do you even know Will?"

"We're just...old coworkers," Kyle lies.

Will and I both facepalm.

"What are *you* doing here?" he asks her.

"Just dropping off some files from the station," Kat answers, annoyance in her tone.

"That's sweet of you."

"Let me in, Kyle," she orders, "don't make me hurt you."

"Funny," Kyle says, "you seemed very keen on hurting me not too long ago."

"You know what? You're right," my sister says in a sinister voice, "either way, I *do* want to hurt you, so excuse me."

Muffled shoving sounds come from the living room, followed by a pained groan from Kyle.

"No!" he shouts. A warning.

I hear movement. The sound of footsteps grows closer.

There are too many people in Will's bedroom for all of us to hide. Before any of us can think of doing anything, the door slams open.

Kat stares at the group, her face full of shock.

"Daniel?" Kat asks. Her eyes then turn to her 'partner' in the police force. "Will..."

"Hello, Miller," Will responds dryly. "Although, I guess it's *Reeves*, isn't it?"

8-Daniel

I rush after Kat as she bolts out the door. As she runs past the gravel driveway, I catch up and reach for her arm, missing and grabbing her hoodie instead.

"Kat!" I yell. "Listen to me!"

"I'm not listening to *anything* you have to say!" she screams back at me. "You're nothing but a liar and a traitor! I should have known..."

"What Dad is doing is wrong, you have to know that!"

"He's our father! It shouldn't matter what—"

"But it *does*," I interject. "What would Mom say about what he's doing?"

"You shut your damn mouth!" she cries, pulling her arm away.

Kat's entire body begins to shake, furiously. She looks outward between me and the road ahead of us, her eyes frantic and wild.

"I... it's too much." She folds her arms, clutching the fabric of her hoodie. "Why would..."

She used to have panic attacks fairly often. Kyle was the one to help her with them, but they only got worse after he left.

Tears rolling down her face, Kat's entire body trembles.

Trying to recall what Kyle used to do for her, I step back to give her some space.

"You're okay," I tell her, "just breathe through it."

Shooting me an aggravated look, she sits down on the road, reluctantly following my instructions.

Still a couple of feet away, I sit down as well to meet her at eye level. I pull my phone out to text Kyle to meet us here, but there's no need. His truck turns onto the road and pulls up a couple of feet behind us. He hops out, heading right toward Kat.

"Hey! Hey, it's okay!" Kyle holds out a cautious hand. "I'm here, I'm right here, Kat!"

He keeps his distance, not daring to get too close, but his calming words continue to let Kat know he's there.

The whole scene reminds me of our time in the gazebo, when Alyssa had her attack. At the time, Kyle thought the best action was to give her space, but that wasn't what she needed.

Like no time had passed, Kyle thought he knew what to do because of how he cared for Kat, so when he told me to back off, that was based on his own experience. Kat has always been very closed-off. In moments like this, she just wants space.

Alyssa is the opposite, craving emotional support from others. But how could I have known what Alyssa needed? I've only known her for a few days, while Kat and Kyle have *years* of history.

How is it that Alyssa and I were able to connect that way in such a short amount of time? It's like every thought I have corresponds to her, a twisting feeling in my gut that's hard for me to grasp. I was guessing, acting on nothing but instinct to help her.

But...it didn't feel like a guess. It felt like I *knew*, like I could feel it just as easily as she could.

To my surprise, everyone else gets out of the truck.

Alyssa's eyes dart between Kat and me. The feeling comes again, that certainty. I don't know how, I don't know why, but I *know* that look on her face. She's apprehensive, watching Kat, but there's a wave of curiousness in the air around her.

It's so blatantly obvious to me, but...why?

Will had said something earlier today about the connection between two Guardians. Don't they start out by reading each other's emotions?

After a few minutes, Kat finally starts to calm down. Her breathing begins to steady. She grips her shoulders as the trembling in her hands starts to ease. With a calming breath, her glassy eyes focus on nothing but Kyle.

"Kyle," her voice breaks.

He takes that as a signal and gets closer to wrap his arms around her.

"It's okay baby," he whispers.

Kat, still crying, holds on to him like a lifeline.

After a moment, Will crouches down beside them. He eyes his former partner. "We shouldn't be out on the road like this, let's head back."

When we get back to Will's place, Kyle leads Kat to the bathroom to wash her face and steady herself.

In the living room, I sit on the old worn-out sofa and bury my head in my hands.

Alyssa hobbles over on her crutches to sit next to me. For a moment, neither of us speak. The dreaded silence is filled only by the distant sounds of water running in the bathroom, and Kat and Kyle talking.

I feel the press of a hand on my lap as Alyssa finally speaks. "You okay?"

"Yeah," I chuckle tiredly, lowering my hands. Looking up, I see her mournful, caring eyes as she studies me. "It's been a weird day," I admit.

She lets out a small, humorless laugh. "Yeah..."

Her knee brushes against mine. The cast on her left leg sends a rush of guilt through my stomach. Alyssa got hurt, and it's all my fault. This wouldn't have happened if I hadn't brought her to the gazebo. Hell, maybe if I hadn't brought her to the *cabin*, she'd—

"WHAT THE HELL?!"

Kat and Kyle storm into the living room. Kat's cheeks are flushed red with anger. Kyle's wide eyes are ridden with guilt.

"What does any of this have to do with *our mother*?" she asks me.

We explain everything to her. From our mom teaching me about the cabin, to waking up Will. When we get to the point of Kyle's escape, and Kat hears about the fact that Alyssa was at headquarters that night, her face is white as a ghost. By the time we've finished explaining, Kat is completely livid.

"This is insane," she exclaims. "You're all *insane!*"

"Kat..." Kyle tries to reach for her, but she backs away.

"No! This is crazy!"

"It's the truth," Madison tries to be reassuring, "I just found out myself."

"I know it's hard to believe," I meet my sister's eyes, "but the main thing is that Dad *can't* know about any of this."

"You're asking too much. You haven't seen him lately," she says. "He's well beyond pissed off."

"I can't go back right now. Alyssa—"

Kat pulls her hoodie off from over her shoulders to reveal a giant, dark bruise on her upper right arm. "*Please.*"

When Kyle sees this, I swear I hear him growl under his breath. "What did he *do* to you?"

"Nothing worse than what he did to Will," Kat waves him off. "And just like him, I'm still standing on my own two feet."

"That's fair," Will says, "but your dad isn't the senseless violence type, he either thinks he's punishing you, or sending a message to your brother."

Kat's bruised arm gnaws at me with guilt. Dad hurt her because of me, because I avoided him for so long.

I can't keep running from him. At some point I would have been forced to go back. Keeping Dad away from Kat is worth it. Keeping him away from the others is worth it.

"I'm going back."

The relief in Kat's eyes is evident. She smiles, her shoulders relaxing.

I walk down the hall after preparing for the drive when I catch Alyssa through a cracked-open door to one of the bedrooms. Curiosity gets the better of me, and I step inside.

Alyssa sits on a fuzzy blue bean bag chair on the floor next to the window, staring outside. Her crutches rest on the floor beside her. A set of bunk beds against the wall sits there with no blankets or bed sheets. The closet is almost completely empty, aside from a few hangers on the rack. When she sees me come in, she shifts in her seat.

"This was you and your brother's room?" I ask her.

"Yeah, it was," she says. "It hasn't changed a bit."

"It's pretty empty."

"Like I said." She tucks a strand of hair behind her ear. In the sunlight, Alyssa's auburn-brown hair looks crimson. Her deep brown eyes are sad and longing.

Something about the bedroom doesn't sit right with me. A dreary weight falls on my chest. The empty beds behind Alyssa leave me with a feeling of dread, an eerie chill crawling up my spine. It takes me only a second to realize that this somberness isn't coming from my own emotions, but from hers.

I sit cross-legged on the floor next to her. "So, I figured out something interesting today."

"Oh yeah?" she asks.

"Remember what Will said? About the Guardians being connected?"

"Yeah, they start sharing their dreams."

"Right, but the first sign of that is being able to sense each other's emotions." As we talk, I twist my mother's bracelet around my wrist.

She thinks on this for a moment before she speaks. "In the gazebo, when I had that panic attack," she starts, "you knew I needed help, that I needed—"

"Comfort," I say, "yeah."

Alyssa looks at me in awe, like we had just single-handedly put a thousand-piece jigsaw puzzle together. "I think I've somewhat noticed it before that," she admits, "back when you were *stalking* me."

She says the word *stalking* sarcastically, like she was making an inside joke.

"Heh, yeah," I laugh awkwardly, "not my finest moment."

"Mm, not your worst, either," she says with a smile.

"Wait, what was my worst?" I ask her, dumbfounded.

Her eyes meet my gunshot wound, and I catch her meaning.

"Ah," I say, not really knowing how else to respond.

Alyssa sighs, looking out the window again. "Be careful out there," she says.

"Always," I reply with a snarky grin.

"I'm serious! The next time I see you, you'd better still be breathing, okay?" She cracks another small smile.

I laugh and stand up, grabbing Alyssa's crutches and offering a hand to help her up.

"Okay," I promise her.

Kat and I leave Will's house and get in her car. It's a white 2009 Camry that I have never seen before.

"Where did you get this?" I ask her.

"In a parking lot somewhere downtown," she says blankly.

"*Great.*" I roll my eyes.

The rest of the ride to the base is quiet. Kat has nothing more to say to me. She thinks that everything we told her is crap.

I don't blame her, of course. It's a lot to deal with. I just wish we were actually *at* the cabin so she could see for herself. Part of me wants to get out of the car and prove it to her, but I can't do anything about it now. What my sister chooses to believe is out of my control, and that unfortunately includes our father.

When we get to the old, abandoned warehouse, I catch the familiar smell of smoke and oil. Needless to say, I didn't miss it.

Kat stands directly behind me as we go inside, no doubt to make sure that I don't run off.

Charles walks up to me, the front of his curly gray hair wet with sweat.

"Hey, there he is! Where have you been hiding?"

"Just been out on a job," I answer. "Where's my dad?"

"In his office," Charles answers, pointing upstairs. "Hey, uh, be careful up there, okay? He's in another mood."

Another mood. It might be worse than I thought.

I nod and make my way upstairs. Kat follows.

We climb each rusting metal step, walking towards the room that Charles pointed to.

At the top of the stairs, my hand rests on the metal railing.

Kat stays behind me, making sure I actually get to Dad's office.

When we reach the door, I sigh before poking my head in.

Dad sits in his metal fold-up chair in his office, sharpening one of his knives with a whetstone. The eerie scraping sound of the knife doesn't calm my nerves any more than if he were actively pointing a gun to my head.

"Come on in, son," he urges, his eyes staying on the knife in his hand.

Kat turns around and leaves without a word.

Reluctantly, I walk forward. I don't say anything or try to defend myself. Keeping a straight face, the two of us wait in silence for a few long, agonizing seconds while he finishes sharpening.

Finally, he puts the knife and the whetstone down on the small table next to his chair and stands up.

"Where have you been?" His voice is like a growl, quiet, but harsh.

My dad is taller than me. My forehead meets him at his eye level.

"I've been working on a job." I try not to show any emotion in my words, especially fear. I've gotten pretty decent at that over the years, but this time it's harder than usual.

"And what kind of job would that be?" Dad asks.

"I can't tell you that," I answer.

"Oh? And why is that?"

"You didn't tell me anything about the job you went on the other day," I point out. "I'm just following your example, keeping it on a need-to-know basis."

He studies me for just a moment, trying to catch me in a lie.

I keep my stone-cold composure. My fingernails dig into the palm of my clenched fist. Jacob Reeves isn't getting anything out of me today.

"Alright then," he says after a little while, "go downstairs and do some training."

"Yes sir," I say blankly.

Before I can leave, he stops me again. "And Danny," he says, "we're gonna have a meeting tomorrow. I expect you to be there."

A meeting?

"Yes sir," I obey.

While trudging toward the training room, Kat passes me on her way to exactly where I just came from. She doesn't even look at me as we cross paths.

In the training room, two others are already there, giggling and whispering. They see the son of their boss, the great Jacob Reeves, and the whispers cease, replaced by nervous silence.

I pick a punching bag to work with on the other side of the room, away from them. Taking off my leather jacket, my phone slips out of my pocket. I quickly pick it up and bury it back in my jacket.

I curl my hands into a fist, keeping my thumbs on the outside, and start swinging at the punching bag. A couple of punches is all it takes to get into a rhythm, as I've done multiple times before. With each swing and each breath before my punch, my mind spirals.

I think about how they have to work without me to figure out how to find Kaedrik. I think about how I left while Alyssa's brother is still out there, with no control over his hold on the dark magic. I think about how my sister refused to believe us when we tried to tell her the truth. And then I think about what Dad did to Kat on my behalf.

With each heart-wrenching thought, my punches get more and more aggressive. I'm starting to get tired. The wound on my side aches. In a final burst of anger, I thrust my fist at the bag harder than before and my right knuckle starts bleeding from the impact.

"Agh!"

When I look down at my bloody hand, another spot of red gets my attention. Lifting my shirt, I notice that the stitches in my bullet wound have torn.

"Damn it!" I growl under my breath.

One of the guys, Sam, walks up to me, noting the red on my shirt. "Whoa, are you okay there, man?"

"I'm fine," I answer through gritted teeth.

"Need some help with that?" Sam offers. "I have the keys to the infirmary, they gave it to me to stock up after the supply run this afternoon and I haven't had a chance to give it back."

Taking a breath, I nod in response.

I follow Sam to the infirmary, a makeshift room on the second floor where we store the medical supplies. On the way there we pass by Pierce, who sees the blood soaking through my shirt and takes his own key out to open the room.

Pierce fixes my stitches. I catch the silent judgement on his face from exerting myself to this point. When he's done, I thank him and head right back to the training room.

"Are you sure that's a good idea?" Sam asks, following me down the hallway.

"I need to hit something," I say dismissively.

Sam bites his lip, unsure of my answer, before chuckling.

"Need a sparring partner?" he asks.

For a moment I study him, searching for any mockery in his words, but there isn't any.

"Sure."

We move over to the mat in the middle of the room. I hold my hands up in a ready stance as Sam makes the first move. He lunges at me with his fist.

I lean to the side to evade him. The force pulls his body forward, and I use that to my advantage. I hold my foot out, making him fall flat on his face.

"That was dirty," he laughs.

I remember what Dad used to tell me as we sparred when I was fourteen.

"Dirty is the point of the game," I repeat to Sam, offering a hand to help him. Echoing my father's words leaves a weird taste in my mouth.

He takes my hand and I pull him back up to a standing position.

We go again. This time, Sam starts with throwing a few fake-outs. He whips his fist toward me but pulls it back before it makes an impact. He's trying to scare me, but he only succeeds in annoying me.

I throw an uppercut and hit him right in the chin, making him double back.

"All that does is waste time," I tell him.

The two of us go at it for a while. I start to lose track of time. Before we both know it, it's late. I grab my jacket from the floor a few feet away, and we both head upstairs to get some sleep.

Specs of little lights float around the strange bedroom underneath the gazebo, as tiny and beautiful as fireflies. The same strange woman sits at the desk. She twirls her hair, red as a rose, as she writes in a notebook.

I step forward to get a closer look. It's the journal we found.

Getting closer shifts her attention. She turns around to face me and smiles.

"You again," I say, "who are you?"

"A friend," she answers. "My name is Mala."

"The journal belongs to you," I realize. "You know about Kaedrik."

"I'm so sorry Daniel." Mala's smile shifts to a frown. "But Kaedrik is much closer than you think." She stands up and sets the journal down on the desk.

"What does that mean?" I ask.

"Just trust me, I am doing everything I can," she insists. "You and I will meet again soon enough."

"Hold on a minute!"

"Say hi to William for me." Her form fades as a blinding light consumes the room. I cover my eyes with my arm for protection.

When I look back up, the scene has shifted back to my father's office. My dad stands in front of a shadow-like form. As they talk, I can't make out any other features.

"Have you found it yet?" asks the shadow.

"No, I haven't," Dad answers. "There's no sign of this place, if it even exists."

A gust of dark magic swirls around my dad in a harsh wind. "Are you questioning me, mortal?" the shadow asks.

Dad looks down at his feet. "No, of course not." I've never seen my father so nervous. "I only meant that I have never seen something like this—"

"Shut up," the shadow commands, "someone is watching us..."

Suddenly pulled back again by the bright, intense curtain of light, the scene before me shifts to the alley. I stand there, confused, before the Light Door appears, and a familiar face walks out.

"Daniel! Oh my gosh, are you okay?" Alyssa asks as she runs up to me and pulls me into a hug. Her cast and crutches are absent here, so she moves around perfectly fine.

"I'm okay," I tell her.

I can't physically feel her, but seeing her here and holding her close brings me a sense of relief.

"Are you real?" she asks me. "Is this...dream sharing?"

"Yeah," I answer. "I think so."

Alyssa hangs her head down, thinking. She looks back up at me.

"Listen to me," she says, "Will knows about—"

I wake with a sudden start. Early morning sunlight brightens the room. Sitting up from my cot, I grab my jacket off the floor. As if triggered the second I made any movement, the fire alarm sounds, and then instantly shuts off again. My father's signal. Sluggish and tired, I force myself up onto my feet, and head to the meeting.

The *meeting room* is just an empty room on the first floor, now flooded with each of the Riot members. There's another door at the front, where my dad and Kat enter from.

I make my way up there, trudging forward to where Dad can see me, as proof that I actually showed up to this stupid thing.

Once he has eyes on me, he raises a hand and everyone is dead silent.

"Alright!" Dad demands. "For the past few days, I've been working on a partnership deal. I've kept this deal close to the chest, but today he is ready to introduce himself."

The room is filled with whispers. The door behind my dad and sister opens, and a young teenage boy steps out.

Ryan.

My heart skips a beat. He's so pale that his skin is almost white as paper. His eyes and the veins in his arms are pitch black.

Some of the Riot members start quietly giggling and scoffing at the thought of Jacob Reeves bringing in a teenage boy.

"Kaedrik, the floor is yours," my dad says.

I feel like all the air has been sucked out of my lungs.

Even my sister, who has kept a straight face the entire time, shifts nervously in her stance at the sight of Ryan Haller.

"Thank you Jacob." His voice still very much sounds like a kid his age, but this is definitely not Ryan Haller talking.

"Your boss and I have been working on a very special project," he says. Kaedrik stands firm in Ryan's body. He carries himself in a stiffer and more authoritative way than a sixteen-year-old normally would. His arms are crossed behind his back, and he raises his head high, making himself look taller than he actually is.

Standing next to my dad, though, it shouldn't be as intimidating as it is. He's much taller and broader than Ryan, and yet, through stature alone, you can tell who's really in charge.

"A way to ensure the Riot's growing ranks for a very long time. We are not yet prepared to share the specifics, but rest assured it will be beneficial for us all."

All of the crew members look around at each other suspiciously. Some of them are still laughing.

Landon speaks up. "Jacob, what's the deal with this kid?"

Dad clears his throat indignantly. "This *kid* has more power than you could ever imagine. If you put your trust in me, then you put your trust in him."

"The world can be ours," Kaedrik says. "The Riot will be the ones to fulfill my plan and snuff out the Light."

My father, more than likely, is expecting everyone to cheer and agree with him. However, nobody indulges him. Everybody else is too stunned and confused to say a word.

As Kaedrik and my father dismiss everybody, whispers flood through the crowd. Dad calls me back up to his office, probably to discuss my involvement in his *project*.

When I get there, both he and Kat are waiting.

"You lied to me, Danny," he says. His brow furrowed in disappointment.

"I don't know what you're talking about," I tell him.

"You've been harboring the Willis traitor, and you helped him bring back Will Haller."

There's no way. There's absolutely *no way*. How could he know about Will?

Kat's head hangs down low, once again staying silent.

Of course. How could I have been so *stupid*? I should've known that she would tell him everything. Kat has never been able to admit how bad our father is for us. He's our only parent. *Of course* she would tell him what she saw if it meant keeping *herself* safe.

"Tell me, son," Dad starts, "what business do you think you have with a man like Haller?"

"What business do you have attacking a police officer?" I bite back.

"*Excuse me*? I am your father!" He sneers. "You do *not* talk back to me."

I start to back away, but before I can reach the door, a towering body stands firmly behind me.

Landon is blocking my exit. He grabs onto me, his arms around my neck in an unbreakable grasp. The hold blocks my airway, making it hard to breathe.

Dad lunges forward and punches me in the gut. The searing pain causes me to cry out in anguish as it hits my bullet wound.

"Kat!" I cry out in a last-ditch effort for my sister's help.

Tears fill her eyes, but she stays silent.

"She's not gonna help you, son," my dad says, tauntingly.

I thrust my elbow back towards Landon, hitting him in the side hard enough for him to let me go.

My dad doubles back as my fist collides with the bridge of his nose. "Agh!" he cries out. "You think you're a *man* now, Danny?"

He signals Kat to help him. The weight in my chest is heavy with betrayal as she obeys him, effortlessly. She runs towards me and punches me square in the face. The impact causes me to fall back and land on the ground.

"Attagirl, Katrina," Dad says.

As she stands over me, I notice her aim a small glare at Dad that he doesn't see. She's always hated that name.

Kat presses a foot on my stomach. The rough grip of her boot digging into my bullet wound feels like fire. Landon hands her the gun from the holster on his belt. She switches the safety off and aims at me.

My heart races furiously in my chest. "Kat..."

"Don't worry, I'll make sure they spare Alyssa," she says, choking up, "but I *won't* say the same for Kyle."

"Stop."

Kat, looking confused, does as Dad says. She steps off me and turns the safety back on the gun in her hand.

Our father offers a hand to pull me back up to my feet.

Hesitantly, I take it. My stomach twists as his fingers curl around mine when he pulls me up.

Dad then innocently brushes off my shoulders, as if the only injury I have is simply from falling on my ass.

"I'm gonna let you go, and then I'm gonna give you two choices," he tells me, his tone still quietly menacing. "If you choose to come back, then I will know that you want to be a part of this family, and this team."

I keep as straight a face as possible, but on the inside, I'm gagging at the thought of Jacob Reeves' idea of *family*.

"If you choose to stay with Willis and Haller, then, just like them, I will *hunt you down*."

He opens the door for me. I inch outside tentatively without saying anything. Landon and Kat are hesitant.

My father stops me one last time before I leave. "I know you'll make the right choice, Danny."

Outside the base, I start running. The muscles in my legs are weak with a burning feeling.

After a while, I finally make it into town, but don't stop running, not even when Milam Street is in my sight.

As I dip into the alley, the Light Door appears. With the little energy I have left, I pace forward past the cabin.

My head is still spinning from my father's ultimatum. He was going to kill me. *Kat* was going to kill me. And Kaedrik? Why is he here? How did he find my dad? What are they working on together?

As these questions circulate through my panic-stricken mind, I pull out my phone and make my way to the gazebo. The journal that we found might have more answers about Kaedrik. We'll need anything we can use to defeat him.

My thumb mashes the button on Kyle's contact with frantic haste. With each ring, I grow more and more anxious.

"Hello?" he asks once he finally picks up.

"Put Will on the phone! Now!"

Before he can respond, there's a loud crash. For a moment, I can't understand what's going on between the several voices over the muffled audio.

Then Will's voice shouts in the background, "Leave her alone, Jacob! She's got nothing to do with this!"

A scream that sounds like Madison rings in my ears.

"That's not what I've heard," says a frighteningly familiar voice.

Dad.

More crashes. The sudden sound of a gunshot. Then, screaming in the background. *Alyssa.*

"No! Please!"

"Let go of her!" Madison yells.

More crashing. Dad says something that I can't make out.

Heat rises in my throat. No. Please, God, no. This isn't happening.

"Hey asshole!" Kyle calls. I hear a smack, some sort of impact. Either Kyle or my dad must have just taken a hit.

"I'll deal with you later, Willis," dad growls.

The call drops. Deafening silence rings in my ears.

9-Alyssa

I watch apprehensively as Daniel and Kat roll out of Will's driveway.

Kyle makes his way to the kitchen without saying a word, gritting his teeth in frustration. He grips his hand around Daniel's bracelet, which he had been given moments ago for safekeeping.

I admire my own bracelet. The swirled designs on the thick golden band match up perfectly with Daniel's. The only difference between the two bands is our names. Where Daniel's first and last name is etched into the metal, mine reads 'Alyssa Haller'.

This bracelet used to belong to Will, so how long ago did my name replace his?

My uncle comes up behind me, and I can't tell if it's the Guardian senses that help me notice him, or my peripheral vision. My head turns, not having the energy to bother with adjusting my crutches to face him.

Madison, who sits behind me, puts a hand on my shoulder. "He'll be alright, Lyz."

"We don't know that," I tell her. "I've been to their base. If he's found out, there's no telling what could happen."

Will aims his eyes up toward the ceiling, then looks back at me. "If there's one thing I know about Jacob Reeves, he may be ruthless, but he's completely clueless and self-oriented," he says, "and Daniel is a tough kid. He'll get out of this."

The words bring me back to what Will had told us earlier at the cabin. A question that had been circling my thoughts for a while comes to the surface. "Was he always like that?"

"For the most part," Will admits, "Jacob put on the 'fun guy' mask when he was around Hillary, until around the time Kat was born."

Will fumbles with the back of his hair as he continues. "Once he got comfortable, he didn't feel the need for the mask. He got angry around her, defensive," he says, "but he was never physically violent...until she died."

"Kat told me what happened," I recall, "the robber that broke into the house and shot her."

"Kat doesn't know the real story, Lyz," Will tells me, crossing his arms.

"What?!" Kyle asks, swinging the kitchen door open, eyes wide.

"What are you talking about?" Madison asks.

Will sits down on the couch, his hand raised defensively. "I'd rather talk about that when Daniel gets back," he insists, "it's his right to know the truth."

That's a fair point. Still, I'm itching with curiosity.

Sitting down with my uncle, I struggle to adjust onto the old cushion with my cast and crutches. Will helps me down and takes the crutches, setting them on the floor beside him. I want to say something to him, but I don't even know where to start.

Will sees me contemplating and speaks up first. "Lyz, I know that no apology can make up for what I've put you and your brother through, but...I will do *anything* I can to be better for the both of you."

My cheeks flush at the slight implication I hear in his words. "I appreciate that, but Will..." I hesitate, "Ryan has been under my care for a long time. Now more than ever, I don't want that to change."

Will places a hand on my shoulder reassuringly. "I understand."

The tightness in my shoulders relaxes. A breath of relief escapes. Only a few days ago, Will threatened to take Ryan away. He even brought up getting a lawyer involved to keep me from protesting. But here, now, the trust in his eyes feels like a weight has been lifted from my chest.

That night, I lay in my bed with so much anxiety that I can't even close my eyes, let alone fall asleep. I lay there with my casted leg elevated by a ramp of pillows that Will had constructed for me.

My thoughts stay on Daniel, hoping that he can make it back here safely. Thinking about what could happen if he's found out makes my skin crawl. He's spent so long trying to stay off his father's path. He's made every effort to do good, to lean closer to the light and far away from the shadow of Jacob Reeves. And now he's back in that base, shrouding himself in that shadow again, solely for the sake of his sister.

A part of me can't help but blame myself. I pushed him. The anger I felt when I learned the truth about his involvement with the Riot urged him to prove himself. I've felt the desperate determination lingering behind those eyes. Daniel wants so badly to prove that he isn't his father. But he doesn't need to. I know that. I've known that for a while.

Oh god. Maybe that's why he felt he had to leave. I never told him.

These thoughts stay with me for hours, and I don't even realize when my eyelids grow heavy and I fall asleep.

In the kitchen, still at Will's house, something looks different. Things have changed around. The wallpaper consists of putrid yellow and white stripes, rather than the base sky blue that I grew up with. The wooden kitchen table is newer, more refurbished. It no longer has the bite marks on one of the corners on the left from when Ryan was a teething toddler.

Looking down, I notice my cast and crutches are gone, and I feel a temporary sense of relief without the physical strain.

Will sits at the table with a can of beer in his hand. He looks younger, not as much gray visible in his brown hair. A young woman stands, leaning against the table next to him.

The woman is beautiful. Her caramel hair is pulled into a neat bun, a few curly strands running along the front of her face. Her green eyes are kind and reassuring, but I can plainly sense the sadness behind them. She wears blue scrubs and white tennis shoes. A name tag is clipped to her shirt. Moving closer, I can see it says: Hillary Reeves, E.R. Nurse.

Daniel and Kat's mother.

"I can't go on like this, Hill," Will says.

I watch in awe as the two of them speak, mesmerized by this vision of an old memory.

"Willy," Hillary sighs, "you've been through a lot. I understand that, and I am so, so sorry." She chokes up.

Will takes a big sip of his beer, avoiding her eyes.

"I can't do this alone," she pleads, "you were the one who found the cabin. We've protected it since we were kids."

"So, you should know how to handle it," Will bites. "You figured out how to make those healing tonics on your own."

The tonic we had used to help Will earlier today. The initials on the tag. H.O., Hillary, and O must be her maiden name.

"I'm sorry it didn't work on your sister," she apologizes.

Will doesn't respond, he just glares at her.

"Willy, please. We don't know when, or if, there will be another Guardian," Hillary points out, "I need you."

Will slams his beer can on the table and stands up.

Hillary jumps, her eyes wide with fear.

"And I needed you to save my sister," he says.

In a split second, the scene changes. Will's house is gone. Everything is. It's pitch black, I can't see anything. Then, a chill runs up my spine.

"Poor foolish child," says a cunning, familiar voice, "so small, so clueless."

"Kaedrik!" I snap.

"Ahh...maybe not so clueless after all," he says in a sly tone.

"Let go of my brother!" I scream.

"Fear not, Lyz...I'm coming for you too," Kaedrik whispers.

A blast of light fills my surroundings. I look around, finally able to see. I'm in the woods in front of the cabin.

"H—how did...?"

With a sudden windy wisp of the trees, a strange woman appears in front of me. Her hair is very uniquely bright red, like Peck's vibrant feathers. It falls past her shoulders, the top ends braided together in a way that almost looks like a crown. She's wearing a silky white gown that falls all the way down to the ground. It's detailed with beautiful gold stitching on the bodice, the ends of her sleeves laced to match. Her eyes are golden yellow, glimmering like the sun.

She looks at me with a warm smile. "Hello Alyssa." Her voice is elegant and welcoming.

"Who are you?" I ask, cautiously inching closer.

"My name is Mala," she tells me. "I've been watching you for quite some time. You've done well in your short time at the cabin."

"How do you know me?" I ask her.

"I know all of my Guardians, dear," Mala says.

"Your Guardians?" I repeat.

She puts her finger to her lips to shush me. Just then, the Light Door appears next to her. "You have someone waiting for you."

I apprehensively head towards the door. Before I open it, I turn back to Mala. "Can you help me get my brother back?"

She puts a hand on my shoulder assuringly. "I already am."

I can't place it, but somehow it feels like I've seen this girl before. Something about her reveals a sense of trust. I do what she says and open the door.

On the other side, in the alley, Daniel is standing there.

"Daniel! Oh my gosh, are you okay?" I ask, rushing up to him. I wrap my arms around him, hugging him tight.

"I'm okay," he says to me.

"Are you real? Is this...dream sharing?"

"Yeah." He runs his fingers through his hair.

I look down at my feet, remembering my conversation with Will this evening. Something happened to Hillary that Daniel doesn't know about. I have to let him know.

"Daniel, listen to me," I start, "Will knows about—"

When I wake up, I curse under my breath. I didn't have enough time to tell Daniel the truth. I pull myself out of bed, grabbing my crutches.

In the hallway, a crisp, buttery smell fills the air. I hobble towards the kitchen, where Kyle and Will are making pancakes and scrambled eggs for breakfast.

Madison stands at the coffee pot, prepping the grounds and water for brewing. "Good morning, sleepyhead," she says.

"Good morning," I respond with a tired grunt. "What's all this?"

Kyle flips a pancake onto the pile of others that he's made, held by an old-fashioned ceramic plate. He looks over at me and smiles, proud of his culinary work. "I figured we could all use a good breakfast."

Will stirs the liquid eggs with his spatula. "I'm just making sure Willis doesn't burn down my kitchen."

Kyle looks at him, playfully offended. "I can work wonders in the kitchen, thank you very much."

Kyle's phone rings next to him on the kitchen counter. He picks it up and all I hear is a second of shouting before a loud crash erupts in the living room.

Every person in the room freezes. Shock fills the air before Will runs toward the noise.

Kyle clutches his phone in his hand as he and Madison follow.

I move as fast as I can with my crutches.

Jacob Reeves and a few of his crew members flood through the door.

He sees Will and grunts. "So, it *is* true," he says, "welcome back to the land of the living, old friend."

My heart races. My blood runs cold.

He signals two of the Riot members, and they walk up to me, grabbing me by both my arms.

I try to thrash away, but it only makes my crutches fall out from under me. My casted foot meets the ground, and I yelp in pain as fire spreads through the nerves in my leg.

Madison tries to run towards me, but another Riot member shoves her to the ground and points a gun at her. She lets out a frightened scream.

"Leave her alone, Jacob!" Will shouts, facing me. "She's got nothing to do with this!"

"That's not what I heard," Jacob snarls.

Will lunges at Jacob, who dodges and kicks Will in the ribs. He retaliates with a punch that sends my uncle crashing into the bookshelf. Jacob doesn't stop. He pulls out his gun, and I watch in horror as his finger squeezes the trigger. The thundering sound of the gunshot makes me scream. The bullet rips through Will's shoulder and he shouts in agony.

"No! Please!" I demand, trying to break free from the tight grip.

"Let go of her!" Madison screams, still at gunpoint. Tears stream down her face, making a strand of her long black hair stick to her cheek.

Jacob walks over to me, his expression unsettlingly calm. He tilts my head up by my chin and tucks a loose strand of my hair behind my ear. His face is rugged, contorted with anger. Up close, the smell of cigarettes and burnt plastic enters my nose.

"So, this is my son's little friend," he whispers.

I pull away from him, not saying a word and keeping a straight face.

Jacob calmly walks to the coffee table, then, with a vindictive smile, he flips it over, making me jolt.

"I am not a patient man, Miss Haller," he says.

"Hey asshole!" Kyle shouts.

Just as Jacob turns to face him, Kyle's fist collides with his jaw in a satisfying *crack*. Jacob rubs his chin from the impact. I didn't think the man could possibly look more annoyed.

A Riot member swiftly wraps his arms around Kyle's arms and waist. He pulls and thrashes, trying to break free. Another man gets in a few hits of his own, punching Kyle in the gut and causing him to collapse weakly on the floor. The phone in his hands drops to the ground beside him.

Jacob doesn't leave it there. He kicks Kyle in the side, and then grabs him by the underarm, forcing eye contact. "I'll deal with you later, Willis."

He drops Kyle's arm, making him slam onto the floor. Jacob eyes the phone on the ground next to Kyle. The screen is still lit up from whoever had called moments before. I can't see the contact's name, but Jacob does. He smiles sinisterly and crushes the phone with his boot.

Jacob walks back up to me and one of the guys holding onto my arm pulls a small syringe from his pants pocket. He hands the needle to Jacob, who sticks it in my arm, injecting some sort of liquid.

"What do you want from me?!" I ask him frantically.

"Shhh."

The muscles in my body start to feel weak. My eyelids grow heavy. I don't have the energy to move or speak as Jacob and his men take me to their black windowless van. As they drag me across the gravel of Will's driveway, the two men holding me by my arms toss me into the back of the van. A few of the other Riot members sit in the back as well to keep an eye on me. By the time they start to drive off, my vision goes black.

As my eyes start to open, blurred shapes start to come into focus. My clouded mind starts to slowly register my surroundings. A worn out and empty room, similar to where I found Kyle when he was taken.

A member of the Riot stands in front of me by the door. When he sees me waking up, he leaves the room without a word.

My muscles are heavy with fatigue. My wrists and free leg are zip-tied to a metal chair, the plastic cutting into my skin. My casted leg is tied to the chair with a piece of rope. I guess they didn't have a zip-tie big enough. A piece of duct tape covers my mouth, preventing me from screaming for help. As if anyone could hear me.

Jacob and a couple other Riot members walk through the door.

Following hesitantly behind them is Kat.

Seeing her again after yesterday, I wonder if Daniel is still here. Maybe he knows that his dad took me. He can find me and get me out of this place.

"Nice to see you again, Alyssa," Jacob says in an eerily welcoming tone. "Your uncle and I are old friends. Last time I saw you, you were a toddler."

I shudder at the thought of this horrible man reminiscing about the 'good old days' with my family.

"Oh, where are my manners?" Jacob says. He rips the tape off without warning.

A sharp sting replaces the tape.

"How did you meet my son?" he asks me sternly.

I don't trust myself to lie well enough, so I say nothing. Anything I tell Jacob could screw us over.

"Look at me, young lady," Jacob orders. His authoritative voice reminds me of an angry father disciplining his child. It sends a chill up my spine. "You can't keep your mouth shut forever. I have my ways of dealing with little *brats*."

I stay silent, shifting in my seat, trying to struggle out of the zip ties.

Jacob grabs the head of the metal chair and I stop. He sees the fear in my eyes and smiles. After a moment of pause, he lets go of the chair and faces Kat and his men.

"What should we do with her, sir?" one of the Riot members asks.

Jacob stays silent for a moment. He grips the handle of his knife that's kept in the holster of his belt. After an agonizingly quiet minute, he speaks up. "We'll use her as bait," he says. "Send for him, but tell him I'm gonna need a minute to myself."

One by one, the members file out of the room, including Kat.

I am now left alone with Jacob Reeves.

He takes his knife out of the holster and fiddles with it, seamlessly. "Tell me this," he starts, "what do you think the chances are that Danny will come running back here to save you?"

"W-what does that mean?" I ask him, confused and worried by the implication. "He's not here?"

Jacob looks at me with intrigue. He circles my chair, still fiddling with the knife. "No ma'am. He left this morning, I assumed he was going to you...he didn't abandon you, did he?"

There's no way. He wouldn't. I don't believe Daniel would do that.

Jacob sighs. "That boy," he says, clicking his tongue, "he has a knack for leaving people behind. He's left his father, his sister...and now you."

I remember how much it hurt for Kat when Daniel wasn't around. He thought he was doing the right thing. But was he?

I feel sick. Weak. I'm not thinking clearly.

"I'm really sorry, Alyssa," Jacob says from behind me. "That kind of pain just *cuts deep*, doesn't it?"

A searing pain shoots through my back near my right shoulder. I scream through the sharp sting of the knife. "Stop! Please!"

Jacob ignores me. He moves on and grabs my left hand. Keeping my palm wide open, he digs the knife into my skin and slices across my hand.

I let out another scream. Tears roll down my face at the same time as the trail of blood trickling down my palm.

He moves behind me again, and this time comes back with a plastic bottle filled with some sort of clear liquid. He holds the bottle over the fresh cut on my palm and pours.

Fiery agony spreads throughout my surrounding nerves as the strange liquid soaks into my hand. Crying out louder than before, I end up choking as my voice strains. Tears flood my face as the pain subsides. The smell is familiar. *Alcohol.*

"That pain? I feel it every day," Jacob says softly as he comes back up behind me. "You should consider yourself lucky, little girl."

He holds the bottle over the cut on my shoulder.

I close my eyes, bracing myself for what's coming.

He pours the alcohol onto my shoulder. Its piercing burn is too much for me to handle.

"*Make it stop!*" I shout.

By the time the pain settles again, my vision is clouded. I can't focus. Jacob's blurry figure heads for the door. His mouth moves, but the sound doesn't register with me. He exits the room, and I am left alone.

Time goes by, I'm not sure how much, and my mind clears. The searing pain of steel and alcohol has mostly subsided. The blurred details of the empty room sharpen as my eyes come into focus. I still feel queasy from the liquid he knocked me out with. In some small part though, the silence alone gives me a morbid sense of ease.

That feeling doesn't last long at all as the door opens again. In walks the last person I ever expected to see.

"R—Ryan?"

Tears immediately form in my eyes. I haven't seen my brother in *days*. I wasn't even sure if he was still alive. And now here he is, right in front of me.

His eyes are completely black, as are the veins in his arms. Ryan was already pale, but now his skin is almost as white as a ghost.

He grins at me maliciously. The curl in his chin looks so foreign coming from my little brother.

"It's so nice to finally meet you in person, my dear," Kaedrik says.

"What have you done to him?" I ask weakly.

"I've done a lot of things to a lot of people, Alyssa," he replies. "You'll have to be more specific."

I glare at him sternly, not saying a word. He knows exactly who I'm talking about.

"Ah yes, Ryan. He's proven himself to be quite the useful host," he patronizes. "But, enough about him, I want to talk about *you*."

"Me?"

"Indeed, I know everything about you, Alyssa Haller." Kaedrik bends down on his knees to meet me at eye level. "You see, typically Mala's Guardians mean nothing to me, they're mere...*playthings*, but lately they've become somewhat of a nuisance as I progress closer to my freedom." He rests a hand on my casted leg.

 192

I try to pull away, but his grip, along with the rope holding my leg in place, makes my effort useless. "I haven't done anything to you," I say, struggling.

"True, not directly...not yet," he snarls, "but I could sense your Guardianship all the way from that disgusting otherworldly basement."

If Kaedrik knows that I'm a Guardian, does he know about Daniel? And if he does, has he told Jacob? I'm not sure. I feel like if Jacob knew, our conversation earlier would have been much different.

"What does any of this have to do with my brother?" I ask him.

He smiles, little waves of a dark shadow emanating from his hand. "Oh yes," he says, "Ryan found something of mine, and I want it back. Getting under your skin is...an added bonus."

"What did he find?" I wonder.

What could Ryan have *possibly* found that got him involved with Kaedrik?

"None of that matters now," he replies. He presses his fingers into my cast, and his dark magic circles my leg like a twister.

It burns into my skin even worse than the alcohol. The bones in my ankle pop in place with an unbearably sharp *snap*.

A scream escapes from my lungs as the pain sears through my body. After a horrifically long few seconds, the pain recedes. My cast disappears in black smoke.

I look down at my leg, rotating my ankle. I'm completely healed. Well, my leg is. The cuts from Jacob's knife still remain.

"Why would you help me?" I ask Kaedrik, perplexed.

"I need you in good shape," he says, "because *you* are going to help *me*."

I glare at him. He can't be serious. "*Never,*" I tell him spitefully.

"My dear, we share a common goal," he says with a sinister smile, "with your help, Jacob Reeves can meet his ultimate demise."

"What?" I ask, "He's your business partner, why would you want to—"

"He's served his purpose," Kaedrik claims. He takes a strand of my hair between his fingers and twirls it. "I have something *far more useful* now."

I pull my head away. "You can't make me do anything for you," I say, stern and quiet.

Kaedrik pulls back, laughing. "Oh child! I can make you do whatever I like," he says, "amplifying your distress, and in turn causing you to...*shoot a friend*, for instance."

The last time I was at this base, when Daniel told me his truth. I remember not feeling in complete control of myself. I thought it was just my nervous state...it was him.

"No!" I shout. "You won't get away with this!"

Kaedrik just lets out a mockingly big laugh. "And how do you expect to stop me? By separating me from your brother?" he asks, "I wonder if you know yet how to do that."

His words make me pause. I remember what the journal said. Kaedrik's statement only confirms my worst fear. The only way to free Ryan is to kill him. My chest grows heavier, tears rolling down my cheeks.

"You can't win without losing something," Kaedrik says, watching my pained realization with a smirk, "but if you do this...I can give you what you desire."

His smile on my brother's face is filled with deviant intent, but his eyes are serious.

I can't tell what his real intentions are. I don't trust it.

Kaedrik sees my hesitation and stands up. A roll of duct tape materializes in his hand. He rips off a piece and places it over my mouth. "Think about it, dear. You'll know when I need you."

Kaedrik walks out the door without saying another word. I'm left on my own once again.

Nobody else comes in for a while. Not even Jacob. I start to nod off in the lonely silence. My mind is blank with exhaustion.

I'm woken by the sound of the door slamming shut. My vision is still blurry, and, for the first couple seconds after opening my eyes, I can't tell who's here. When the room finally comes into focus, I see a tall blonde figure standing firm with her arms crossed.

Kat stands in front of me, her posture is stiff and serious, but her eyes are full of regret.

She rips the tape off my mouth, but stays quiet. Neither of us say anything for a few seconds. I don't think either of us know *what* to say.

Finally, I ask her a question. "Where's Daniel?"

"He's gone," she sighs.

"Is he coming back?"

She pushes her hair behind her ear and tugs at the ends — her nervous habit. "I don't know," she admits, "but I know my dad is counting on it, that's why you're here."

I remember what Jacob had told that other Riot member a while ago.

We'll use her as bait.

"He's using me to lure Daniel here."

"Yeah," Kat confirms. Her voice is quiet, almost in a whisper.

"What happened?" I ask her sternly.

"That's not important."

"What are you doing here, Kat?" I ask, sighing.

"I just was just wondering...can you tell me what you and my brother have been doing?" she asks. "I can convince them to let you go, but I need the *truth*, Lyz."

I scowl at her. "There's nothing I can tell you that you don't already know."

Kat scoffs at me. "You can't expect me to believe all of that."

I roll my eyes. "You saw Ryan, what do you think?"

Kat stops for a moment, processing. She hangs her head low in shame. "I don't know what to think," she admits.

"I understand, really, it's a hard truth to swallow," I tell her, "but it *is* the truth, Kat."

Our conversation is interrupted by a knock on the door.

Kat sighs heavily, "I've got to go."

She holds out the piece of duct tape. She has to put it back on. "I'm sorry."

"Fine," I respond plainly. An apology from her means nothing right now.

She puts the tape over my mouth and before she walks out the door, she turns around to meet my eyes. "I...I hope they come for you," she says, her voice breaking slightly.

She leaves, and once again I am on my own. Trapped here in the silence, I think about Daniel. The last time I saw him, he was on his way here with Kat. What could have led him to leave? Then my thoughts turn to the dream I had last night. I remember seeing Hillary Reeves' sad expression as she spoke to my mourning uncle. I wish I could've warned Daniel about the information Will has on his mother.

As these thoughts stir in my mind, I feel an object pressed into my bound right hand. Whatever I'm now holding has a bit of weight to it, but not too much. It feels like some sort of handle. I take a hold of it with my other hand and feel a thin piece of metal with a serrated edge.

A knife.

Before I can even wonder how a knife materialized into my grasp, I remember what Kaedrik said to me earlier.

You'll know when I need you.

He wants me to use the knife to escape, and then to kill Jacob. I feel dizzy with unease as the thought circles through my head. Obeying Kaedrik like a slave is the *last* thing I want. Jacob is a monster, but so is Kaedrik. I can't listen to him, I won't.

But I've snuck through this warehouse and escaped before. If I can cut myself free, maybe I can make it back before Daniel gets here and puts himself in more danger.

I adjust the knife with my hands, trying to get it inside the zip tie and between my wrists. My fingers fidget with the handle, nearly dropping it a couple of times. Squirming to get the knife into place, the serrated edge of the blade digs into my skin. I wince as the knife leaves a few stinging cuts on my wrists.

Gritting my teeth, I push the knife against the ties, moving it up and down in a sawing motion. A couple seconds later, I hear a snap as the zip ties fall off. With my hands free, I scramble to cut the rope and the last zip tie on my legs.

I crack open the door as slightly as I can to make sure that the path is clear. I don't see anyone, but I wait a while to be certain.

When I finally leave the room, I run as fast as I can down a flight of stairs and into the closest hallway, looking around frantically for an exit. The sound of metal pounding under my feet makes more noise than I intended.

"What was that?" a gruff voice asks in the distance.

As footsteps approach, I hurry in the opposite direction, toward a strip of hallways.

Last time, Kyle and I escaped through the window. Now I have no choice but to find a door that will lead me outside. I tread carefully through the halls, wary of each step, each small noise, each little movement. A few times, I hear approaching footsteps, and I shuffle to hide behind a wall to avoid passing Riot members. When they walk by, I hold my breath, anxiously waiting for them to leave so I can make my escape. This works for a while, until I find myself backed into a corner.

The next hallway I venture into is a dead end. I turn to leave, but a voice makes me freeze with panic.

"He's not here yet...if he doesn't show up in the next hour, send someone to get him," commands Jacob Reeves.

Before I can make any decisions, Jacob and three other men pass by the hallway. Some misguided shred of hope leads me to pray that I am out of his line of sight. But unfortunately, that's not the case.

He turns his head and sees me cowering in the corner. Jacob smirks like a predator catching sight of his prey. It makes my blood run cold.

"Boys!" He signals his men. "Get her!"

I try to run to the side and get past them, to no avail.

Jacob pushes me against the wall, his arm presses right underneath my neck, his tight hold is enough to keep me in place, despite my thrashing. He gestures with his free hand, and two of his men grab my arms. The other gets a syringe out of his pocket, the same as before. He quickly injects it into my arm.

"Agh!" I let out.

Jacob lets go of me.

I fight through the exhaustion as the drug starts to take effect, trying to take the opportunity to run. One of his men grips my shoulders forcefully before I can take more than a step. I attempt to struggle out of the hold, but the other man punches me in the stomach, making me double over.

Jacob bends down on one knee and grabs a fistful of my hair to force my head up. The corner of his mouth curls up in a sinister grin. He's caught his prey.

"You should've stayed put, little girl," he says, turning to his men. "Gordon, Suggs, take her downstairs. I'll deal with her later."

10-Alyssa

As Jacob's men drag me down the steps of a basement, the drug wares me down. I start to feel weak and sluggish, my eyelids weighing heavily, along with the rest of the muscles in my body.

I'm taken to the basement. A giant furnace heats up the room and support beams stretch to the ceiling. A long metal chain sits next to one of the support beams. Other than that, there's not much else down here.

The men sit me down against the beam, wrap the chain around me tightly a couple of times, and lock it. One of them comes around and puts a piece of duct tape over my mouth. As the Riot members leave, I can hear one of them snickering. They know I won't last long.

Left alone once again, tears roll down my face. I'm here to lure Daniel into a trap. All this pain and torture, it's either to send him a message, or to make up for the Riot failing to get rid of Will.

Eventually the drug lulls me to sleep. I don't have any dreams, I don't see anything. My mind is completely quiet.

A while later, the tug of the metal chains pulling from behind jostles me awake. Someone has come to untie me, probably to take me to Jacob. Or, for all I know, it could be Kaedrik. I didn't do what he asked. My thoughts turn to the worst-case scenario as I struggle in my restraints. Still lethargic from the drug, the movement sends me into a weary panic. I wiggle restlessly in a desperate attempt to free myself from the grasp of the chains. My chest heaves as my screams are muffled by the duct tape.

Whoever is behind the post stops what they're doing and turns to my side.

"Hey! Alyssa, it's me! You're okay!"

More tears roll down my cheek as I register the person in front of me.

Daniel tears the duct tape from my mouth.

The weight in my chest immediately falls. A breath of relief escapes as I scan his emerald eyes, confirming that he's *actually* here in front of me. Joy settles every anxious nerve beneath my skin.

But the feeling dims as I remember Jacob's plan. "You can't be here! It's a trap!" I warn him.

"I know, don't worry," he says reassuringly. "The others are keeping my dad and the Riot distracted."

I let out a quivering sigh of relief at his words.

Daniel goes back to the lock on the chain. Within seconds, it falls in my lap.

I stand up and pull Daniel into a tight hug. "*Thank you*," I say, my voice breaking with a wash of relief.

"Of course," he replies softly. He holds onto me tight, as if letting go would put me back in those chains. His hands fall over the cut on my back, and a small wince escapes through my teeth before he quickly retracts them.

I don't mind at all. His touch is comforting. It's safe. I'm *finally* safe.

Daniel then pulls back for a second, looking perplexed. "Your ankle..."

"Kaedrik. Long story," I answer, "he's here and he has Ryan, just like we thought."

"I know, I saw him before I left," he says.

"Why *did* you leave?" I ask.

The sound of pounding footsteps comes from upstairs.

"Long story," he says, "we need to get out of here."

The footsteps get closer and I brace myself. The two of us are about to be caught. I close my eyes and hide behind Daniel as I hear someone scuffling downstairs.

"Guys! We need to go, they'll be back soon!" says a familiar voice.

I open my eyes, Kat stands by the railing of the stairs, her expression anxious. She's holding a white plastic bag in her hand, but I can't see what is in it.

I want to say something, maybe to thank her, but she's right. I don't know what their plan is, but we need to leave before the Riot realizes.

Daniel and Kat lead me through a section of hallways. Soon, I start to feel nauseous. My head feels light and my stomach is in knots. After a few minutes of running, I have to stop. I'm unable to hold it back. The double dose of the drug was too much for my system. I lean down and throw up right in the middle of the hallway.

Daniel and Kat rush to my side. Kat holds my hair back.

"What did he do to you?" Daniel asks. Regret and anger simultaneously fill his voice.

"Propofol. It knocked her out...but it messed up her system, made her feel sick," Kat explains.

As I come to a pause, I hear Riot members calling out in the distance. I force myself back up. "We...have...to get out of here."

The three of us run the rest of the way. I still feel queasy, but I hold myself back as much as physically possible.

Finally, we make it outside, where Kyle and Will wait outside in the truck.

A wave of relief washes over me when I see them. I look at Will, who watches me approach with the release of a worried breath he'd been holding.

Daniel and Kat quickly help me into the back seat. They set me by the left window in the passenger side so I can get some air.

Once we're in, Kyle quickly drives away.

The car ride back to the cabin is sullen and quiet.

Daniel sits in the front with Kyle, stealing glances at me through the rearview mirror, as if he's worried that I would disappear the second he looked away.

Will is in the back with Kat and myself, rubbing his shoulder. I remember when the Riot first got to his house. Jacob shot him. I then realize that I'm not so sure how long ago that was, because I had been in and out of consciousness.

"How long was I gone?" I ask them.

"Just over a day," Will answers, gently placing a hand on my knee.

I press my lips together, processing that information. I'm not really sure what else to say.

We finally get back to the alley, and before I can walk through the door, I throw up again.

Kat directs the other guys to head to the cabin and leans down to help me. With the plastic bag still in her hand, she takes out a water bottle and a box of pills.

"What is that?" I ask her.

"Zofran," she says. "Anti-nausea, it'll help."

She takes out a pill and hands it to me with the bottled water.

I swallow the pill, take a sip of water, and put the cap back on the bottle. "Thank you," I tell Kat.

"It's no problem, they had it in the Riot's med bay."

"That's not what I mean," I say.

Kat shrugs with a passive smile. "Yeah, well," she starts, "you and your uncle make a damn good argument."

I frown, confused, but she waves off the subject.

A moment later, I take Kat through the door. The astonishment in her eyes reminds me of my first time here. I lead her up to the cabin, where the guys are waiting inside with Madison, who stayed behind to look after the Dark Door.

When she sees me, she runs to wrap her arms around me in a long, tight hug.

"Are you okay?!" she asks me frantically.

I pull back when I start to feel nauseous again. "I will be," I tell her. As I sit down on the couch, Will notes my healed ankle.

"How did that happen?"

I sigh and my stomach knots just thinking about it. "Kaedrik did it," I tell them.

Daniel crosses his arms, his eyes unwavering in my direction, filled with concern. "You saw him too?" he asks.

"You *knew* about this?" Kyle wonders.

"Dad introduced his new *partner* to the entire group this morning," Kat explains. She says the word 'partner' with clear disgust in her tone.

"It's not much of a partnership," I explain, "Kaedrik wanted me to kill Jacob."

Shock and confusion fills the room.

"Why would he do that?" Daniel wonders.

"He's toying with him...but Jacob isn't the only one," I explain.

"What do you mean?" Madison asks.

"Kaedrik views the Guardians as inconsequential — he's been messing with us from the start, like we're nothing but *pawns*," I tell them. "And now he's doing the same thing to Jacob."

"Does Kaedrik know that Daniel is a Guardian? Because if he's with the Riot right now..." Kyle starts.

"I...I don't know," I admit, "but we should assume so, even if it didn't seem like Jacob knew anything."

Kat sits down next to me and gives me the water bottle. "He doesn't," she says, "Dad has no clue what's going on, I know it."

"How?" I ask her.

"Because he let Daniel go. If he knew what was going on, he never would have done that."

"If that's the case, then why take Alyssa to bait Daniel into coming back?" Madison wonders.

"There were a few different reasons behind Alyssa's kidnapping, I'm sure," Will says, "hurting me being one of them."

I feel a build-up in my stomach and run to the kitchen. I'm able to make it to the trash can just before throwing up again. Everyone follows behind me and I can't help but feel embarrassed.

After I've let it all out, Daniel takes the trash can from me, takes out the bag, and heads outside. Kat runs to get the pills she had gotten for me.

"I'll go brew some of the forest tea, it'll help," Kyle offers. He goes to work, brewing a cup.

I head back to the living room where Kat is waiting and sit down, grabbing the fluffy purple blanket sitting on the head of the couch. I take the pill and water bottle that Kat offers. Instead of letting myself feel awkward and helpless, I ask Kat a question that's been on my mind since we left the base.

"How did you know what would help the sickness?"

Kat sighs and doesn't say anything for a moment, until she finally turns to face me.

"Well, for one thing, it's not the first time I've seen my dad use propofol during an interrogation," she admits.

Her face is sad, like she was visiting a memory she didn't want to remember. I recall the dream I had of her mother. Hillary was a nurse, maybe Kat picked up a couple of things from her, or she read up on some medical facts out of curiosity because of her late mother's profession.

Kyle comes back with a cup of tea and sets it in front of me on the table.

Begrudgingly, I take a sip. The unpleasant earthy liquid leaves a lingering aftertaste, and I can't help but gag.

Daniel enters the room at roughly the same time.

I look over at Will. "You need to tell them."

206

Will glances at Daniel and Kat.

"Tell us what?" Daniel asks, curious.

Will sighs. "Lyz, now isn't a good ti—"

"Will knows what really happened to your mother," Kyle interjects, agreeing with me. He sits down next to Kat, placing a gentle hand over hers. "It wasn't a robber."

Both siblings direct their attention to Will.

Carrying a sad expression, he starts to explain. "Your mother and I were going through a rough patch. My sister had just died, Alyssa and Ryan were left with me, and the door in the basement was getting worse. I wanted to leave this life."

He gestures to the cabin. Daniel looks confused.

"Leave? I didn't know you could just *choose* not to be a Guardian," he says, looking at me.

I say nothing, looking down at my feet. If I had that choice, with *everything* that's been happening, would I take it?

No, I — *maybe*? I don't know...

"Guardianship can end in one of two ways," Will says. "You can choose to leave it behind, which I honestly don't recommend, or you stay a Guardian until the day you die. A new Guardian is chosen immediately after."

I hesitate before asking. "You don't recommend it? Why? What happens?"

Will sighs before elaborating. "Renouncing Guardianship is like going through heavy withdrawals. I get these constant headaches, nausea, sometimes I feel a lot more irritable. And at night?" He lets out a dry, humorless laugh. "I *hardly* ever get the nightmares anymore. But anytime I do, I wake up feeling groggy and almost sick. It's called sleep inertia, and it messes you up for a good while during the day."

Daniel winces.

Will's explanation actually starts to make a lot of sense. No wonder he was so rough with Ryan and me. Whether it was emotional or physical, the man was *miserable*.

"A few months after I left, I got a phone call from your mother telling me who the next guardian was," Will starts. He turns his head to Daniel, who leans in and cups his hand over his mouth in disbelief. "You."

Will's tone is attempting to be comforting, but I can sense that it only makes Daniel feel sad. Through our connection as Guardian partners, I feel the sorrow looming over him as Will speaks. When he doesn't say a word, Will continues.

"I came over to the cabin one last time, Hillary begged me to help teach you, but I...just couldn't," he says, "we had a really bad fight, but then we heard a crash in the basement."

Everyone perks up, intrigued or shaken by the turn of the story.

"We went downstairs and found that some sort of demon had escaped from the Door. It was the same dog that the two of you found. A demon from Kaedrik's prison," Will gestures to Daniel and I.

"That dog has been out there for years..." Daniel realizes.

"Not necessarily," Will interjects. He moves closer to me and rolls up his sleeve, revealing the bracelet he had given to me. I had left it in my room before Jacob took me. Will takes off the thick golden band and hands it back to me.

"Hillary and I were able to fight it off with our bands," he continues, "you have no idea how helpful those can be, I can show you if you're up for it."

"Absolutely," I respond, making eye contact with Daniel. I remember the shield that came up when we were fighting the dog.

Will sighs heavily as he continues his story.

Daniel moves from his spot standing near the coffee table to sit with his sister. Kat takes his hand and the two of them continue to listen to Will with a sadness in their eyes that searches for an answer they might not be able to handle.

"I was trying to fix the door when the dog got a hold of your mother. It started dragging her in," he says, "I stopped what I was doing to help her, but she insisted that I keep fixing it so that nothing else could get out."

Kat starts to tear up. Her fingers tighten around Daniel's.

"Even today I feel sick to my stomach knowing that I listened to her," Will says, choking up a little. "That damn dog pulled Hillary through that door, trapping her in and signing her death warrant."

"Dad...he told us it was a robber..." Daniel says.

"That's what I had to tell him," he explains, "he couldn't know the truth. It broke my heart, and it broke his soul."

"It did more than that," Kat says, "he wasn't just broken when Mom died, he was *vengeful*. I remember him screaming on the phone with the coroner because they wouldn't let him see the body."

"There wasn't anything to see. Hill was *gone*." Will shakes his head. "The coroner owed me a favor. He wouldn't let your dad in no matter what, just kept telling him *the damage was too severe*."

"He was your *friend*!" Kat yells "Why would you—"

"Kat," Kyle speaks up calmly, squeezing her shoulder.

Will steps closer, leaning forward in front of her. "I had to keep the cabin a secret. He couldn't know the truth. But I know what that did to him, to both of you." He looks at Daniel as well. "I'm so sorry."

Daniel's green eyes are glassy, but stern. As if he was actively trying to force the tears away before they came. "If you knew that I was the next Guardian, why didn't you look for me?" he asks.

"Kid, you are what *started* my investigation on the Riot," Will explains. "Yes, I wanted to stop your dad, but I opened the case to find *you* and try to help."

All those years of Will being obsessed with the Riot...were to find Daniel. It makes so much more sense now, why it pulled Will's focus all the time.

"I had no idea that you already knew about the cabin," he says, "if I had known you would be there, that would have been the first place I looked."

I stand up to give Daniel a hug, but when I lift myself up, my head spins. I feel faint. The room around me lurches sideways as I lose my balance and find myself suddenly on the ground.

"Alyssa!" Madison yells.

As everyone crowds around me, my eyes grow heavy and my vision blurs to darkness.

210

"You didn't really think you could slip through my fingers that easily, did you Alyssa?" Kaedrik's voice booms over me.

I'm still in the cabin, but everyone else has disappeared. I look outside the window in front of me. A gust of wind pushes against the window under the clouded skies. The walls around me seem to shake. The magic that kept the cabin's sky sunny and warm is evidently failing.

"You and your Guardian partner will be defeated, and I shall finally be free!" Kaedrik's voice bellows around me.

I'm left petrified and frozen under the force of dark magic, but then a familiar bright light engulfs my surroundings.

"I'm here Alyssa," says a different voice, "I won't let him hurt us...not again."

Mala...

11-Daniel

Distract them. Find Alyssa. Save her.

I repeat the plan in my head over and over again. My left leg bobs up and down. Leaning forward in Kyle's truck, I'm fully prepared to leap out the second we reach the Riot base.

Kyle notes my obvious impatience from the driver's seat. "We're almost there," he says.

I don't say anything, my nerves are shot. All I can do is nod in reply.

Will keeps his eyes locked on the road intently from the passenger seat. When it comes to his niece, he has more regrets than I do. But this...this is something that neither of us will ever forgive ourselves for.

Kyle comes to an abrupt stop in the middle of the road and any grasp I had on my nerves is gone.

"Kyle, *what the hell*?!" I snap, admittedly harsher than I mean to.

"The bridge," he says, staring out the window.

Following his gaze, I spot the old railway bridge halfway hidden in the trees. It was one of the spots where Kyle, Kat, and I used to hide out a few years ago to get away from, well, *everything*. Looking closer, I see my sister sitting at the edge of the bridge, legs swinging freely above the water.

"In case you forgot, nobody in this car is on her good side right now," I remind Kyle.

"I know," he says, "but look at her. Didn't you tell me that she hasn't been here since I left? Something is up."

That was true. The last time I saw Kat on that bridge was just before Kyle left the Riot, the two of us were here together. I had gotten into a fight with dad, probably over something stupid.

Kat had brought me out here, split her sandwich with me, and listened to me rant for hours. It was one of the only times we could really get stuff off our chests. Probably the only time we could really *feel* anything out loud.

If Kat is here now, something must have rattled her. But I remain skeptical, too much has happened.

"I think we can talk to her," Kyle says.

"The last time we talked to her, she almost shot me, Will *did* get shot, you got beat up, and Alyssa got kidnapped," I point out, "and I would *really* like to get back to helping her, guys!"

Will rubs his shoulder where my dad shot him. "Let me talk to Kat."

I can't help but scoff. "Will, I've heard my sister's reports to my dad when she was undercover. She didn't exactly use kind words about her *partner down at the station.*"

"Daniel, let him try," Kyle pleads, "I think we can sway her."

I sigh and pinch the bridge of my nose with one hand, waving the other hand in exasperated agreement.

"Come on, Dan, she's your sister," Kyle says, "she won't bite."

I look up and glare at him. "Oh, shut up, yes she will, and *you like it.*"

The bridge isn't the most stable structure, but the wooden boards and rusted metal beams are strong enough to hold all four of us.

Kat spots us before we reach the bridge. Instead of running away or threatening to shoot anybody, she just stays seated at the edge of the bridge, looking annoyed.

"What are you guys doing here? Shouldn't you be rescuing Daniel's girlfriend?" she asks.

"She...she's not my—!" I struggle to finish the sentence before Kyle speaks.

"What are you doing up here, Kat?"

"Just enjoying the view," she sighs.

Kyle sits down next to her, his feet dangling beside hers over the bridge. "What happened?" he asks.

She doesn't answer.

Will takes a couple steps closer. "Do you remember the Nelson case, Miller?" he asks. His eyes dart to the structure below him every time he hears a creak at his feet.

"It's *Reeves*, you know that," she responds irritably, "and...yeah, why?"

"Adam Nelson was accused of money laundering, and I was about to leave the precinct to make the arrest, but the file was missing, why?"

"I stole it," she remembers, "I saw his face when we questioned him, he didn't seem like the criminal type."

"You would know," I remark, crossing my arms.

Kat flips me off.

"How could you have possibly known that Nelson was innocent?" Will continues.

 214

"I don't know, I just had a feeling," she admits, "I took the file so I could check it out before it was too late."

"His brother was making the copies and selling them under Adam's name," Will said. "You brought him in the same afternoon."

"And *you* threatened to have the captain suspend me for a week for stealing the file," Kat bites.

"I was trying to teach you to be careful," Will explains, "but I admit it was a rough time for me, I was a lot more drunk back then, and Ryan was failing summer school. I'm sorry."

Kat scoffs.

"I'm not making excuses. I *am* sorry, Kat," he says, gentler this time.

For the first time since we've been here, she looks up at Will. Tears well in her eyes. "I'm so sorry about Alyssa," her voice breaks, "and Ryan."

Will swallows hard. "Are they okay?"

"I don't know what's going on with Ryan. He doesn't *seem* hurt. But Alyssa..." Kat then turns her eyes to me, and I know the answer to that question. She's nowhere *near* okay.

"She's alive," she finally answers Will.

A large sigh of relief that I didn't know I was holding escapes from me. "Kat," I say tentatively, "we need you to help us get to her."

She sighs. A tear falls down her cheek. Kyle raises a hand to wipe it away, but she smacks it and wipes the tear herself.

"You know he's expecting you to come for her, right?" she says. "You're walking right into his trap."

"I don't care. She needs our help."

"Okay," Kat sighs, "count me in."

Kat sits next to me in the back seat of the truck and directs Kyle to drive to the back of the building. Which is strange to me. Dad usually holds his captives in the rooms upstairs, where the closest entrance is the front.

"He moved her after she tried to escape," Kat explains, "she's in the basement."

My heart races in my chest. My cheeks flush with heat. *He's going to kill her.*

"She tried to do *what*?" I ask frantically.

"Oh no," Kyle says. He remembers.

When Jacob Reeves takes someone down to the basement, they don't come back.

Kat takes both of my hands in hers. "Hey, look at me, Dan," she says, "she'll be okay, but we've got to go *now*."

"We'll go to the front and distract them," Kyle says.

I nod and follow Kat out of the truck and through the back entrance to the warehouse.

We don't have to worry about sneaking past many Riot members. Most of them are afraid to be near the basement. However, when we make it to the basement door, two of the men are guarding it, likely at my dad's orders.

I recognize them, Brad Gordon and Alex Suggs. Gordon was always a pretentious hothead, but Suggs and I have done a few jobs together. He's a good guy. The two of them plant themselves in front of the door, rooted like pillars. Unmoving. The only thing standing between me and Alyssa.

Kat motions for me to stay put against the wall, out of sight, as she steps out to talk to the guards.

Reluctantly, I obey.

Kat walks toward Gordon and Suggs with a stiff, intimidating demeanor. She's mimicking our father. Using his reputation, and ours as his children, to command respect. I've seen her do this a million times. Hell, I've done it when I needed to, but it doesn't make it any less unsettling.

"Jacob is changing the guard," Kat says in a serious voice, "move aside."

Suggs starts to do as she asks, but Gordon stops him with a raised hand.

"Not so fast, *princess*," he snarls, "the boss gave us specific instructions to watch the brat until *he* said otherwise."

A wave of anger passes over me when Gordon calls Alyssa a brat.

The feeling is gone as quickly as it came when Kat raises her voice. "I have just as much authority as my *father* does, Gordon." She says the word 'father' with a chilling emphasis. "Or did you forget who you were speaking to?"

Suggs pulls Gordon by the arm, dragging him out of the way of the door. "Brad, let's go," he says, "I'm starving anyways."

Gordon doesn't argue. He just sneers at Kat before turning away and leaving the room.

Alex turns around as he walks and gives Kat a respectful nod. "Some of us know when to not be a total dick," he laughs, "have a good shift, ma'am."

"Thank you, Alex," Kat replies.

When the coast is clear, she motions for me to meet her at the door.

I run from my hiding spot.

"I'll keep watch out here while you get Alyssa," she says.

"Thanks, Kat."

She smirks, waving her hand to urge me inside.

As I rush down the stairs and into the basement, I see her.

Alyssa is chained to one of the wall posts, unconscious. She looks so pale and quiet. The girl with the fierce determination that I've come to know just sits there. Helpless. She's malnourished, but she's *alive.*

I start to reach for her hand to wake her up. Ice runs through my veins when I notice an inflamed red gash across her palm. Then, looking up at her face, I see a bloody stain on the back of her shirt.

He *cut* her.

I've seen him use this interrogation tactic before. Seeing the blood on Alyssa, I can't help but choke up a little bit. My face is red hot with guilt and anguish. This is all my fault. I drove him to this point. My dad came after Alyssa because of *me.*

"Oh god. I'm so sorry..." I say, though I know she can't hear me.

Muffled voices come from upstairs. Kat is talking to someone, probably trying to keep them from coming down here.

I have to hurry. I maneuver around the beam to where the lock is and fumble in my jacket for my lock picking set. As I start to work on the lock, Alyssa stirs awake. She thrashes around frantically, so I shuffle around the beam to face her.

"Hey! Alyssa, it's me! You're okay!" I say.

218

When she sees me, her eyes brighten. Tears spill down her cheeks. She looks like she's about to burst with joy, or post-traumatic relief, or both.

When I tear the duct tape off her mouth, her smile quickly morphs into fear.

"You can't be here! It's a trap!" she pleads.

"I know, don't worry," I tell her. "The others are keeping my dad and the Riot distracted."

She sighs, the worry in her expression easing with my reassurance, and I move back to the lock. A couple of quick seconds later, it falls undone to the floor. She stands up, and I meet her eyes again. Hopeful this time. Safe.

"*Thank you*," she says with a quivering breath.

She wraps her arms around me in a hug.

I hold onto her, never wanting to let go. The feel of her messy auburn brown hair over my hand fills me with ease, grounding me in the realism of her touch.

"Of course," I say, my voice breaking.

I rub her back gently to comfort her. Coming across the slice in her shirt, I feel the cut on her back. She cringes slightly at the touch, and I immediately pull my hand away from the sensitive spot. Blood lightly paints my fingertips, but I don't care. My fingers gently caress her back, careful not to touch her wound again.

I got to her before Kaedrik or my father could do any worse. She'll be okay. And I will *never* let them touch her again.

When Alyssa tumbles to the floor, everyone panics. Before I have her in my line of sight, Will demands that everyone back up. I maneuver between the three other people in front of me. When I get behind Will, I see what he was warning us about. Small waves of dark magic emanate from Alyssa's healed leg. The magical energy resembles that of the Dark Door in the basement.

"This was Kaedrik," Will deduces, "he healed the bones in her leg."

"But *why* would he do that?!" Madison asks, eyes wide.

"Because he left traces of his magic inside to corrupt her," he answers.

"We have to do something!" I say frantically. "How do we help her?!"

"I... don't know. I've never seen this," Will admits.

My heart is racing. I can't lose her, not again.

"Kyle, run to the gazebo, see if you can find anything there. Tonics, *anything*," I order. "Will, time to teach me how to use the bracelet."

"Dan, the gazebo is *miles* away," Kyle says.

"And the bracelet doesn't have healing properties," Will interjects. "I know, I've tried."

"I don't care!" Rolling up my sleeves, I quickly bend down to meet Alyssa on the floor. "We have to do *something*!"

Will pulls me back up. "Dan, it's not gonna work!"

"It has to!" I growl, pulling myself away from his grip. My eyes turn back to Alyssa, desperate for an answer.

Kyle stares at me with a concerned, furrowed brow. With an understanding nod, he starts to make his way out the door but is stopped when Peck flies in front of him furiously.

"Don't..." Will whispers.

A bright flash of soothing warm light swallows our surroundings. I cover my face with my arm. When the light recedes, a familiar face stands in Peck's place.

"Stand back!"

Mala pushes past us and runs to Alyssa's side. She places a hand on her leg, and small rays of light chase after the dark magic. It seems almost surreal, watching Mala outside of a dream. I almost don't believe it. Her bright red hair falls messily in front of her face as she works. She mutters something to herself, and though I can't make out most of what she's saying, I catch one phrase." ...won't...I won't lose another one."

The expression on Alyssa's face, though unconscious, goes from being contorted with pain and anguish, to relaxed and calm.

Mala, however, appears stressed.

After a moment, Alyssa's eyelids start to lift open and my shoulders fall with relief.

As she stirs awake, Mala pulls away. Both the light and dark traces of magic fade away from Alyssa's leg.

"W—what happened?" She looks around to see everyone gathered around her but stops when she notices Mala at her side. "How...?" she starts.

"I apologize for revealing myself this way," Mala says, standing and offering a hand to help Alyssa up. She takes it, and Mala continues, "but if I hadn't released you from Kaedrik's grip, you would've been lost to your friends and family. I...I couldn't let that happen again."

"Who are you?" Madison asks.

"Mala," Alyssa answers, "Kaedrik's opposite, remember? This cabin belongs to her."

"Actually," Mala interjects, "this cabin was created for its Guardians. It belongs to you. I am merely the supplier."

"*Merely*?" I say.

"So, wait... you've been Peck this whole time?" Kyle asks.

"Yes," she answers, smiling at me. If I had to guess, she's remembering the ten-year-old little boy that gave her that name.

"It was the only way I could help without compromising myself."

"But why hide for so long?" Kat asks, studying Mala with suspicion. "You saw how often they could have used your help."

Mala sighs and stares out the window for a short moment before answering the question. "Kaedrik can sense when I show my true form, as I can sense him," she explains, "in order to assist you at all, I had to stay...*under the radar*, as you might phrase it."

"Peck, the dreams..." I realize.

"Both were my best attempts at helping you along," Mala confirms.

"All this time we all thought Peck was a male..." Kyle realizes aloud.

Kat rolls her eyes and flicks his shoulder.

Mala holds up a hand, as if excusing the thought.

Will puts a hand on Mala's shoulder in comfort. Something about his gesture seems odd.

"Will, have you...did you know about this?" I ask him.

Will looks in Alyssa's direction, then nods his head in affirmation.

"*Are you kidding me*?!" Alyssa asks angrily.

"Lyz, she asked me not to tell you, for her safety *and* yours. The night that I shared your dream, she came to me afterward and begged me to keep it a secret," he says. "If she had revealed herself beforehand, Kaedrik would have sensed it, and you would have been in even more danger at the Riot base than you already were."

Will has a point. But the emotional connection between myself and Alyssa shows her apparent discontent.

Alyssa stands there quietly, arms folded, waiting for more answers.

"How long *have* you known about her exactly?" she asks.

Mala steps up, her posture is firm and proper, but her eyes betray her nerves.

"I revealed myself to William and Hillary when they found my cabin as children," she admits. Mala can see the expressions of confusion and hurt that surround her, particularly in Alyssa.

She stares at Will with betrayal in her eyes. The sting of the secret pangs in my chest, but it isn't coming from me.

Will doesn't meet his niece's eyes as Mala continues.

"You must understand, back then I had a better hold on Kaedrik's prison," Mala explains. "Things have only gotten worse over the years, he's grown more powerful, I...I had no choice but to hide and do what I could to hinder him from afar."

Alyssa gathers herself and ends her sullen silence with a question. "What does Kaedrik plan to do once he escapes?"

Mala looks at her, perplexed. "Kaedrik has always been one for threats and theatrics, I would've thought he'd boast about his plans."

Alyssa looks down at her feet. "He told me bits and pieces."

Mala's face clouds with guilt as Alyssa's time with the Riot is mentioned. "Kaedrik wants to rewrite the world in his own image," Mala starts. "This world that I have created is full of life and growth, but his idea of *creation* is dark, twisted...and sickening."

She stares wistfully out the window, then she turns back to face us with fiery determination.

"By revealing myself to you in this form I am alerting Kaedrik and breaking my solemn oath to stay in hiding," Mala says, anger in her soft and quiet voice. "But I would break a *thousand oaths* to protect this world. If Kaedrik is to sense my presence for the first time in eons...it will be as a *warning*."

"So, how do we stop him?" I ask her.

"We need to find the key," Mala responds. "When I first locked Kaedrik away, I created a key to his prison. Keeping it safe was the first job of the Guardians."

"Well, where's the key now?" Kat asks.

Mala looks at Madison. "It was taken by the first Guardian, Draven," she says and puts a hand on Madison's shoulder, "my son, and your ancestor."

"W—what?" Madison asks.

"Impossible..." Alyssa says under her breath.

The events of Madison's arrival come to mind. "No, it's not," I tell Alyssa. "That's how Madison found the cabin."

"Oh my god..." Kyle exclaims.

"Will, Alyssa, and I can enter the cabin because we're Guardians," I say. "Madison was able to do it because she's related to one."

"Not exactly, Daniel," Mala corrects me. "If that were the case, then Kat or Ryan would have no problem entering this place. Madison was able to enter because she is also *my* descendant."

"That...actually makes a lot of sense," Alyssa admits.

"But wait," Kat interrupts, "if Madison's ancestor was the first Guardian, why were Daniel and Alyssa chosen next instead of her?"

"Because Guardianship is not hereditary to my bloodline, nor is it always to those of past Guardians," Mala answers, "I choose the Guardians based on who I deem as worthy, not through genetics. It just so happened that this time, my Guardian's successors shared a relation."

Madison pulls away from Mala's attempt to comfort her. "So, I wasn't *worthy* enough for you?" she asks.

"Madison, no, that's not it," she replies, "after the turmoil that was caused by Draven, I couldn't risk my own family line continuing Guardianship."

"*Turmoil?*" Madison growls.

Alyssa takes her hand from behind. "Maddie," she whispers.

"Wait," Kyle interjects, "you said that your son took the key to Kaedrik's prison."

"Yes..." Mala sighs. "We should talk about this in my dorm."

"We're not gonna hike all the way back to your bedroom to hear you finish your story," Alyssa states.

Mala waves her hand and a bright flash of light covers the room. When the light recedes, all seven of us are standing in that same bedroom we found underneath the gazebo.

Kat and Madison look around in amazement while Alyssa eyes the top of the stairs and shudders nervously.

Mala makes her way towards the desk where we found the journal. She opens the drawer and shuffles through other papers before turning to me. "Where is my journal?" she asks with hints of panic in her voice.

"It's not in there?" I try to think back to the last time we had it.

"Oh!" Kyle says, facepalming. He walks over to the bed, leans down, and grabs the book from off the floor.

"Why was my journal tossed onto the floor?" Mala sounds almost like a parent trying hard not to yell at her children.

I remembered when we found the line in the journal. *The host can be freed when blood is shed.* When we saw that, I threw it out of anger. If I told Mala what really happened, she would only justify the need to kill Ryan in order to defeat Kaedrik.

My eyes meet Alyssa's. She doesn't need to hear that again. "When Alyssa got hurt, I dropped the book and ran to help her."

Alyssa and Kyle hear this, and Alyssa perks up. She doesn't say anything, but she looks at me, confused.

Mala just takes the book from Kyle and wipes off a layer of dust. "Please be more careful next time." Mala continues her story as she flips through the pages of the book. "Kaedrik and I weren't always enemies. There was a time when we were...very close. But, as I was an entity of creation, and he an entity of decay, he grew jealous of my work and tried to create something of his own."

"Did it work?" Alyssa asks.

"It did. You two have seen his creation when I led you to it, the dog in the alleyway," Mala admits. "When Kaedrik unleashed his demon into this world, it destroyed everything...I was *devasted*. I banished Kaedrik *and* his creation to their prison, the Dark Realm."

Kat leans in, intrigued by the story.

"I went to my son, Draven, and together we created a pocket realm between your world and the Dark Realm as the last line of defense in the event of his escape."

"If Draven was your son, and he helped you make this *whole* place, why did he take the key?" Kat asks.

"Draven was the Guardian of this realm for a long time. I did what I could to shield him, but...Kaedrik's whispers were slowly driving him mad," Mala explains. "He couldn't bear it and begged me to release him."

"You *can* just choose to leave..." Alyssa says quietly.

I shift uncomfortably in my stance.

"It was then that I chose his son, Cai, as the second Guardian," Mala says, setting the book down gently on the desk. "When Draven left, he no longer had me to try and block out Kaedrik's voices. My son fell corrupt to his influence."

She hangs her head low, and my mind begins to wander. Mala had a son...that Kaedrik could easily manipulate...

"Draven killed his wife and Cai just to get the key from Cai's grasp. Draven tried to free Kaedrik, but instead I was forced to lock him in the prison realm as well," Mala finishes.

"The key is with Draven on the other side of the Dark Door?" Alyssa asks.

"Is he even still alive?" Kyle asks.

"I honestly don't know, but I don't believe he still has it," Mala says, "Kaedrik has been able to bleed through his prison enough to invade your dreams and take a host body. The only way he can do that is with the key."

"So Kaedrik has it?" Will summarizes.

"Yes, in order to reach through our world, even as restricted as he is, he needs to project himself and the key to the outside, so Kaedrik will have the key in this realm," Mala explains.

"Kaedrik is Draven's father, isn't he?" I ask her.

Mala's chest heaves. Her eyes are glassy with regret.

"Yes, Daniel."

Madison's breath hitches. She stares down at her feet, avoiding looking at anyone, even Alyssa. Mala sits down at her desk, ashamed.

"Hey, no," Kat speaks up. She faces Madison and Mala determinedly. "We're not about to *sit here* and let you guys feel guilty. And we're *definitely* not taking this as a loss."

"Kat's right," I say, taking Madison by the hand. For a moment, I look over at Alyssa, who's smiling. "All of you learned to accept both of us, despite *our* family, so we're gonna return the favor."

Kyle grins and comes over to give Madison a reassuring hug.

Alyssa walks up to Mala and extends her hand. "Come on," she says gently.

Mala takes her hand and the two of them come to meet the rest of the group.

I stand with Alyssa and meet Mala's eyes. "Mala, we're gonna get that key from Kaedrik and keep his ass locked up. I promise you."

Mala beams at the two of us with pride. "I knew I made the right choice," she says, "I want to show you something." She leads us to her desk. From one of the wide drawers behind her, she pulls out a wooden box. She opens it, and I see multiple healing tonics like the one we used to help Will.

"Hillary's tonics," Alyssa says.

The mention of my mother's name gives me a pause. "Wait, what?"

"The night the two of you first shared your dreams, I gave Alyssa a glimpse into the past, hoping it would be of some help," Mala says. She takes a tonic out of the box and shows me the tag. Just like the last one, the initials on there are H.O.

"Hillary O," Alyssa points out.

"Oaks, my mother's maiden name," I say.

Kat hears this and leans in. "Mom made these?"

"That's how you woke me up..." Will realizes.

"Do you know how she made these?" Kat asks Mala.

"I only know that your mother was able to combine her medicines with a sample of my power to do it," Mala admits.

"Uh, Hill had a journal that she kept somewhere around the cabin. I could help you look," Will offers.

Back at the cabin, everyone spreads out.

Kat and Will dig around for Mom's journal, while Kyle and Madison are in the kitchen making dinner plans.

Alyssa and I sit with Mala to figure out how to get the key.

The cabin has gotten a lot more crowded lately. It's almost hard to believe that last week it was just me and Kyle here. Now, we have so many more friends to help us out. I'm grateful for it. I don't feel as lonely as I once did.

"How do we get the key from Kaedrik?" Alyssa asks.

"Unfortunately, I cannot be of much help," Mala admits. "My presence at the Riot's headquarters would start a battle with Kaedrik that we are not yet prepared for."

"She's right. Taking Kaedrik head on for the key is too much of a risk," I say. "You shouldn't go back there either, Alyssa."

Alyssa scoffs. "I can't just do *nothing*!"

"I don't want to risk my dad hurting you again," I tell her.

"Well, you can't go either," says Kat coming down the stairs with Will. "Remember dad's ultimatum?"

"What's she talking about?" Alyssa asks me.

Sighing heavily, I stand up. "That morning, before he took you, he let me go," I say. "He said that, if I came back, he'd know I want to be a part of the family."

"And...if you didn't?" Alyssa asks, standing to meet my eyes.

"Then he'd kill him," Kat answers for me.

"Jacob, you *asshole*," Will growls under his breath.

Alyssa just sits there, stunned. The fear and guilt surrounding her face are just as apparent in her emotions. But something else lingers around her, a sense of unresolve.

"I have to go," I say.

"Are you *insane*?!" Kat exclaims.

"Now hold on, kid," Will says.

Even Kyle bursts through the kitchen door. "Absolutely not!"

Madison follows behind him, curious and concerned.

 230

Alyssa still doesn't say anything. I can feel her confliction like a whirlwind of thoughts and emotion. It's almost overwhelming. She takes a single step away from the group before pausing. Her eyes close as she takes a deep breath.

"Hey," I tell her, grabbing both of her hands. "I can do this."

"Every time one of us goes to that base, we pay for it," she says quietly.

Before I can say anything else, she pulls her hands away from me and walks off without another word.

Madison starts to follow her but pauses. "Look, I know I haven't been here for very long, but Alyssa has been my best friend for *years*," she says. "I've seen enough to know that she cares about every single person in this room. She can't afford to lose anyone else. Just keep that in mind while you make this decision, please."

With that, she leaves to follow Alyssa.

Awkward silence fills the air. It's nearly suffocating.

"I need some air," I say.

Sitting on the front porch, I think about what my father said. The words of his ultimatum replay in my mind like a broken record. Truthfully, those words have haunted me ever since they were spoken. Sometimes it's hard to believe that a father, even one like Jacob, could do such a thing.

The debate rings in over and over in my mind. Would he *really* kill me if he saw me again?

I have to go back. It's the only way to get the key while ensuring that nobody else gets hurt.

Kat opens the door and sits next to me on the steps of the porch. For a minute, neither of us say anything. We just sit there, watching the trees and feeling the gentle touch of the wind.

Kat then takes a deep breath. "You don't have to go, you know."

"Yes, I do," I tell her. "I don't want to put anybody else in danger. If I do what Dad says, I can get close enough to find the key."

"Daniel, you know him. He's not gonna be that easy," she says. "It has to be me."

"What are you talking about?" I ask.

"He trusts me. He thinks that I'm looking for you *right now* to bring you in," she says. "I can go back to get the key and everyone there would be none the wiser."

"*No*. It's too dangerous."

"Hey, I can handle myself. You know that."

She's right. Kat is the only one who wouldn't cause any alarm from Dad or Kaedrik. The thought of putting her in harm's way makes me really uneasy, but it's the only logical option.

Sighing, I stand up. "I'm not telling Kyle," I say. "That's all you."

Kat stands and lets out a small nervous laugh. Then, both of us head back to the living room.

Inside, Kyle, Mala, and Will are waiting.

"We have a plan," I start.

Kat steps up. "Daniel isn't going back to the Riot," she says, "I am."

Will and Mala eye each other with furrowed brows.

Kyle, however, isn't having it. His eyes deadpan as the corners of his mouth lower into a frown. His posture is stone cold and steady. "No."

"I wasn't asking," Kat snaps.

"Well, I'm *telling* you that you're gonna get yourself killed!" he bites back, edging closer to her.

Kat crosses her arms, her mouth forming into a defensive scowl. "Kyle, I'll be fi—"

"No!" Kyle yells, his voice slightly breaking. "I *can't* lose you again!"

When she hears this, Kat relaxes her shoulders. Her eyes soften. A brief moment of silence fills the air as the tension releases.

The pain in Kyle's face reminds me of when he first left the Riot. For several mornings, I came to the cabin to find him sitting on the front porch, his eyelids heavy with exhaustion. We'd sit together in silence for a few minutes, until he felt comfortable enough to open up. Thinking about how Kat was hurting after he left took its toll on him. And seeing how Kat took his absence, watching her grow more distant and harsh over the years, it broke my heart.

Kyle's confession seems to have shifted something in her. She steps up to him, leaning close to his face. When she grabs his shirt by the collar, twisting the fabric in her grip, for a second I think she's about to hit him, yell at him, or both. But instead, without warning, she presses her lips against his and kisses him.

His eyes widen with shock. Kyle's hands wrap around her waist as he takes the moment in for the short time he has before she pulls back.

Kat straightens up, her fingers still tight around his shirt. She stares deep into Kyle's eyes. The corner of her mouth lifts into the slightest smile as she looks at him. "Not gonna happen," Kat says. "You can't get rid of me that easily this time."

Kyle lets me take his truck to drop Kat off.

She sits in the passenger seat with her arms crossed, her gaze set outside.

After a few minutes of not saying anything, I decide to break the silence.

"So... what was that back there?" I ask her.

"What do you mean?" she replies without turning her head to me.

"The kiss?"

"Oh," she says. Her eyes fall to her knees. She pushes a strand of hair behind her ear. "Just tried to get him to shut up."

"Uh-huh," I say, glaring at her.

She shifts uncomfortably in her seat, and the teasing edge slips away from me into a genuine question. "Are you wanting to get back together?"

Kat doesn't say anything for a moment, then she grunts, spreading out her hands. "I don't know," she finally answers.

"For what it's worth, he feels awful," I tell her. "We've talked about it a lot."

"Daniel, he *left* me," her voice instantly grows sterner. "I get that being partners in a criminal gang isn't the most *romantic* thing. But I thought we were doing fine, and then he just... left me."

"For the *same* reason that you left," I point out, "to get away from what he knew was wrong, and to help with something bigger than himself."

Kat turns her head back to the window. Her elbow rests on the car door as she rubs her temple. "It still hurts."

My hand reaches for her shoulder. "I know."

Kat was devastated when Kyle left. She didn't leave her room for three days. When she finally did, she was different, colder.

For months, my stomach turned every time I saw her, because *I* was the reason he left her. And, at the time, she had no idea.

"Maybe," Kat says out of the blue.

"What?" I ask.

"You asked if I wanted to get back together," she says. "My answer is *maybe*."

The slight hint of hope in her voice makes me smile. I don't press any further, keeping my focus on the road as Kat continues to gaze out the window.

At the Riot base, I park just outside of view of the building. Kat gets out of the car and walks around to my window.

"Good luck," I tell her.

"You too," she replies.

Kat walks off and I turn the car around to head back to the cabin. The further away I drive, the more my chest tightens. As my sister willingly enters the lion's den, I can only hope that she won't get caught.

12-Daniel

It's past midnight by the time I park Kyle's truck by the alley. The fatigue from driving, along with stressing over my sister's safety, has me worn out.

As the entrance to the cabin appears, a strange bark sounds in the distance, so loud that someone could probably hear it two states over.

A chill runs up my spine as the sound dies.

Kaedrik's demon dog. If the dog is here, could Kaedrik be close somewhere?

I rush into the cabin before I risk any more time.

Kyle and Alyssa sit in the living room talking. Both of them have a mug of tea in their hands. An untouched third cup sits on the coffee table in front of them.

"That's for you," Alyssa says, "Mala sensed when you were on your way back, so I brewed you a cup. It's chamomile, none of that gross broccoli stuff from the forest."

"Thank you," I say, taking the cup. A sigh escapes as I shake off the nerves from hearing the barking, trying to mask my unease.

Alyssa gives me a look, our emotional connection probably giving me away. I decide to change the subject. "Are you doing okay?"

Alyssa's cheeks flush a little. She seems embarrassed. "Yeah," she says, "I'm sorry for walking out like that."

"Don't worry about it," I smile, taking a sip.

Kyle doesn't say anything. He just takes a sip of his tea and shoots me a pissed off look.

"She's gonna be okay, Kyle," I tell him.

He slams his mug onto the coffee table. The impact causes some of the tea to splash onto his hand, making his skin a little red, but he doesn't even flinch. He stands up and meets me face-to-face.

"Let me make something clear," he snarls, "if Kat gets killed out there because of you, I'm *done*."

"I understand."

I'm well aware of where his anger is coming from. Kyle is afraid. He doesn't want Kat to get hurt, and he blames me for letting her go. Hell, I blame myself. I didn't want her to go, but Kat insisted. Kyle has spent so long regretting his past mistakes with her. Now that she's fallen in with the group, he just got her back. I know how scared he is that this plan will get her killed.

Kyle walks past me and makes his way upstairs. I sit next to Alyssa, who gives me a reassuring half-smile.

"He's just scared," she says.

"I know," I sigh. "He just doesn't want Kat to get hurt."

Alyssa looks down at her cup, seemingly ashamed. Our connection reveals a looming sense of sorrow over her, though you wouldn't know it by reading her expression. "Did she choose to go because of me?" she asks. "Because of how I reacted to you offering to go?"

"No, not at all," I tell her, "Kat went back to the Riot because she's the only one that wouldn't have to hide. Plus, I think she wants to prove herself."

"How do you mean?" Alyssa asks.

"Well, she seemed determined," I explain, "I think she wanted to know for herself that she could do something good."

"She saved me from Jacob," Alyssa points out. She eyes her leg and frowns.

"She did," I nod, "but it takes more than that most times."

Alyssa yawns and adjusts the blanket she has wrapped around her like a shawl.

"You should get some rest," I suggest to her.

She nods tiredly in agreement, puts down her cup, and heads to bed. I stay up for about another hour, thinking more about my sister's predicament, before going to bed as well.

I'm standing on an old cement sidewalk. Across the street from me is a high school: Fairplay High. I see a two-story brick building and several cliques of students walking toward the door. This is where I had stopped the day we found Alyssa. The noise in the trees. The same chill in the air crawls up my spine.

Why would Mala show me this?

An all too familiar growl stops me in my tracks. Kaedrik's demon dog runs up the road and past the school. As he runs, he drops something out of his mouth.

I can't make out exactly what it is, but it looks like some sort of golden necklace. A bright sparkling light emanates from whatever charm is attached to it.

All of the students are far enough away that they don't notice the dog. Or so I thought. Just as suddenly as the demon dog appeared, so does a familiar face.

Ryan Haller walks by. His curly brown hair falls in front of his face as he walks with his head lowered toward his phone. The necklace gleams in the light magic, catching Ryan's attention. He picks up the golden chain. The light from the necklace dims, and now I can make out the charm attached. A golden key, about two inches long with small red rubies, hangs from his hand as he walks off.

"So that's what he took," a voice says behind me. I turn to see Alyssa.

Her eyes widened with awe.

"Alyssa?" I ask. "Are you...?"

"I'm here," she answers.

We're dream-sharing again.

"What were you talking about?" I wonder.

"When I was...taken," she hesitates, "Kaedrik told me that Ryan took something of his."

I think back to the charm on the necklace. A key, one that belonged to Kaedrik.

"The key to the Dark Door," I realize.

The scene of our joint dreaming venture shifts to a sickeningly familiar setting: the Riot base. As I look to Alyssa, her feelings of fear and dread flood my mind.

In an attempt to comfort her, I grab her hand. "Hey...it's okay."

Alyssa gives me a small smile, a mix of appreciation and nervousness.

The base is completely empty and still, until the sudden sound of someone crying echoes behind me. Alyssa and I turn around. Kaedrik, still in Ryan's body, stands over Kat, sobbing on the floor. She's covered with bruises and cuts.

"Did you really think you could steal from me?" Ryan says in Kaedrik's threatening voice.

"No," Kat cries. Her head sinks to the floor, not making eye contact. "No, please!"

Forced to stand there and listen to my terrified sister's cries, my chest aches with remorse.

"Kat!" I call out.

Alyssa grips my arm. "It's a dream, Daniel. She can't hear you."

Kat doesn't answer. Another voice slowly merges with hers. My heart starts to sink. What does this mean? Another possession? Then the second voice shifts from crying to speaking.

"Stop it! Please! I beg of you!"

The voice belongs to an adult male, but I don't recognize it.

"The key is mine, and soon your pathetic world will be in my grasp as well," Kaedrik patronizes.

"No! Please!" says the other voice as Kat's fades away. My sister stays silent on the ground.

"Silence!" Kaedrik orders. "This is a fate you cannot escape."

Although it seems like he's talking to the strange voice, Kaedrik still faces Kat, never breaking his gaze.

"Father...please don't do this."

Kaedrik just laughs menacingly in response as a wave of darkness surrounds Alyssa and I. I can't see anything at all in the chaos of Kaedrik's magic. A short moment passes before I can finally see Alyssa again. She looks shocked, like she figured something out.

"Father..." she says, quoting the strange voice.

"Draven," I realize. It was him that was talking to Kaedrik.

"He was weak," says Kaedrik out of nowhere. He's nowhere to be seen, but he can be heard everywhere. "Though, I will say, he lasted far longer than the Haller boy."

Alyssa is red with rage.

"In the end, they all fall to me," Kaedrik continues, "Guardians, mortals. The two of you will be no different."

I can't take it anymore.

"You're wrong! I don't care how many threats you throw at us!" I shout. "The Guardians are stronger than ever. The cabin is stronger than ever. Whatever plan you and my father have, we will be there to stop it. You're gonna rot in that prison forever!"

"Your father?" Kaedrik asks, then he realizes, "Daniel Reeves..."

I wake in a cold sweat, quickly checking my phone on the nightstand for the time: 8:13 a.m.. Before I even get out of bed, footsteps run up the stairs.

Alyssa bursts into my room, eyes wide. "What did you *do*?!"

We spend the next few minutes in the kitchen going over everything. The dog, the key, Ryan...Kat.

Alyssa sits down with a cup of coffee.

Meanwhile, I stand up and lean against a dining room chair, fidgeting nervously with my gold bracelet as we talk.

Eventually, Will comes in and we relay everything to him.

"And Kaedrik told you about this?" Will asks Alyssa when we explain that Ryan found the key.

"Yes, he said that Ryan found something of his that he wanted back. That's why he took his body," she explains. "Now we know what Ryan found."

Mala walks into the kitchen, tired and sluggish. "Good morning to you three," she yawns.

Will steps in front of her. "Mala, what were you trying to tell the kids last night?"

"What are you talking about?"

"Uh, the dream? You are the one that gives us those, right?" I ask.

"Well yes, but I didn't give you anything last night. Are you sure it wasn't Kaedrik?" she asks.

"I've been suffering through Kaedrik's nightmares since I was ten years old," I remind her. "His are always dark and threatening, while yours are always trying to send a message. Last night we got both."

"I...don't know what to say, it wasn't me."

"Could it have been Draven?" Alyssa asks.

"What...?" Mala says.

"We heard his voice. He was in pain...just like Kat."

"How do you know it was him?" Will asks us.

"Because he called Kaedrik *father*," I answer.

"My son..." Mala says under her breath. She sits down next to me at the table.

Up until now we didn't know whether or not Draven was still alive.

"One thing I know for certain is that my sister is in danger," I say. "I'm going after her."

"*What*?" Kyle says from behind me.

I turn around to see that both Kyle and Madison have joined us in the kitchen. Kyle is fuming. His expression holds way more anger toward me than it did last night.

Madison maneuvers around him to sit next to Alyssa.

"What happened to Kat?" Kyle asks, his tone serious, almost threatening.

"When Alyssa and I dream-shared, we saw Kaedrik hurting her," I admit. The caution in my voice makes it sound like I'm trying to calm down a spooked horse. It's not a tone that I've ever used with my best friend.

Kyle pushes me back with both of his hands. The impact almost causes me to fall into Mala's lap.

"ARE YOU OUT OF YOUR DAMN MIND?!"

The eyes around the room are wide with shock. Will looks ready to interject, a hand pressed on the table ready to push himself up. Madison and Mala both look at Kyle, almost frightened. Alyssa, however, watches him with sadness across her face.

"Kyle, it was a *dream*. We don't know if it actually happened. It could just be a warning," I tell him, regaining my balance. I know where this anger is coming from. I won't fight him on it.

"Daniel is right," Mala says. "I can feel Kaedrik, and Katrina—"

"Her name is *Kat*," Kyle grits through his teeth.

Mala nods and mimics my cautious tone to finish her thought. "No harm has come to her as of yet. There's still time."

"I can get Kat out of there before Kaedrik even touches her," I try to reassure him, and myself.

"I'm going with you," Kyle insists.

"Okay," I agree.

"Hey," Alyssa adds in. "I think you guys are ignoring something *kind of* important: Kaedrik knows that Daniel is the other Guardian now."

"What? How?" Madison asks.

Alyssa explains our confrontation with Kaedrik as I sit down at the table and bury my head in my hands.

How could I have been so *stupid*? If Kaedrik knows that I'm a Guardian now, my father definitely does too.

"We all make mistakes, kid," Will says to me. "Besides, they would've found out at some point."

"I know. I just can't believe that I..."

"You saved me," Alyssa says, "again."

"What are you talking about?" I ask.

"Ever since I had that reaction to Kaedrik's magic in my leg, I've been feeling this darkness pulling at me every now and then," Alyssa turns to Mala, "I was able to resist it...until last night."

Mala glares at Alyssa with a look of sympathy and guilt.

"Oh my god, Lyz," Madison gasps, "what happened?"

"Kaedrik's words, his power, I was frozen," Alyssa continues. "But Daniel, you drove him away last night, and when you did that, I stopped feeling that pull. It's been gone all morning."

She moves around the table and wraps me in a hug. "You made a mistake, but in doing so you kept me away from the darkness."

Her hug is warm and reassuring. A feeling of peace washes over me, which I recognize now as her emotions. Our Guardian connection is stronger now. It's easier to tell which feelings are hers, and which are mine.

After a moment, we pull away, and I can't help but feel a bit disappointed.

"Go get your sister," Alyssa says.

The ride to the Riot base is silent and awkward.

Kyle scowls as he focuses his eyes on the road.

I've thought about saying something a couple of times, maybe apologizing, but he's not in the mood to talk right now. It's best to give him his space.

At the base, a familiar, eerie sense of decay fills the air. It's the same feeling in my dreams. I've been around the Riot base since my dad revealed Kaedrik's involvement, but I have never felt anything like this around here until now.

"Something's wrong," I tell Kyle.

"What is it?"

"Kaedrik is up to something," I explain, "I don't know what it is, but it's bad."

Kyle and I take the side door that leads to the facilities hallway. That's where the Riot keeps things like the laundry room, the supply closet, and the garage entrance.

Back when he was still a member, Kyle, Kat, and I would use this way to sneak in and out of the base. We would go see a movie, hang out at a local fair, take a hike on a trail, whatever. Of course, I was always a third wheel with those two, but I never minded.

We move through the halls for a while, peeking through any door we can to try and find Kat. After a few minutes, a couple of voices approach. I push Kyle into one of the empty rooms and partially close the door to stay out of sight.

"What are you—" Kyle starts.

I cover his mouth with my hand. "Shh!"

"You're sure you checked everywhere?" my dad asks somebody.

"I was out for days looking for him," Kat replies. "What do you think?"

Kyle and I exchange an anxious look. *We found her.*

"Then he's made his choice," Dad says.

"You gave the boy an ultimatum," says another voice. Kaedrik. "Daniel made his decision, and I expect you to hold him to it."

"You don't mean...?" Kat asks.

"If you see your son again, I expect you to make good on your word," he says, "and kill him."

A portion of Kat's expression is visible through the open crack of the door, bewildered and speechless.

"No. You wouldn't...right?" she asks.

A moment of silence.

"You can't!" Kat yells. "He's my brother!'

My father speaks in a stern, low voice. "He's made his choice. Now Danny can live with the consequences, or die with them."

I step away from the door, baffled. Jacob Reeves has been a complicated brute of a man my entire life, but I never *actually* thought he would go this far. Sure, I remember what he said to me before he let me go, but I don't think either I or Kat would have expected him to go through with it.

"So much for family," Kat says before she storms off.

Damn. Now we have to wait for Kaedrik and my dad to leave. This just got a lot harder.

"Do I need to be worried about her, Jacob?" Kaedrik asks.

"No, she'll get over it," Dad says. "Besides, we had a deal."

Kyle and I lean in closer. What is he talking about?

"I suppose we do. You provide your services, and I leave the girl out of my plans so that she may stay by your side," Kaedrik says. "But, know this, Jacob. If she interferes, your daughter will be the test subject of my new power."

Kaedrik and my dad walk through the hallway talking for a little longer. When they're finally gone, I turn to Kyle.

"What did he mean by *new power*?" I wonder.

"I don't know," Kyle replies, "but we have to get out of here and find Kat."

We move through the halls again, listening for footsteps and hiding in corners when necessary. When we're able to get upstairs, we run to Kat's room. Kyle knocks twice, pauses, then knocks twice again. Our code we used a few years back when we wanted to sneak out of the base.

Kat swings the door open a split second later. "What are you guys doing here?!" she asks frantically.

"We came to save you," Kyle says. "Do you have the key?"

"No, I don't have the key! I've barely been gone for twelve hours!" Kat says in a scream-whisper as she pulls both of us into her room. "You guys need to get out of here, now!"

"Dad made a deal with Kaedrik," I tell her. "If he finds out that you're a spy, he's going to use you to test out some kind of magic for his plan."

"What deal?" Kat asks.

"Your dad's work in exchange for your life," Kyle says. "Kaedrik made a deal to spare you in his plan so that you can stay by your dad's side when Kaedrik does...whatever he's doing."

"Wait...*what*?" Kat asks in disbelief.

Kyle and I explain everything we heard downstairs. By the time we finish, Kat looks mortified.

"I can't believe this," she says, "he wants to drag me down with him."

"If he's willing to kill his own son, I believe it," I say.

She looks at me with sad eyes. "You heard that?"

I nod in reply.

"We're not going to let him drag you down," Kyle says, "but we have to go back to the cabin, all of us."

"What about the key?" she asks.

"We'll figure something out," he replies.

"Kyle—" Kat starts, rolling her eyes.

He waves her off. "We need to *go*."

The three of us head downstairs. We try to stay as quiet as possible, so we don't alert anyone. We head down the hall to the door that Kyle and I entered from. I grab the handle and try to pull the door open, but it won't budge. I switch the lock to unlock it and pull again, but it still doesn't open.

"*What the hell*?" I say under my breath.

"Going somewhere?"

Kaedrik stands behind us with five Riot members in front of him, all of them have their guns aiming at us. Standing next to Kaedrik is my father.

"You shouldn't have come here, Danny," he says.

"I thought you wanted me to come back," I say snarkily.

"Too little, too late," he replies.

Kaedrik raises his arms, and a charcoal-colored smoke leaves them and moves towards the five Riot members...and Kat.

"No! Stop!" Dad shouts at his partner.

"We had a deal, Jacob," Kaedrik says.

The smoke creeps up, starting to cover Kat completely.

"No!" I shout.

In an instant, I roll up my sleeve to reveal my bracelet and think of the shield that had protected Alyssa and myself from the demon dog. The shield appears as quickly as the thought crossed my mind, and I stand in front of Kat. Suddenly, a bright force field of light forms and encases the two of us.

"How did you *do* that?!" Kat asks, bewildered.

"I have no idea," I admit. "Are you okay?"

"I think so," she says.

The forcefield dissipates, and the smoke is gone. Kat seems unaffected, but I can't say the same for the other Riot members.

Their skin is pale white. The veins in their arms are black, just like their eyes. They look just like Ryan, except that the black smoke that transformed them is shooting out of their backs. All five of them have a maniacal expression on their faces, like animals ready to pounce.

"What the hell is that?" Dad asks. He didn't know what Kaedrik's plan was. He really *was* being played for a fool.

"A simple test on my new project," Kaedrik replies. "My army of darkness." Kaedrik keeps his stance like a statue. He speaks so low that I almost don't even hear him. "Get them."

The possessed Riot members immediately charge toward us.

As the one on the left starts to make a move on me, I slam my shield into his ribcage. While he's disoriented, I lunge my fist and land a punch right across his nose. I turn around to the member attacking Kyle and swing my shield out, knocking the side of his head.

The movement with the shield is a little awkward since I'm not very used to it, but at the same time, I can't help but have a little fun with this. I feel like a superhero.

Before I can turn my attention to the next possessed person, one of them, Aiden, I recognize through the possession, grabs my arm. I try to yank it away, but he's too strong. He pulls my shield off my arm and throws it to the floor. As the metal hits the concrete, the clanging noise of the impact is loud, echoing throughout the room. The shield slides on the floor and the second it settles, it disappears and is replaced by my bracelet.

My dad walks up to the bracelet, bends down, and picks it up. "What is this thing?" he asks.

"The Guardian's weapon," Kaedrik replies.

"The *what*?" Dad asks.

I struggle to break free of Aiden's grasp. Kat and Kyle have also been grabbed by the others — Derek and Charles.

Kaedrik gives me an evil, twisted smirk before answering my dad's question. "Your son has been lying to you, Jacob," he says, "Daniel is an accomplice to the one who keeps me in my prison."

250

"What are you talking about?" Dad asks him, seemingly irritated.

"He has been working against you, Jacob," Kaedrik claims.

My dad stays quiet as he walks up to me. He gets close, less than an inch in front of my face. "Is this true, Danny?" he asks me. He makes his tone waver to sound sad, but I can tell that it's an act.

"It didn't have anything to do with you until you started working with *him*," I answer, eyeing Kaedrik and trying to pull away from the possessed member's grasp, "until both of you took a *kid* hostage."

He doesn't say anything for a solid minute. He just stares at me with anger and disappointment in his eyes. Then, my dad turns to Aiden as he grips my arm. "Finish him."

He doesn't listen. Aiden just continues standing there as if he didn't hear my dad's words.

"I don't think so, Jacob," Kaedrik says. "They don't take orders from you."

"These are *my* men!" he shouts.

"Weren't you listening? It's *my* army," Kaedrik says. He turns to Charles, who is holding Kyle by both of his arms. "Put them away."

They drag the three of us downstairs to the basement, the same place where we found Alyssa when we rescued her. Derek locks a chain on my wrist, his face blank and unwavering from Kaedrik's grasp. Aiden does the same to Kyle and Kat before the three of them leave, locking the door behind them.

"Some rescue mission," Kat snarks.

Kyle grunts in frustration before turning to me. "What do we do now?"

"I...I don't know," I admit.

At some point the others will have to notice how long we've been gone, and they'll come to help. I just hope that they won't be too late.

13-Alyssa

Not long after Daniel left, Will elected to gather supplies from my place.

After seeing him off, I went to Mala's crypt hoping to find anything that might be useful. Her journal drew my attention, but after about an hour, I gave up trying to decipher it.

Mala's writing switches from English to some other weird indistinguishable language. Maybe it has something to do with her being an immortal entity? Maybe she gets it mixed up in her head when she's writing? Like dyslexia?

Admittedly, the language wasn't the only reason I put the journal down. Flipping through the pages, I saw it:

Taken by his darkness...only way...kill them...the host can be freed...when blood is shed.

The only solution we've found to my brother's possession. Thinking about it makes me sick, especially after what Kaedrik said. *You can't win without losing something.*

I push the thought away. Moving on to Hillary's vials, I look through Mala's desk to search for a recipe or something to help us replicate the healing tonics.

After a while, Madison comes down the stairs. "Any luck?"

"Not really," I answer, "I need to take the journal to Mala and ask for a translation."

Madison doesn't say anything, but she nods in agreement. She walks around the room anxiously, like she's avoiding something.

"Weren't you at the cabin with her earlier talking about your heritage?" I ask her. "How did that go?"

Madison groans with exasperation. "She just kept apologizing for taking the Guardianship out of the family," she answers. "All she did was explain herself and give excuses of *duty* and *caution*. It was infuriating."

"Well, she knows that she took the Guardianship away from you. She just feels bad," I say in Mala's defense before coming up with a different question. "Do you even want it?"

"Not really, to be honest," she says. "It seems terrifying."

I see what she means. Between demon dogs, creepy basement doors, and having a dark entity put traces of bad magic in my leg, Guardianship hasn't really been all sunshine and rainbows. It hasn't been all bad though. I met Daniel and Kyle, and we became good friends. Kat and I even got pretty close. My uncle and I are starting to do better.

"Do *you* want it?" Madison asks me.

"I didn't at first, but it's had its moments," I say, "plus, there's no way I would have known where Ryan was, let alone be able to try and help him, if it weren't for this place."

As we're talking, I'm still crouched down on the floor looking through Mala's desk. Madison bends down to my level and hugs me. With so much going on, I honestly hadn't thought about Ryan for a minute.

I remember when he first disappeared, Madison was the first person who was there for me. We've been through so much together. It's nice to know that even in a situation that's much bigger than anything we've seen before, we're still doing it together. I'm so glad that she's here. Honestly, I'd have fallen apart ages ago without her.

"Let's head back to the cabin and talk to Mala," I suggest.

Madison reluctantly agrees.

On the way, we talk about a few different things that I didn't cover when she first showed up. I tell Madison about how I first met Daniel and Kyle. When I get to the part about Kyle and the pizza delivery, she laughs so hard that the sound echoes through the trees.

When we get back, Mala is standing in the living room. Her gaze is fixed on the floor. She grips her arms tightly, muttering quietly to herself. "No...*no*..."

I run up to her. "Mala! What's wrong?"

She doesn't hear me. "No..." she lets out again.

Panic rises in my throat.

Madison's bright blue eyes are wide with concern. The two of us stand there, urgently trying to think of a solution. Before we can try to do anything, Mala wakes up from her trance.

"*Stop*!" she shouts.

"What happened?!" I ask, holding onto her shoulders to keep her grounded.

"Daniel is in trouble!" she states, sweating.

"How do you know?" Madison wonders.

"I can sense them. My connection with Daniel is strongest, but I feel Kyle and Kat as well. Kaedrik has them," Mala answers.

"We have to go get them!" I decide.

"You can't go by yourself," Mala shakes her head, "you need to call your uncle."

Without a second thought, I pull out my phone.

Will answers on the first ring. "Hey Lyz, I'm almost back, is everything okay?"

"Daniel and the others have been taken," I tell him. "I'm going to help them. Meet me at the base."

"Jacob got a hold of them?" he asks.

"No," I reply, "Kaedrik."

Will doesn't even hesitate. "I'm almost to the cabin, I'll give you a ride," he offers. "Hand the phone to Mala."

I give it to her, and she takes it with a puzzled look. "How do I use this?"

"Put it to your ear and talk to him," I tell her quickly.

She does as I instruct her, and she and Will talk for a minute. I can't really hear what Will's saying, so all I catch is a one-sided conversation from Mala:

"You want me to *what*?...Are you sure she's ready?...I *know* that, William, but I don't think—...I haven't done a blessing in over a decade...I understand that it's serious, but so is this! What you're asking is a huge risk—!"

Finally, she just sighs.

"Alright, fine. Just remember whose idea this was."

Mala then gives me the phone back.

"What was he asking you to do?" Madison asks.

"Sometimes, in dire situations such as this one, I can provide a Guardian with a little extra assistance. I call it a blessing," Mala explains. She holds out both of her hands, "Alyssa, come here."

Tentatively, I do as she says, and she takes both of my hands in hers.

She starts chanting in some strange language that I can't understand. Could this be the same language she wrote in her journal? It must be, because just like in that book, she switches to English.

"Let the light of lights guide you in your journey!...Hold the power in your heart with the care of the creator!...Unleash thine eternal rays with justice and compassion!" Mala proclaims loudly.

A bright yellow aura of light surrounds the two of us as Mala continues to chant. Her eyes glow with the same light as the magic around us. The light is warm. Safe. Powerful.

I look over at Madison, who is just as in awe as I am.

When Mala is finished, her chanting stops. The light in her eyes fades away with the rest of the magic. "This will help you while I cannot," she says, "but it's temporary. It'll only last a few hours."

"How do I use it?" I ask her.

"It will come as you need it."

Will enters right at that moment. "Come on, let's go," he says.

Before I leave with Will, I turn around to face Madison. "Are you coming, Maddie?"

"There's not really much I can do out there," Madison answers. She walks up and gives me a hug. "I'll ask about the journal."

On the way to the Riot base, I can't help but feel a knot in my stomach.

The last time I was there, all the pain, the torture...a small, terrified part of me desperately doesn't want to revisit that.

"Are you okay, Lyz?" Will asks.

"Hmm? Oh, I...uh..." I start, unsure of how to answer the question.

"It's okay to feel nervous," my uncle says. "I know you went through a lot when you were there last."

I shift nervously in my seat. "I'm going to save the others, no matter what," I assure Will, "but I'm scared."

"Of Kaedrik, right?" he asks.

"Actually, Jacob."

Will gives me a look, showing his intrigue.

I take a deep breath before explaining. "When they kidnapped me, I knew what to expect from Kaedrik. I see it almost every night. But Jacob was different. I had no idea what he was going to do. What he was capable of."

"Ah, I see," Will says, nodding. "Trust me, you're not the first Guardian to see Kaedrik as predictable. I bet if you ask Daniel, he'd tell you the same."

I guess that makes sense. Daniel has been a Guardian for a little over fifteen years. Of course he'd also be fed up with Kaedrik's threats.

"Let me tell you something about Jacob," Will continues, still keeping his eyes on the road. "He's nothing but a broken man who chose a bad path."

There was a time when I used to think similarly about Will. But it's probably best not to say that out loud.

"Ever since I met him, he's tried to be in control," he says, "and, now that both of his children don't want to follow him anymore, he's lost that control. Jacob doesn't like that, so he's grasping at straws."

"It didn't seem like he was *grasping* at anything when I met him," I point out.

"He was," Will assures me. "Working with Kaedrik, trying to hurt me, that's why he took you in the first place, to try and get that control back."

I never thought about it that way before. My chest tightens thinking back to how Jacob got to be that way in the first place, losing Hillary. Losing his wife like that...it must have been heartbreaking. My thoughts then shift to how much it affected Daniel and Kat. Kat especially. For fifteen years they were trapped under Jacob's control with no hope for escape.

It makes me wonder...

"Will, you spent *years* chasing the Riot for Daniel," I start. "If you had found him earlier, would you have taken him in? Like you did with Ryan and I?"

Will sighs heavily. "I used to think about that *all the time*," he says. "Honestly? I don't know. I wasn't exactly great with you two..."

"Personally, I think things would have been better if you did," I rest my hand on Will's shoulder in reassurance. "But that's not your fault."

Will grins, which feels a little strange to me. I've hardly ever seen my uncle smile over the years. At the same time though, it's a pretty nice change of pace.

At the Riot base, I hesitate to get out of the car, but force myself through it. My friends need me. Whatever *blessing* Mala gave me should be enough to protect us, right?

Will's plan doesn't involve sneaking in. He says they know we're coming — they're probably counting on it. His statement doesn't make me feel any better, but I follow him regardless.

He finds one of the entrances on the side of the old warehouse building and slams the door open. The noise should have announced our arrival, but nobody comes after us. The halls are silent.

We exchange confused looks before moving forward. Will and I run swiftly through the hall into the stairwell. In the wide-open space, I realize why nobody was waiting at the door.

Several Riot members fill the room. They stand at the ready behind Kaedrik and Jacob.

Kneeling on the floor in front of them are Daniel, Kyle, and Kat. My friends, forcibly held into place by Riot members that have been...changed. They look so similar to Ryan's possessed state, with their pale skin and blackened eyes. Smoke falls off their backs, shifting in sync with their movements. I've never seen anything like it.

My head turns to Will, who is equally shocked at the sight.

"Welcome, Guardians!" Kaedrik says with mock enthusiasm in his voice. The wicked grin that spreads across my brother's face makes my skin crawl. He gestures to the possessed members. "Do you like what you see?"

"What did you do to them?" Will asks sternly.

"They are the next phase of my plan," Kaedrik answers. He slowly paces across the room with his hands folded behind his back. "I call them my Stygian Soldiers."

"You stole their bodies! Their will!" I shout.

My uncle looks at me for a moment, then moves on and turns to Jacob. "How could you let him do this to your men?!"

"I'll do anything to get her back," Jacob replies with a snarl. "You know that, Will."

Realization hits like a slam in my chest. My eyes dart between Kaedrik and Jacob. *That's* why they're working together. Kaedrik must've promised to bring Hillary back if Jacob worked for him. But why would Kaedrik need someone like Jacob? Was it just for these *Stygian Soldiers*? Or is there more in this for him?

"Alyssa!" Daniel yells frantically. The Stygian holding onto him covers Daniel's mouth with his hand before he can get another word out.

"Let them go, Kaedrik!" Will shouts.

"I'm afraid I can't do that, William," Kaedrik replies.

I can see the fear in Will's eyes. It must have been years since he was this close to Kaedrik. Last time he was, he lost his Guardian partner.

Kaedrik waves his hand at the Stygian Soldier holding Kat down. The Stygian moves aside, allowing his master to step up and grab her by the hair.

Daniel shouts indiscernibly behind the Stygian's hand.

"Kat!" Kyle yells as he tries to reach for her against his captor.

She wriggles restlessly in Kaedrik's grip, grunting and gritting her teeth. "Let go of me!" she bites.

He ignores her. "You Guardians and your compatriots have been a thorn in my side for far too long," he grips Kat's neck with his other hand, "it's time you children learned. You cannot escape the darkness." Kaedrik tightens his grip on Kat's neck, strangling her.

I see the guys squirming helplessly in the Stygians' hold as Kat is choking.

"NO!!!" I shout, reaching out my hand and running to stop Kaedrik.

Before I can get very far, a ball of light shoots out of my palm. It hits him square in the eye, sending him tumbling backward, away from Kat.

She gasps for air, and once she composes herself, tries to escape. However, Jacob steps in and grabs her while the Stygian soldier runs to aid his master.

"Dad!" she exclaims, trying to pull away.

"Not so fast, young lady," Jacob snarls.

I pull back my hand and look at my bracelet, turning frantically to Will. "What was that?"

"I'll explain later, but right now I need you to do it again!" he says hurriedly.

"But *how*?!" I ask.

"It's all about willpower, Lyz!" he says, "I still have a lot to teach you."

Kaedrik growls furiously as he holds a hand over his eye.

"No...no, *no*!" he yells. He almost sounds *desperate*.

The outburst makes me panic for a moment. He's still in Ryan's body, did I hurt him that badly?

As he's scrambling, something falls out of his pocket, a necklace. He quickly puts it around his neck.

I recognize it from my dream: *the key.*

Kaedrik straightens up, his face clearer now. There's no wound where the blast hit him.

I let out a breath of relief.

He takes a short moment to compose himself, then smiles deviously before giving an order to his Soldiers. "Get them!"

All three of the Stygian Soldiers come charging towards Will and me. Two more appear, running out of the hallway we came in from. Daniel and Kyle try to run, but Kaedrik forces them back down with his magic.

Will grabs his gun from his holster and starts shooting at the Soldiers, but the bullets don't seem to be affecting them at all.

Trying to summon another light blast, I aim my arm out, focusing on the threat in front of us. Another light shoots toward one of the Stygian Soldiers, knocking him to the ground.

Will curses. "This isn't working! Lyz, you need to use the blessing!"

"I don't even know how that works!" I yell through the chaos.

Two more Stygians get close. I shoot the one in front. He falls, pushing back the other Stygian behind him like a couple of dominoes.

"Just relax and breathe," Will instructs. "Focus on Ryan. You'll figure it out."

"Ryan? *What*? How am I supposed to do any of that when there are monster soldiers coming at me?!" I blast another Stygian that runs up behind Will.

"That's part of the job, Lyz," Will says. "You can do this."

Something in the corner of my eye stops me in my tracks. Jacob raises his gun at Will.

"Look out!" I shriek.

An even bigger ball of light emits from my hand and hits Jacob in the chest. The impact knocks him back a couple steps.

Kat takes her chance to break free. She quickly steals her father's gun, but seems to take something else as well before running to join Will and myself.

"I couldn't let you two have *all* the fun," Kat snarks.

"Give Alyssa some cover," Will orders.

"Yes sir," she answers as she moves in front of me to aim at the Stygians.

I don't know what Will expects me to do. How does the blessing even work? Would it kill somebody? No, Mala wouldn't give me something that dangerous, right?

But we're in a rush. As Will instructed, I take a breath and focus on my brother.

When I first asked Ryan to move in with me, we were both so hopeful and excited to leave Will's house. The day he moved in, we ordered takeout and marathoned his favorite superhero movies until three in the morning.

When Ryan went missing, the weight of the loss was unbearable. I didn't know if I was ever going to see him again. I *certainly* didn't know that he was being possessed by a dark entity. In that moment, I wanted to do anything and everything I could to bring him home, to protect him and keep him safe.

Past Will and Kat. Past the angry cluster of Stygian Soldiers. Past a fuming Jacob Reeves. Kaedrik stands behind all of them, shouting orders.

It's him. It's *Ryan*. He's so close that I could just run up and wrap him in a hug. But I can't. His mind is so far away, I don't know if I'll ever reach it.

A look in Kaedrik's eyes catches my attention. He studies me, like he's looking for something specific. It almost...humanizes him.

Is it...? No, it can't be.

Ryan?

The entry from Mala's journal: *The host can be freed when blood is shed.*

It makes my skin crawl. I hadn't had the stomach to ask Mala about it. The only way to save my brother is to *kill* him. It's not fair. It eats me up inside every single day.

"Alyssa!" Kat calls.

Before I can react, a yellow aura of light surrounds me, even brighter than when Mala gave me the blessing.

Only this time, I'm hovering almost fifteen feet up in the air. Looking down, everyone is just as confused and bewildered as I am.

I don't waver, remembering what Will said.

Stay focused.

Channeling all those feelings, hope, joy, even fear, I let it build up inside me. The light gets even stronger. Flashes of bright white light covering the entire room. It's the same light from Mala that I've seen time and time again, except...it's not.

It's me. It's all *me*, I can feel it.

When the light fades, whatever magic that carried me into the air gently lowers me down. The Stygian Soldiers slowly turn back into humans.

Kaedrik folds onto the floor. His dark magic no longer holds Daniel and Kyle in place. They take the chance and run up to meet me.

"How did you do that?!" Daniel asks, his expression filled with amazement and wonder.

"Turns out Mala has a few other tricks up her sleeve," I answer.

Kaedrik stands up, grunting wearily. "You...ruined...*everything*..."

"*Daniel*," Kat whispers. She hands him the object that she must have taken from Jacob.

Daniel's Guardian bracelet. When did he lose it?

He takes the bracelet and slides it back onto his wrist, nodding in thanks.

"You will *all* pay for this!" Kaedrik yells. Black smoke falls off his body. He stands firm, preparing for an attack.

I do the same. Closing my eyes, I recall every threat that Kaedrik has made. Not only to me, but also to my brother. I remember when I first saw Ryan right here at this warehouse.

Ryan's face, but not Ryan's *soul*.

The yellow aura enflames around me once more. A new orb of light magic fills both of my hands. I let the light build. It's warm, safe. A force of power to protect the people I love.

This time, I focus on more than just Ryan to channel the light. I think of Madison, who's been by my side through everything. Will, the *last* person I would have ever expected to count on for guidance. Then Kyle, whose kind heart has shown so much support and love despite the short time we've known each other. And Kat, her boundless strength as she's changed into someone I'd *gladly* fight beside. Even Mala, with her determined spirit as she guides us through the Light.

Then, my thoughts shift to Daniel. My destined Guardian partner, fated to save the world with me. At first, I never could've imagined how we could work together to guard the cabin. Especially after learning about his involvement with the Riot. I didn't think I could trust him. But, through these past few days, we've connected. We've supported each other, shared our burdens. Even when Jacob tried to trick me into thinking that Daniel abandoned me, he proved him wrong.

He's not a criminal, or a flake. Daniel is loyal. He's a protector. A Guardian.

The light releases from my hands and flies toward Kaedrik. He screams in agony, falling to the floor.

While he's disoriented, Daniel runs to yank the key from around his neck. He grabs a hold of it, turning to head back our way.

My shoulders relax, we've almost made it.

Suddenly, Kaedrik grabs Daniel by the wrist before he can make his exit.

"Daniel!" I shout. My heart lurches in my chest.

A small black cloud of black smoke forms in Daniel's hand. When the smoke clears, the key is gone.

"Mark my words...*Guardian*," Kaedrik says through gritted teeth. "I *will* get out of my prison, and when I do, you will watch as I destroy everything and everyone you ever loved!"

Daniel yanks his hand away from Kaedrik's grasp. "Not if I can help it," he remarks before bolting toward us.

✦14-Alyssa

"This way! Let's go!"

Daniel, Kyle, and Kat lead us through the halls of the Riot base. My heart pounds in my chest as they direct us seamlessly to an exit on the side of the building. Outside is a parking lot full of several black vans like the one Jacob's men threw me into. To the left, Kyle's old blue truck is visible, sitting alongside one of the vans. Will's vehicle is across the lot, right where we left it.

A strange feeling nags at me. Something about Ryan...

Tentatively, I suggest to the others that we stop by my apartment.

Will gives me a questioning look. Just this morning I was avoiding that place. "Are you sure?"

I nod. "I just...have a feeling."

Daniel eyes me affirmingly. Maybe he can feel it too? Through our connection?

"Alright," Will shrugs, "let's go."

Kyle takes his truck and follows Daniel, Will, and I out of the Riot base, Kat riding with him.

We approach the door to my apartment, and I dig through my pockets. When I find nothing but the bare cloth of my jean fabric, a knot forms in my stomach.

Next to me, Daniel raises an eyebrow. His expression then quickly softens as he approaches the doorknob. He pulls what looks like a lockpicking set out of his jacket pocket and crouches down. "Don't worry about it."

"Uh dude? You're picking a lock in front of a cop," Kyle points out.

Daniel stops what he's doing and looks up at Will nervously.

He shakes his head. "I don't see anything, just get the door open."

After Daniel's fiddling, it unlocks. As he pushes the door open, memories fill my mind. Calling Ryan's name with no answer, searching desperately through the apartment for him. A hole forming in my chest from thinking he might have run away because of me. Every gut-wrenching second of that night comes back to me in a wave of regret.

Daniel must feel my unease. His voice in my ear is low when I feel the press of a hand on my shoulder. "It's gonna be okay."

Ryan's room is a mess. There are clothes everywhere, and his desk is covered in papers and computer wires. I wince —how long has this place gone without being cleaned?

"What are we looking for, exactly?" Kat asks.

"I'm...not really sure," I admit. "Anything that looks like it involves Kaedrik, or even Mala. I just have a hunch."

I look through the drawers in Ryan's desk while Kyle looks through the papers on top. Kat and Will look through the closet, and Daniel starts with Ryan's computer.

"What's the password?" Daniel asks me.

I only know it because I've had to check my brother's homework for school overnight, when he's asleep. "RHolla16," I answer.

Daniel smiles, and I roll my eyes at the ridiculous password. "Ryan can be an old-fashioned dork sometimes."

A pile of old papers in the bottom right drawer of his desk catches my attention. The handwriting looks familiar.

Is this from Mala's journal?

"Is that what I think it is?" Kyle asks.

I flip through the pages and scan what I can make out between her language. *Dangerous. Must be protected. Magic is waning quickly.* Each phrase I catch goes into detail about the key to the Dark Door.

"How could Ryan have gotten these?" I ask, looking over at Will.

He takes the pages from my hand and examines them, then looks up to the ceiling. "Mala gave me these pages *ages ago* for safe keeping. I took Ryan to my house while you were away, I needed to get some cash from my savings," he explains. "I got a phone call from the chief and found Ryan in my room after I was done. He must've taken them then."

"But *why* would he take them?" Kat asks.

Daniel and I exchange a look.

Last night's dream. Ryan had picked the key up after the demon dog dropped it.

"Because Ryan had the key," Daniel answers before I can.

"But how did he know about the pages?" I ask, "Much less where to find them?"

Will strokes his beard. "Lyz, did you notice Ryan acting strange before he disappeared?"

"I don't know about *strange*. He was still mad at me for leaving him when you kicked me out," I say.

Will's eyes fall to the floor.

A twinge of guilt knots in my stomach. That came out wrong.

"He was looking kind of sick," I continue, shifting my tone. "Not as pale as he is now, but enough for me to notice."

Will nods, his hands resting on his hips. "I think Kaedrik got to him quicker than we realized."

"How do you figure?" Kyle asks.

"Since Kaedrik got a hold of Ryan, he can give Ryan dreams," Will starts, "just like he can give the Guardians."

"I didn't know that..." I say under my breath.

"Kaedrik must've gotten to Ryan before everything. He visited Ryan in his dreams and answered some of his questions," Will deduces.

Daniel crosses his arms and narrows his eyebrows. "If that's the case, then why are the pages *here* and not with Kaedrik?"

"Because he didn't need them," I add. "He just needed to get closer to Ryan."

"Um, guys?" Kat interjects, "I think Ryan was poking around a bit longer than that."

She shows us a shoebox with printed photos inside and hands me one of the pictures. A clear shot of the demon dog in front of Ryan's school.

"What is this?" I ask.

I don't remember Ryan *seeing* the dog in the dream. How could he have known?

The rest of the pictures in the box are just as shocking. There are pictures of me asleep in my bed the night I had my first dream as a Guardian. Another photo shows Will pulling the chest of his old Guardian items out of the closet. Kyle and Daniel walking down the street. Them talking to me at work. Several pictures of Jacob Reeves at the warehouse, with Daniel and Kat standing behind him. Other Riot members, Jacob in his office, different rooms at the base.

Ryan was *studying* them.

No.

"*Ryan* wasn't poking around," I realize. "Kaedrik was. This is how Kaedrik found out about the Riot."

"He got to him long before any of us noticed," Will said.

"Oh my god..." Daniel exclaims.

"I know, this is insane," Kyle agrees.

"No. I mean *yes*, the pictures are disturbing," Daniel stumbles, "but I found something."

I sit next to him while he tilts Ryan's laptop toward me.

A Word document is pulled up on the screen. It looks like a letter from my brother addressed to me. A few years ago, I tried to get him into therapy, but I couldn't afford the payments after a while. He *did* tell me that writing letters was a suggestion Dr. Levine gave him.

Alyssa,

Something is wrong with me. I keep having these weird nightmares. And, call me crazy, but some of the stuff I've seen in my dreams has...ended up being real. I could've sworn I saw a weird dog on my way back from school a couple weeks ago. Since then, I've been feeling really off. Do I need to be put on meds or something? Or maybe it's just in my head? I don't know.

I've been thinking a lot about how our parents died. Will barely told us anything about it. I started getting curious, so I snuck into his room yesterday. I found this weird chest in his closet. There were a lot of useless papers and stuff in there, but I did find something: Mom's necklace. I stashed it under my bed. I don't know why Will had it, but it should be yours.

Things are really crazy right now. I think I blacked out for a second when I opened that chest. I'm scared, Lyz. I don't know what's going to happen, and I don't know if you're going to believe me.

I know we don't always understand each other, but I hope I can show you this letter one day.

Please keep an open mind. I need you, Lyz.

Ryan.

A tear rolls down my cheek. These are my brother's words, not Kaedrik's.

I wipe the tear away with my T-shirt sleeve and turn to Will, confused and skeptical. "You had my mom's necklace?"

At first, Will doesn't respond. He scratches the back of his neck nervously.

"I tried to give it to you with the bracelet, but it was gone," he admits. "I'm sorry, Lyz."

In a huff, I look under the bed, using my phone flashlight. The light shines on something metal between the mattress and the bedframe.

"Get up," I order Daniel.

He doesn't hesitate and shuffles off of the bed. When I lift the mattress, Daniel holds it for me while I grab the golden chain sitting on the frame. The chain is thick and twisted, like yarn. The matching golden heart charm is slanted. I hold the necklace in my hands with a misgiving feeling in my stomach.

"Are you okay?" Daniel asks me.

"Yeah," I answer, "I just never thought I'd see this again."

"Can I see it?" He asks curiously.

I drop the necklace in his palms. He looks at it for a moment, and a wave of tenderness washes over me through our emotional connection. Daniel opens the clasp, holds the necklace in front of me, and closes it around my neck. As he does this, I pull my hair out of the way.

"Thank you," I tell him, feeling a flush of heat in my cheeks.

Daniel smiles softly.

"So..." Kyle asks, "what now?"

"It's best to steer clear of Kaedrik and Jacob right now while we figure things out," Will says.

A wave of exhaustion drifts over me. I look at Daniel, whose eyes meet mine at the same time.

"We can stay here tonight," I suggest.

With that, Kyle and Will drag out mine and Ryan's mattresses, setting them in the middle of the living room. I gather some spare blankets from the hallway closet. Kat and I share a mattress, and Will takes the other. Kyle lays on the couch next to Kat, and Daniel takes the other couch behind us.

We stay up for a while, talking and laughing, an attempt to gain some sense of normalcy. But a sense of tension still lingers through the air.

How long until Kaedrik builds up enough strength to come after us again? And when he does, how will we stand a chance against his new army?

In my bedroom, I stand in front of my bed, and a half-packed duffel bag. This is the night Will kicked me out.

I don't understand. Why would my dream show me something that I was already around for?

Footsteps creak in the hallway, growing louder as they approach me. Scuffling to meet me at my bedroom door is Ryan. My heart drops, but I'm left skeptical.

"What do you want, Kaedrik?" I ask him, scowling.

He doesn't say anything. He just comes up to me and wraps me in a hug.

"I missed you, Lyz," he says.

My breath shortens in shock at his words. I don't want to believe it, I can't. Kaedrik has played too many tricks on me in the past.

I push Ryan off me. "I'm not falling for this!"

He looks at me with soft, understanding eyes. "He's not here," he says. "It's me, Lyz. I promise."

My throat catches. It can't be him. It's not possible. A part of me desperately still doesn't want to believe it, waiting for the rug to be pulled out from under me the second I start to hope. Ryan is gone.

He's not coming back.

But…if Kaedrik were going to pull this trick, making me believe that my brother was standing right in front of me, wouldn't he have done it from the start?

Ryan's deep blue eyes examine mine. He's not studying, he's not looking at me like someone planning their next move.

The furrow of his brow, the lump he catches in his throat. He's sad.

This isn't Kaedrik. It's him.

It's Ryan.

I pull my brother into a tight hug. "How…?" My voice quivers.

"I don't know, honestly," he says. "It felt like…waking up."

He stops in his tracks, looking up in alert.

A chill runs down my spine.

"We don't have a lot of time," Ryan says. He pulls something out of his jacket pocket.

It's the key to the Dark Door.

"Take it," my brother insists, pressing it into my palm insistently.

"How did you…?"

"Just trying to give my big sister a leg up," he shrugs. His face changes, looking more sad and guilty, "I'm so sorry, Alyssa."

I hold my brother close. "What? No," I tell him, "you have nothing to apologize for."

He smiles gently.

I switch topics, trying to take advantage of what little time we have.

"Do you know how to break Kaedrik's possession?" I ask him, a desperate crack in my voice.

Ryan shifts in his stance. "The host can be freed when blood is shed—"

"It won't come to that. I won't let it."

"Lyz, It's okay. You have to stop him, I get it." he says, not meeting my eyes.

I shake my head, tears now streaming down my face. "No! I'm not giving up!" I shout. "I can't lose you!"

Ryan hugs me again, this time tighter. "It'll be okay," he repeats, his voice breaking.

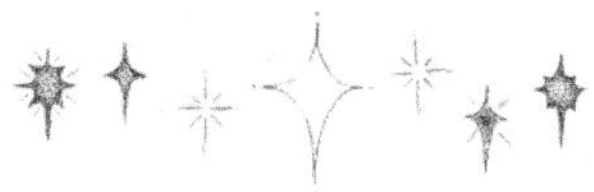

"Ryan!"

I wake with a jumpstart, gasping for air as Will runs to my side.

"Alyssa! Are you okay?" he asks.

Everyone else starts to wake. Including Kyle, who seems to have rolled off the couch and onto the mattress with Kat.

"What's going on?!" Daniel asks as he gets up off the couch behind me.

"I...I saw him," I huff through tears.

Will's eyes widen as if I had just told him I saw a ghost. Although, I might as well have.

I relay the dream to everyone. Halfway through my explanation, Kat interrupts me.

"Alyssa, what's in your hand?" she asks.

It's not until she says it that I feel the press of the metal in my palm. I look down at my right hand where the key to the Dark Door rests.

"Ryan gave it to me," I answer.

"How is that possible?" Kyle asks.

"I don't know," Will says, "but Lyz, I'm not so sure that this is a good thing."

"What are you talking about?"

"William is absolutely right."

Mala and Madison appear from the kitchen, where Will came from. Madison looks tired, like she's just rolled out of bed like the rest of us. Her hair is disheveled, and she's wearing an oversized T-shirt. Mala, however, has her bright red hair pinned in a delicate twist, and her white dress drapes neatly on her figure.

"Mala! What are you doing here?" Daniel exclaims.

"We didn't want to risk Kaedrik coming after you here," Madison answers for her ancestor.

"Alyssa," Mala starts as she bends down to my level, "Ryan's ability to communicate with you...it isn't very promising."

"What does that mean?" I ask her.

"It means that the connection between your brother and Kaedrik could be growing stronger," she explains. "It may be harder to bring him back."

"But that doesn't make any sense!" I point out. "If the connection was growing stronger, why would Ryan be able to give me the key? Wouldn't Kaedrik have stopped him?"

"I...I don't know, which is why I said it *could be,*" Mala admits. "But we can't afford to take any risks."

"How do we save him?" I ask her straight up. "That riddle in your journal is crap! We're *not* killing him! So, how?!"

"My journal?" she asks, her brow furrowed.

"Alyssa…" Madison says as a familiar eerie feeling grabs my attention.

"I feel it too," Daniel says.

Will and Mala also stop in their tracks.

"It's Kaedrik," Will says.

"You need to go," Daniel points to Mala.

"I can't," she says. "If I use my magic to teleport, he will sense where I am going. He will sense the cabin."

"Hide in my room." I direct her before turning to Madison, "you should go too."

Madison nods, and the two of them run to my bedroom.

Daniel and I reach for our bracelets. I give Will the key for safekeeping.

Kat cocks her gun and conceals it on her waist.

Kyle borrows Will's pistol. It seems strange, watching him hold such a deadly weapon. Despite what I know about his past, seeing Kyle with a gun feels out of character for him.

Outside, Kaedrik is a yard away from my front door. He stands there, stoic, solid, with a devilish smile.

I speak up first. "What are you doing here?"

"How brave of you, Alyssa. First one on the front lines!" Kaedrik replies in a patronizing tone. "I simply came to retrieve what you stole from me."

I glance at Will, who nods. He's not letting go of the key, no matter what.

"I didn't *steal* anything from you," I remark.

"I'm well aware of the tricks that your brother pulled," he says, annoyed. "I intend to deal with that act of insolence soon."

Kat steps up and aims her gun at Kaedrik.

I rush to push her hand down before she can put a bullet in my brother's head.

"No! Don't hurt him!" I yell.

"Whoa! Kat! What are you doing?" Kyle shouts.

"What are we supposed to do?!" Kat asks, impatient, "we can't just give him the key!"

"Well, how about I make the choice simpler for you," Kaedrik offers, crossing his arms with a knowing smirk. "Give me the key, and I will let Ryan go."

A small gasp escapes under my breath.

Everyone looks to me, awaiting my answer. Before Daniel even reaches my line of sight, I feel his desperation. The sense is overwhelming, like a whirlwind of anxiety as he awaits my answer.

Will sees the look on my face and lays a hand on my shoulder. "Lyz, you *know* you can't make that bargain."

"If you refuse, I will kill your brother the moment he is no longer useful." Kaedrik continues, "and believe me, that time *will* come."

My eyes dart between him and Will, who looks at me sternly.

"I know how much we want to get Ryan back, but we *can't* risk it," he says, "we can't let Kaedrik get out. That's our duty."

It should be an impossible choice. But, as much as I want to, and I really, *really* want to, I know better.

I was chosen to protect the world from this monster. I *can't* make this deal.

"No," I answer plainly, glaring at Kaedrik.

Will lets out a breath of relief. His eyes are somber, but his proud smile tells me that I've made the right choice, no matter how much the pit in my stomach tells me otherwise.

Kaedrik growls. Then, his tone changes, and he just chuckles. "Well then," he says, "it seems that we *are* at an impasse."

A surge of his dark magic surrounds me.

No, it's *inside* me.

Kaedrik stands perfectly still. He doesn't look like he's doing *anything* at first.

A sharp pain suddenly shoots through my left leg, causing me to fall to the floor.

"Alyssa!" Daniel calls as he bends down to help me.

"What's going on?!" Kyle asks.

"I told you that I would deal with Ryan's and your insolence," Kaedrik repeats.

I grab my calf as Kaedrik's magic stabs me with several fiery twinges. It feels like needles piercing through every nerve in my calf. Tears roll down my face as I try to clench my teeth through the pain.

"What did you do to her?!" Daniel snarls at Kaedrik.

"Something I was saving for a rainy day."

"I thought Mala got rid of any traces of Kaedrik's magic!" Kyle remembers.

"She must not have gotten all of it," Will says.

"Indeed, I have my ways of staying hidden in the shadows," Kaedrik confirms. "Now, give me the key, or *both* of the Haller siblings will die a slow and *painful* death."

I shout as the pain spreads up my leg.

"Daniel!" Will shouts. "Shoot him!"

Daniel aims his bracelet while Kaedrik raises his arms as smoke is released from underneath.

"The shield!" Will says.

Daniel does what Will instructs and leaves my side to form a shield from his bracelet.

Just as quickly as the shield is formed, a golden yellow field erupts from the metal. As Kaedrik's smoke moves toward us, the force field prevents any of the dark magic from passing through.

"Mala's tools won't save you forever, Guardians," Kaedrik snarls.

"I wouldn't count on that, Kaedrik." Mala appears in a short burst of yellow light. She stares down her former lover with centuries-old rage. Madison stands by her side.

"What are you doing?!" Will asks frantically.

"No more hiding," Mala answers him, "you need us."

"You are a fool, Mala," Kaedrik says.

"And *you* are a tyrant who is incapable of learning his lesson!" Mala bites back. "You have no one to blame but yourself!"

Mala stretches out her hand towards me. A warm ray of light covers my entire body, easing the pain of Kaedrik's magic. I take a breath of relief and slowly sit up.

"Don't get too comfortable," Kaedrik warns me. "My power has been growing inside of you for *days*. You can't be freed so easily."

Black tufts of magic circle me furiously as a battle between light and dark rages in my calf muscles. With his words, the fiery sting of the magic grows against Mala's warmth. It ebbs and flows, fighting against Mala's resistance.

I let out a scream, gripping my leg once again and breathing deeply through the pain.

"No!" Madison bends down next to me, her hand on my leg. "What do we do?" Her desperate eyes lock on Mala.

As she sits there with me, I notice something strange. Her hand feels unusually warm. It's almost *hot* to the touch. In an unexpected flash, another ray of light similar to Mala's escapes her hand.

"*Madison*!" Mala shouts.

As both of their light surrounds me, the black swirls of magic leave my body, and retreat back to Kaedrik.

"Interesting..." he says to himself.

The two lights fade, and, finally, I'm able to stand. Daniel's shield returns to his bracelet, and he smiles.

A wave of relief washes over me that I recognize as his. I turn my attention back to Kaedrik and aim my bracelet in his direction. "I think we're done here," I tell him. "You need to leave."

Kaedrik relaxes his shoulders and calmly turns to walk away. He pauses and turns his head toward Daniel and Kat. "Your father will be *thrilled*."

In an instant, Kaedrik disappears in a cloud of charcoal black smoke.

"I bet he will be," Kat remarks with a scoff.

As the smoke dissipates, I turn around to wrap Madison in a hug. "*Thank you.*"

"I... I don't even know how I did that," she admits.

"The light magic from your bloodline is starting to come to the surface," Mala answers. "Madison, you must be more careful in the future!"

Madison frowns, disappointed. The two of them remind me of how Will and I used to be at each other's necks.

The others start to head inside, but Daniel stops me.

"You had us worried there for a second," he laughs nervously.

"I know," I say, dipping my head down, "I shouldn't have even *thought* about Kaedrik's offer. I didn't mean to scare you guys."

"Oh, I wasn't talking about that," he says, running a hand through the back of his hair. "I'm just...I'm really glad you're okay."

The softness in his voice makes my cheeks flush. The corners of his mouth lift into a bright smile. Something tugs lightly in my chest. A small, warm pull before I even fully understand it. I step forward and wrap my arms around his waist. His body jerks at the sudden impact, but after a moment, I feel his hands press against my back as he returns the embrace. When I pull back, he looks at me, curious.

"What was that for?" Daniel asks.

Warmth returns to my cheeks. I find myself unable to meet his eyes. "Nothing," I say quietly, "and...everything."

He smiles, and gives me an understanding nod, not saying anything. With that, he opens the door and we head inside together.

Kyle drives me, Daniel, and Madison back to the cabin.

Will drives his own truck behind us with Kat and Mala. Frustrated, Madison spends the first half of the car ride venting about her ancestor.

"She's always telling me not to stand too close to her when she does magic!" she says. "It's so *stupid*!"

"Well, you were in her path when she was healing Alyssa," Daniel recalls.

"But I was able to help! You all saw that!" she remarks. "It's like she thinks I'm a loose cannon!"

"Remember what happened with Draven? She's just trying to keep history from repeating," I point out to her. "It's why she picked Daniel and I as her Guardians."

"I get that," Madison says, giving me an assuring look. "But I'm *not* my ancestor. A little trust wouldn't kill her, would it?"

"No, it wouldn't," Kyle answers. "But you need to be a little patient with her. She's been trying to keep an apocalypse from happening for millions of years, and now she's losing her grip on it."

Madison just sits there, her head down, not saying a word.

"She's just trying to be careful," Kyle finishes.

During the rest of the car ride, Daniel gives us the details on Kaedrik's "Stygian Soldiers".

"So I'm guessing we haven't seen the last of those guys?" I say.

"Not by a longshot," Daniel confirms. "But we don't know how long it takes for Kaedrik to gather that kind of magic."

"Not to mention, you probably set him way back with those *crazy* light powers!" Kyle adds, smiling. "How did you *do* that?!"

I tell them about Mala's blessing. The look on Daniel's face, and his thoughts through our connection, fills me with a wash of amazement and pride.

"What did it feel like?" Daniel eventually asks me.

"Like a release," I tell him. "Everything I fought for *literally* gave me strength. It was...like a weight off my shoulders."

His smile brightens.

We tell Madison about the pictures, and the letter that we found in Ryan's room. I show her my mother's necklace. She tears up at the sight of my new family heirloom, knowing what it means to me.

Finally, we get to the cabin and meet up with the others.

Once Kat sees me, she walks over with a guilt-ridden expression, gathering her hair to one side.

"I am *so* sorry about what happened out there," she says. "I shouldn't have aimed at Ryan so quickly."

"I appreciate it," I say, though the act still doesn't sit well with me.

"Alright," Will walks up behind her, holding the key to the Dark Door, "we need to hide this thing."

"The safest place would be my quarters," Mala continues for him. "However, we must take extra precautions to ensure that Kaedrik will not find it."

"Daniel, Alyssa, and I can't know where it is," Will says, "Kaedrik can still invade our dreams."

"Neither can Madison or I. Once either of us leaves the cabin, Kaedrik will have an eye out for us," Mala claims.

"I can find a good place for it," Kyle offers.

"I'll go with you," Kat volunteers.

Will nods and hands Kyle the key.

Mala moves to face them both. A flash of light surrounds the room, carrying Kat and Kyle away.

Once they're gone, Daniel grabs me by the shoulder and directs me to my uncle. "Hey, Will, I have a question," he says. "It involves the two of us."

286

Peeling his hand off my shoulder, I glare at him, raising an eyebrow.

Will crosses his arms, though not in an intimidating way. If anything, he just looks really tired. "What's up?"

"Do you have time to teach us about these bracelets?" Daniel asks.

Will's grin tells me that he's been waiting for this question for quite a while. He looks over at me, indicating whether I feel the same way.

"I'm ready. I want to learn," I say. "For Ryan."

Will looks at both of us proudly. I know that when Daniel first became a Guardian, before his mom died, Will wanted nothing to do with this place or its magic. But I can see it in his eyes. He's ready now too.

"I'll teach you everything I know," he says. "Mala can show you how to use her blessing, and Hill..." my uncle chokes up.

I feel a heavy weight in my chest, but it's not mine.

"Your mom's research will help the both of you along too," Will finishes, clearing his throat.

Daniel holds up the golden bracelet that used to belong to Hillary Reeves. He stands there, silent for a short moment, as if he were making a silent promise to his mother.

Quietly, I do the same.

I'll bring you back, Ryan. No matter what.

"Alright, kids." Will clears his throat and straightens up. "Let's go make some Guardians out of you."

15-Daniel

Will leads us to an open space to the left of the cabin. He turns to Alyssa and folds his arms.

"Alright, Lyz," he starts. "When you made those light blasts from your bracelet back at the Riot base, what were you thinking about?"

"Kat was in danger," she answers, "I was scared out of my mind, but I knew she needed help. I had to save her."

Will nods with an approving grin, then looks over to me. "When Kaedrik's pet attacked, and you used the shield, what was going through your head?" Will asks me.

It feels like ages ago. Kyle was missing, Peck—er—*Mala* left the cabin, and we chased after her. But, when the demon dog lunged after us, all I could really think about was keeping it away from Alyssa.

"I was worried about Kyle, and I didn't want the dog to hurt Alyssa," I summarize.

"Right," he responds, "what's the pattern in both instances?"

Alyssa thinks for a moment.

"We were both protecting someone," she answers.

"Exactly. The two of you are *Guardians*. Your entire purpose is to guard and protect," Will explains.

"Those feelings of preserving the good in your life and keeping it safe are where your power comes from."

Will's words sit with me for a moment. I had never really thought about Guardianship in that way. I was always so focused on keeping track of the Dark Door, finding Alyssa, and keeping suspicion away from the Riot and my dad. I guess with everything I was trying to keep intact, I never stopped to really think about what it was all for.

Will claps his hands together. "Okay kids, who's up first?"

Keeping quiet, I feel like the shy kid in gym class that doesn't want the teacher to call on them. Will's method of training is so much different compared to my dad's. Where Jacob Reeves hits first, asks questions later, Will already seems much more communicative. Thankfully, Alyssa is the first to volunteer.

"Can you guys show me how to make that shield? And the force field?"

"Absolutely," Will says. He gestures at me. "Dan, help her out."

"What do you want *me* to do?"

"How did you make the shield?" he asks. "What were you thinking? What were you feeling?"

"Uh yeah, okay," I start. "Earlier today, at your apartment, I saw the smoke coming, and I knew what it could do. I ran to protect everyone."

"But what were you *feeling* when that happened?" Will asks me again, furrowing his brow.

"Scared, mostly. And angry," I realize. "Angry at my dad, and Kaedrik."

Will nods. "You know, when Hillary and I were a little younger than you both, she was the first one to form the shield," he says.

"We got into a fight about...well, *something*, I don't know. She was so mad that the shield just appeared and hit my chest, knocking me to the ground." He chuckles at the memory.

"So...to form the shield, I need to be angry?" Alyssa asks her uncle.

"No," Will answers, "but you can focus that anger. Shape it, and it'll give you the tools you need."

Alyssa sighs, a slight sneer across her lips. She closes her eyes and takes a couple of deep breaths.

Will comes up to me and whispers something in my ear. "Can you give her something to block?" he asks.

I see where Will is going with this. With a nod, I stand a couple yards away, facing Alyssa. A light blast forms in my hand. The moment she opens her eyes, I aim right for her and throw the orb of light in her direction.

"What are you doing?!" she shrieks. Alyssa holds her arms up in protection, and just as she does so, the golden shield forms from her bracelet. The light blast bounces off of the shield and escapes to the bright blue sky above us.

"Look up, Lyz!" Will calls out, smiling.

Alyssa does as instructed. She stares in awe at the beautiful golden shield that is now attached to her arm.

"Whoa..." she says.

"Nice!" I exclaim. "No hard feelings?"

She pauses for a second with a sly look on her face. Alyssa's shield disappears, and a light blast takes its place in her hand. In a split second, I barely register the light hurtling toward me before it knocks me onto the grass.

"Not anymore!" she answers, laughing.

 290

"I deserved that," I admit. As I start to get up, Alyssa offers me a hand. I take it and stand up.

"Alright you two, be careful with those," Will warns, "those light blasts don't hurt us or Kaedrik as badly, but they do hurt normal people—"

" — And the Stygian Soldiers," I remember.

"The point is, those are literal balls of *fire*," Will says, "so don't be stupid."

"What else can these bracelets do?" Alyssa asks curiously.

"You'll find out in time," Will says, grinning. "This training is to help you harness and control these gifts, *you* have to discover what they are. That's part of your journey as Guardians."

Mala's bright red hair pokes out of the front door of the cabin as she meets us outside. I'm surprised she didn't teleport, but my irises are thankful that she didn't. Kat and Kyle follow behind her.

"How are they progressing?" Mala asks Will.

"Well, we just got started, but Alyssa's a quick learner." His prideful smile as he looks at his niece says more than the words can.

Alyssa blushes.

"I don't envy you guys having Will as a teacher. He was rough on me when I was his partner," Kat says.

"*Will* was rough? You trained with Jacob!" Kyle points out, raising an eyebrow.

"My statement still stands," she responds, smiling at Will.

"I was only rough on you because *you* were too rough," Will retorts, laughing. "I was trying to humble you a bit."

"I guess that's fair," Kat chuckles.

"And what of Daniel?" Mala asks Will.

"I mean, if you're not going to show us some new tricks, Will, I think I've got it down," I shrug, "Shield? Check. Light blasts? *Decade-long* check."

"Alright hotshot," Will chuckles, "let's see how you handle the blessing. What do you say, Mala?"

"Great idea! *Please* humble my baby brother for me, Mala," Kat says snarkily. "Lord knows he needs it."

As I glare at Kat, I notice how tired Mala looks. The bags under her eyes look heavy enough to drag her down. Her focus is off, like she's trying not to fall asleep.

"I'm afraid I won't be much help," she says, yawning.

"Are you okay?" Alyssa asks.

"Oh, I'm sure I will be." Mala sluggishly rubs her forehead. "I just need some rest. I think I'll retreat to my room for a while."

"Alright, feel better," I say.

A flash of light fills the space, carrying Mala to her quarters.

"She's been like that since we got to the gazebo," Kyle frowns, resting his hands on his hips.

Will looks back at the forest, his eyes focused intently in Mala's direction.

"Will?" I ask. "You good?"

He shakes it off. "Yep, let's keep at it."

Alyssa readies a light blast while I form my shield. She throws the glowing orb in my direction, but misses. The light swings past me and hits a tree standing a couple yards away. I expect the tree to catch fire, but instead, the light is absorbed into the tree's bark. I jump back, my heart pounding in my chest. Alyssa shrieks behind me.

"What the hell?!" I yelp, turning to Will.

"You've never seen that before?" he asks.

"No! I haven't seen the trees *eat* a ball of fire before!" I shout back, staring wide-eyed at the tree.

Will is unphased. "Mala made this place with her light magic, and these blasts *are* light magic, so hitting anything here with those just kind of 'feeds' the realm."

"That's...unexpected," I say.

After Alyssa and I have gone a few more rounds, Kat steps up to Will. "Hey, do you think you can help me figure out Mom's tonics?"

"Now?" Will asks.

"If you can," Kat says, "we found a couple of them in Mala's room."

"Madison told earlier that she might've found a recipe in Mala's journal," Alyssa states. She turns to Will. "You should go."

"Alright, but you two keep practicing," he says, "Willis, do you think you can make sure that those two don't kill each other?"

"Yes sir!" Kyle answers with a salute, giggling.

Kyle watches a few feet away as Alyssa and I get back to it. For a while, we're just going through the motions. I can see Alyssa getting gradually more frustrated as she stumbles through dodging and blocking light blasts with the shields. The longer we train, the closer we get to each other. I hit Alyssa with another light blast. She yells and lunges her shield at me. In a split second, I hold my arm out, blocking her on instinct. Ignoring the stinging pain of metal slammed against my arm, I grab the edge of her shield, yank it off out of her grasp, and toss it to the ground. Without a second thought, I sweep out my leg, knocking Alyssa to the ground.

My breath catches as I realize what I've done. Alyssa grunts frustratedly, picking herself up off the ground.

"Hey!" Kyle shouts as he runs to us.

"What was that for?!" Alyssa asks, exasperated.

"I'm sorry! You were coming at me, it was a reflex!" I say, offering a hand. "Are you okay?"

"I'm *fine*," she says sternly as she walks away to sit on the porch.

Kyle turns to me, accusingly. "Dude, what happened?" he asks.

"I didn't mean to!" I say defensively.

"Tell *her* that," he says.

I head to where Alyssa is sitting on the wooden porch steps with her head dipped down to her lap. I sit next to her, and, thankfully, she doesn't move away.

Kyle stands at the bottom of the stairs, leaning on the railing.

"What's wrong?" I ask her.

She lifts her head slowly. I feel her equal parts sadness and embarrassment through our connection as she lets out a sigh. "I'm sorry I got so pissed off."

"Don't apologize, it was my fault," I say. "Do you want to tell me what's going on?"

"I was having fun at first," she shrugs. "But you were just faster. I had a hard time keeping up. You're the one who's actually *had* training before."

She has a point. We had very different upbringings. Alyssa doesn't have the same kind of experience with combat that I had gotten from my dad.

"If you want, I could teach you a few things," I offer.

Alyssa smiles. "I'd like that."

"Why don't you guys take a break first? You've been at this all afternoon," Kyle points out.

"Pick this up tomorrow?" I ask Alyssa.

She nods, and the three of us head in to make some lunch.

Alyssa's eyes are wandering and unfocused with exhaustion.

I rub my aching shoulder as I make my lunch.

While we're eating, Madison comes in. She sits at the table and presses her hands against her brows, sighing.

"You okay?" I ask her.

"Not really," she answers. She stares off into the distance, as if she's focused on something else.

"What's wrong?" Alyssa asks.

At first, she doesn't answer. Alyssa grabs her shoulder and shakes her, trying to get her attention. "Maddie!"

"Oh, um...sorry," Madison says, out of her trance.

"What's going on with you?" Alyssa asks her.

Madison sits down at the table across from Kyle. She runs a hand through her long black hair, exasperated. "I was trying to read through Mala's journal, and I fell asleep—"

"Uh oh," I say, knowing where this is going.

Alyssa and Kyle perk up at my reaction.

"Was it a nightmare? Did you see Kaedrik?" Alyssa asks.

"Yeah," she replies, "I didn't even know I could get those. I thought it was just a Guardian thing."

"Well, it's not a good sign," Kyle points out, "but it could be because of your relation to Draven. He *was* the first Guardian."

"What happened in the dream?" I ask Madison.

"He was threatening me," she starts, "saying that he'd come after my family."

Alyssa sighs, annoyed. "Yeah, he does that."

I can't help but crack a small smile. I've been dealing with Kaedrik's threats for over a decade. They get old after a while. It's just nice to know that after so many years of working through those dreams on my own, someone else finally understands that feeling.

"But it wasn't just that...I *saw* him," Madison says.

"*Kaedrik*?" I ask in disbelief.

"No," she says, "I saw Draven."

Kyle chokes on the sandwich he had in his mouth.

"What happened?!" I ask her.

"What did he say?!" Alyssa wonders just as quickly.

"Guys, he was very vague," she says, "all he said was *I'm here*."

"Do you think that means he's nearby?" I theorize.

"I guess," Madison says, "but couldn't that also mean, like...a *spiritual* thing?"

"That's a good point," Alyssa agrees, "based on the way his mom has helped us out, not everything is literal."

I think back to the dreams over the past few days when I had started seeing Mala in person. She was never very straight-forward.

"I wish I got more from him," Madison sighs, "I'm sorry."

"Don't be," I tell her. "Honestly, you got more than Alyssa and I ever do in a dream."

Madison scoffs in disbelief, but Alyssa nods at me. She knows I'm right.

As we're talking, a throbbing pain seeps into my forehead. I shout, pressing both palms against my head.

"What's wrong?" Kyle asks.

The room around me is spinning. My head pounds furiously. In a loss of balance, I fall out of my chair.

Alyssa also clutches her head and falls to the floor, unconscious. Whatever is affecting us got to her quicker than it got to me.

"Alyssa!" Madison yells.

"Dan!" Kyle rushes over to me.

The pain grows worse by the second. My head is throbbing. I melt down to the floor. Gritting my teeth through the pain, I try to speak.

"Get... help..." I instruct them. Kyle frantically runs out of the room.

Madison follows behind him.

My hands grip the sides of my head. The searing pain causes me to pass out right there on the kitchen floor.

"Finally."

I'm on the floor of my dad's office again. He stands there with Kaedrik, who seems to be reaching out to something with his dark magic.

"Daniel!" Alyssa says from behind me.

The second I see her, something inside me unclenches. We both get up from the floor, and I watch as Kaedrik spreads his dark magic throughout the room.

"After countless centuries," he says, "I have finally found it."

Alyssa eyes the scene in front of us and then turns to me. "What are we looking at?" she asks, "can they hear us?"

"I'm not sure," I admit to both of her questions.

My dad steps away from Kaedrik and sits down at his desk. He opens one of the drawers and pulls out a black pen and a map. I walk up to him and look over his shoulder.

"It's a map of the town," I tell Alyssa.

"Where is it?" my dad asks Kaedrik.

"In an alley downtown," Kaedrik answers, "right between a bakery and an herb shop."

"That's on Milam Street," Dad says before circling it on the map.

"Shit..." I say.

"They've found the cabin..." Alyssa breathes.

Dad stands up out of his desk chair. "What are you locking onto?" he asks, raising an eyebrow.

"When I left to retrieve the key, I met someone that I wasn't expecting...a descendant."

Madison.

"My son's bloodline still lives on," Kaedrik continues, "and with it, the key to my freedom."

"Speaking of that damn key, how are you going to find it?" Dad asks.

"The same way I found it at the Haller girl's dwelling," Kaedrik says. "Mala needed our son to make the key with his magic, dark and light, to ensure its effective use."

"If there's dark magic in the key, then you can sniff it out," Dad deduces.

I wake with a gasp.

Kyle and Kat are on either side of me.

Will stands over Alyssa as she wakes up as well.

"What happened to you two?" Kat offers a hand, and I take it.

"We got pulled into a dream," Alyssa answers as Will helps her up.

"What did you see?" he asks her.

"Kaedrik knows where we are," I tell him.

The air grows thick with quiet tension.

Will is white as a ghost.

Kyle covers his mouth.

"Shit..." Kat lets out.

Mala then comes running into the kitchen. "Where's Madison?!" she asks frantically. "Something dark is coming this way. I can feel it."

"She didn't bring you down here?" Kyle asks.

"No, she didn't come to get me. Something is wrong!" she answers.

"Kaedrik is using her," Alyssa realizes, eyes wide. "We have to find her, *fast.*"

16-Daniel

Mala and Will look justifiably mortified as we relay the details of the dream. Will strokes his beard, deep in thought. "After all these years," he sighs, "he's found us."

"We *must* retrieve the key before they arrive," Mala says, "Kat, Kyle, please come with me. You know where it is."

The two of them stand with Mala, ready to be teleported, when Mala stops. She bends down and starts coughing.

"Mala!" Will calls.

My pulse races as we rush to her side. She falls to the floor, her coughing fit worsening as if the air were being sucked out of her lungs.

"What's wrong with her?!" Kat asks.

"I—I don't know," Will admits.

When Mala's coughing fit recedes, her eyes close as she slips into unconsciousness.

"Damn it! Kaedrik is getting stronger," Will says. "He must've found a way to get to her." He turns to the group. "Two of you need to get to the gazebo and get that key," Will instructs. "Kat, go grab a tonic!"

"Is that really going to work on her?" I ask him as Kat bolts up the stairs.

"We're about to find out," he answers. "Daniel, Alyssa, one of you needs to stay here with me."

"I'll stay," I volunteer, turning to Alyssa.

She nods approvingly before Kyle puts a hand on her shoulder. "Let's go."

Kat comes back down a moment later with the healing tonic.

Will gently pours it into Mala's mouth and then turns to me. "I need you to hit her with a light blast," Will instructs, his brow arched.

"*What*?!" Kat and I say in unison.

"She'll absorb it, remember?"

"Oh, right!" I exclaim, shuffling to Mala's side.

"Try to make it as big as you can," he instructs.

Closing my eyes, I take a deep breath and focus on summoning the magical orb of light energy. As I feel the warmth leaving my palms to form the blast, my hands shift around the orb to shape and expand it. I open my eyes to a ball of light in my hands, bigger than I've ever seen. Rather than throwing the blast at my target like normal, I bend down and gently place the light on top of Mala.

She absorbs the energy instantly. Her eyes stay closed as her body relaxes, chest rising and falling slowly.

"She's still breathing," Will says. "At the very least, we helped her stay alive. That's what matters."

"*Thank God*," Kat exhales.

After we move Mala from the floor to a more comfortable spot on the couch, we have nothing to do now but wait patiently for Alyssa and Kyle to come back. Will goes upstairs, while Kat and I stay in the living room with Mala.

"That magic you did earlier was pretty impressive," Kat says after a beat of silence.

"Thanks. I'm still getting the hang of it."

She sighs, running a hand through her hair as her eyes stay on the fireplace in front of her. "A few weeks ago, I did *not* think this would be how my life turned out."

"Are you disappointed?" I ask.

She pauses for a short moment. "No, not really," she admits. "You're here, and I'm on good terms with Will, and...Kyle."

"How's that going?" I ask her.

She shrugs. "It's going. We were talking while we were out hiding the key."

"What did you guys talk about?"

Am I being nosy? Maybe. But I've been watching these two for years. Excuse me for wanting an update.

"We mostly talked about *us*," she says, "and whether or not it's a possibility."

"What does he think?" I ask curiously.

"He wants to give it a shot, but he knows I'm still trying to figure things out."

That sounds about right for both of them.

"Okay," I say to her, "you know he'll wait for you as long as he needs to."

Kat doesn't say anything, just nods.

Alyssa and Kyle finally come back with the key after a while.

Will walks downstairs when he hears them return. "I've been working on a plan," he says. "It's not ideal, but it'll keep everyone safe, and it'll keep the key away from Kaedrik and Jacob."

"Okay, what've you got?" Kyle asks.

"We need to leave the cabin," he says. "We'll take Mala, and the key, and everything else we need with us."

My heart pounds in my chest at his words. "*What?*"

302

"This way, when Kaedrik and Jacob get here, they won't find anything," Will explains.

"Yeah, except for *the door*!" I point out.

"Which they can't open without the key," Alyssa realizes.

I turn to Alyssa, desperate. "You can't seriously be considering this!" I plead. "We're supposed to *protect* this realm, not *abandon* it!"

Alyssa's eyes lock onto mine. I feel her stern determination through our Guardian connection. "Daniel, what we're *supposed* to do is protect everyone from Kaedrik," she says to me.

Kyle steps up next to me. "If he's here, but Mala and the key *aren't*, then he can't do anything,"

I can't believe everyone, especially Kyle. After *everything*, they're all prepared to just pack up and leave?! My stomach clenches and my face feels hot. There has to be some other way. There *has* to. We can think of something. Another plan to keep Mala and the key away.

When nothing comes to mind, I frustratedly throw my hands in the air and grunt. Taking a couple steps forward, my fist meets the wall in front of the kitchen.

"Daniel!" Kat yells.

I don't answer, not trusting myself to respond. But I stop to listen nonetheless.

"It's the *only way*," she says. "It's going to be fine."

Damn it.

She's right.

Taking Mala and the key away from the cabin is our best chance at stopping Kaedrik and my dad from doing anything. As much as I hate to admit it, there's no other option.

"Fine," I sigh, defeated, "let's pack up."

Kyle pulls Will aside for a moment while Alyssa, Kat, and I start packing up the living room. Their voices are too low to catch, but hopefully it isn't more bad news. When they're done, both of them come back out. Will waves for Kat to join him upstairs to pack the tonic ingredients and my weapon supply.

Meanwhile, Kyle, Alyssa, and I gather food and any other essentials.

"Do we know where we're taking everything?" Alyssa asks as she empties out the pantry. "Because we can't all just hide in my apartment again."

"I talked to Will," Kyle says. "My family has a vacation house a couple hours out of town. They mostly use it for winter getaways, so it'll be empty this time of year."

I freeze mid-reach of a loaf of bread, giving Kyle a curious look. "You never told me about that," I point out.

Kyle's face falls. His shoulders go rigid as he avoids my eyes. "It wasn't important until now."

I set the bread into the plastic bin to load onto the truck. "What do you mean *not important*?" I ask.

"Just drop it, Dan," he exhales.

"No, hold on! Your family has enough money for a *second home*? You told me you were homeless before you joined the Riot."

"I was!" Kyle insists, now yelling.

"Can we please worry about this later? We have a job to do," Alyssa interjects.

I ignore her.

"You and I don't keep secrets! Why didn't you tell me about this?"

"I said drop it, Daniel!" He pushes a hand against my chest, making me stumble backward into the pantry shelves.

The back of my head and shoulders ache from the impact. A tin can rolls off the shelf on my left, falling to the floor with a clanking metal sound ringing in my ear. The aggression behind his movement, and the look in his eyes...

This is nothing like the fights we had in the Riot's training room. This is real, raw anger.

Picking myself up, I shove him back. Hard.

Kyle regains his balance just before landing against the edge of the table.

"Guys, stop!" Alyssa speaks up, placing herself between us.

Neither of us says anything. Kyle's chest rises and falls. His face is deep red with anger. He steps forward, jaw clenched. The wooden floor creaks beneath him as he approaches.

My chest heaves. Every breath comes out like a gasp. Looking my best friend in the eye, it's hard to recognize his features as he stares me down with an intensity I've never seen from him before. Something clinging desperately to whatever he's been hiding. He takes a breath, and I swear I can almost see a quiver in his jaw.

"Why didn't you just *tell me*?" I say. "I thought I could trust you, Kyle."

Either he doesn't hear me, or he doesn't care. Without warning, his fist collides with the bridge of my nose. I double back, my hand over my throbbing face.

"Because it's none of your damn business!" he answers.

"That's *enough*!" Alyssa shouts.

The sound of footsteps quickly grows louder as Kat and Will enter from upstairs.

"What happened?" Will asks.

I snap my head around.

Alyssa shoots both Kyle and I with an irritated glare. "Both of you are acting like idiots!" she yells. "Fighting about Kyle's family is *not* the issue at hand right now! You two need to get your heads out of your *asses* so we can get out of here before Kaedrik and the Riot show up!"

"Alyssa..." I let out, a small crack in my voice.

"I..." Kyle starts, but the words escape him just as quickly.

"I don't want to hear it!" she snaps, leaving Kyle and I speechless. Without another word, she starts picking the cans up from the floor and packing them in the bin. I can feel her irritation as blatantly as the pain across my nose.

Will crosses his arms, eyes darting between us and the mess of the pantry. "What the *hell* is going on?"

Dreaded silence fills the air for a few long, agonizing seconds before Kyle finally answers. "I told Daniel about the house," Kyle sighs, looking right at Kat.

"Oh." Her voice is quiet, almost indiscernible.

"So you *knew* about this?!" I ask my sister.

"Yes," she answers, "but Daniel, it's not what you think."

"Honestly, I don't know *what* to think right now!" I admit, throwing my hands in the air. Out of the corner of my eye, I catch Alyssa's glare. When my voice rises, the sense of her anger intensifies.

"Daniel, you need to calm down." Will orders.

"Kyle's family kicked him out," Kat explains, talking over Will.

Kyle pauses for a moment. He buries his head in his hands shamefully.

"What...?" I ask, dumbfounded.

"Remember that friend Kyle had? He joined the Riot to help him?" Kat asks me.

"Yeah," I reply, raising an eyebrow.

"They were smuggling knives, and—" Kat says.

Kyle comes up next to her and interjects. "My stepdad runs a big air conditioning company. They work at the corporate level," he starts. "Years ago, my old friend from high school, Jim, got me to steal some money from my family's bank account to buy a set of tactical army knives from this old handler. He was going to sell them for more than they were worth and get me the money back."

Unbelievable. I never knew that Kyle was capable of something like that.

"My stepdad found out, and he kicked me out on the spot. I couldn't even pack my things." His eyes meet the wood floor below him as he speaks. "So *yes*, Daniel. I was homeless."

"What about your mom?" Will asks.

Kyle's frown drops even more. "She had SPD."

Kat puts a hand on his shoulder, "Schizotypal Personality Disorder," she explains.

"She was always spacing out. She couldn't tell what was real," Kyle says.

"My sister was diagnosed with that before the accident," Will mentions. "I had no idea, kid, I'm sorry."

"I remember that," Alyssa says.

Kyle nods and continues his story, looking in my direction.

"Jim and I drove up here, and he was *dumb enough* to try and sell those knives to your dad."

"Kyle, I..." I try to say, but he holds up a hand to let him finish.

"Jacob said that we owed him, so I thought that if I joined up with the Riot and worked for him, I could pay off the debt and he would leave Jim alone," he sighs, "but he sent a team to shoot him down a week later while you and I were at that bank job out of town."

"Oh." It felt strange to both of us when he sent us to that small bank in Bloomington, nearly an hour away for something seemingly unimportant. Now I know why.

"Kat was the only person I'd ever told about Jim, my family, or even when my mom died a few months later," he says, his breath trembling. "When you asked me to help you here, I wanted to be defined by who I am now, not by my past mistakes."

"I understand that, you know I do," I say, "I'm so sorry."

Kyle pulls me into a quick hug, accepting my apology.

When we let go, I notice Alyssa standing by my side. I feel a twinge of guilt, seeing how she just watched us fight like a couple of rowdy kids. She must've sensed it though, because she gives me a knowing smile.

"Come on," she says, "let's finish this up."

A little over an hour later, we've finally finished packing. Everything we have is loaded into Will and Kyle's separate trucks.

Carefully, I carry Mala to Will's truck. Her breathing is ragged. I feel her chest slowly rising and falling against mine as I lay her in the backseat.

The drive with Will is filled with nothing but the low volume of a country radio station. Eventually, I find the courage to ask him something that's been gnawing at me.

"Was my dad any better before?"

He doesn't say anything for a moment, staring into the distance past the car window as if reliving an old memory.

"He wasn't as vengeful," Will says, "but he was still very damn cocky and manipulative."

"And you guys were friends?" I ask.

"At first, yeah," he answers. "After a while I stuck around just to look after your mother. She was like another sister to me."

"I've lived with that man my whole life," I say. "When I got older, I could tell when he was lying, but he still got under my skin. He still had this...*hold* on me and Kat."

"He's your father," Will points out. "Pointing you in his direction was easy for him for a long time. But now both of you kids have the opportunity to make it a hell of a lot harder."

Nodding, his words sit with me for a second.

That's definitely the plan.

A beat of silence passes before I change the subject. "Why didn't my mom tell me the truth about Kaedrik?"

He sighs. "I don't think she meant to lie to you, Dan. You were just a kid. I think Hill was trying to ease you into all this. She just...didn't have the chance to explain."

Will finally pull up to a two-story white home with big glass windows and a porch that wraps around half of the house.

"You've got to be kidding me," I say.

With Mala in my arms, I stare in awe as we step in.

The interior is just like someone would expect from a vacation house in the woods. The walls are decorated with deer antlers, an unlit stone fireplace stands firm at the center of the living room, and three black leather couches with old, knitted blankets draped across the top. The kitchen is behind the living room, an open concept space with no walls separating the two. Stepping further inside to look around, almost every towel, oven mitt, and picture frame in the kitchen says the phrase: *live, laugh, love.*

There's another door on the left wall next to the dining room table. I lay Mala down on the couch with a blanket atop her and go to investigate. Through the door, I see a separate patio with a hot tub.

Will follows close behind.

"Unbelievable! The guy can afford a *hot tub*, but he chooses to share a bathroom with me!" I exclaim.

"I'm not complaining," Will laughs. "Come on, help me unload."

A sudden unexpected barking catches our attention. Curiously, both of us follow the barking to one of the three bedrooms. When we open the door, a black labrador jumps up and uses his paws to lean on my stomach.

"What the hell..." Will says.

The dog seems friendly, so I pet his back and scratch behind his ears. My hands catch on the green collar around his neck with a golden tag bearing the dog's name.

"Obie," I read. "That's an unusual name for a dog."

Obie wags his tail and pants, delighted to be called by his name. "Arf!"

"Where did he come from?" Will asks.

My phone buzzes in my pocket. I answer with one hand and continue petting Obie with the other. "Hello?"

"Hey, we're like fifteen minutes away. How close are you guys?" Kyle asks.

"We just got here," I answer him, leaning the phone away from Obie as he curiously tries to sniff it. "Hey, does your family have a dog that you know of? Maybe one left behind at some point?"

"Um, no. My stepdad is allergic. Why?"

"Arf! Arf!" Obie barks.

I hold out the phone for Kyle to hear. "That's why. You might want to pick up some dog food on the way up."

"He was just in one of the bedrooms?!" Kyle summarizes as I help him unload his truck.

"Yeah. We have no idea where he came from."

Kyle and I take a couple of boxes and set them in the living room for now. The door to the hot tub meets my line of sight, and I punch Kyle in the arm.

"*Ow*! Dude!" he yelps.

"Look at this place! I never knew that you used to live like this!"

Kyle just laughs. "I can't wait to see your face when you find the game room," he says before walking away to keep unloading the trucks.

I stand there, baffled. "There's a *game room*?!"

After everything is put away, we reconvene in the living room. Mala is still on the left couch, passed out. Alyssa, Will, and I sit together in the center. While there is plenty of room on the third couch to the right, Kat and Kyle sit on the floor, giving Obie plenty of scratches and attention.

"So, what do we do now?" Alyssa asks.

"We're going to wait out Kaedrik and the Riot," Will explains. "In the meantime, we'll do what we can to help Mala, look for Madison, and prepare for the worst-case scenario."

Almost as if on cue, a familiar light fills the room and nearly blinds us. We look at Mala, now back in bird form and still unconscious.

Obie barks and tries to run to her, but Kat holds him back.

"*Shit*," Will says under his breath as he picks her up gently. "She's getting worse."

17-Alyssa

Will takes Mala to the bedroom downstairs and shuts the door, so that the dog, Obie, can't hurt her. He comes back seconds later, his eyes drifting outward as he frowns, as if lost in thought.

It's been a few days since I've seen Mala in her bird form, after she saved me from Kaedrik's magic. I'd almost forgotten she could do that.

"Is there anything we can do to help her?" Kyle asks.

"The tonic didn't work when we tried it," Kat informs us.

"It helped a little bit," Will corrects her. "Right now, all we can do is keep her alive. Which means we *need* more of those tonics."

"Why don't I just hit her with another light blast?" Daniel asks.

"You did *what*?" I ask him.

"We don't know how well that will work outside the cabin, especially if Kaedrik is already there," Will explains.

Daniel lets out a low growl.

"*This* is why I didn't want to leave!" He shouts. "All we can do is sit here and do nothing!"

"We *are* going to do something," I tell him, sensing the bitter strength in Daniel's emotions. He's afraid, and he's hurting. There's a sharpness in his wide green eyes: a fear of the unknown.

I grab his hand on one side and pull him into a hug. "Like Will said, we can make the tonics, find Madison, and prepare for a fight." I direct that last part to everybody. "Because there *will* be a fight, and we need to be ready."

Daniel returns the hug for a short moment before pulling away. "Are you sure you're ready for that?" he asks me.

He's reading my emotions too. As much as I try to hide it, I feel like a nervous wreck. My stomach twists, cold and heavy as my fingers curl tighter around Daniel's hand.

Am I ready for this? To fight Kaedrik when he has such a tight grip on my little brother *and* my best friend? If I lose, they could *both* be gone forever.

Straightening my shoulders, I answer Daniel's question. "Kaedrik threatened everything I love. He won't get the chance to follow through with those threats."

Daniel eyes me curiously, no doubt sensing my unease as our Guardian connection betrays my attempt at feigning bravery.

"You Guardians aren't alone either," Kyle says with a soft grin. He gestures to himself, Kat, and Will. "We're with you guys."

"Always," my uncle says.

Obie barks, as if joining in. His tongue sticks out of his mouth as he pants, a smile across his face.

"Alright then," Daniel says, squeezing my hand. "Let's get to work."

Daniel and I are out in the backyard area of the house, training. It's too dangerous to use the light blasts out here in the open. So, rather than our magic, we focus on hand-to-hand combat.

Kat and Will sit at the table on the back porch, coaching us while working on the tonics.

Will had recommended that we call the station to look for Madison, so Kyle, standing with them, is pacing back and forth with his phone to his ear.

Between Kat, Will, and Daniel, I start to find a pattern in my movements that works and feels comfortable. "Steady your breathing", "watch your feet", "switch things up". With every instruction, each moment of trial and error, the movements become easier.

Daniel throws a punch toward my left shoulder. I quickly step to the right, his fist sailing past before he stumbles forward. While he's off balance, I turn and knee him in the stomach. He doubles down on the ground, wheezing.

"Oh god! I'm sorry!"

"Don't be...that was good!" He grins weakly through heavy breaths. "You just hit my side, and it's...still a little sore."

A grimace crosses my face. Memories of the day I shot him at the Riot base come back to the surface. The sound of the gunshot, Daniel's blood, the gun shaking in my hands.

"I still feel bad about that," I say with a nervous laugh, offering to help him up.

He takes my hand and shakes his head with a winded smile as I pull him to his feet.

"Alyssa! You can't stop like that in the middle of a real fight, you have to keep going!" Kat calls out from the porch.

"Relax, Kat!" Daniel yells back. "We're just training!"

Kat puts down Mala's journal and marches toward us. "She needs to stop pulling her punches," she says, her eyes narrowing toward Daniel. "You *both* do. Don't think I didn't notice."

"But she's—"

"I'm gonna stop you right there," Kat interrupts, raising a hand. "If you say *but she's a girl*, I'll hit you in that same spot. And you *will* feel it in the morning."

At this point, Kyle leans over the porch railing, facing us. He moves the phone away from his ear for just a moment to speak up.

"Do it!" he calls out jokingly.

I can't help but giggle a little.

"No! I was *going* to say that she's just starting to learn this stuff!" Daniel says defensively, "and we have time! We can teach her what she needs to know and still pull back just enough to not kill anyone."

Kat doesn't seem to agree with her brother. Her brow furrows as her mouth curls into a frown. "Did you forget what we're dealing with?" she asks.

"Of course not," Daniel answers, eyes narrowing to his feet.

"This is *Kaedrik and Jacob Reeves* we're talking about," she says. "Both of them have been able to get under your skin. They will scare you, make you doubt yourself, and you'll lose focus on the fight. We *can't* afford that."

"I know, but—"

"Alyssa has been able to snap out of it before, and so have you, and that's great. But I'm trying to teach you guys how to keep moving so you don't have that problem as much," Kat continues. "*Especially* Alyssa, because she's not used to combat, and—"

"Guys!" I shout to get their attention. Both siblings turn to me with shock in their eyes. "Daniel, it's alright. I need this."

He hesitates for a moment, then nods. He can read my earnestness just as easily as I can read his hesitancy.

Kat smiles, satisfied with the resolution.

We both go at it for a few more rounds until it starts to get late. Will suggests that we take a break, and Daniel and I head inside.

After grabbing a couple glasses of water, we meet them back on the porch.

Kat slams the book closed and onto the table before she pushes out of her chair and stomps away. "Without Mala, we can't understand anything that *damn book* is saying!"

Kyle hears this and quickly makes his way to her side. "What can we do to help?"

"Mala was helping Madison interpret the book," Will points out, sighing. "Things would be a lot easier if she were here."

"The police went by her house, but they didn't find anything," Kyle says. "I can't exactly send them towards the cabin to check."

A tight knot forms in my stomach. My best friend is being used by Kaedrik and Jacob. This whole time, I thought I could protect her. I'm a *Guardian*, that's my job. Between Kaedrik taking over Ryan's body, and Jacob nearly killing Will, I'd thought that if I kept Madison out of it, she wouldn't get hurt.

Maybe that was just wishful thinking.

Maybe her heritage connecting her to Mala and Kaedrik would have gotten her involved regardless.

I step to the side, focusing my attention on the forest in front of me to avoid the crashing waves of guilt trying to drown me.

In an instant, I feel a hand on my shoulder. Turning my head, I see Daniel standing beside me. He doesn't say anything at first, his gentle green eyes just look softly into mine. The smile he gives me is kind, reassuring. His hand is cold and grounding from the glass of ice water he was holding.

"Hey, it'll be okay," he says.

I take a deep breath, but don't respond. Daniel's hand slips away from my shoulder, leaving a different, more empty kind of cold on the skin under my shirt.

It's late. The stars in the night sky shine just a little brighter than they would back home. The sound of crickets and cicadas fills the trees.

"We should all get some rest," Will says.

No one argues. We pack up and head inside.

Will takes the bedroom downstairs, while the rest of us trudge upstairs tiredly. There are only three bedrooms upstairs. Kat and Kyle agree to share one, and Daniel and I take the other two.

After changing into my pajamas, I crash out on the bed. Unable to fall asleep, I lay awake for a while, my muscles sore from training. My thoughts drift off as I continue to worry about Madison, until my eyelids finally start to feel heavy.

Standing in the garbage-ridden alley on Milam Street, the Light Door is nowhere to be seen, and neither is Daniel.

I step closer, trying to summon the door. Nothing. No bright flash, no delicate red entry to Mala's cabin. Though, if she's out of commission, I might not be able to get in at all. If that's the case, though, then how am I here? The dreams come from Mala, don't they?

My head jerks around as a black van pulls up in the parking lot behind me. I recognize it. It's the van that the Riot threw me in. A chill crawls up my spine. When the doors open, my breath stutters as Jacob exits the vehicle.

Kaedrik steps out next and opens the door behind him. "Let's go, dear," he says as he helps someone out of the van.

Madison.

She follows Kaedrik with no hesitation. Her face is blank, almost dazed, and she doesn't say a word. Kaedrik leads her to the alley, and the Light Door appears for her in an instant.

The wide-eyed shock on Jacob Reeves's face is strange, seeing how his partner works with plenty of dark magic.

Madison turns the golden doorknob, and the three of them make their way into the forest. I follow closely behind them.

As we walk up to the cabin, another presence looms behind me. I turn my head to find Daniel walking with us.

"What's going on?" he asks, quickening his pace to catch up to me.

"They're here," I tell him.

We follow them up the porch stairs, through the front door, and into the house.

Jacob stops when he sees a picture frame hanging on one of the wooden walls.

Looking over his shoulder, I see it's a photo of Hillary.

He examines the photo of his dead wife intently, picking it up off the hook. In an instant, he scowls and throws the frame to the ground. The sudden sound of glass shattering onto the floor makes me jolt.

"Where is this thing, Kaedrik?" He asks, his face contorted with rage.

Daniel shifts uncomfortably, eyeing the broken frame with a furrowed brow.

"Ease your temper, Jacob!" Kaedrik snaps. "We're close."

Jacob snarls and folds his arms impatiently.

Ignoring him, Kaedrik turns to Madison. "Where is the door, child?"

Trapped in her lethargic state, she leads both of them down to the basement. Her steps are slow, but even and methodical. Her face is blank, emotionless. She looks weary and tired as she directs Kaedrik right toward the object of his freedom.

I turn to Daniel, frantic. "What do we do?!"

He blinks, his head snapping away from the photo. "We stick with the plan," he says. "They can't do anything without the key."

"What about Madison?" A rush of panic creeps into my bloodstream.

The aching regret in my chest is overwhelming. Madison looks so...lost. Kaedrik has taken over another person that I care about.

"We can go after her once they leave the cabin," Daniel decides, placing a hand on my shoulder.

My head turns toward the basement, then back to Daniel. I nod in agreement.

Downstairs, Kaedrik stands in front of the Dark Door, basking in the desolate energy emitting from it. Even in a dream, the power from the Dark Door sends a chill up my spine. Jacob stands a few feet behind his partner, gripping Madison's shoulder. Not that it takes much effort — the trance she's in keeps her from moving away from him.

"My men are on their way," Jacob says. "We'll find that key soon, even if we have to turn over every leaf in the forest."

"The key is not here," Kaedrik says. "The Guardians, and your friend, William, have it in their possession."

A cold weight sinks into my stomach, and Daniel stiffens behind me. His jaw tightens, and our eyes meet, the realization hitting both of us at once.

He knows.

"Well then how the hell do you expect to open that thing?" Jacob asks, gesturing a hand to the door.

"My insolent son created that key. He was a product of both dark and light magic," Kaedrik says, turning to Madison. "His blood runs through her veins. This girl has the power to make another key."

Daniel's face pales, white as a ghost.

I turn to him and find only a few words. "Can...can he do that?"

"I—I don't know," he admits.

The view in front of us starts to fade. Kaedrik, Jacob, and Madison's figures blur into darkness. I reach out a hand to my friend as the details in her face disappear before my eyes.

"Madison!" I scream.

Instead of her answer, another familiar voice reverberates around us in the darkness. "Guardians...it is time."

My vision clears, the darkness filtering out just as quickly as it came.

Daniel stands next to me. "What just happened?" he asks.

Unfamiliar, tall trees surround us, and the distant sound of birds squawking echoes through the woods. Turning my head, Kyle's family's house is right behind us. The same tall windows and the wrap-around porch.

The front door of the house swings open. To my surprise, Will makes his way down the steps of the porch to meet us. He seems a bit disoriented, rubbing his face with his hand. The bags under his eyes are darker than usual, and he trudges toward us slowly.

"Will? Are you okay?" I ask as he approaches.

He grumbles, straightening up despite the obvious exhaustion. "Dreamshares are a bitch for me nowadays."

I nod, remembering what he had told us a few days ago about his drawbacks.

Another bright beam of light appears in front of us. I expect to feel Mala's familiar warm glow, but the power from this light feels different. It's colder, just slightly, sending a shiver up my arms. Rather than the yellow hue I've come to know, this light is solid white. It's frigid, a sense of eeriness follows as it engulfs our surroundings.

When the light fades, a gruff man stands in front of us. His jet-black hair reaches just past his shoulders. His thick beard stops past his chin. The man wears torn blue jeans, hunting boots, and a grey T-shirt covered by a black lightweight jacket. The most notable feature about him are his golden-yellow irises, not at all human. They glow brightly in the sunlight.

He doesn't say a word at first, but his presence is familiar just the same. Daniel and I exchange a look.

"Draven?" Daniel asks.

The man nods silently in confirmation.

Will stands there, speechless with his mouth agape.

"What's going on?" I ask.

Draven stiffens his shoulders and takes a deep breath. "With my mother incapacitated, you will need all the help you can get in order to keep my father in his prison."

"What can you do?" Daniel wonders, stepping closer.

The immortal former Guardian turns to me with a knowing look in his eyes. "As Mala has done once before, I will give all three of you a blessing of my power," he says.

At this, Will blinks. His mouth clamps shut as he snaps out of his awed gaze. "Hold on, this is a bad idea," he says, pulling me and Daniel aside in a huddle to face away from Draven. "He may be Mala's son, but he's also Kaedrik's. How do we know that his blessing isn't going to include dark magic?"

I turn outward to the immortal former Guardian. "Have you done this before?"

He sighs heavily, dipping his hands into his jean pockets. "Unfortunately not, so there may be some risks. However, Mala is still unconscious, unable to even visit you in your dream world, and my descendant is in the hands of my father."

I flinch, shifting uncomfortably as he mentions Madison.

"This is the only chance you three have to acquire light magic strong enough to stop him," Draven states. "I do not see another option. But, as you all stand as fellow Guardians, I won't force it. The choice is yours."

My eyes shift to Daniel. I don't need to sense his emotions to know that we're thinking the same thing.

He nods affirmingly. "We'll do it," Daniel says before turning to Will. "We have to."

Will sighs but nods his head in agreement. "Alright."

The corner of Draven's mouth lifts into a soft grin. Despite his rough appearance, he seems gentle and kind. Stepping closer to us, his boots make a rigid crunching sound in the gravel.

"Gather round and take each other's hand," Draven directs.

We do as instructed, and the four of us make a circle as we lock hands. Draven begins chanting the same words that Mala used when she gave me her blessing. Just like his mother, he switches between English and their other language.

"Let the light of lights guide you in your journey!" he yells.

The swirling yellow magic begins to surround us. Across from me, Daniel's mouth is agape as he watches the powerful light. Will grips my hand tightly.

"Hold the power in your heart with the care of the creator!" Draven chants.

Suddenly, I notice small black streams weaving through the light. This blessing is our only hope. I take comfort in knowing that this darkness is not coming from Kaedrik himself. Focusing on that, the thought repeats in my mind as a distraction from the memory of Kaedrik's intensive power.

"Unleash thine eternal rays with justice and compassion!" Draven shouts. He continues to chant in his incomprehensible language as the stream of light, and darkness, grows bigger. A familiar yellow aura surrounds us all, and Draven's eyes glow like the sun, just as his mother's did.

The magic intensifies, like a heater blasting pressured hot air into my face. I shut my eyes and breathe through it, squeezing Will's hand. He grunts through the pressure of the spell. When he feels my hand firm around his, he relaxes.

Finally, the spell ends, and the whirl of magic dissipates. I open my eyes, and find Daniel and Will still surrounded by the yellow aura. Looking down at my hands, the glow still encases me as well.

"I sincerely hope that this gift serves you well, my friends," Draven says. He turns to walk away, but I quickly stop him.

"Wait!" I say. "Are you out there? In our world? Can you help us?"

Draven turns around. A smirk grows across his face below those saddened golden eyes.

"I am right where you need me to be," he answers. "Now, you all must go home. Be well, Guardians."

I wake in a cold sweat. The bedroom is bright as the open window lets in the warm morning sunlight. I catch my wild eyes and messy hair in the mirror above the wooden dresser. Without a second thought, I pull on my purple hoodie and run downstairs.

Daniel has already beaten me to it. He and Will are standing in the living room, whispering in a rushed tone. They stop when they see me coming.

Will yawns and rubs his eyes, the sleep-inertia getting to him. Regardless, he turns and crosses his arms, his brow furrowed with intrigue. "Tell me everything."

Kat and Kyle meet us in the kitchen. Though they both look equally exhausted, once they catch on to the conversation about the key and Madison, they come into focus very quickly.

"Kaedrik is forcing Madison to create a key? How does that work?" Kyle asks.

"It makes sense," I say. "Draven made the first key. Madison is his descendant."

"Yeah, but Madison is nowhere *near* Draven's level of magic," Kat points out. "She wouldn't know how to do that."

"She doesn't have to know what she's doing if Kaedrik is controlling her," Daniel points out, running a hand through his hair.

"We're going after them, right?" I ask, turning to Will.

"Absolutely," he answers with a long yawn. "We need to get back to the cabin as soon as we can."

I feel a sudden shift in my emotions, something that almost feels like curious possibility. Looking over to Daniel, his face is lowered and focused.

"I should stay here," Kyle states. "Someone needs to look after Mala."

Kat takes hold of Kyle's hand. "I'll stick around too."

Will nods approvingly, then faces Daniel and I. "Get ready to go. We're leaving as soon as possible."

Back in my room, I change out of my pajamas and dig through my bag of clothes. I rummage through the bag and pull out a pair of blue jeans and a gray t-shirt. As I get myself dressed, Madison's near lifeless body from the dream flashes across my mind. Her eyes were so dull, her movements stiff. She was like a *puppet*, with Jacob and Kaedrik leading her along.

Stop it. Dwelling on it won't save her.

As I slide my white tennis shoes on, somebody knocks on my door.

"Come in," I say.

Daniel walks tentatively through the door. He holds his mother's golden bracelet in his hand rather than on his wrist.

"What's up?" I ask as I tie my hair up.

"Have you felt any different since Draven's blessing?" he asks me.

"No, have you?" I wonder, growing concerned.

"I haven't felt anything. That's the problem," he says. "How do we know it worked?"

"It's not exactly an instant change," I tell him. "When I had Mala's blessing, I didn't feel anything until I actively tried to use it."

Daniel frowns, staring down at his shoes.

"*Did you* try to use it?" I ask him.

"I thought of something that might help," he says, fiddling with the bracelet. "Mala has teleported us around the cabin before, and..."

"And you thought you could try to use the blessing to teleport us *to* the cabin," I finish for him.

"Yeah," he confirms with a nervous chuckle.

I think about his theory for a moment. If we could teleport, how would we do it?

"What have you tried so far?" I ask him.

"I tried picturing where I wanted to go in my head," he answers. "The cabin, the forest, even the alley. Nothing worked."

"What feelings were you channeling? I know that's what Will has been teaching us, but when I last had the blessing, that was a *big* part of it."

Daniel's eyes meet the floor again. I feel a sudden rush of shame coming from him, like he already knows the answer to my question won't help his case.

"I guess I wasn't really *channeling* anything," he admits, crossing his arms. "I was too focused on my dad."

"What do you mean?" I ask, tightening my hair into the finished look and sitting on the edge of the bed. I can already feel the shorter strands of my hair loosening away from the tie and waiting to fall back to the front of my face.

"I'm angry, Lyz," Daniel says. "I hate it, but he's winning, and it makes me *furious*. I can't stop thinking about it."

"Well, there's your problem," I say, "I know it's hard to keep your dad out of your head. My suggestion? Focus on saving the cabin."

"I'm trying, but—"

"No, I mean *use that as your channel*," I clarify. "That anger you're feeling, while it's completely valid, it's not the focus that Will taught us."

Daniel sighs and sits next to me on the edge of the bed. "You're right. I should've known that..."

As I clasp on my mother's necklace and slide my Guardian bracelet onto my wrist, the sullen look in his eyes catches my attention. I don't need our Guardian connection to know that there's something *else* bothering him.

"What's wrong?" I ask him, resting a hand on his shoulder.

He sighs again, covering his forehead with his palm. "I shouldn't have jumped to just being so angry at him. That's what *he* does," Daniel answers. "I hate when I get like that. It makes me feel like I'm going right down the same path."

"Hey," I stop him, "you are *not* your father."

"Lyz—"

"Listen to me. I know we haven't known each other very long, but in the short time that I've known you, you have grown *so much*," I continue. "I truly don't think you have to worry about that."

The connection between us feels particularly sharp as I sense Daniel starting to let go of his earlier tension.

"Someone said this to me once," I start with a soft smile. "*He may have raised you, and he'll always be a part of your life, but you chose not to let him into your* heart. *In the end, that's what really matters.*"

"Who told you that?"

"Madison," I answer. "Right after I moved into my apartment."

Daniel raises an eyebrow at the mention of her name. A flicker of realization crosses his face. He moves our hands to lace his fingers between mine.

"We'll get her back," he says, meeting my eyes.

I nod, trying for an affirmative smile.

God, I hope so. I hope we won't be too late.

Daniel and I walk together to meet Will at the truck.

Before we make it out the front door, Kat and Kyle stop us to say goodbye.

"You guys be careful," Kyle warns. "Call us if you need us."

He pulls both of us into a hug.

Kat pats Daniel on the shoulder from behind.

"Give him hell," she says, softly bumping him on the shoulder with her fist. Daniel and Kat both exchange an understanding look.

"I will," he replies.

"Are you two ready to go?" Will asks, opening the driver door to his truck.

"Yep, let's hit the—"

"Hold on, I want to try something," Daniel interrupts me. He stops in his tracks and holds out a hand, closing his eyes. I know right away what he's doing.

Will looks confused, but I nod at him, silently communicating to let him try. He seems to get the message and doesn't object.

For a moment, nothing happens. I step up next to Daniel and take hold of his free hand. He notices, his fingers jerking at the sudden touch, but he doesn't stop. Closing my eyes, I mimic him. I focus my attention on the cabin, and Madison.

As I attempt to channel my thoughts and emotions, heat surrounds my body, covering me like a blanket. Just as the warm power starts to intensify, I hear a distant voice.

"Hey guys!"

In an instant, the warmth around me is gone. Rather than feeling the gravel driveway under my feet, the bottom of my shoes press onto something softer. Blades of grass tickle my ankle under

my jeans. I open my eyes and recognize the bright mystical forest that surrounds the cabin, which rests on the hill up ahead, just barely in sight.

"We...we did it!" Daniel says, eyes wide with awe. He lets go of my hand, and a strong nervous feeling leaves a pit in my stomach.

Is that coming from him? Or me?

"That was incredible!" Will gapes. "I was *never* able to teleport that quickly!"

"Uh...shit," says the same voice from earlier.

The three of us turn to see Kyle standing a few feet behind us. He awkwardly holds a blue shoebox in both of his hands.

"What are you doing here?!" Daniel hisses.

"I just came outside to show you guys this!" Kyle said defensively, holding up the box.

Stepping closer, I see the little red bird inside the box. Her eyes flutter open. Her breathing is slow, but more evident than before. She chirps at the three of us, quiet and faint with every bit of energy her little body can allow.

It's Mala.

She's still in bird form, but she's *finally* awake.

18-Alyssa

In her bird form, Mala is still sluggish and weak. But her eyes are open, and she's moving.

That simple fact fills me with more hope than I've had in a while.

"Why is she still a bird?" Daniel asks.

"Because she's still healing," Will answers. "She isn't strong enough to transform back just yet."

"She can't be here like this. Kaedrik is here, and she's vulnerable," I point out.

In Kyle's hands, Mala tweets weakly. Her silver wings fluff at her side.

"You're right, but she'll be able to heal faster while she's under this sunlight," Will points out.

"I'll take her to her room," Kyle offers.

Daniel shakes his head. "Too risky, there could be Stygian Soldiers swarming that place," he says.

I look up at the wooden cabin hiding in the distance between the trees. This area has always been so calming, so quiet. It feels out of character, knowing the storm we're about to approach up at the cabin.

"Hide over here by the entrance," I suggest. "Keep your phone on you in case we need backup."

Kyle nods in agreement, and the rest of us trek further towards the cabin.

Each step closer to Kaedrik makes me feel uneasy. Knowing what he's done and what he's capable of makes me want to turn around and hide in the forest with Kyle and Mala. But I'm starting to recognize that this feeling of fear is just the effect of being near Kaedrik's magic. I ignore the part of my mind telling me to run away. For Madison. For Ryan. For me.

Inside the cabin, Daniel walks toward the shattered frame that held his mother's picture. He stares intently, face contorted with anger as he picks up the frame and shakes off the small glass shards. Thankfully, the photo inside isn't damaged.

Daniel places the frame face-up on the coffee table. "Let's go," he says.

Will, Daniel, and I move slowly into the kitchen, towards the basement. The air is still, quiet. The door to the basement stands unassumingly in front of us. I can hear the distant whirs of Kaedrik's magic. His and Jacob's distant, muffled voices make me tense up.

Will places a hand on the knob. He turns to the two of us, face hardened. "Make sure you're ready. Stay sharp."

Daniel tenses up, his knuckles white as he clenches his fist. His gaze is firm on the basement door. I take a deep breath, my hand reaching for my Guardian bracelet.

My heart races in my chest. Nervousness forms in my stomach that I'm *almost* certain is coming from me. But then, I look back to Daniel as he lets out a short, silent breath, his shoulders tense, and it's anyone's guess as to who it came from.

Will opens the door, and a gust of wind smacks across my face. When we enter the basement, the first thing I see is Jacob Reeves leaning against the cement wall with his arms crossed. Light moves back and forth on his face as the unstable Dark Door's magic waves in front of the ceiling light. Kaedrik stands behind Madison, who is still in a trance. He leads her hands like a puppet master, using her magic to create his own key to open the Door.

Jacob looks up as we enter, greeting us with a conniving smirk.

"Well, *look at this*!" he shouts.

Kaedrik ignores him, focusing on the spell.

"Aren't you guys a little late to the party?"

"Oh, I think this party is just getting started, *Jake*," Will snaps.

Daniel gives Will a quick look. I guess he's never heard anyone call his dad "Jake" before.

"You know, I'm surprised to see you still kicking around, *Willy*," Jacob says, taking slow steps toward us as he talks, like a lion preparing to pounce. "I hope you're not still mad about that, by the way."

"Nah, I beat your ass plenty of times in high school," Will says, "we're even."

Jacob scoffs, shouldering the comment as he creeps his way toward me.

"Nice to see you again, Alyssa."

I dip my head down, avoiding eye contact.

Daniel throws a hand in front of me in a protective motion and steps up closer to his father. "*Don't.*"

The word comes out sharp and quick. The fury in Daniel's expression is plain to see.

He stands there, stiff, motionless, creating a wall between me and Jacob. I feel it through our connection: pure unbridled *hatred*.

My breath catches. I've never seen him like this.

Jacob studies him for a moment before sighing.

"I'm disappointed, Danny," he says. "I really thought that you had more respect for your father than this."

"*Oh no*," Daniel's low voice sends a shudder up my spine, "I lost all respect for you a *long* time ago."

Jacob doesn't respond. Instead, his face hardens as he takes a couple steps back and snaps his fingers. Black smoke drifts off the walls and gathers behind him, taking the shape of nearly a dozen Stygian Soldiers.

I clench the fist that holds my gold bracelet, feeling the warmth in my palm from the light orb preparing to form for me. It waits for me to allow it to grow, anticipating the brewing fight.

Jacob solemnly points in our direction. "Get them."

They listen, effortlessly. All at once, the Stygians charge at us.

How is that possible? I thought Kaedrik controlled the Stygian Soldiers. Did he somehow use his power to grant Jacob command?

The first one reaches Daniel, who quickly blasts him with a familiar beam of light. At the same time, Will is covered in a bright yellow aura as he calls on his blessing when a Stygian lunges at him. He uses the newfound strength to catch the fist before it hits him, pushing back with a strength I've never seen from him before.

As a Soldier from the left runs at me, I duck under his side, allowing his built-up momentum to send him slamming into the cement wall. I call up the light to knock him out.

Another soldier appears behind me and grabs my right wrist. With the bracelet on my left, I summon the shield and hit him in the face. When he still doesn't let go, I use my blessing to create a bigger blast and shoot it at his foot. The Stygian Soldier tumbles backward and lets go of my wrist.

"Jacob, don't let them get close!" Kaedrik calls out, still holding onto Madison and crafting the key.

I start toward them, but another Stygian Soldier tackles me and pins me to the ground. I try my best to struggle away from him, but his hold is too tight. The smoke coming off his back sends a wave of anxiety and fear at the touch.

"Alyssa!" Daniel yells as he kicks off a Stygian. Another one jumps onto him just as quickly.

Will tries to come to my aid, but Jacob rushes in front of him. He signals for two Stygians to hold Will by the arms. As Will tries to pull free from their grip, Jacob steps forward a few paces and punches him hard in the gut. The Soldiers drop him, letting his knees crash to the floor.

"Not like high school, is it, Willy?" Jacob asks him tauntingly.

Will holds onto his stomach for only a moment before he regains himself. He returns the favor with a punch at Jacob's abdomen. "Yeah, back then you didn't leave yourself open," he says as Jacob doubles down onto the floor.

One of the Stygians rushes to help him, but Jacob swats him away furiously. "Get off me! Kill them!" he demands.

The hold of the soldier on top of me is too much. I summon all of my strength in an effort to push him off, but these soldiers are much stronger than a regular Riot member. One hand grips my wrists tightly behind me, while the other presses with a crushing weight against my back. The power from the smoke sends a chill up my spine.

Panic settles in my gut. My eyes frantically dart everywhere, looking to Will and Daniel.

Across the room, Daniel struggles, just as I do, trying to break free. Will attempts to get closer to Jacob, fighting off Stygians one by one. Turning my head, Madison meets my line of sight. She's helpless. She's lost complete control over herself. Taken away from her by a man with my brother's face. As I look up at him, the distinction becomes painfully clear. The difference between Ryan and Kaedrik.

I *refuse* to give in. I *can't*.

As these thoughts flood my mind, they gradually flush out the anxiety. The warmth starts to pull its way through my body. Draven's light surrounds me as his blessing comes to the surface. The light gets brighter, even brighter than Will's. With each passing moment, I feel stronger. My hands break free from the Stygian Soldier on top of me. He fights back, but I push him off me almost effortlessly.

The Stygian smacks onto the ground, disoriented. When he refocuses, he tries to lunge at me again. I shoot a light blast at him before he can touch me, sending him back, slamming against the wall.

"Lyz! A little help?" Daniel calls. The soldier that tackled him is grabbing his wrists. But Daniel is the only one that hasn't used Draven's blessing yet.

Before I can react, I can hear Kaedrik cackling some distance behind me.

"Almost there!" he laughs. "My freedom is at hand!"

In front of him, the shape of a black key starts to form in his hand. The metal of the key is obsidian, with something blue shining from the handle. It's not finished though. Some spots on the key are faded, translucent. They fill in as Kaedrik and Madison continue the spell.

Soldiers stumble behind me, as Will aims his gun at the one attacking Daniel. "Go!" he yells as the shot echoes through the room.

With no hesitation, I run to Madison and Kaedrik.

Kaedrik sees me coming and holds out his hand. A ball of pitch-black energy, the polar opposite of our light blasts, forms in his hand. He throws it with precision, a sharp flick of his wrist. I duck my head down and the blast hits the corner of the ceiling behind me.

Before he can throw another blast, I yank Madison away from him.

The key falls into Kaedrik's hand, and he scowls at me, furious. "*That was a mistake.*"

He balls his fist, and waves of dark magic circle his hand. A strand of black energy circles me.

All of a sudden, I feel a twinge of pain in my left calf. The sensation that I know all too well quickly grows, spreading through my leg like wildfire. Draven's blessing fades, and I drop to the ground, letting go of Madison.

The pain surging through my leg is unbearable. I curse myself. Kaedrik was able to manipulate me *again* through my stupid leg. I crawl on the floor towards Kaedrik, using my arms to push forward.

Kaedrik cackles. "Ever so resilient, aren't you?" He bends down to meet my eyes.

Ignoring him to focus through the pain, I muster just enough strength to form another ball of light in my hands. Kaedrik signals one of his Stygians, and they grab my wrist before I can aim at him. The soldier steps on my back to hold me down. The rough bottom of his army boot presses into my back with an inescapable grip.

I can't see behind me, but Will and Daniel's struggles echo over the walls. The Stygians must be holding them back too.

"Daniel! Use it!" Will calls out.

"It's not working!" Daniel grunts through whatever grip he's trapped in.

Kaedrik smirks and motions for Madison. "Come my dear." His voice is soft but demanding. "Let's finish this."

Madison remains still and blank-faced. She does as he says without any objection.

"Ma—" I try to call for her, but the rest of her name is squashed by another wave of pain in my leg. "Aghh!!!"

The two don't bother to look in my direction. Kaedrik places his hands on Madison's shoulders as she holds her arms out in front of her with the key in one hand. I can only watch as the dark magic surrounds the key, filling in the holes in the black metal. After a few moments of Kaedrik doing the spell, the key is complete, and the dark energy dissipates as it falls into Madison's hand.

"Yes...YES!" Kaedrik exclaims. He takes the key from Madison and steps in front of the door. "Keep them contained, Jacob," he orders, "in order to cross, I need to step away from this host."

I perk up and raise my head as much as I can in my captive position. He's going to release Ryan?

"How long will you be gone?" Jacob asks from behind me.

"Not long at all, my friend," he assures. He says *friend* as if he didn't ask me to *kill* Jacob just a few days ago. "I will return soon."

Kaedrik inserts his key into the door...and it opens. A cold dread rushes through me. All I can do is watch, sprawled on the floor, clutching my leg as the agonizing pain is overpowered by the realization: We failed.

As the Dark Door slowly swings open, the desolate black energy from Kaedrik's prison fills the room. The power coming through the door is so strong that it pushes back on my face like the wind. Kaedrik lifts a hand up and reaches it through the door, testing it. He pulls his hand back quickly, and, with no warning, my brother's body suddenly collapses to the ground.

"R—Ryan...?" I mutter, searching for signs of movement.

He lays there, motionless.

Jacob makes his way over to me and the Stygian Soldier holding me down, his boots at my eye level.

"Line them up against the wall," he orders.

The soldiers do as instructed and drag Will, Daniel, and I to sit against the cold cement wall of the basement. Jacob and the Stygians seem to have done a number on Daniel and Will.

Will's face is covered in bruises, and a line of blood runs down his forehead.

Daniel has a black eye, and his lip is split with blood.

At this point, the bright yellow aura that Will and I had is gone. Unlike last time though, I can still feel the energy from Draven's blessing dormant inside me. Maybe I can call it back once I find the right moment to strike.

"The jacket, Danny," his father demands, "no tricks."

Daniel glares at Jacob without saying a word as he pulls his black leather jacket off his arms and hands it to him. The handle of his gun, the one I'd shot him with, sticks out of his white shirt. Jacob motions with his hand for Daniel to give it to him.

"Come on now, son." he prods.

Daniel growls under his breath, and hands it over. Jacob takes the gun and examines it for a moment before aiming it right at Daniel's chest.

"Consider this the last time you disobey me, Danny," he says.

"*No!*" I scream.

Before I can even think, my arm extends in front of Daniel's chest. Jacob squeezes the trigger, and a rush of adrenaline runs through me. The sound of the gunshot thunders through the basement, loud enough to feel the vibration against the wall.

A light flashes suddenly from my Guardian bracelet. The golden shield materializes in front of Daniel before the bullet reaches him. With a metal clank, it ricochets and rolls onto the floor across from us.

I look to my right: Daniel and Will are both wide-eyed with shock. Daniel gawks between me and the shield, then presses a trembling hand to his chest. Stunned and speechless, but *alive*.

Jacob scowls. He grabs me by the shoulder and pulls me away from my spot on the floor.

"Dad, stop!" Daniel calls out.

"*Jacob!*" Will warns him.

He ignores both of them. His cold stare is focused on me.

I don't falter. I don't give in. I don't cry for mercy. I meet his eyes with my own stoicism.

Jacob is quiet at first, his warm breath brushing over my face, until he finally speaks. "I've just about *had it* with you getting in the way, Alyssa."

Before I can reply, something leaves the Dark Door. A black raven lands on the floor in front of us. This peculiar bird has a strikingly familiar feature. Wings tipped with silver, like Mala's.

For a single frightening moment, I panic. Could this be Kaedrik? Is he disguising himself the same way that Mala had?

"What the *hell*?" Jacob asks.

The raven squawks, and a hoard of several more pile into the room. The birds swarm around the four of us and the Stygian Soldiers. Their silver wings are sharp as knives, leaving multiple stinging cuts across my arms.

One of the ravens slices across Jacob's forearm, and he instantly lets go of my shoulder. He's so focused on the pain that he quickly forgets about me. I keep my head down, covering my face with my arms, and run to the other side of the room to get away from him. Daniel and Will take advantage of the chaos and make their way toward me.

"What's the plan?" I ask Will, raising my voice so he can hear me through the sounds of Stygians screaming and birds squawking.

"Shoot the damn bastards and close the Dark Door before anything else gets out," he answers, "especially Kaedrik."

Quickly, I turn to Daniel. "What happened with your blessing?"

"I don't know!" he yells through the chaos. "I can't get it to work!"

A few of the birds turn their attention to us. One of them lands directly on me. The talons of its feet dig into my shoulder as its wings slice across my cheek and arm.

I grit my teeth through the pain, looking back at Daniel. "Never mind, just blast them!"

I summon the light with my bracelet, and knock the bird off my shoulder. Before it can hit the ground, the bird crumbles into ash.

Daniel, Will, and I do what we can to take out the birds.

Jacob sees us and takes out his gun to shoot the birds himself. The bullets don't seem to be as effective.

The ravens that Jacob hit drop to the ground, silent for only a brief moment before waking back up and rejoining their friends. The Stygian Soldiers don't have much for defense, and just swat them away only to continue getting cut by the razor-sharp wings. The three of us are struggling, but at least the light blasts are actually killing the birds and weakening their numbers. One by one, a few of the birds fall, and black specs of ash hit the ground like snow. It's not enough, there's too many of them.

Will doubles back when a couple of birds claw him in the chest. He's managed to reactivate Draven's blessing. His eyes glow brighter than fire, but the yellow aura around him seems weaker than it was before.

Now that I know for certain the blessing still works, I call on it. The warm glow gives me a rush of energy. I still feel the sting of metal slicing through my skin, but it feels lighter, not nearly as painful. With one hand, I hit the ravens with my blasts, and with the other I form a shield with my bracelet to cover myself. As the birds come into contact with the golden metal of my shield, they scratch at it with their claws. I hold it up to assess the damage for a quick moment, but I don't see any marks left on it.

Daniel is *really* struggling. Still unable to use Draven's blessing, he shoots the ravens with his bracelet. He's only able to pick off a couple of them before they start retaliating. I can feel him growing more frantic. The demonic birds come to slice their wings at Daniel's face and claw him in the ribs.

Before Will or myself come to his aid, I feel a shift in Daniel's emotions. Where at first, he was afraid and disoriented, his mood begins to shift. He finds Jacob in his line of sight. A wash of irritation fills the air around me, quickly morphing into *raging* indignation. A flicker of light surrounds him before quickly retreating. Will notices it too and stops in his tracks.

Then, like igniting a spark, the yellow aura of the blessing returns to Daniel's body. The light of the incredible power flows through him seamlessly. The ravens nearby burst into ashes upon the formation of his intense light.

But there's an alarming difference between Daniel's blessing and ours. A few waves of dark magic surround him. They're not big, but they're visible. It doesn't seem to affect his power, though. The blast he sends from his hand to hit a nearby raven is pure Light magic.

As the three of us, now equally enhanced by Draven's blessing, throw light blasts at the ravens, more of them start to flood through the door.

"We have to close it!" Will exclaims.

"How do we do that?!" Daniel asks.

Will gazes at the Dark Door for a moment. His expression reads as steady, yet there's something behind his eyes that he won't say out loud. He shakes it off and turns his head to Daniel.

"I'm gonna try *physically* closing the Door, but it needs something stronger than that," he starts, eyeing Daniel. "I need you to fire at it with your bracelet to push it closed."

"What do you want me to do?" I ask him.

"Stay on the birds. Don't let them leave the basement," he orders.

I nod in agreement, and turn my attention back to the birds, focusing my aim on the ravens that are closer to the basement door. Looking over my shoulder, Jacob is still shooting at them with his gun, cursing as they resurrect and claw at him further.

He shouts, turning to the Stygians. "Retreat!"

They do as he says and scatter out of the room. Before Jacob himself makes his exit, he bends down and picks up Ryan's unconscious body.

"*Stay away from him*!" I yell, turning on my heels to run in his direction. Before I can get close, one of the ravens slams into me. Its claws dig into my arms, leaving scratches stinging across my face. The impact causes me to fall back, stumbling onto the ground.

"Lyz!" I hear Will shout. He meets me on the floor as I sit up. "You alright?"

"Forget about me! Where's—"

But Jacob is nowhere to be found...and neither is Ryan.

"*No!*" I scream, darting toward the exit.

Will grabs my shoulder. "Alyssa! We *need* to get this door closed. We can go after them when the job is done."

Panic rises through every nerve in my body. "But he's—"

"*I know*," he says. "I know. But if Kaedrik gets out, there's no point."

My lungs feel heavy as I look between the exit and the Dark Door. I can't believe this is happening. Ryan was *so close*.

But Will is right. This is too important to risk.

Solemnly, I nod. With a reassuring look, Will runs to the Dark Door. He pulls the handle in an attempt to force it toward the striker plate on the door frame. It takes a lot of effort, the dark magic holding it open trying to push back, but eventually he gets close enough for Daniel to do his part.

Daniel shoots out a beam of light. It's similar to our light blasts, but more concentrated. The beam hits the door, pushing it further to a close. Though, as close as the two of them are, it's still not enough.

As Daniel and Will continue to push on the Door, I see a hand stretch out from the inside.

Fear and urgency well up in my stomach. Will notices it too and presses harder on the Door, shifting the weight into his upper arms.

The hand continues to emerge from the Door: first an arm, then a shoulder, and then, finally, a face. I can't even settle in the relief that we're not looking at Kaedrik.

The creature is some sort of demon. Its gray skinny body is transparent but dark, like a shadow. His aged face is *blank*. No nose, eyes, or mouth. The demon's head has no hair, only black singe marks.

Will frees one of his hands, propping his right foot against the frame to keep a hold on the door, and reaches for his gun to shoot

at the creature. The bullet passes right through him and hits the wall of the basement. Will's attempt only angers the creature. It growls and grabs him by the neck.

A fearful scream escapes my throat.

"Will!" Daniel shouts.

"Do NOT stop!" my uncle barks. He uses his free hand and drops his gun to quickly take the original key out of his jacket pocket. "Alyssa!"

He throws the key to me, and I catch it. Will unhooks his foot from the frame of the Door, but keeps a tight grip on the handle.

"*What are you doing*?!" I yell.

"It's okay..." he says.

"No! We can figure something out!" I cry. "Will, *please*!"

"You guys take care of each other," he says softly. He looks over at Daniel. "All of you."

The shadow demon pulls Will inside the door, its grip still clamped, unbreaking, around his neck. His fingers tighten around the doorknob, and for a split second, I hear him gasp as the creature yanks him inward.

Daniel's beam of light pushes the Dark Door forward. An aching pit forms my chest as I watch the door slam shut...trapping Will inside.

The world around me goes quiet, like all the air in the room was sucked in through the door with him.

Daniel's sudden voice makes me jolt. "Alyssa, you need to lock it," he says firmly, though a crack forms at the end. "Now!"

The key rests lightly in my hand like a phantom as I force each step forward. My arms feel heavy, weighing me toward the floor. Yanking Kaedrik's key out of the lock, I toss it to the ground. My heart beats thunderously in my chest, the only discernable noise as I take the golden key and insert it. With the securing twist, a wave of light runs across the Dark Door, fixing the damage and refurbishing the wood to be stronger than ever.

My knees give out from under me. Kaedrik's key falls from my hands. Tears stream down my face.

He's gone...Will is gone.

I'd lost him before, after Jacob attacked him. But that felt so different. I felt defeated, alone. Before Will and I were able to talk about things, to heal. Back then, I *hated* him for separating me from Ryan, but now...

I just feel empty.

Daniel meets me on the floor and wraps me in his arms, pulling me tightly against his chest. He says something, but I don't hear the words. Everything sounds like I'm underwater, drowning in inescapable grief. His hands run up and down my back, trying to be soothing, trying to keep me grounded.

My chest tightens, hard and painful. Each breath turns sharp and uneven as I try to gasp for air.
The room spins around me uncontrollably. There's no space for anything in me. No breath, no thought, no *light*.

And then the dam finally breaks. Crying out through the tears, my scream fills the room, so loud that my vocal cords feel hoarse. A light erupts from my body as the sound rips through my throat, reducing the rest of the ravens to ash.

Daniel whispers apologies, but I can't bring myself to focus on his words. Through the blur in my vision, I see the light in his blessing dim. It flickers, once, twice, then leaves, as does the darkness that had joined it.

Another, lighter voice suddenly breaks through the tension. "What...happened?"

My head snaps around to find Madison slowly picking herself up off the ground. Shock and relief runs through my mind when I see her stand up, *finally* in control of herself again. I want to react, to hug her tight and be happy that she's okay. But the loss still weighs on me, keeping me catatonic on the floor. My eyes dart back to the Dark Door, waiting, *praying* that it will somehow find a way to open and bring my uncle back.

"Kaedrik almost escaped," Daniel answers for me. "But Will...he stopped him."

I don't see her reaction, but I hear the quiet gasp as she realizes what Daniel means. "Oh no..."

Daniel takes hold of my hand, his fingers curling around mine in a slow, cautious movement. He squeezes, gently, trying to get my attention. "Alyssa," he says quietly. "Hey...look at me."

With the last shred of strength I have, I turn my head, forcing myself to look away from the Dark Door. My breath shudders as I slowly meet Daniel's eyes.

"We should go." His voice is low, barely above a whisper.

He helps me up, his grip on my arms the only solid thing in the room. When I attempt to stand, my knees feel weak, like twigs about to snap in two. He catches me when I falter, until I'm back on my own two feet again.

Daniel walks to the other side of the room and picks his jacket up off the ground.

Madison bends down to grab Kaedrik's key off the floor beside me, her hands visibly shaking as she picks it up. She then steps toward me and holds tightly onto my arms. Maybe to try and be comforting, maybe to keep me from melting back onto the floor and sobbing even more.

As my foot presses off the last step of the cabin porch, the normally calming air of Mala's forest feels uncomfortably cold against my skin. Firm hands stay on my shoulders, guiding me through the forest until we reach the Light Door. I smell the shift in the air from the trees blowing in the wind, to the garbage cans in front of us in the alleyway.

Kyle is parked in front of us in what I can only assume is a stolen blue minivan.

"I figured we'd need a getaway vehicle," Kyle says as we pile into the van. "What...where's Will?"

I hold back a sob forming in my throat.

Daniel shakes his head.

Kyle's mouth lowers into a frown as the realization hits, and he starts the car without another word.

Letting my head rest on the window, I watch buildings, cars, and tall trees as we pass them by. My eyes stay firm on one spot in front of me out the window, relentlessly holding back tears.

My brother is missing. *Again*. Will is gone. I've lost everything that really matters.

Kaedrik is trapped. We won.

But at what cost?

19-Daniel

From the front seat of the van, I turn to check on Alyssa. She keeps her gaze out the window, unbreaking on the passing trees that speed by. I want to say something, do something, *anything* to comfort her, but any time I've tried to say something, or put a hand on her knee, she dismisses me, and pushes it away. Even Madison is rejected in her efforts.

I look over at Kyle next to me. Though nobody dares to talk about what happened out loud, Will's absence, as well as my dismissal when he asked, was enough for him to not press any further. His eyes are focused on the road in front of him. Mala, still in her bird form, rests on the flat surface above the speed dials on Kyle's side of the car. After a few minutes of long, dreadful silence, I speak up.

"How much farther is your place, Kyle?" I ask.

"We still have about forty-five minutes," he answers.

I lean back in my seat, exhausted. I start to close my eyes, allowing myself a moment to rest after everything that we've been through today. Of course, it doesn't last long. I feel the pull of the vehicle as Kyle makes an abrupt stop.

"Guys..." Kyle alerts us.

Mala wakes up, chirping with vigilance.

A black van is parked in front of us, blocking our path forward. Standing in the road beside the van are my father and Ryan.

I hear Alyssa's short gasp from the backseat when she sees her brother, but with the angry scowl across his face, not to mention the way he still stands proudly next to Jacob, I'm pretty sure this is still Kaedrik.

My father points at me and motions to come to him. The mood in the van rapidly shifts into panic.

"I have to go out there," I say aloud.

"Are you crazy?" Madison cries.

"No, Daniel!" Kyle says.

"Guys... I need to do this."

"No." From behind me, Alyssa's voice is quiet. Broken, but firm in her stance.

"Alyssa—" I start before she interrupts me.

"No! You don't *have* to do anything! Stop trying to act like some sort of martyr!" She unbuckles her seatbelt and stands up in the car, gripping onto my shoulders as if that alone can keep me from leaving. "I can't lose anyone else today, Daniel. If you do this, your dad will *kill* you," she cries, the words trembling but fierce. "You can't just throw your life away for him!"

"I'm not doing it for him," I tell her.

"Then *why?*"

My chest heaves. An unexpected rush of emotion suddenly falls over me. Fear curls in my stomach, because, once I step out of this van, I may never see her again.

Her brown eyes are wide with worry. Her cheeks are flushed, wet from the tears that fell after losing Will. I would do *anything*

352

to keep those tears away. To stop her from worrying. I want to protect her. Keep her safe after everything that's happened. After all, it's my fault.

The feeling in my chest loosens, replaced by a soft flutter in my gut. It's familiar: longing. It's a feeling that's been lingering inside me from the moment I met her.

I lean my head forward and kiss her, holding her cheek with my hand. Warmth floods through my entire body as our lips meet. In reality, the moment goes by quickly, but it feels like I'm sitting there with her, just the two of us, for hours.

Alyssa is still, quiet, but a small shudder of breath escapes from her as I begin to let go.

I pull away, slowly, then finally answer her question.

"I'm doing this for you."

Alyssa is left shocked and speechless. Her eyes flicker over my face, and, for a moment, even the empathy link feels silent.

Next to her, Madison is wide-eyed and just as frozen.

Kyle just smirks, not saying a word.

With that, I get out of the car before anyone else can say anything, and tread forward to confront my father.

Outside, Kaedrik is standing there, visibly angry. He knows he's lost his chance at freedom.

My dad smiles knowingly as I approach. "Hey there, Danny," he greets.

"What do you want?" I snap.

"My partner here wants to have a chat with you," he answers.

Kaedrik steps up.

"How are you still here?" I ask him. "We fixed the door."

Kaedrik studies me for a second, annoyed. "Yes, and thank you for that, *boy*," he says, as if the word leaves a bad taste in his mouth. He looks tired, more so than he was almost two hours ago.

"I will not let this *annoyance* of a setback go unpunished," Kaedrik states. He turns his head to my father. "Jacob."

Dad moves toward me and grabs my shoulder. He pushes me against the front of the van.

From behind me, Alyssa's shrill, panicked voice calls my name. I turn to her, Kyle, and Madison and hold my hand out to stop them.

"Stay there!" I shout. "I'll be okay!"

"*More lies*, Danny," my father says as he punches me in the gut near my gunshot wound, causing me to double down onto the ground. I clutch my stomach. My knees collapse onto the gravel road. Dad picks me up by the collar of my jacket, forcing me to stand. I barely have time to let out a heavy breath before he lands a punch right on my nose. My face burns, only worse after our fight in the basement.

Covering my nose with my hand, a drip of blood runs down my face.

Dad shoots me a look of disappointment. "You see what you've done here, son?" he says. "The mess you've made?"

I wipe the blood from my mouth before speaking. "*You're* the one making the mess, Dad," I snarl, gesturing to Kaedrik in Ryan's body. "*You* hurt people. You let a demon take control of a *teenager*."

I never knew Ryan before all of this, but I've heard a bit about his life from Alyssa. He's a *really* smart kid in high school — he's working on building his own *computer*. He has a sister that loves and misses him. And Will...who may never get the chance to repair things with Ryan the way that he and Alyssa did.

"I held up my end of a business deal," Dad argues, "enabling my partner to have a body."

"Kaedrik isn't your partner, he's using you!" I tell him, though trying to reason with my father feels like grasping at straws. "He'll throw you away as soon as he's done with you!"

"Well that's just insulting," Kaedrik says. "I'll have you know that I value your father's contribution...and his loyalty."

Dad scowls and hits me again in the stomach, making me fall face-first to the ground once again. Before I can pick myself up, a small gust of wind rushes past me. Looking up, I see a small red bird with silver-tipped wings race toward Kaedrik.

"*Ack*! What are you—NO!" he yells as Mala claws at his face. Kaedrik melts down to the ground, screaming in pain.

Taking advantage of the confusion, I push past my dad, slamming into him with my shoulders and bolting toward the van. The sudden impact makes him tumble to the ground.

"You ungrateful *shit*!" he yells as Mala zooms across his face to follow me.

"Drive!" I yell to Kyle.

He already has the key in the ignition. Kyle curves past the two, leaning so far off the road that one of the tires rolls onto the grass. Once we're clear of them, Kyle races onward toward his family's lake house.

The rest of the car ride back is somehow quieter than before. My whole body aches from the amount of hits I've taken today. Rubbing my eyes with my hands, my blood coats my fingertips.

A hand emerges from the seat behind me, holding out an old blue and yellow beach towel that had been sitting on the floor of the van. Turning to look, I notice Alyssa doesn't meet my eyes as she hands it to me. "Here. clean yourself up."

I nod and take the towel. She doesn't ask me anything about the kiss, and frankly I'm too hesitant to say anything.

Kyle and Madison don't dare to bring it up either, but I can plainly see Kyle smiling smugly at me, hiding it from the girls.

When the four of us are finally back at Kyle's house, Kat runs in from the kitchen to meet us.

"You're back! Did you—" she stops when she notices the absent member of the group. "Where's Will?" she asks.

Alyssa doesn't say anything. She just turns her head away, looking outward at the trees surrounding us to keep herself from crying again.

We all head into the living room, and I pull Kat and Kyle aside to fill them in while Alyssa and Madison sit on the couch, placing Mala on the cushion next to them.

Both Kat and Kyle's faces drop when I tell them about Will's sacrifice.

"Poor Alyssa," Kyle says.

"Will..." Kat lets out with a shaky breath. "I can't believe he's gone."

"Me neither," I say, placing a hand on her shoulder. "Alyssa's not ready to talk about it yet, so just...give her some space. Please?"

 356

"Of course," Kat says.

"Are you guys going to talk about the *other thing* instead?" Kyle asks with a sly grin.

When my face turns beat-red, Kat raises an eyebrow and crosses her arms. "I hope this *other thing* explains why you look like shit?" She asks me curiously.

"Yes," I say immediately.

"Nope," Kyle says at the same time, chuckling.

I shoot him a sharp look and groan, rubbing at my temples.

Kat doesn't let the matter go. She steps closer, tilting her head in my direction as she studies me. "*Daniel...*"

"It's not important right now!" I snap.

Just then, a flash of light flickers through the windows of the building.

"What *now*?!" I ask, exasperated.

We rush inside to find Alyssa and Madison knocked onto the floor, surprised to see Mala awake and in her human form. She smiles softly and helps both girls back to their feet.

"Kaedrik's power has weakened, and the Dark Door is stronger than it has been in decades. I am so proud of you, my Guardians," she says, "I'm proud of *all of you*."

"It's not much of a win," I point out to her, "we lost Will."

"Yes, I know," she replies, giving Alyssa a sad, mournful look. "I am *so* sorry."

Alyssa doesn't look in her direction, instead turning her eyes to the door.

Through our connection, I can feel a sense of hopeless wonder from her. She's silently hoping that her uncle will walk through that door at any moment, and that everything will be okay again.

"Unfortunately, William's journey in Kaedrik's prison is one that he'll have to make alone."

Alyssa's eyes widen at Mala's words.

"He's alive? You can feel him in there?" she asks.

"Well, yes, of course, but—"

"We have to go back for him!" Alyssa pleads.

"My dear, going into the Dark Realm is far too much of a risk," Mala says.

"We can handle it!" Alyssa argues.

"While that may be true, that's not what I mean," Mala says sternly.

For a moment, the room is dead silent. The air is harsh and awkward.

"Alyssa, we cannot risk reopening Kaedrik's prison, even for William," she says. "I am sorry, but as a Guardian, you have to consider the well-being of *everyone* in your world, not just his."

"Mala, you can't be *serious*," Madison speaks up. "This is her uncle that we're talking about. He's her *only* family left."

She pauses for only a brief moment before continuing.

"I...I am well aware, but my decision stands," she says decisively. "It is far too dangerous."

Though Alyssa's face is red hot with anger, she takes a deep breath. I half expect to feel a sense of dread wash over her. In this moment, it's almost like she lost Will all over again, but instead I sense her affirmation.

"Fine, I understand," she says with a sad tone. "It's too risky." She excuses herself and slowly makes her way upstairs to her room. I follow her, and she doesn't stop me. In fact, she waits for me to catch up at the top of the stairs and shuts the door behind me.

"Lyz—"

"If Will is alive, there's a chance that I can save him," she says.

I smile at her, knowing *exactly* where this is going. "You're going through the Dark Door to get him, aren't you?" I ask.

She hesitates for only half a second, as if she were thinking hard about something, before answering me. "Yes," she says.

"Then I'm going with you."

"Daniel—"

"You shouldn't go in there alone. You're going to need help over there," I tell her. "Besides, we're partners. We're in this together."

Alyssa blushes, and turns away, but after a short pause, she turns back to face me and smiles. I can see it in her eyes, how certain she is. A feeling of warmth falls over me, followed by that same certainty. We may not know what we'll find behind that door, but both of us will do everything we can to get Will back. And we'll do it together.

Later that evening, Kyle and I are doing the dishes in the kitchen. As much as I want to tell him what Alyssa and I have planned, I know that there's a chance Mala will hear me.

"I talked to Madison earlier," Kyle says. "She's been getting better at reading Mala's journal. She and Kat are going to look through it together tomorrow and try to figure out those tonics."

"That's good," I say. "That'll come in handy."

"How's Alyssa doing?" he asks.

"She's...processing," I say to avoid the topic of my previous conversation with her.

"Did you guys talk about it yet?" he asks.

I raise an eyebrow. "Talk about what?"

Kyle rolls his eyes at me and chuckles, "*The kiss.* God, you're hopeless." He whacks me lightly upside the head with a small plastic cutting board.

I yelp. "I don't think now is a good time, dude."

"Well yeah, of course let her process what she needs to about Will," he says, "but I think you guys should at least *talk about it.* Let her know that you care, and you're here for her."

"When I want your dating advice, I'll ask my sister," I reply snarkily.

"*Hey*! She'll just tell you everything I did *wrong*," Kyle says.

"Exactly," I laugh, throwing the kitchen towel in my hand at him. "It's perfect."

A few minutes go by before we hear a knock at the door. Kyle leaves the kitchen to answer it with a curious look on his face. I put down the plate I was drying and follow him.

Obie runs down the stairs and beats us to the door, barking non-stop. I grab hold of his collar and back him away from the door. "It's okay, boy," I say.

Kyle opens the door, and a gruff adult man stands outside. The man is wearing a black zip-up jacket and green camouflage hunting pants. Sunglasses cover his eyes. His hair and his beard are as black as coal.

Obie breaks free of my grasp and lets out a strange loud bark...one that I've heard before. With no warning, he bursts into flames.

"*Whoa*! What the hell?!"

As I jump back, I see the rough texture of his skin. His bright, fiery eyes and small tufts of smoke falling off his body. The man at the door is unphased, bending down to pet him.

Kyle, gathering his composure after seeing the dog catch on fire and turn into a demon, clears his throat.

"Uh, can I help you, man?" Kyle asks.

Before he even takes off his sunglasses to reveal his bright golden yellow eyes. I recognize him.

"Draven."

To be continued in...

Book Two:

The Darkness We Fear

Acknowledgements

This story has been close to my heart for a very long time. I am so grateful that I finally get to share it with the world. I wrote this book for the people that have those influences in their life that they can't escape from. The ones that feel stuck, and hopeless. You are *not* alone, please know that. No matter how long it takes, no matter how impossible the battle may seem, there *is* hope for a better ending. There *is* light...and it's you.

I could not have done this without the help of the amazing people in my life.

Thank you to my fiancé, Brendan. You have always supported me through day one. Listening as I work through ideas, helping me when I was stuck, picking me up when I was down. Your constant love and encouragement never ceases to amaze me, even after I've completely talked your ear off about the storylines. I love you, and I *cannot* wait to be your wife.

Alex, there is no doubt in my mind that we were meant to meet on TikTok. It still amazes me that I've found my twin just by commenting on one simple video. You have been one of the greatest friends I've ever had. The support you've shown for me inside and outside of this book's process is unmatched. Thank you for your friendship, thank you for *everything*.

Miss Gilmore, before I came to you for help, I was so overwhelmed with how much editing I had to do that I thought this book would never see the light of day. But thanks to you, it did. You encouraged me, taught me, and made me feel like nothing could stop me from reaching my goal. I will forever be thankful for that.

Thank you, Mae, for being such a kind and wonderful editor. I reached out to you with hope, with a vision. But I was out of work, and not in a good place financially. You waited patiently for me to be ready, and when I was, you showed the care and attention that this book needed. That *I* needed. Thank you so much, and I can't wait to work with you again on future projects.

Miles and Gracie, your friendship has meant the world to me. To have people in my life that I share a connection with, that share the same interests as me, that make me feel *connected* has been such a blessing. You both mean the world to me.

The Highlands Writers Guild. I found them when I first started out in college, when I was looking for a community of people who liked to write as much as I did. And boy, did I find it. This community has grown tremendously in the time that I have been with them, and I am so grateful to be a part of it. I hope that each and every member of this wonderful group sticks to their passion, and with it, they reach for the stars.

Last but not least, my wonderful family. My mom, my stepdad, my sisters, my grandpa. Everyone that has watched me turn this book from an idea to a published piece. They have always been my biggest cheerleaders, and I love them dearly for everything they've done for me.

And to you, my incredible reader.
Go. Find your light, and let it guide you to a brighter future.

"Your dad will always be a part of your life. But you chose not to let him into your heart, and that's what matters. You are not like him, and you will always be better than him. Your being here is proof of that."
– Brendan King

This man has been my rock. My best friend and my biggest supporter. When the world around me feels dark, his is the light I choose to follow.

Thank you for always being there for me, baby.

Want to learn more about Kyle? Keep reading!

Kyle's Story — A TLWG Prequel

What am I doing?

My hands shake with the heavy gun pressed between them. I didn't want this. I didn't want any of it. I don't care what this guy did. He doesn't deserve this. Nobody does.

"Please!" The store owner, Harold Croft, is sprawled on the ground in front of me, begging for his life. "I'll get Jacob the money! I have a family!"

He caught his son buying guns from Jacob and stopped the transaction. Pissed, Jacob has been making the man repay the money for the guns *monthly*. He owns a convenience store, the same one we're standing in now, holding him at gunpoint.

Guilt washes over me as I relay the message that Jacob Reeves had ordered me to pass on. "Jacob doesn't do extensions," I say quietly. "You had a deal, and you're past the deadline."

Behind me, Brad Gordon is grunting impatiently, waiting for me to pull the trigger. Daniel Reeves just watches, not saying a word. I click the safety off and steady my hands, ready to fire.

"Please, *no*!" Croft begs.

It all feels so wrong. This man is innocent. The only mistake he made was owing a debt to a madman.

We have that in common.

The store owner's terrified dark eyes remind me of Jim. Jacob confronted us on the street after Jim had sold him those damn

Read the entire prequel, and learn more about Kyle's origin on the author's website:

www.aurorakingwrites.com

See you in Book Two!

About the Author

Aurora King became an indie YA fantasy author in 2026. She loves exploring themes of found family, strength, resilience, and love. Much of her inspiration over the years has come from movies and books of fantasy and action.

She lives in Carrollton GA with her fiancé, Brendan, and their orange and white cat, Dewey. She fell in love with writing in her sixth-grade reading class when they read The Lightning Thief by Rick Riordan.

When Aurora is not writing her book, she's writing for her college newspaper as a features editor while pursuing a degree in Digital Media and Communications. She also spends time with the campus creative writing club, the Highlands Writers Guild, where she continues to grow alongside fellow storytellers.

To learn more about her journey and her series, visit her website for art, updates, and inquiries. Because the Guardians' story is only just beginning…

www.aurorakingwrites.com
Instagram: @aurora_day_writer
TikTok: @aurora_day